ABOUT BEDTIME STORIES

Bedtime Stories is a popular channel on YouTube, which has captured the imaginations of audiences across the world. With more than half a million subscribers and a truly unique brand, the Bedtime Stories team – comprising of Richard While, Simon Andrews and Mikey Turcanu – creates a universe which is built on a combination of haunting imagery, articulate storytelling and character driven narration.

We focus on actual recorded events which seem to defy explanation. The world of Bedtime Stories does not exist in an alternate universe. It exists in *our* universe. Real people. Real towns and cities. Real history. There is truth in every tale. This leaves the viewer with a lingering sense of foreboding about the world we inhabit, inviting us to question what is really possible.

VOLUME 1

BEDTIME STORIES

RICHARD WHILE

Copyright © Richard While 2022

The right of Richard While to be identified as the author of this work has been asserted by him in accordance with the Copyright, Designs and Patents Act, 1988.

This book is sold subject to the condition that it shall not, by way of trade or otherwise, be lent, resold, hired out or otherwise circulated without the publisher's prior consent in any form of binding or cover other than that in which it is published and without a similar condition being imposed on the subsequent purchaser.

Chapters 7, 12, 18, 20 and 24 written by Dwain Reynolds
Chapters 26, 29, 31, 33, 35 and 37 written by Red Fawcett
Chapters 15 and 17 written by Simon Andrews

Edited by Hazel Walshaw

First published in the United Kingdom in 2022

Cover design by Tom Mulliner

Cover and Chapter artwork by Mikey Turcanu

Cover and Chapter artwork Copyright © Bedtime Stories 2022

CONTENTS

About Bedtime Stories i
Author's Note ix
Foreword xi
1: The Flannan Isles Lighthouse Mystery 1
2: The Strange Death of Zygmund Adamski 11
3: Rudolph Fentz; The Man Out of Time 19
4: The Ilkley Moor Alien 23
5: The Curse of the Ourang Medan 31
6: Bones on Mars 37
7: The Last Moments of Elisa Lam 51
8: The Legend of the Mothman 61
9: The Mandela Effect 69
10: Who Are the Men in Black? 75
11: The Peculiar Death of Christopher Case 83
12: The Mysterious Murders of Hinterkaifeck 91
13: The Body on the Reservoir 101
14: Doppelgängers and the Strange Case of Emilie Sagée 111
15: The Black-Eyed Children 117
16: The Disappearance of Kenny Veach 125
17: The Ghosts of Stocksbridge Bypass 133
18: The Curse of Carl Pruitt's Grave 141
19: The Dyatlov Pass Incident 147
20: James Dean's Little Bastard 165
21: The Wraith of Trench Pool 173
22: Secrets of Celle Neues Rathaus; A Nazi Occult Tale? 179
23: There is Something in the Woods 187
24: The Alien of Varginha 201
25: The Crosswade Interlopers 209
26: The Baby Aleshenka 215
27: What Killed Olivia Mabel? 225
28: There is Something in the Water 231
29: The Devil Made Me Do It 239
30: The Man From Taured 249

31: The Nightmare 255
32: The Evil Within 263
33: The Boys From Yuba City 271
34: The Strange Death of Gaurav Tiwari? 281
35: The Mysterious Disappearance of Flight 19 289
36: The Lead Masks of Vintém Hill 299
37: The Curse of Atuk 307
38: The Watervale Runner 315
39: Who is the Grinning Man? 323
40: 25 Cromwell Street 331

AUTHOR'S NOTE

This book contains all the transcripts of the first 40 episodes of the Bedtime Stories YouTube channel, but rather than being a mere "copy and paste" job, this work should really serve as a companion piece to the series. We have updated many of the stories with new information, which only came to light after their corresponding episodes were published. We have also taken this as an opportunity to expand on some of the explanations and correct any mistakes which were made in the original work.

For our American readers, please appreciate that, although we may share the same language, British English is different in many ways to the Olde English used by the United States. We get many comments on our channel about how we say and/or spell certain words, with "disorientated" being the most commonly called out. We would not say "disoriented" in this country, and we appreciate that you may find our longer version of it irritating, but we will defer to the way in which we were educated.

Elsewhere, other colloquialisms are used, such as "torch" instead of "flashlight", "trainers" instead of "sneakers" and "bonnet" and "boot" instead of "hood" and "trunk". We spell "offence" and "defence" with a "c", not an "s" and there are many other British English quirks you may find throughout the book, which may cause you to raise your eyebrows. Rest assured we are currently working on a glossary of British terms/spellings, which we hope to include in future books, but for the time being, Google is a good translator!

FOREWORD

There has never been a time in history in which the horror genre has grappled so much for our collective attention in the creative spaces dominating pop culture. Everywhere we turn there are scares waiting to be made, whether it be in the booming independent horror film industry or the ever-eclectic horror gaming scene. Everyone wants a piece of the pie, to get their hands dirty, to relish in the revelation that someone, somewhere can't fall asleep at night because of the stories we've told. It shouldn't be as addictive as it is, chilling the spines of people we've never met. But that's how horror strengthened its grip in the first place, isn't it?

Throwing the unknown onto the unknowing is a tale as old as time.

Thus, the question becomes why? Why do we keep returning to the dusty cellar with cobwebs aplenty and a foul stench run amok only a ghoul from hell could love? Why do we walk through the cemetery at night, tempting the undead with our fate dripping from our brow like wax sliding down the vampire's candlestick? Why do we, after all these years, still not check below our bed for the bogeyman and various monsters which lurk in the shadows, fuelling our nightmares and sucking our souls until the final breath expires and the executioner's axe swings silently towards death?

Why do we care at all?

If we didn't, we wouldn't end up on that carousel of creeps for the umpteenth time. We'd run away and never look back. We'd surround ourselves with safety, turning the other cheek to even the slightest sign of fear. We'd grab that blanket from our youth, the kind with tattered edges and fading colours, and wrap it around ourselves so tight we'd blockade ourselves from feeling anything at all. We'd jump into an abyss of abnormal comfort. It would suffocate us until we forget what it's like to feel our blood pumping and experience something that reminds us of our own existence. We'd be nothing but mammals, numb to life.

The fact of the matter is that horror makes us feel alive. It validates our role on Earth, of our necessity to engage with fight-or-flight and know our priority is to live. Humans are literally wired to feel adrenaline. Cortisol and healthy stress are necessary to life. Without it, we'd halt evolution, halt expansion and growth and the bettering of our understanding the world around us. We must care, for caring is just as important as returning to the terror itself.

Do we consciously acknowledge this when we see a ghost, get lost in the corn maze, or hear a thump in the night? Of course not. Horror is a master of twisting our subconscious, where this urge to feel dread ultimately resides. So much of what makes horror great is that it enables us to fill in the blanks. Steven Spielberg once curdled the blood of millions of moviegoers because of a broken shark which made empty spaces feel like a runaway train of tension. It's not about what's out there, but rather what could be out there. It's not about what we've seen or heard, but about what others have seen or heard and the waiting period between now and whenever it might happen to us.

The Bedtime Stories team excels at creating these experiences, mastering the art of horror and its connection to our humanity. They've found the chisel to sculpt endless scares which resonate with us even after the final page has been turned. It's been their modus operandi since the beginning, understanding their audience's innermost desires, their subconscious hope to feel the very life force that woke them up that morning, so as they might not go back to sleep. Why slumber when the nightmares are right here, anyway?

Like those who choose to stay awake, we marvel at the inspiration Bedtime Stories effortlessly puts into all their projects, from their YouTube channel to this very book you've picked up. Despite the ballooning amount of horror projects spanning the cultural lexicon, their originality never ceases. They continue to find new ways to bring us back to that place where all we want to do is hide, and yet we stay awake, regardless. They put nails to the chalkboard, but the sound changes infinitely, each scratch more cacophonous and calculated than the last.

Above all, they've embraced what horror means to them, what horror means to us, and what horror means to you. They've given us the chance to cast the spotlight on the why, while still leaving our hearts racing in the darkness, chasing the feeling to live.

Top5s

For Thomas, Callum, Hudson, Alexander and William

Remember; truth is stranger than fiction…

1
THE FLANNAN ISLES LIGHTHOUSE MYSTERY

In December 1900, three lighthouse keepers, stationed on an isolated group of islands in the North Atlantic, vanished without trace. Was their disappearance the result of a freak accident? Or was there something more sinister at work?

There was a sharp intake of breath from the ship's crew as the looming spectre of Eilean Mòr emerged from the mist. The towering cliffs of this small islet were an imposing site to behold, no matter how many times one encountered them. Beneath their feet, the vibration of the engine seemed to dampen as the vessel slowed its approach. Standing at the prow, a lone figure kept his eyes fixed on the lighthouse jutting from the summit of this brooding landmass. It was little more than a silhouette beneath the veil of fog. That, in itself, was a concern. In these conditions, it should have been lit.

The man's name was Joseph Moore, a lighthouse keeper from the Isle of Lewis. It had been six long days since he had received orders from the Northern Lighthouse Board to return to his post at Eilean Mòr. He had hurriedly made his way to the harbour at Breasclete, where the

Hesperus had been waiting to take him to the nearby Flannan Isles, but poor weather conditions had prevented them from sailing until this morning. The journey had been an anxious one and he had spent the majority of the trip in deep thought, pacing fore and aft across the ship's deck. Any attempts to engage him in conversation had been met with little more than grunts or nods, and he had refused any breakfast, taking only a few mugs of coffee for sustenance.

The reports had clearly troubled him. As soon as he had heard about the lighthouse having been dark since the 15th of December, he'd had an unshakeable feeling in the pit of his stomach that something had gone terribly wrong. He wasn't quite ready to accept this possibility. The three men, stationed on the islet rising from the waves in front of him, were not just his colleagues, they were his friends. As the ship approached the east side of the island, an ominous atmosphere descended over the scene. The Flannan Isles had a haunting loneliness to them at the best of times, somewhat punctuated by the fierceness of the seas around them, but on this morning, as the Hesperus came about, there was something else in the air. Something which suggested all was not quite right.

Captain Harvie noticed immediately that the ensign was not flying on the flagstaff. Joseph Moore had also noticed that none of the provision boxes had been put out to be restocked and there was no welcoming party from any of the men he had been sent to relieve. The eeriness was suddenly amplified beyond words. Three long blasts on the ship's foghorn split the air as Harvie attempted to notify the lighthouse keepers of their arrival. When this failed to elicit a response, he ordered that the crew set off a signal rocket from the deck below, but still there was no reply from the three men.

Save for the crashing of waves against the cliff faces, and the cawing of seagulls overhead, an oppressive silence hung over the island in front of them, which sat heavy in the heart of Joseph Moore. A short time later, a crewman by the name of McCormick, approached him. He explained that the captain had ordered the two of them to take the ship's launch across to the east landing, and to report their findings. The relief keeper made his way towards the waiting boat. He couldn't have known it at the time, but he was about to step into one of the world's most haunting and enduring mysteries.

Every day across the globe, people go missing in their thousands. Thankfully, most turn up alive and well. For others not so fortunate, their remains are often found weeks, months, or even years later, having perished through misadventure or foul play. But every so often there are cases in which the missing individuals are never seen or heard from again. They simply disappear into the vastness of the world we inhabit. Vanishings like this occur in both urban and rural settings, but in either case there are often obvious explanations. After all, there are plenty of sinister people with sinister motives, just waiting to take advantage of any given opportunity. But what about more isolated incidents? Where a group of individuals, stationed on a remote, uninhabited, and almost inaccessible island, miles away from the evils of the world, simply vanish without trace?

On the evening of the 7th of December 1900, almost three weeks before the Hesperus arrived at the Flannans, Superintendent Robert Muirhead stepped off the east landing of Eilean Mòr and climbed into his waiting launch. Having shook hands and bid farewell to his colleagues, he now headed out to a larger steam vessel anchored offshore, which would take him back to the mainland. As his small boat made its way over the choppy waters, he looked back at two of three men he had left behind. They were 43-year-old James Ducat and 28-year-old Thomas Marshall, and they were stood on the east landing waving to him. The third man, 40-year-old Donald MacArthur, was atop the cliffs towering above them, manning the lighthouse as procedure dictated. It was strictly forbidden to leave the light unattended at any time, and so he could not join his colleagues in waving off their supervisor. As Muirhead waved back, he would not have known that he would be the last person to see these men again. For when the relief vessel arrived 19 days later, they were nowhere to be found.

The Flannan Isles, a group of seven small islets situated some 20 miles west of the Outer Hebrides in Western Scotland, were to be the setting of this strange disappearance. The islands were named after the 7th century Irish priest, St. Flannan, and for as long as anyone could remember they had remained uninhabited. The settlers on the neighbouring isle of Lewis, and the rest of the Hebrides, always viewed this bleak and deserted group of craggy rocks with great superstition. Many fishing boats and merchant vessels had foundered there over the years, and although the Hebrideans often ferried sheep to graze on the Flannans' lush turf, they believed it very unlucky to spend a night there.

During the 1890's the Northern Lighthouse Board decided to construct a lighthouse on Eilean Mòr, the largest of these seven islets. It took four years and building work was constantly hampered by the tempestuousness of the wild Atlantic Ocean, which made it very difficult to land supplies. Nevertheless, the lighthouse was completed and went into operation on 7th December 1899. It had no wireless communication and the only way of contacting the mainland was by using visual signals, which could be seen by the Hebrides on a clear day. The lighthouse would have been operated by up to three men at a time, with a fourth keeper on shore rotating in as relief.

The mystery began on the night of the 15th of December 1900, when a sudden squall broke out in the vicinity of the islands. The first signs of anything amiss came when the captain of an American steamer, the SS Archtor, making its way from Philadelphia to the port of Leith in Edinburgh, passed close to Eilean Mòr just before midnight and noticed that the lighthouse was eerily dark. This was almost unheard of for an operational rock station like the one on the Flannans, and was reported when the ship reached its destination three days later.

Even so, although a dark lighthouse was considerable cause for alarm, no immediate action could be taken due to the harsh weather. The Hesperus was due to set sail on the 20th of December, carrying fresh supplies and the relief keeper, Joseph Moore, but because of the unfavourable conditions, it was unable to set out until dawn on Boxing Day, the 26th. As Moore and McCormick reached the east landing, Moore instructed his colleague to wait below whilst he made his way up the steps leading to the plateau where the lighthouse stood.

Moore called out to the three men as he negotiated the steep incline, but there was no reply. Upon reaching the lighthouse, he found the entrance gate to the compound and main door both closed. Inside, nothing appeared out of the ordinary. The lamps were cleaned and refilled, the beds were unmade as if the men had just awoken, the washing up was done, and there were cold ashes in the grate. After his initial observations, he spotted an over-turned chair in the kitchen and then noticed that all the clocks had stopped, which only added to his concerns.

Returning to the Hesperus, Moore relayed his findings to the captain, then made his way back up to the lighthouse with more men, in the hopes of conducting a wider search. At the east landing, everything had been intact, but the west landing provided considerable evidence of storm damage. A box at 110 feet above sea level had been smashed and its contents strewn about; iron railings were bent over; the iron railway by the path was wrenched out of its concrete housing, and a rock weighing more than a ton had been displaced above that. On top of the cliff, at more than 200 feet above sea level, turf had been ripped away as far as ten meters from the cliff edge.

Further investigation revealed that the keepers had kept their log until 9am on the 15th of December and their entries made it clear that the damage had occurred before their disappearance. The only other considerable piece of evidence was that two sets of oilskins were missing. Only one set of the outdoor gear remained by the entrance, suggesting that one of the men must have ventured outside without wearing his protective clothing. This was surprising considering the severity of the weather on the date of the last log entry, and especially during a harsh North Atlantic winter.

Of the keepers themselves, there was no sign, either inside the lighthouse, or anywhere else on the island. They had simply vanished. Moore and three volunteer seamen remained behind to attend to the duties of getting the lighthouse back up and running, whilst the Hesperus returned to the shore station at Breasclete. From there, Captain Harvie sent a telegram to the Northern Lighthouse Board dated 26th December 1900, stating:

> "A dreadful accident has happened at the Flannans. The three keepers, Ducat, Marshall and the Occasional have disappeared from the island... The clocks were stopped, and other signs indicated that the accident must have happened about a week ago. Poor fellows they must have been blown over the cliffs or drowned trying to secure a crane or something like that..."

Whatever the cause of the keepers' mysterious disappearance was, several embellishments have been added over the years, such as the classic "half eaten meal" which was supposedly found on the keepers' kitchen table. This is common in many vanishing tales, but in this case, it is a complete fabrication. Even the over-turned chair has been called into question, with no mention of this in the original accounts. The stopped clocks is another aspect for many looking for something out of the ordinary, but there is nothing even remotely strange about this fact. All clocks of that era had to be wound in order to continue ticking away. With no one around to do this, they inevitably ceased to function. Another point of contention are the log entries, which are listed as follows:

> "December 12. Gale north by Northwest. Sea lashed to fury. Never seen such a storm. Waves very high. Tearing at lighthouse. Everything shipshape. James Ducat irritable."

Later, on the 12th: *"Storm still raging, wind steady. Stormbound. Cannot go out. Ship passing sounding foghorn. Could see lights of cabins. Ducat quiet. Donald MacArthur crying."*

> "December 13. Storm continued through night. Wind shifted west by north. Ducat quiet. MacArthur praying."

Later, on the 13th: *"Noon, grey daylight. Me, Ducat and MacArthur prayed."*

There was no log entry on the 14th. The final entry was supposedly chalked on a piece of slate, which would normally have been transferred to the logbook at a later time:

> "December 15. 1pm. Storm ended, sea calm. God is over all."

These entries would have made for disturbing reading, if not for the fact that they are mostly fictitious. The reports on the weather are probably true, but the comments regarding the keepers' mental states do not make any sense when considering the context. A Northern Lighthouse Board logbook is an official process-bound document. It is not a diary for an employee to record his personal thoughts, especially regarding other members of the team. It seems rather odd to suggest that Marshall would have written such statements about James Ducat. Ducat was Marshall's superior, and it would have been today's equivalent of an employee writing on an office message board or an official report that their boss was in a foul mood. Had the men survived, the NLB would have rightly asked Marshall to explain why he had written such personal remarks. The comment about MacArthur crying is also completely out of character, as he had a reputation for being a tough old seadog.

In fact, all three men were highly seasoned and rather hardy. It was a prerequisite for the job, so the idea of them cowering beneath a violent storm, which they would have been more than used to as it was a common sight around the Flannans, is an insult to their memory.

Finally, there is no mention of the damage recorded at the west landing, which was present in the original logbook entries according to Joseph Moore. The source of these false additions has been traced back to an American pulp magazine published in 1921, many years after the incident took place. This was perhaps a harmless attempt by the publication to add more intrigue to the mystery, but it has ultimately become confused with fact. In any case, no bodies were ever found. No other clues were uncovered, and we can only speculate as to what really happened on those windswept isles, in that cold December, during the last year of the 19th century.

Theories have ranged from the mundane to the extreme, with the most fantastical mentioning sea monsters, boats filled with phantoms, kidnapping by foreign spies, and even alien abduction. There are two or three more rational explanations, however, and one of these involves the occasional keeper, Donald MacArthur. It has been suggested that, despite the log entries being fictitious, MacArthur's mood at the time was highly irritable. He wasn't a full time lightkeeper and was only used to spending a few weeks on station at a time.

At the Flannans, he was covering for an assistant lightkeeper by the name of William Ross. Ross was on long term sick leave and, incidentally, would quite literally drop dead in the light room of the Eilean Glas lighthouse 16 months to the day after the tragedy at Eilean Mòr. As a result, MacArthur had already spent most of October, all of November, and the beginning of December on the Flannans by the time Superintendent Robert Murihead visited them on the 7th of that month. The fact that a superintendent took the trouble to visit the keepers at such a remote station in the middle of December is quite unprecedented and suggests that he did so because there were issues brewing between the men.

It is highly likely that Muirhead made the trip to calm the situation and assure MacArthur that he would be relieved on the 20th by Joseph Moore. In MacArthur's eyes, though, this simply translated that he would have to spend yet another two weeks away from his family. It is not difficult to imagine what may have transpired from this situation. Some have suggested that MacArthur possibly suffered a bout of cabin fever and took the lives of Marshall and Ducat. He then threw their bodies and himself from the cliffs rather than face the consequences of his actions. There was little if any evidence of any kind of a struggle inside the lighthouse, so if this line of thinking is to be taken seriously, it would require that MacArthur lured the other two men to their deaths whilst outside.

One of the most prominent theories suggests that the men were swept away by a freak wave. It postulates that Marshall and Ducat had gone to secure some of the damaged equipment at the west landing, leaving MacArthur to man the lighthouse. A box containing mooring ropes and other essential items was apparently wedged in a fissure on the cliffs at 110 feet and it is thought that one of the men got into trouble trying to retrieve it. The other man then rushed back to the lighthouse seeking assistance from MacArthur and as they worked to rescue their colleague, all three of them were taken unawares by a freak wave. Whilst this is probably the most convincing explanation, it is not without its flaws.

First of all, it is clear from the log entries that the disappearance occurred in the late afternoon on the 15th. In the years since, many lightkeepers have questioned why Ducat would have left it so late in the day to try and retrieve the box of supplies, especially with the fading light and deteriorating weather conditions. They agree that any lightkeeper worth their salt would have carried out this task in the morning. Ducat had more than 20 years of experience to call upon and was, by all accounts, one of the best lightkeepers in the service. So why would he have unnecessarily risked his life, and those of his subordinates, when the west landing was being hammered by 30-to-40-foot waves, and the wind was building up to just below storm force?

On the subject of the wind, a relatively new theory, put forward by Keith McCloskey in his book, *The Lighthouse*, suggests that a vortex may have been responsible. Many lightkeepers who served on the Flannans will attest to just how strong the winds can get on those isles, with some of them describing how they had been lifted off their feet and carried through the air for quite a distance. Because the Eilean Mòr lighthouse is constructed on sloped ground, the wall around the complex is lower on the west side than at ground level in front of the winch house, which means it offers no protection from westerly winds and causes something of a wind tunnel effect through this narrow passageway.

McCloskey postulates that high winds on the afternoon of the 15th December may have caused shutters or doors around the complex to bang and slam, and that two of the men donned their oilskins and ventured out to remedy the situation. As soon as they turned the corner from the living quarters into the area immediately in front of the winch house, a high wind may have carried them over the low wall and then straight over the 200-foot cliffs to the north of the lighthouse, which are only 15 or 20 feet away. He goes on to say that the third man may have gone out to investigate when his colleagues did not return, not bothering to put on his oilskins as he wouldn't have been outside for too long, only to turn the corner and suffer the same fate. But if this is the case, why didn't other lightkeepers, stationed on the Flannans, also succumb to this strange weather phenomenon? Surely it wasn't so unique that it only ever occurred once?

The riddle of the Flannan Isles has been an endless source of fascination, one which has inspired stories, films, poems, songs, and even an opera, but the whole truth may never be known. Something about the mystery of these three men, isolated at the edge of the civilised world, and surrounded by the vast and hostile Atlantic Ocean, not only sends a chill up the spine, but it also tugs at the heartstrings. They left their families with a promise that they would return over Christmas, but instead they were never seen again. James Ducat was married, with four children and MacArthur, married, with two children. Whilst Marshall was single at the time of the disappearance, he must have had children at some point in his life as there are descendants of his alive today. There would be no closure for their loved ones, only heartbreak and confusion.

The lighthouse itself remained manned and without further incident up until 1971, when it became fully automated. It is still in operation to this day, and the isles are now only visited occasionally for maintenance purposes. Over the years, the islands never could quite live up to their cursed reputation, as nothing out of the ordinary ever took place there again, but the mystery of Eilean Mòr lives on, perhaps forever more.

In closing, we leave you with the words of Superintendent Robert Muirhead, who, in his official report of 8th January 1901, said of the keepers:

> *"I visited them as lately as 7th December and have the melancholy recollection that I was the last person to shake hands with them and bid them adieu."*

2
THE STRANGE DEATH OF ZYGMUND ADAMSKI

In June 1980, a man was found dead in a coal yard more than 20 miles from his home with suspicious burns to his neck and shoulders. Who—or what—could have been responsible?

Strange disappearances such as that which occurred on Eilean Mòr are certainly mysterious and intriguing. But in cases where someone goes missing, only for their body to re-emerge days or even weeks later, these often take a turn for the chilling or downright disturbing, sometimes even, the truly bizarre. Especially when none of the evidence points towards a satisfactory explanation. This was certainly the opinion surrounding the death of Zygmund Adamski, whose passing appeared so unnatural, that many believed it to be the work of something beyond our understanding. It was not so much the cause of his death that was considered strange, but the circumstances in which his body was found.

Zygmund, a coal miner who lived in the village of Tingley in West Yorkshire, England, had spent most of his early life in his native country of Poland. But in 1960, at the age of 37, he and his wife Lottie decided to relocate to the UK, where they hoped to make a fresh start. After arriving in their new home, they quickly made new friends and soon settled into the small-town life of rural England. To anyone who knew them, they were a perfectly happy couple and not disposed to confrontation with others. So perhaps it comes as no surprise that Mr. Adamski's sudden disappearance and subsequent death was so unexpected that it was to leave behind a tantalising conundrum, which remains unresolved to this day.

At around 2pm on 6th June 1980, 56-year-old Zygmund left his home, on foot, to buy some groceries from the local shop. As he was leaving, he engaged in friendly conversation with a neighbour before setting off on the mile-long journey into town. The weather had been glorious, and all had seemed well on that peaceful summer afternoon, but unbeknown to himself, his wife, or anyone else who knew him, Mr. Adamski would never be seen alive again. For almost a week, it seemed to anyone who knew him, that he had simply dropped off the face of the Earth. And to this day, his whereabouts during that time have remained a complete and utter mystery.

Five days later, on the 11th June, his body was found in a coal yard at Todmorden, more than twenty miles away from where he lived. Trevor Parker, the coal yard owner's son, had opened the compound gates at 3:45pm in preparation for the afternoon shift, when he spotted Adamski's body lying on top of a twelve-foot-high coal pile. He immediately called the police and a constable, Alan Godfrey, arrived on the scene at ten-past four.

When questioned, Parker stated that the last time he had been at the yard was 11am that morning and that Adamski's body had not been there at that time. He had also closed and locked the gates as he had left, and no one, to his knowledge, had visited the coal yard since. This indicated that the body must have been dumped there sometime during those intervening five hours. PC Godfrey radioed for an ambulance shortly after arriving and it was quickly established by paramedics attending the scene that Adamski had suffered a massive cardiac arrest. However, on closer examination, and due to several suspicious elements, authorities began to suspect foul play.

Firstly, and probably most disturbing of all, were the second degree burn marks on the back of his neck and shoulders. These were covered with a strange gel-like substance, which more than likely indicated that someone had tried to treat these injuries whilst he was still alive. Secondly, the way in which he was found, as well as the overall appearance of his body, was not consistent with a death by natural causes. One of the strangest anomalies was how Adamski was attired. It was as if he had been crudely redressed, after his death, by someone who was unfamiliar with the process of dressing. He was wearing a coat, which was buttoned up the wrong way. His trousers and belt were not fastened properly, and neither were his shoes. His wife would later report that the shirt he had been wearing on the day he vanished was now missing, as were his wallet and watch. But overall, his clothes were in good condition, which ruled out the probability that he'd been sleeping rough for the past five days.

Another odd factor was how spotlessly clean his body appeared, as if he had just stepped out of the shower, and even though he had been missing for nearly a week, he showed only one day's growth of stubble. Remarkably, there was no trace of coal dust on his skin or clothing, which excluded the possibility that he had climbed the coal pile by himself before succumbing to the heart attack.

Finally, and perhaps most perplexing of all, was the fact that there was no sign of any footprints in the coal pile itself, or any indication that it had been disturbed, by someone climbing it or otherwise. Zygmund was found lying on his back, face towards the sky and, by all accounts, it seemed as if he had literally been dropped there from above. PC Godfrey went on to describe how Adamski's face had looked contorted with terror, which was later confirmed by the coroner, who said that he must have known great fear or pain at the time of his passing.

During the post-mortem it was concluded that Mr. Adamski must have died between the hours of 11am and 1pm on Wednesday, the day that his body was found. He had eaten well during the time he was missing, although not on the day he had died. It was revealed that the burns to the back of his neck and shoulders had been inflicted only two days prior to his death. The strange gel-like substance which had been applied to the burns was tested by a home office laboratory but could not be identified, and there were no records of him having visited a local hospital for any such treatment.

There seemed to be no apparent reason for Adamski's sudden disappearance. He was a good-natured man with few, if any, enemies. He was of a sound mind, and he had been due to attend a family wedding the day after he had vanished, which—it was reported at the time—he had very much been looking forward to. There was a great deal of mystery surrounding the case and some very odd aspects which could not be ignored, especially the peculiar burn marks. Strong hints of alien abduction were in the air by the time the story broke and hit the tabloids in the following weeks, and regardless of how far-fetched they may seem, it is impossible to completely dismiss them.

Todmorden and the surrounding areas are a known UFO hotspot, and the complexities of this theory are further borne out by the involvement of PC Alan Godfrey who would, himself, later become an alleged alien abductee. And it would be remiss to tell the tale of Zygmund Adamski and not include the experience of Alan Godfrey, as over time, the two have become inextricably linked. In November of 1980, six months after finding Adamski's body, Godfrey was on duty in the early hours of the morning when he was dispatched to investigate bizarre reports of a herd of cows, which had been seen appearing and disappearing all over a local council estate.

Driving down Burnley Road towards the location of the latest sighting, he saw what he thought was an overturned double-decker bus about 200 metres ahead of him. Believing it to be a shift bus for the local coal miners, and thinking that a terrible accident might have occurred, he slowed down to observe the scene. However, on closer inspection he discovered that the object was not a bus at all and that it was, in fact, hovering five feet off the ground. He tried calling for backup but found that neither his personal radio, nor his dash radio was working. Not knowing what else to do, he noted the time and began sketching the object.

After completing the drawing, which took him all of thirty seconds, he looked up to find that the strange looking craft had vanished. Surveying the scene for any further sign of it, he suddenly realised that his car was further along the road, almost a quarter of a mile distant from where he had originally stopped. Upon checking his watch, even though only a minute seemed to have passed, he found that he had lost almost half an hour; time which he could not account for. Later, he would discover that the soles of his standard issue police boots were split at the toe, in a way that suggested he had been dragged along the ground.

Shortly afterwards, he returned to the police station and asked a couple of colleagues to help him search for the missing cattle. The cows were eventually located in a rain-soaked field, the only access to which was through a locked gate. Although the recent rainstorms had softened the ground, there were no hoof prints to be seen. Like Zygmund Adamski, they seemed to have simply been dropped there. As standard procedure dictated, Godfrey reported his encounter with the strange object later that morning. He discovered that another driver on the same road, only three miles further along, had seen a white light and had reported it to Todmorden police.

Two weeks passed by without further incident, but the report of Godfrey's experience was somehow leaked to the press, causing himself and his department a great deal of embarrassment. Despite being an outstanding officer, with two commendations for previous police work, Godfrey found himself being alienated by his colleagues and slowly pushed out of favour with his superiors. With his once solid career effectively ruined, he eventually left the police force.

Some years later, he would undergo hypnotic regression, and over several sessions he recounted some disturbing memories. He woke up in a white room where a tall, bearded man, along with a black dog stood at the end of the bed he was now lying on. The man was human, or at least, he appeared to be, and he was wearing a kippah. Godfrey recalled that he was placed on a cold, hard table while the man performed physical examinations and spoke to him telepathically. He said his name was Josef. Meanwhile, approximately eight creatures with odd-shaped heads watched on as Josef removed his shoes. There was no real conclusion to his recall, he simply 'woke up' and that was the end of it.

Recounting the case of Zygmund Adamski, Godfrey was to relate how it had been one of the strangest cases he had ever been assigned to, but regardless of his own experiences that same year, he was somewhat unsure of whether UFOs had actually been involved in Adamski's death, though he didn't rule out the possibility. Some twenty-five years later, British UFO Research Association (BUFORA) investigators interviewed members of Zygmund's family and found that he had not, in fact, been looking forward to his Goddaughter's wedding. There had been a family feud during this period and a female relative had moved in with the Adamski's. This relative had taken out a restraining order on her own husband and relations were very bitter between the two.

In light of this, two overriding theories have transpired regarding the whereabouts of Mr. Adamski during those five days. BUFORA concluded that Zygmund had been kidnapped by the female relative's husband and held in a shed for the duration, where he had been tortured with battery acid before finally suffering the fatal heart attack. This could well have been the case, and it is quite plausible that when Mr. Adamski died, the estranged husband had panicked and dumped the body at the coal yard. But there are still many unanswered questions over this explanation.

By all accounts, Adamski was a neutral bystander in the family feud, so why had he been kidnapped? What could this course of action possibly achieve? Secondly, Zygmund had obviously been in a state of undress at some point during his disappearance, but why? And what was the ointment found on his skin? If his captor had wished to do him harm, as suggested by the burn marks, why had it been applied? Why had his body been dumped on top of a coal pile in broad daylight and not hidden in a more discrete location and at a less obvious time of day? And how did the person who dumped his body even get access to a locked coal yard and then manage not to leave a single trace of having been there? Finally, and perhaps most importantly, why was no one ever arrested or charged for the kidnapping? It is clear that this theory has many loose ends, which are yet to be tied up.

Another angle to consider is that, during the 1960s, when Adamski travelled to live and work in the UK, Poland was very much a satellite state of the Eastern Bloc. Theories have inevitably arisen surrounding Zygmund's possible placement as a KGB agent and that he was assassinated due to a defection on his part. This is not as farfetched as it may at first appear as recently, the Skripal poisoning would seem to suggest that assassinations of this nature can and do occur. There is, however, an overwhelming intimation amongst conspiracy theorists that the latter was nothing more than a false flag event. Many others believe that extra-terrestrials were somehow involved and that they had abducted him at some time on 6th of June as he had made his way to the local shop. From that point on he had been held in a kind of suspended animation, thereby explaining the lack of stubble growth and the appearance that he'd been eating healthily. When he was pulled out of this state, possibly for examination, he was so overcome with shock that he suffered a massive cardiac arrest and died.

But the possible involvement of UFOs raises even more perplexing questions. It was reported that Zygmund's wallet and watch were missing. What could extra-terrestrial beings possibly want with his valuables? This point alone leads many to believe that the reason for his disappearance has a far more earthly explanation. Secondly, accounts of most alien abduction cases suggest that although the experience is very frightening, and at times mild physical discomfort is felt, the captors themselves are benign and do not wish to harm their subjects. Why then had Adamski sustained various malicious looking burns? Could it have been accidental on their part? Hence the supposed effort to treat him, as indicated by the strange ointment which, oddly enough, could not be identified by modern science.

Finally—and the question must be asked again—why would his captors dump him on top of a coal heap in broad daylight? Why leave a mystery at all? Why not hide the body where no one would ever find it? Was there a feeling of guilt amongst those who took him; a feeling that he should be returned to his home?

Whichever way you look at it, there is no denying that there is more to this mystery than meets the eye. Although the family feud scenario is probably the more plausible of the two theories, it is by no means conclusive. And any other assumptions, regardless of how fantastical, are by no means ruled out. There could be a hundred other reasons why Zygmund Adamski disappeared on that fateful day, but whatever the explanation, it will forever be consigned to pages of history as yet another unsolved case.

3
RUDOLPH FENTZ; THE MAN OUT OF TIME

In 1951, a man was said to have appeared out of thin air in the middle of New York City. He was killed shortly afterwards, but when officials searched his body, it left them wondering not so much where he came from, but when.

Time travel has been a much-loved staple of science fiction stories for well over a hundred years. The prospect of going back in time to right our wrongs or going forward into the future to see what's in store is an exciting one. But what if it was more than just mere science fiction? What if, every now and then, certain people experienced so-called time slips, which made them question the stability of our otherwise unshakeable reality? And what if they never made it back to their own time?

On a warm summer night in June 1951, the bustling streets of Time Square were suddenly brought to a complete stand still. Onlookers were startled when a young man, said to be in his late 20s, seemingly materialised out of thin air. This man, it was stated, looked entirely out of place and time. His hair style was said to be about 70 years out of date, his face half obscured by mutton chop sideburns, and the style of his clothing was strikingly similar to fashions prevalent in the mid-1800s. Witnesses reported that he seemed distressed and confused by his surroundings, and that he suddenly flew into a panic and ran. Less than a minute later he was lying dead in the road after being struck down by a passing car. This man's sudden appearance would have been strange enough, but when officials at the morgue searched his body, they found a whole host of bizarre items on his person, which baffled local authorities. These included:

- A copper token for a beer worth five cents, bearing the name of a saloon which was unknown, even to the older residents of the area
- A bill for the care of a horse and the washing of a carriage, drawn by a livery stable on Lexington Avenue, which was not listed in any address book
- Approximately 70 dollars in old bank notes Business cards with the name Rudolph Fentz, listing an address on Fifth Avenue
- A letter sent to this address from Philadelphia, dated June 1876.

What was even more intriguing was the fact that none of these items showed any signs of ageing or degradation, particularly the letter, which did not look anywhere near its supposed age of 75 years.

The case was assigned to NYPD Captain Hubert V. Rihm of the Missing Persons Department, who used much of this information to try and identify the strange man. His first port of call was the Fifth Avenue address listed on the business card, but this turned out to be a dead end. The owner said that he had never heard of a Rudolph Fentz. To make Rihm's task even more difficult, Fentz's name was not listed in any current telephone or address book, his fingerprints were not recorded anywhere, and no one had come forward since his death to report him missing.

Nevertheless, Rihm continued his investigation, and after much searching, found the name of a Rudolph Fentz Jr. in a 20-year-old telephone book, dating back to 1939. As it turned out, Fentz Jr. no longer lived at the listed address. Instead, it was now occupied by a middle-aged couple, who remembered the previous owner, saying he was a man of around 60 and that he had worked nearby. After his retirement in 1940 he had apparently moved away, though they could not say where. Even so, this lead proved to be invaluable, as it allowed Rihm to track down the bank which had facilitated Fentz Jr.'s business account. From there, Rihm discovered that Fentz Jr. had died five years earlier, in 1946, but his widow alive and living in Florida. Rihm was able to contact her, and when the conversation turned to matters regarding Fentz Jr.'s father, she simply said that he had disappeared in 1876 aged 29. He had left the house one evening for a stroll and had never returned.

So, what happened to the original Rudolph Fentz? Did he accidentally travel forward in time by 75 years, leaving his young son behind to age naturally over time and die before his reappearance in 1951? We are not so sure.

During the 70's, 80's and 90's, this story was reported almost exactly as it is told today, as fact. That was until 2001, when a folklore researcher named Chris Aubeck investigated the case. He was unable to find the original story reported in any newspaper at the alleged time of the incident, and no record of a Rudolph Fentz having ever existed. Aubeck concluded that the people and events described were all a work of fiction. However, he could not find the source of this fiction. Another researcher, Pastor George Murphy, claimed in 2002 that the original story was published in a September 1951 issue of Collier's Magazine, as part of a series of short stories entitled, *I'm Scared*. Murphy's investigation led him to conclude that the author was none other than the renowned science fiction writer Jack Finney.

And so, the strange case of Rudolph Fentz was finally put to rest as nothing more than an urban legend, or so everyone thought. No original copies of the Fentz story have ever been found, and Finney died in 1995, before he could be questioned about it. Another twist emerged in 2007, when a researcher working at the Berlin News Archive, found a newspaper article from April 1951, reporting the story as it is told today. This would have been five months before Jack Finney's short story was said to have been published. What's more, other researchers have come forward claiming to have found evidence of the real Rudolph Fentz and proof of his disappearance in 1876.

Could the Jack Finney angle, as purported author, be a well-placed cover up in order to disguise the truth as a work of fiction? Why has no one come forward with examples of this new-found evidence?

The likelihood is that the story of Rudolph Fentz is completely fabricated. That said, many are far too quick to dismiss this case on the assumption that time travel is impossible, when in fact this is not entirely accurate. In the quantum realm, at least, some subatomic particles do not appear to obey the rules of causality and can randomly travel forwards or backwards through time. Even in the macroscopic world, it has been physically demonstrated that time dilation occurs at significantly high speeds, or inside deep gravity wells, meaning that some version of forward time travel—as supposedly experienced by Mr. Fentz—is, in essence, possible. This is not mere theory, but scientific fact, although you would have to be moving at phenomenal speeds to observe any such dilation.

But if there is any truth to this tale, how could Rudolph Fentz have travelled 75 years into the future, when the fastest method of transport in his day, the steam train, would have been capable of no more than 60 miles per hour? Did he unwittingly slip through a crack in time during his evening stroll? This sort of phenomenon is not unheard of. Throughout history there have been many accounts of people experiencing sudden and unexpected time slips, though they are usually deposited back in their own time relatively unscathed.

Unfortunately, until we find an intact copy of the original Jack Finney story, or someone comes forward with evidence proving beyond a shadow of a doubt that Rudolph Fentz did exist, or even a clipping of the original news report that was said to have been published at the time of his death, the origins of this tale, whether fact or fiction, will forever be in question.

4
THE ILKLEY MOOR ALIEN

On the morning of 1st December 1987, a man walking across Ilkley Moor in Yorkshire, England, saw and photographed what he believed to be an extra-terrestrial being. Is there any truth to his story? Or was it all a hoax?

Ilkley Moor in West Yorkshire, England, looks very much like one might expect. Wide open expanses of boggy grasslands, a harsh, yet oddly beautiful landscape of low hills and shallow valleys littered with outcrops of rock and odd thickets of trees and wild brush. An eerie place, steeped in mystery and obscurity, it has been said that Ilkley Moor can scare you to death during daylight, but at night it's far worse. Especially in winter, when the northern fogs descend. Situated between the towns of Ilkley in the north and Keighley to the south, the moor is home to many myths and legends. There are countless boulders and large rock formations with strange markings carved into them, some of which are said to date back more than 10,000 years. Over the centuries, locals in the outlying settlements have described all sorts of bizarre phenomena, from weird lights in the sky to reports of strange creatures roaming the moorlands. And one of these encounters, which took place during the 1980s, would go on to make international headlines.

The story begins at 7am on the morning of 1st December 1987, when Philip Spencer, an off-duty policeman, set off towards his father-in-law's house, situated in one of the neighbouring villages. Under normal circumstances he would not have elected to walk across the moor in the dark, and the prospect of doing so was a foreboding one to say the least, but it was a short-cut, and far quicker than walking the perimeter roads. As an amateur photographer, Spencer had hoped to capture some of the famous Ilkley Moor light anomalies, which were caused by the rising sun hitting the early morning mists, so he had taken his camera with him.

Due to their size (roughly 40 square miles), coupled with the thick fog and high winds, the moors could be unforgiving at the best of times, and it was all too easy for someone lose their way whilst hiking across them. So, as a precautionary measure, Spencer also packed his compass. It was a cold morning and the frosty ground crunched underfoot as he stepped off the perimeter road and into the gloomy wilderness beyond. A chance passer-by might well have seen his dark silhouette fading away into the darkness of the thick fog and thought one of two things; either he was a very brave man or completely mad.

Despite Spencer's own reservations, the walk was uneventful and, in actual fact, rather pleasant, but at some point during his journey, he noticed that the day had suddenly dawned. This struck him as odd as he didn't recall seeing the sun rise over the eastern horizon. He did not dwell on it too much, and as he reached a small coppice and was getting ready to take some photographs, a slight movement to his right caught his attention and he turned his head. The image of what he saw standing there would stay with him for the rest of his life.

No more than fifty meters away, on the slight incline of an escarpment, stood a small greyish-green figure, roughly four feet in height. At first glance, he thought he was looking at a young child in a costume, but as his eyes adjusted it became obvious that the small figure was not human in the slightest. Or even an animal for that matter. In fact, it was like nothing he had ever seen before. Its head was abnormally large, and it had big, black, almond shaped eyes. It was gesturing with one of its hands as if to say, *do not come any closer*.

Spencer was utterly bewildered, but after his initial shock had subsided, he raised his camera and snapped a single photo of the strange creature just before it turned and retreated the rest of the way up the escarpment. Although he was some way behind, Spencer hurried after it and reached the crest of the rise just in time to see a dome shaped saucer shooting off into the sky at phenomenal speed. So fast, in fact, that he didn't have time to take another photo. The police officer stood in silence, looking up at the dark clouds, dumbfounded by what he had just witnessed. When he finally came to his senses, he scanned his surroundings for any clues that might explain what had just happened but found nothing. There was no sign whatsoever of the creature or the strange craft ever having been there. Feeling somewhat disorientated, he took out his compass to get a bearing on his location. Whilst he was sure he was facing north, the needle was, oddly, pointing south.

Fortunately, he knew the moors quite well and, thinking the compass may be faulty, decided to disregard its reading altogether and go with his gut instinct. Continuing his journey, he eventually reached his father-in-law's village, which confirmed that the compass needle had indeed been pointing in the wrong direction. A few other anomalies became apparent when Spencer checked the time on the village clock. It indicated that it was just after 10am, at which point he remembered thinking earlier on that it was much lighter than it should have been. His walk across the moor should have taken a little over an hour at most, yet he had started out at 7am and had arrived at his destination a full three hours later. Even with his stopping to take photographs, this should not have been the case. He now realised that either he had set out later than he thought, or he was missing time, the prospect of which he found unsettling, given what he had just witnessed.

Remembering the photograph he had taken, he managed to get the film from his camera developed within 24 hours. Upon examining the shots, he discovered that he had indeed captured an entity of some description, although the image quality was fairly poor. Despite this, he knew he had something of importance and through the proper channels, he was able to contact a UFO investigator by the name of

Peter Hough. During their initial telephone conversation, Hough was sceptical of the police officer's account, thinking that the story sounded far too good to be true.

However, upon meeting and interviewing Spencer, and after viewing the accompanying photograph, he was convinced that he was dealing with a man of integrity, and that the case was genuine. Hough's next step was to have the photograph analysed by several specialists. It was first sent to a wildlife photography expert who confirmed that the creature in the image—if it was a creature at all—did not match the description of any wild or domestic animal local to the area. If anything, it appeared more humanoid in shape. The next stage was to send the image and its negatives to Kodak Laboratories in Hemel, Hempstead, where analysis confirmed that whatever had been captured on film was indeed part of the original photograph, and not superimposed.

Finally, it was sent to the United States for computer enhancement and further examination. Dr. Bruce Maccabee, an optical physicist for the United States Navy, expressed his opinion, concluding that the slow shutter speed used for low light conditions made the film far too grainy for proper analysis. He closed his investigation stating, "I had great hopes that this case would prove definitive. Sadly, circumstances prevent it from being so."

Somewhat indifferent to Maccabee's comments, Hough turned his attention to other aspects of the case, such as the compass and the scene where the encounter had allegedly taken place. Both were examined by a local university, and neither was found to exhibit any signs of radiation. However, it was confirmed that the polarity of the compass needle had been reversed, suggesting that it had been subjected to a strong magnetic field at some point in time. With that, the investigation was effectively drawn to a close.

Over the next few months, Spencer began to have strange dreams and, as a result, became deeply troubled by the missing time he had experienced. Hough suggested that he undergo regressive hypnosis as soon as possible. They contacted Dr. Jim Singleton, who agreed to conduct the session at the home of Arthur Tomlinson on 16th March 1988. Also in attendance was Matthew Hill, a journalist friend of Hough's, whose responsibility it was to operate the recording equipment. Under hypnosis, Spencer described an extraordinary encounter, saying that he had been walking along the moor when he had suddenly spotted the strange creature just ahead of him.

It was said to have been around four feet tall, with a large head and dark eyes, and greyish-green skin. It had unusually long arms, but short legs, which appeared thin, almost as if they were in a state of atrophy. One of its most striking features was its exceptionally large hands. Spencer was astonished when the entity began to approach him and found that he was stuck to the spot, unable to move. He then recalled floating in a horizontal position, no more than two feet above the ground as the creature walked ahead of him, pulling him along as a child would a helium balloon. They finally reached a strange craft at the top of an escarpment where he immediately blacked out.

Upon waking, he found himself in a bright, round room, where a voice told him not to be afraid. He discovered that he was able move freely but remained still as he was examined by three more humanoids, similar to the one he had encountered earlier. He was then shown two films, one of which depicted mankind's continual destruction of the planet through war and other means, such as pollution and deforestation. The second film remains a mystery, as Spencer was instructed by his captors never to talk about it. And he has since refused to do so, even under hypnosis.

Afterwards, the voice asked him if he understood what he had been shown, which he acknowledged with a nod before blacking out again and finding himself back on the Moor. A small movement to his right caused him to turn his head and that's when he saw and photographed the small humanoid figure, although at that exact moment he did not recall his abduction, or ever having seen the entity before.

So, the question remains; what exactly did Spencer photograph that day? Is there any truth to his tale? At least as far as the image is concerned, it can't be debunked for the same reasons that it can't be given as proof; the image quality is too poor to provide any conclusive determination one way or the other. Whilst it could well be a genuine picture of an extra-terrestrial entity, it could just as easily be a bush of some variety, or even a mannequin.

Some years later, another investigator visited the scene of the encounter and photographed himself at the same distance and location in order to get a sense of scale. This demonstrated that, whatever had been photographed had been around the height reported by Spencer. Furthermore, there was no bush or hedge in the exact spot where it had been standing, somewhat ruling out the possibility that the anomaly was part of the foliage. Despite this, sceptics have been quick to dismiss the case as a hoax as, indeed, it wouldn't have been too difficult to perpetrate. One thing they have frequently pointed out is the awkward angle at which the figure appears to be standing, almost as if it is being propped up in some way, as a mannequin would need to be. Secondly, the compass could easily have been tampered with before Spencer even set out on his walk.

And finally, particular attention has been drawn to how apparently absurd Spencer's abduction experience sounds. For instance, why would beings of a higher intelligence show him, a simple policeman with no power whatsoever to do anything about mankind's wider problems, a film about our gradual destruction of the planet? Doubters have likened this idea to showing a domestic cat a film on why it should not foul the cabbage patch. That said, sceptics are no more qualified to speculate on the thought processes of extra-terrestrials than anyone else. Who could possibly know the inner workings of their minds?

One undeniable fact of the case is that Spencer has remained steadfast regarding the details of his story. By all accounts he seemed a very genuine individual, who sought little financial gain from his experience. One should question, then, what his motives would have been behind propagating such a hoax, especially as the name Philip Spencer is actually a pseudonym, and his real name remains unknown, so it is quite evident that he has not sought fame either. The community's opinion on the photograph and the alleged alien abduction experience remains split. Believers will see what they want to see, and sceptics will see nothing at all. Ultimately, it all depends on one's mind-set, and for that reason; the case remains wide open to debate.

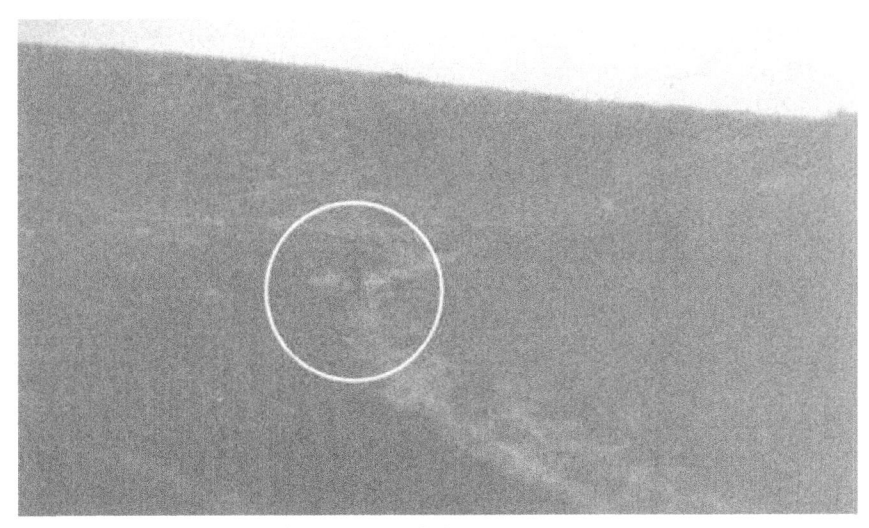

Fig. 1 - *Original image with creature circled*

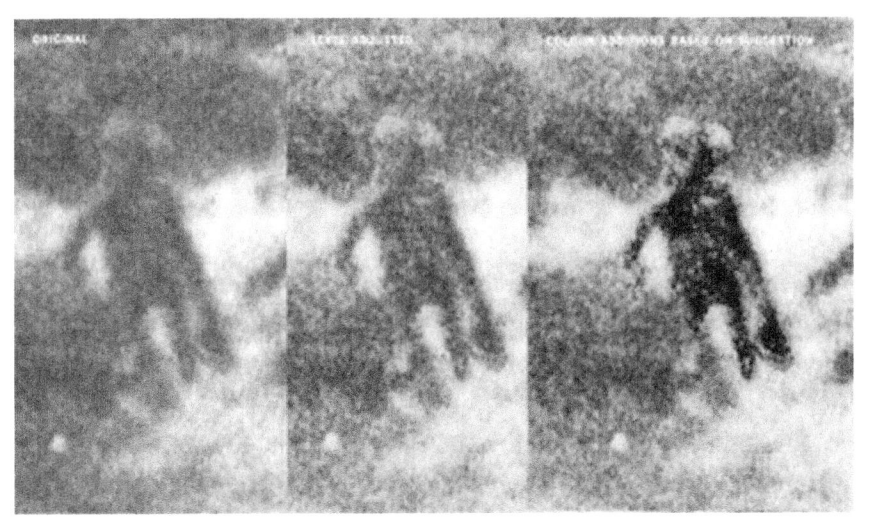

Fig. 2 - *Image of creature with colour enhancement*

5
THE CURSE OF THE OURANG MEDAN

In 1947, a ship was found drifting in the middle of the Indian Ocean. All crew aboard were found dead, yet the ship was undamaged, and their bodies showed no signs of injury. How did they die?

The Strait of Malacca, situated between Malaysia and the island of Sumatra, is one of the busiest and most important shipping lanes in the world, linking major world economies such as China, India, and Japan. Around 260 ships pass through the strait each day carrying approximately one quarter of the world's traded goods. Its significance as a major logistical highway of the seas is matched only by its notoriety, not least because for centuries it was completely at the mercy of pirates, but also because it is one of the most congested shipping lanes in the world. It narrows to just 1.5 miles wide at the Phillips Channel, making it impassable for some of the largest vessels. Perhaps this is to their benefit, as there is, of course, another reason for the strait's unwelcome reputation. Over the last century, it has committed to the deep more than thirty ships, roughly one every three to four years. And one such vessel, the SS Ourang Medan, would meet with such a strange and violent end, that it would unsettle seafarers for decades, and ultimately pass into legend.

In June 1947, so the story goes, ships navigating the Strait of Malacca received a peculiar SOS communication from a then unknown source. Transmitted in Morse code, the message came in two parts, which did not identify the ship or its location, but gave a chilling insight into its situation. It read:

> *"All officers, including the captain are dead. Lying in chart room and bridge. Possibly whole crew dead."*

This was followed only minutes later by a rather distressing conclusion, which simply said, *"I die…"* Nothing else was transmitted after this point and authorities found themselves in a race against time to try and locate ship in question. All other ships in the area were alerted and asked to stay on the lookout for anything unusual, although nothing was found during the initial stages of the search. Eventually, with the help of British and Dutch listening posts, they were able to triangulate the source of the transmission, and the location was found to be far out to sea, in the middle of the Indian Ocean, some way off well-established shipping lanes.

An American merchant vessel, the Silver Star, happened to be closest to the source of the signal at that time and was sent the coordinates. The captain of this vessel , knowing the contents of the SOS, wasted no time in setting a new course and, within a few hours, sighted a ship upon the horizon. The identity of the ship would turn out to be the SS Ourang Medan. She did not appear to be under steam or any form of control and, by all accounts, was said to be drifting aimlessly across the open ocean.

Upon approach, several attempts were made to contact her crew, all of which resulted in failure. There were no signs of life to be seen anywhere, and it was becoming ominously apparent that something had befallen the ship and all those aboard. A deafening silence descended over the scene as the rescue vessel pulled in on her starboard side. The two ships were tethered, and a rescue party was hastily assembled. The crew of the Silver Star began to prepare themselves under a thickening air of trepidation. Unfortunately, their worst fears were confirmed as soon as they stepped aboard and saw that the decks were littered with the corpses of the Dutch crew. Each one was found staring in wide-eyed fear, mouths agape, their faces twisted in horror, and their limbs frozen in positions which suggested they had been trying to fight off something which had been attacking them. Even the ship's dog was found dead, its teeth exposed, and lips peeled back in a vicious snarl.

Searching the rest of the ship, they found the captain's body on the bridge and the rest of the officers in the wheelhouse and chart room. The engineering crew were found at their stations, and the radio operator, the man who had sent the SOS, was found at his post, his body sprawled over the communications equipment. All had the expression of fear on their faces, with arms and legs contorted in the same way. It was obvious that everyone aboard had died in some degree of pain. However, the cause of their deaths could not be determined. The ship was undamaged and although it looked as if the crew had been terrified at the time of their passing, they had suffered no injuries to speak of.

Their bodies would otherwise have been perfectly healthy if not for another bizarre turn of events, which was becoming more apparent to the rescue party with each passing minute. The corpses were already beginning to decompose, much quicker than would naturally be expected. And this wasn't the only strange thing happening aboard the stricken vessel. The crew of the Silver Star also noticed that, although it was a clear summer's day, with temperatures in excess of 37 degrees Celsius (100 degrees Fahrenheit), there was a notable chill in the air. Measurements taken aboard the Ourang Medan put temperatures as low as 4 degrees Celsius (40 degrees Fahrenheit) in some places.

Despite these findings, the captain of the Silver Star made the decision to tow the ship back to port for salvage. But shortly after the two vessels had been tethered together from bow to the stern, smoke began to billow from below the decks of the Ourang Medan, particularly from the number four cargo hold. The rescue ship managed to cut the tow ropes just in time, and within seconds of doing so, the Ourang Medan exploded with such force that her hull was lifted completely out of the water. She quickly broke apart and sank into the dark depths of the Indian Ocean, never to be seen again.

Fortunately, none of the Silver Star crew members were harmed in the blast. Nobody had been on the doomed vessel when she had exploded, as no one had been willing to stay aboard and accompany her back to port, for obvious reasons. It was also lucky that the explosion had not occurred whilst the two ships were floating side by side, and it is down to the crew's vigilance that we have any insight into the incident at all. The story was first officially reported in May of 1952 by the United States Coast Guard, and since then, people have questioned exactly what happened to the crew of the ill-fated ship. As always, there has been no shortage of wild speculation.

Inevitably, comparisons have been drawn to the Philadelphia Experiment, with some theorists suggesting that the Ourang Medan had been part of some clandestine government exercise, which had gone awry. Others have said that the ship had been attacked by forces of a supernatural or paranormal nature, for how could one rationally explain the strange deaths of all those aboard? And of course, there are the doubters who question whether the ship even existed at all. An interesting fact arose when investigators researched the story and found that the name Ourang Medan did not appear in any maritime records and it had not been registered in any known port. But there could be a logical explanation for this.

A German author by the name of Otto Mielke published his research on the case in 1954, which was apparently authenticated by members of the Silver Star's crew, who had been present at the time of the incident. Mielke's work cited several previously unpublished details, which included the ship's last known location, as well as its intended shipping route. More importantly, it made mention of the ship's cargo, a point which seemed to suggest that the Ourang Medan had been carrying unsecured lethal substances, such as potassium cyanide and nitro-glycerine. If true, then this would have been seen by authorities as the height of negligence and a ship carrying such a cargo would never have been allowed to leave port.

It is for this reason that some believe the Ourang Medan was involved in a smuggling operation, and was in fact another ship altogether, hastily renamed whilst at sea in order to disguise her identity, hence not being registered anywhere. This could also explain why she had been so far off established shipping routes, in order to avoid detection. It is theorised that sea water had entered the cargo hold and reacted with the potassium cyanide, which in turn released toxic gasses, poisoning the crew. As the day wore on, the saltwater somehow reached the nitro-glycerine, starting the fire which ultimately caused the ship's violent end.

But if this were the case, then why had none of the rescue party also succumbed to the lethal effects of the cyanide gas, which would have been highly concentrated by the time they arrived? Another problem with this theory is that, whilst cyanide kills quickly and is thought to result in a painful death, the general appearance of the victims would have been very different. Cyanide is an enzyme inhibitor, which ultimately stops blood cells within the body from carrying oxygen. A death from cyanide poisoning is said to resemble drowning; it causes the victim to struggle and panic as their muscles and organs begin to shut down from the effects of histotoxic hypoxia. Once the victim passes away, their body relaxes into a posture more suggestive of a peaceful death.

However, many of the bodies on the Ourang Medan were said to be contorted in pain and terror, as if they had suffered intense muscle spasms, a characteristic which is more typical of nerve agents. For this reason, other researchers have suggested that the ship was not carrying potassium cyanide at all, but another substance known as Tabun. Tabun is an extremely toxic nerve agent, which had been mass produced by the Germans in World War II and had been shared in large quantities with their Japanese allies. During the post-war years following the defeat of the Axis forces, the Western Allies were busy persuading German scientists to defect, and procuring all sorts of enemy war assets, of which Tabun would have been one.

The US was heavily involved in chemical weapon research at this time and elements of the US military could well have commandeered large quantities of the Japanese supplies. It is feasible that in order to avoid the inevitable paper trail, they commissioned a nondescript freighter to transport the goods and employed a foreign crew to further distance themselves from the operation. It is also worth mentioning that Tabun has a very low persistence level, meaning that it would have completely dispersed by the time the rescue crew arrived. It also blocks the neurotransmitter responsible for signalling the muscles to relax, hence the contorted appearance of the bodies.

The story of the Ourang Medan can neither be proven nor disproven. It is entirely possible that it is nothing more than another tall tale of the sea, but the official mention by the US Coast Guard seems to counter this. Not only that, but some researchers have dedicated more than 50 years of their lives to studying the case, so there must be something more to it than mere fabrication. It is not beyond all likelihood that something clandestine was taking place, whether officially or unofficially, and this would also explain the lack of recorded evidence, as is often the case with such matters. The fact is this story is more than half a century old, and any enthusiasm that might have been felt in researching it any further has long since dried up. If the Ourang Medan did exist, nobody is looking for her, and unless someone discovers, by chance or otherwise, her final resting place, we'll never know the truth of the matter. We are, once again, left to wonder.

6
BONES ON MARS

Have humans already visited Mars, either in recent times or possibly even in our distant past? And could images beamed back from various probes provide any proof of this? Or is it just another case of pareidolia? Strap yourselves in; this one is well and truly out of this world.

Mars, Earth's second closest neighbour is cold, barren, and deadly. Orbiting at an average distance of 142 million miles from the sun, human beings are yet to set foot upon this small, unforgiving world. Or are we? Mars is undoubtedly the next steppingstone in our ongoing exploration of the solar system, but does mankind have a much greater link to the red planet than we realise? Have we secretly already visited Mars? Could ancient civilisations have travelled there? Or maybe even have originated there?

Back in 1976, the Viking 1 space craft in orbit around the red planet was tasked with photographing the Martian surface and beaming the images back to Earth for analysis. This was so that NASA could locate and select suitable landing sites for its sister ship; Viking 2. In late July of that year, Viking 1 sent back eighteen images of a region in the planet's northern hemisphere which had, up until that point, remained uncharted. Little did NASA know it at the time, but one of those images would go on capture the public's imagination for decades to come.

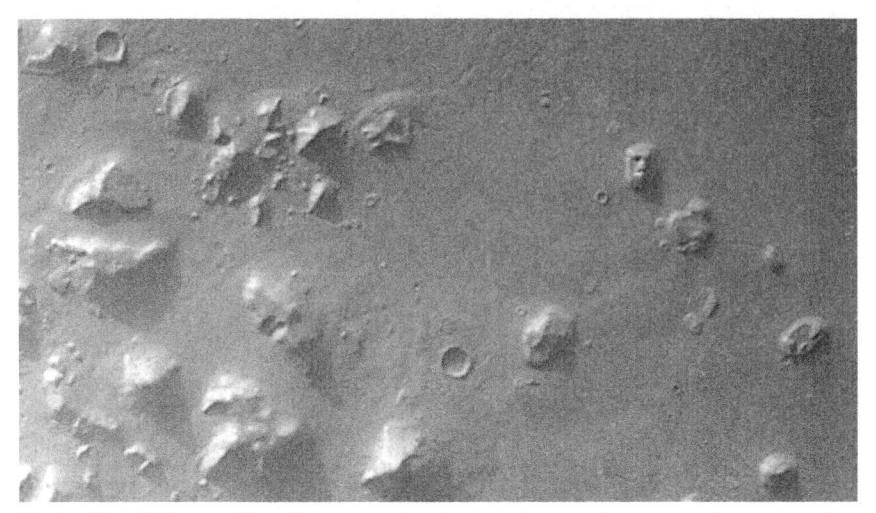

Fig 3 - *The Cydonian Complex*

At first glance it appeared to be nothing more than an expansive and unremarkable plateau. But on closer inspection, tucked away in an area covering no more than 25 square miles, mission controllers were startled to see what resembled a huge human-like face staring back at them. This face was surrounded by several other unnatural looking structures, which initially raised a few eyebrows, but when examined further, NASA officials simply deemed these anomalies to be optical illusions and released the pictures regardless.

The notion of civilisations on Mars had been a huge part of science fiction culture for well over a century by this time, and when the image finally went public in the weeks that followed, imaginations understandably ran wild. Aside from the face, other features within the same area were singled out, such as "the city" and "five-sided pyramid", seen in the top left of Fig 3. Conspiracy theorists claimed that there was no way these structures could have formed naturally, though geologists largely disagreed with this. Even so, the region became known as The

Cydonian Complex and, in the wake of its discovery, inspired many science fiction writers and alternate history theorists alike.

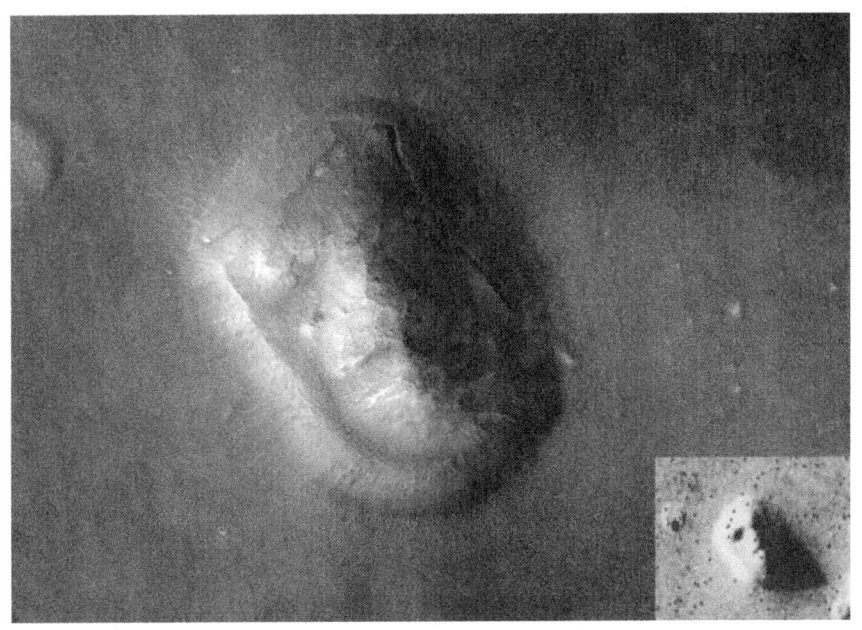

Fig. 4 - *Unmasking the face. Later NASA images showed the "face on Mars" to be little more than a mesa of jagged rocks*

Over the years, sensationalism over the Cydonian Complex gradually evaporated as both the European Space Agency and NASA released more images of the region from different angles and altitudes and at greater resolutions. These revealed "the face" to be nothing more than a large mesa of jagged rocks. The official explanation was that when viewed from just the right angle, tricks of light and shadow combine to give it the spooky appearance of a face looking back at us but, in reality, it bears little to no resemblance as such.

However, some proponents of the theories regarding ancient Martian civilisations remained unconvinced, declaring that these new images were forgeries on the parts of both NASA and the ESA in order to cover up the truth. Subscribers to this belief were largely alone in their assumptions. That was, at least, until 2004 when the NASA rovers, Spirit and Opportunity, touched down on the surface of Mars and began transmitting some very interesting images back to Earth.

Fig. 5 - *Photo taken by Spirit. Some believe this looks very much like a human skull half buried in the Martian soil*

Fig. 5 was captured by the Spirit Rover in 2005, and for almost a decade it sat in NASA's archives without so much as a whisper of anything untoward. It was not until 2014 that the more eagle-eyed observers amongst us noticed something strange and all the attention was suddenly on the rock in the top left corner. On closer inspection it looks very much like a human or humanoid skull half buried in the Martian soil and whilst one might simply put this down to pareidolia, even the most ardent of sceptics would have to agree that its resemblance to a human skull is rather striking.

Spirit continued to send back more anomalies, pictures of rocks which are believed to resemble elongated skulls, similar to those found in ancient Mayan ruins and those of other cultures, the result of a process known as head binding. These images lead many to believe that ancient civilisations were somehow able to travel to Mars, or that they might have even originated there. There are countless prehistoric cave drawings, ancient works of art and paintings from the middle ages which are believed to depict visitations by UFOs and interactions with extra-terrestrial beings. And whilst many sceptics would argue that this is purely down to interpretation, it is not beyond all possibility.

Unfortunately, Spirit became unresponsive in 2010 and Opportunity suffered a similar fate in June 2018, but another rover, Curiosity, which was sent to the red planet in 2011 continues to transmit images to this day. And some of them are quite peculiar to say the least. Skulls aside, other anomalies have also been captured.

Whilst these images are quite compelling for some and hard to believe for others, things are about to get even weirder. In July 2014, an ex-US Marine going under the pseudonym of Captain Kaye reported to the press that he had spent seventeen of his twenty years in the Navy posted on Mars, protecting five human colonies from indigenous Martian life forms. What is even more astonishing is that he is not the first person to speak out in public about these supposed Martian colonies. Three other so-called whistle-blowers by the names of Michael Relfe, Randy Cramer, and Corey Goode have also provided testimonies regarding Lunar and Martian bases and a top-secret space programme, which all seem to corroborate Kaye's account.

Even Laura Magdalene Eisenhower, the great-granddaughter of President Eisenhower, claims that covert efforts were made in order to recruit her as part of a colony on Mars, which was headed by famed physicist Dr. Hal Puthoff. Once again, images from the Martian rovers have played an important role in these so-called revelations, with many conspiracy theorists declaring that they have found proof within those photographs that all is not as it seems on the red planet. They have cited the examples seen in figures 11, 12 and 13.

Fig. 6 - *Photo taken by Spirit. Some believe this to be an elongated skulls*

Fig. 7 - *Photo taken by Spirit. Another so-called elongated skull*

Fig. 8 - *Photo taken by Spirit. Another supposed human or alien skull*

Fig. 9 - *Photo taken by Curiosity. Could this be a thigh bone?*

Fig. 10 - *Photo taken by Curiosity. Many believe this to be the head of a statue looking skyward*

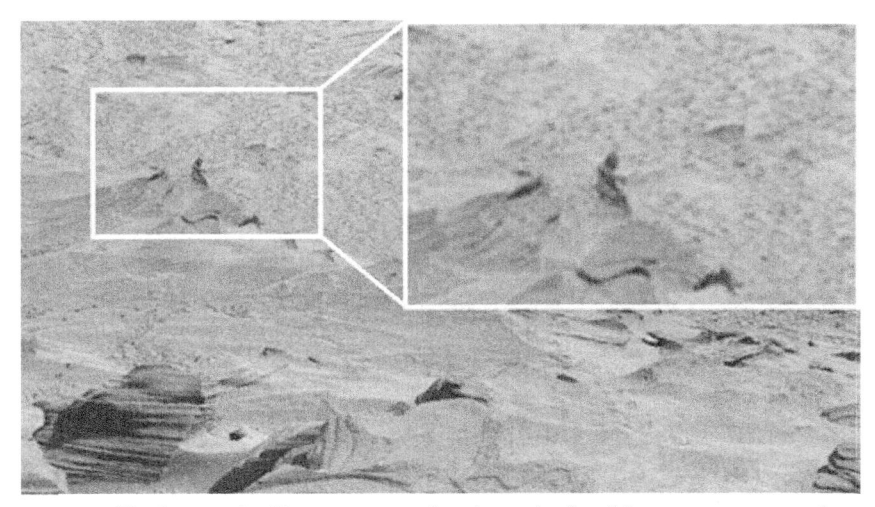

Fig. 11 - *The Sasquatch - This image is said to show a bigfoot-like creature running down the side of a hill*

Fig. 12 - *The Guardian - This shot seems to depict what looks like a small figure running towards the rover whilst waving its arms, as if to ward off an intruder. Particular attention has been drawn to what looks like a plume of dust rising behind it*

Fig. 13 - *The Watcher - This rather eerie image shows what looks like a small dark figure standing on top of a distant cliff, observing the rover as it passes by*

Fig. 14 - *Odd light anomaly - This picture was taken just before sunset and appears to show a light in the distance. Sceptics have said that this could be a geyser.*

Fig. 15 - *This image is said to depict a UFO flying across the surface of the planet during the afternoon. This is rather interesting, as it cannot simply be explained away as a misidentified bird or otherwise. And there are numerous photographs of supposed UFOs on Mars besides this one, so the possibility of it being a one-off anomaly in the photograph itself is also unlikely*

So, do any of these images provide unequivocal proof that the rovers are not alone on the red planet? Or that they have captured pictures of bones, human or otherwise? Unfortunately, not. The images are far from conclusive. The bones and other anomalies are likely nothing more than odd shaped rocks. It is human nature to see familiar patterns, particularly those of faces, when looking at random markings or objects. This is known as pareidolia and is the most likely explanation for what we see in these images.

Another explanation, which has taken hold more recently—especially within the Flat Earth community—is that the reason these images appear to show bones or unnatural abnormalities is because the rovers never went to Mars in the first place. Every single one of those images was taken here on Earth, so it is only natural that you would see Earth-centric anomalies within them. But what of the supposed secret space programme and Martian colonies reported by Captain Kaye and other so-called whistle-blowers? Whilst these accounts do make for a fascinating read, not one of those individuals has provided any proof whatsoever of their experiences. And until they do, we are stuck with the official narrative regarding Mars and the wider solar system.

But do not let that assumption deter you from your belief if you are so inclined to support any of these ideas. The thought of humans having visited or even originated from Mars is a fascinating one. The solar system is ancient and, particularly for those who believe in life beyond the stars, it is highly probable that we will one day find the fossilised remains of an alien life form, within the solar system or otherwise. And let's not forget the slim possibility that what we are looking at in those images are, indeed, bones. Or that Captain Kaye, Michael Relfe, Randy Cramer, and Corey Goode could all be telling the truth. Until we know for sure, we should never fail to keep an open mind.

7
THE LAST MOMENTS OF ELISA LAM

In February 2013, a young woman was found dead on the rooftop of a Los Angeles hotel. The subject of much scrutiny, it became something of an internet sensation in the weeks that followed, and the circumstances surrounding her death are both mysterious and harrowing.

When investigating any inexplicable incident, it is essential for the authorities to recreate an accurate representation of the victim's movements leading up to their death or disappearance. With some of the cases we have recounted so far, it was an overwhelming lack of detail, regarding the final days and hours of those involved, that prevented the riddle of their demise from ever being fully resolved. In the case of Elisa Lam, the issue was quite the opposite. Here, the detectives tasked with solving this mystery were instead faced with an overabundance of information about her final moments. So much so, that it would prove impossible to come up with a satisfactory summary of the incident, as every new piece of evidence that was uncovered only served to undermine their existing and working hypotheses.

Lam Ho Yi or 'Elisa' Lam to her friends, was born in Vancouver, Canada, on 30th April 1991, to parents of Hong Kong descent. Shortly after her birth the family settled in Burnaby, a multicultural city in British Columbia, Canada, and this is where Elisa would spend her formative years. Although she had experienced a comfortable upbringing in a secure environment and had always been a happy child, her teen years would be plagued with depression, brought on by her Bipolar Disorder, which would prove to be highly debilitating. Despite this, she developed an early desire to travel and see the world and refused to let her personal issues get in the way of this dream.

She had enjoyed moderate academic success and it was at the age of 21, whilst attending the University of British Columbia, that she decided to take a trip to the United States, embarking on what she would refer to as her "West Coast Tour", exploring numerous regions, cities, and towns during her visit. Her parents more than likely wondered and worried about the prospects which lay ahead for their daughter. As they waved her off for the last time, they couldn't have known that it would be this trip, and in particular, her stay at the Cecil Hotel in Los Angeles, that would ultimately seal her fate. Sadly, they never saw their daughter alive again.

The Cecil Hotel already had a notorious reputation for its history of macabre events involving guests, with at least fourteen deaths by non-natural causes occurring there, including multiple suicides dating back to 1931 and the violent murder of a retired telephone operator in 1964. Notable serial killers such as Jack Untereiger and Richard Ramirez are also known to have stayed at the Cecil. And as if that wasn't chilling enough, paranormal incidents have been documented there on numerous occasions, with some guests even reporting instances in which they had been choked by unseen hands.

Whilst it is not known for sure whether Elisa stayed here out of choice or convenience, the venue clearly had a dark reputation, and as we will discover, the Cecil would provide the setting for the events which led to yet another unforeseen tragedy. Surprisingly, a significant amount of information is known about Elisa's movements in the days leading up to her disappearance, as she was active on social media, updating her Tumblr account regularly with images and commentary regarding her trip. She travelled alone via Amtrak and intercity buses and it is agreed that she visited San Diego Zoo before finally settling at the Cecil on the evening of 28th January 2013. She was initially allocated shared hostel style accommodation on the fifth floor but was later moved after her roommates complained about her odd behaviour. This is not surprising. Elisa's Bipolar Disorder might have caused those around her to feel uncomfortable.

However, some believe her being asked to switch rooms is a complete fabrication on the part of the hotel. There are those who postulate that a worker there may have been involved in her death and that this small detail was simply an attempt to further portray her as a mentally unstable individual and assuage any blame against themselves. Whatever the truth of the matter, it is known that she settled into a single room by herself on that first night, and that this is where she remained until the day she disappeared. On her second night, she updated her Tumblr status with an ominous post, saying that she was having trouble with "creepers" in the hotel. A small detail, but one which would ultimately contribute to widespread disagreements over the cause of her death. Elisa was last seen on 31st January, buying gifts for her family.

Katie Orphan, the manager of a nearby bookstore, reported that she seemed to be in high spirits, describing her mood as outgoing and happy. Orphan also reported that she was alone at that time. Elisa was scheduled to check out of the Cecil on that same day, but nobody, not even hotel staff recalled seeing her after this date. She had been in regular contact with her parents during her trip, updating them every other day on her whereabouts and intended destinations, and the last time they had heard from her was on the 30th. They did not speak to her on 31st and became concerned by 2nd February when she failed to get in touch. They had tried calling her several times, but there had been no answer. They eventually contacted the LAPD, reporting her as a missing person, and flew to Los Angeles to assist in the search.

Initial efforts to track Elisa down proved unsuccessful. Her belongings were still in her room, untouched, though they could not locate her mobile phone or laptop. Hundreds of man hours went into the search, sniffer dogs were deployed, and flyers were distributed throughout the neighbourhood and posted online, all of which failed to generate any leads. It was becoming more and more likely with each passing day that something unspeakable had happened to her, and her family began to prepare themselves for the worst. On Valentine's Day, two weeks after her disappearance, the LAPD released CCTV footage of her last known sighting, taken from inside an elevator in the Cecil hotel and timestamped at 2am on 1st February.

During the short film, Elisa enters the elevator, presses all the buttons, and awaits a response, but the doors fail to close. She then steps out into the corridor, quickly peeks right, then left and steps back in. She then backs up into the corner of the lift nearest the control panel as if hiding from someone. After a few more seconds, she steps back towards the doorway and leans against the elevator door itself, which has still failed to close. She then steps forward into the corridor, then to her left, then back into the elevator and back out again, this time standing mostly off camera to the left of the doorway. After approximately 25 seconds, she re-enters the elevator with both hands on her head, as if confused. She then spends around 15 seconds pressing every single one of the buttons on the control panel, before stepping back outside of the elevator for the final time. Once again, she stands to the left of the doorway and it is here that the most disturbing part of the video takes shape.

She begins gesticulating in a very strange way, waving her hands out to her sides, palms flat and fingers outstretched, bowing slightly forward whilst rocking back and forth. She continues like this for almost a minute and the last time we see her, she is walking away down the corridor in the direction she originally came from. The elevator door then closes for the first time since the start of the film. The entire video is around four minutes in length; a long time for somebody to consider using an elevator in normal circumstances. Whilst the CCTV footage disturbed a great many people when it was released online, and was rather chilling to watch, it was but a prelude, leading up to the harrowing discovery, made only five days later.

Less than 72 hours after the footage was made public, guests at the hotel began complaining about low water pressure in their rooms. Some also reported that the water coming from their taps was discoloured and had an unusual odour and taste. Hotel staff began to investigate and on the morning of the 19th February, an employee was sent to the roof to check the supply. The water was held in four cylindrical 1000-gallon tanks and was pumped directly from the city's main water board. In one of them, he found Elisa's decomposing body, floating face up, a foot below the surface. The police were called and, by noon that day, the tank had been completely drained so that firefighters could cut it open and retrieve her body, since the access hatch was too small to accommodate the necessary equipment. Her family was notified, and an autopsy was scheduled for later that afternoon.

After two days, the coroner's office ruled that the cause of her death had been accidental drowning, with her bipolar disorder being a significant factor. It was theorised that she had suffered from some form of psychotic break, that she had then made her way to the roof and had climbed into one of the water tanks by herself, not realising the danger in doing so. The full coroner's report was not released until four months later, after a number of delays, and it was reported that her naked body had been discovered in the tank, bloated and greenish in colour, suggesting that she had been there for a number of weeks. Found floating beside her were the clothes which she appeared to have been wearing in the elevator video, as well as her watch and room key. No signs of physical trauma or sexual assault had been noted and there was no evidence to suggest that she had committed suicide. No traces of illicit substances were detected in her blood, although a minute amount of alcohol, as well as small traces of her prescription medication, showed up in toxicology reports.

There were many unresolved issues surrounding the case, and this report did little to satisfy either her family members or the thousands of people in online forums who had been closely following the news regarding her death. Amongst the many unanswered questions was the issue of how she even got up to the roof in the first place. It was reported at the time that the roof was locked off to hotel guests and that any unauthorised access would have triggered alarms. Another query arose over how she got into the tank itself, as each one was eight feet tall and sat on a four-foot-high concrete block, giving a total height of twelve feet. The access port was situated right on top of the tank and there was supposedly no fixed ladder in place, so the question of how she managed to get up there was prominent during the investigation.

Another issue related to this was that the lids on the access ports were said to be quite heavy (approximately 30-40kg), and many people questioned how a petite person, such as Elisa, could have lifted one of them to gain access. Furthermore, they asked how she could have closed the lid after climbing inside. There was no way she could have reached it and, as we have already established, its weight would have made the effort all the more difficult. The biggest queries of all, though, centred well and truly on the elevator video, which, rather than helping the investigation, simply confused things further. It had become something of an internet sensation by this time and assumptions about the cause of her death began to take on a much more sinister vibe.

Whilst a possible psychotic break and accidental drowning are the most accepted explanations, it has been noted that at least two sex offenders were known to have been living permanently at Cecil Hotel whilst Elisa had been staying there. It is no surprise that there are many people who have drawn inevitable conclusions in this direction, theorising that she had been murdered and dumped in the water tank. Even though there was no evidence of sexual assault, the autopsy report did note a subcutaneous pooling of blood in her anal canal, which some observers have suggested is a sign of sexual abuse. The pathologist stated that this could have been due to bloating in the course of the body's decomposition and that her rectum was also prolapsed.

Although Elisa's actions in the elevator are most definitely odd, she does not look like someone who is trying to escape from a would-be attacker. But then, it is not known how much time passed between its recording and her death. Explanations for her strange behaviour and, in particular, her odd gesticulations raise the possibility that she was under the influence of recreational drugs. Even though no illicit substances were found in her blood, these could have broken down during the time her body had been in the tank.

As much as people have speculated over Elisa's actions, the footage itself must be critiqued. Given that the video's running time is obscured, many now believe that parts of it have been subject to editing, either by the police or hotel staff, perhaps to hide someone's identity, though both organisations deny this. In other parts of the clip, it appears as though footage has been slowed down and there are claims that Elisa's mouth has been pixelated in order to make it difficult to read her lips, further fuelling speculation that other parties were involved.

There have also been suggestions angling towards the paranormal, with those who are open to the idea that Elisa was temporarily possessed. They describe her movements as inhuman at times, a possible connection to the Cecil's dark past and reputation for paranormal occurrences. In keeping with these fringe explanations, it is interesting, and as it happens, rather chilling, to note the sheer number of unlikely coincidences surrounding her death.

Comparisons have been drawn between this incident and a film which was released in 2005 called *Dark Water*, a remake of an earlier Japanese film of the same name. In it, a mother and daughter move into a rundown apartment building. A dysfunctional elevator and discoloured water coming from the building's supply eventually lead them to a rooftop water tank, where they discover the body of a young girl. What is decidedly odd about this is the fact that the daughter's name is Cecilia and the mother's name is Dahlia. The Black Dahlia was a nickname given to Elizabeth Short, a murder victim whose last known sighting was at the Cecil Hotel in Los Angeles in 1947.

But the peculiar coincidences don't end there.

A TB outbreak occurred in the neighbourhood surrounding the Cecil in the days after Lam's body was discovered. The screening kits they used to test patients was called LAM-ELISA. sPerhaps even more bizarre is what has recently been dubbed the "cemetery synchronicity phenomenon", which is now attributed to this case. The Last Bookstore—the store where Elisa was last seen alive—uses a registrant privacy company for their website which is based in Burnaby, the suburb of Vancouver where Elisa was from. The address given is a PO Box on Canada Way in Burnaby itself. However, the postal/zip code which is displayed for this address shows up as inside Forest Lawn Cemetery. This is where the remains of Elisa Lam's body now reside.

It is difficult to say what exactly happened during the last moments of Elisa Lam's life, and whether any of the issues surrounding the hotel's rooftop and her odd behaviour in the elevator can be explained. The more rational explanations do seem to answer some of the niggling questions. For instance, visitors to the hotel over the last few years have demonstrated that she could have gained access to the roof via the fire escape, rather than through the fire doors which were connected to the alarm. Videos posted online many years before her death show a number of hotel guests running around on the rooftop of the hotel, somewhat suggesting that the area was not as secure as reported.

Regarding issues surrounding access to the water supply, images taken by news helicopters on the day her body was discovered clearly show that a ladder was chained to the side of one of the tanks and that it was different to the ones being used by firefighters. It is thought that this belonged to the hotel and that it had been there for some time. Also, whilst she might have struggled to lift the heavy lid on the tank's access hatch, it is not beyond all possibility that she succeeded in doing so. Some witnesses suggested that the lids were not that heavy to begin with. Whether Elisa could have closed the lid from inside the tank is now a moot point, as the individual who located her body later stated that the hatch was open when he found her.

As for her strange behaviour in the lift... The chances are that you have already seen the video by now and perhaps found it disturbing, especially if you are inclined to believe that something more sinister occurred. But if you look at it in a way which suggests she is not alone and is in fact playing a game of hide and seek with someone off camera, the video takes on a whole new meaning. It was confirmed by hotel staff that pressing numerous buttons on the elevator control panel causes the doors, and the lift itself, to hold for up to two minutes. Elisa probably would have known this. When she enters the elevator, she is not intending to ride it alone, perhaps not even intending to ride it at all, but use it as a hiding place, hiding from whoever she was with at the time. She steps in, presses all the buttons, and looks expectantly out into the hall in the direction she came from as if waiting for someone to follow her in.

When that person does not appear, she takes a quick look out into the corridor, both left and right and then steps back in. She huddles into one of the corners, ready to jump scare whoever she is expecting. When that person still doesn't appear, she waits by the door then goes back out into the corridor, side and back stepping in an aimless way, which would otherwise look odd, but doesn't if you consider that she is in a playful mood. She then stands just outside of the elevator door, perhaps thinking to herself, *Where the hell are they?*. When she steps back into the elevator, she looks slightly annoyed, realises that the lift will start moving soon and presses all the buttons once again to hold it in place. People have queried why she would have pressed all the buttons to stall the lift, when she could have just pressed the "hold" button, but amateur investigators visiting the hotel in 2014 confirmed that the hold button was, in fact, missing.

When she steps back out into the corridor for the final time, those strange hand movements she exhibits do not seem so strange if you consider that she is talking to someone she knows is there, but we cannot see. Her actions suggest that she is gesturing towards the lift and saying something along the lines of "I'm holding the elevator, where are you?". A smile is also visible on her face at this point, suggesting that, once again, this is a playful interaction. The last thing we see her do is count on her fingers, almost as if she has had enough of waiting and is telling the person that she will count to three and if they haven't appeared by then she will leave. She then proceeds to count to three, waits the customary extra couple of seconds and walks off.

Taking this into consideration, it seems that there was, indeed, another presence besides Elisa, who was with her at the time the footage was captured. Whether they had anything to do with her death is another matter altogether, but the question is who or what was this other presence? Were they real or imaginary? Or possibly even of a paranormal nature? Did they accompany her to the roof? And did they kill her and dump her body in the water tank? Or did she die in some other way, causing whoever she was with to panic and hide her body? Did she climb into the water tank by herself?

Experts have examined the film and deemed that, due to her relatively focused coordination and balance, she does not appear to be under the influence of either drugs or alcohol. She was not suicidal, and even if she was, climbing into a deep, dark water tank seems like a very frightening and undesirable way to go. There is of course the possibility that she was experiencing a psychotic break and hallucinated that the water tank was something else entirely, but if this was the case, why would she have removed all her clothes? Whatever the true circumstances surrounding Elisa Lam's death, there is no denying that there are still many unanswered questions, and that the official narrative, as presented by authorities, does not quite add up. One can't help feeling that something is missing here, and we'll probably never know for certain what it is. Our hearts go out to Elisa's family. May she forever rest in peace.

8
THE LEGEND OF THE MOTHMAN

In 1966, the residents of a small town in West Virginia were stalked by an unknown creature with glowing red eyes. Was he real or just a figment of the imagination? And does recent photographic evidence suggest he may have returned?

We now live in an age where most people carry on their person at least one device capable of photographing or recording any given incident. As a result, reports of encounters with monsters and cryptids have become not only less commonplace, but also far less believable. Of all the alleged incidents that feature such entities, the only available evidence is often the verbal testimony of those who were involved. And because actual proof is often lacklustre or non-existent, it is almost routine for these experiences to be written off as campfire stories or urban legends. But what are we to believe when the incident is witnessed over a sustained period, by multiple members of the same community?

Point Pleasant, West Virginia, is a small town with a big history.

Its population of just over four thousand occupies an area of just three square-miles. One would not think of it as a city, but in fact it is. A city surrounded by lush green countryside, bisected by the vast Ohio River, and steeped in larger-than-life legend. As its name suggests, its character is quaint, peaceful, and above all, pleasant. On the surface at least, no one would ever suspect that it was home to one of the most unsettling ordeals of the last half century; one that still strikes fear into the hearts of many.

During the latter half of the 1960s, reports began to surface of a mysterious and horrifying creature stalking residents on the outskirts and surrounding areas of town. Encounters with this entity were said to be so frightening that at least one person suffered from psychological trauma for many years after their experience. The first sighting occurred on 12th November 1966, when five gravediggers, working in a local cemetery near Clendenin, saw what they thought was a human being fly out of a group of trees nearby. They watched for about a minute as it swooped low over their heads and then took off into the distance.

Two days later, on the 14th, a resident of Salem, Newell Partridge, was at his home watching television when he saw two red objects hovering over a field at the rear of his property. Upon investigating, he realised that the glowing objects were, in fact, a pair of eyes, which belonged to a tall, dark figure. This figure was standing on the branch of a tree about a hundred metres distant when it promptly rose up into the air and flew away over the woods, letting out a blood-curdling scream as it went. His dog, a German Shepherd named Bandit, took off in pursuit and was never seen again.

The following evening, on the 15th, two young married couples burst into the Mason County Sheriff's office in a state of panic and distress. They were Mr. & Mrs. Roger Scarberry and Mr. and Mrs. Steve Mallette, and they had been on their way back from a double date, driving close to the "TNT Area" of Point Pleasant, when they saw a tall grey figure standing next to the road. They reported that it looked like a man, but much taller, possibly seven feet or more, and that it appeared to have a pair of wings folded behind its back. In front of it lay the carcass of a dog, the breed of which was never determined, but was later assumed to be that of Newell Partridge's German

Shepherd. As they passed this strange looking figure, it rose into the air and proceeded to fly after the car. Mr. Scarberry, who was driving, sped up to nearly a hundred miles per hour, but the creature was able to keep up, matching the speed of the vehicle. His wife said that it emitted a high pitch screech as it flew and that it had huge red eyes, which glowed like a pair of car reflectors. As they entered the town, it broke off the chase and flew back in the direction of the TNT Area.

A press conference was held on the afternoon of the 16th, where the Scarberry and Mallette couples gave their accounts of the previous evening. Dr. Robert Smith, a wildlife expert, was also in attendance and offered his explanation to the waiting media, saying that what the two couples had actually seen was an abnormally large crane, which had been blown out of its migration route. These reports would hit the local evening papers on the 16th November as word of the encounters spread through the town like wildfire. This, as with any kind of sensationalism, unfortunately invited many fabricated sightings from other so-called eyewitnesses, and from here on out, nearly all of these alleged encounters should be subjected to a much higher scrutiny. That is not to say that all of them are fictitious, however.

One sighting in particular occurred on the evening of the 16th, at around the same time the first evening papers were being deposited in local mailboxes. Mr. and Mrs. Raymond Walmsley, along with Marcella Bennett and her baby daughter, Tina, were on their way to visit the Thomas family, who lived on the outskirts of town. When they pulled up to the Thomas property, the car seemed to disturb something. As they were getting out of the vehicle, they were shocked to see a large grey figure, bigger than a man, rising from the ground nearby, which they described as having terrible glowing red eyes. Marcella was so alarmed that she forgot she was carrying her baby daughter and, in her panic, dropped her. After collecting herself and her child, she ran to the Thomas home and was let in by one of their children.

The creature shuffled after them and continued to terrorise the household by peering in through the windows. By the time the police arrived, over half an hour later, it had of course vanished, but this was not the last Marcella would see of the so-called Mothman of Point Pleasant. She just so happened to live on the outskirts of town, near the

TNT area, and claimed that after her initial encounter at the Thomas residence, the creature had visited her home on several other occasions, and that she often heard its blood-curdling scream in the dead of night. Marcella apparently suffered with nightmares and other mental health issues for many years after her ordeal.

The "TNT Area" of Point Pleasant would later become heavily associated with the Mothman. It is a large tract of land, dotted with small concrete "igloos", used during World War II to store ammunition. It is also adjacent to the 2,500-acre McClintic Wildlife Station and the entire landscape is covered with dense forest, steep hills, and riddled with tunnels. The press would go on to claim that the area provided a sort of home for the creature during its time there, with most of the sightings having occurred in that area. There were many more reported encounters towards the end of 1966, peaking especially in 1967. During December of that year, the Silver River Bridge over the Ohio River collapsed, plunging a number of vehicles into the icy depths, and killing 46 people in the process. Immediately after this, sightings of the Mothman ceased altogether, leading many to believe that the creature was somehow responsible for this tragedy; that it was, in fact, a harbinger of death.

So, who, or rather, what was the Mothman? Was there any truth to the events that took place? Or was it all just an elaborate hoax, orchestrated with the sole intention of increasing tourism to a failing backwater town?

Ideas have been varied to say the least. Sceptics have largely agreed with Dr. Robert Smith's explanation, maintaining that the Mothman was nothing more than a very large bird and this may well have been true. The Sandhill Crane is a large species of bird, common in North America, which normally averages a height of around four feet, but is capable of growing up to six feet. It also has shocks of bright red feathers around its eyes, somewhat matching the descriptions given at the time of the sightings.

Eyewitnesses have taken great issue with this, rejecting the idea that what they saw was a bird, and countering that they would have known the difference. Firstly, it would have to have been abnormally large in order to match the proportions given by those who encountered the strange being; seven feet tall in most cases. Secondly, the Mothman's eyes were said to glow red, and whilst owls exhibit eye-shine when a light source is pointed in their direction, most other birds do not. By all accounts, the creature's eyes glowed red even when no light source was pointing directly towards it. The high pitch scream it emitted was also said to be far more human-like than bird-like, and Mr. Scarberry would go on to question exactly what kind of bird could fly at over a hundred miles per hour. Finally, whilst it might be plausible for one or two witnesses to misidentify a large bird, it would be highly improbable for so many people to have done so. This is, of course, if many of the eyewitness accounts are to be believed.

Sightings dramatically increased after the Scarberry and Mallette accounts were published in the local papers, and it would only be prudent to assume that some, if not most of them were completely fabricated to further inflame the situation. Even the Scarberry/Mallette sighting is said to have several inconsistencies between how the story was originally reported to the police and what it later became in the press. For instance, other sources have it that the creature did not, in fact, fly after their car, but rather shuffled down the road in pursuit for a very short distance. With this in mind, we are once again at the mercy of speculation, and of this there is no shortage. Tourism to the town experienced a noted increase in the wake of those first sightings and, of course, this has led a number of doubters to believe that the entire episode was a cleverly planned hoax, engineered towards that end.

However, the reason this story captured the imaginations of so many in the first place was the result of those first four encounters. These four sightings all happened over the course of as many days in locations that were many miles apart. They were all strikingly similar, even though nothing had been reported in the press during that time, and despite the fact that none of the witnesses knew each other. Add to this that the Sheriff absolutely believed the Scarberrys and Mallettes, having known them for most of their lives and witnessing first-hand how extremely upset and visibly shaken they were after their encounter. For this reason, many are prepared to extend these accounts a degree of credence.

There could well have been an unknown cryptid stalking the

countryside around Point Pleasant, and if this were indeed the case, what was its purpose, and where did it come from? One theory within the fringe community is that the Mothman is a symbol of impending doom. Completely unrelated to the Point Pleasant sightings, the same creature has allegedly been seen all over the world, and wherever it appears, tragedy soon follows. Indeed, many have likened the Mothman to the strange flying humanoids often witnessed in parts of South and Central America.

The most popular theory amongst believers, though, is that the Mothman was extra-terrestrial in origin. Sometime before the first Mothman sighting, a sewing machine salesman by the name of Woodrow Derenberger, driving along highway I-77 not far from the area of Point Pleasant, encountered a UFO, which stopped his car dead in the road. A being exited the strange craft, sporting a huge inhuman grin. This entity was said to have communicated with Derenberger telepathically, asking about the "strange glow" on the horizon, not realising it was the lights of a distant town.

Derenberger reported that the individual referred to himself as Indrid Cold, a name which didn't mean anything to him at the time, but one which has gained much notoriety over the years. Many alleged alien abductees have reported meeting an Indrid Cold, otherwise known as The Grinning Man. Cold was said to have asked Derenberger many questions about the people and surrounding areas, then thanked him and left in his strange craft. Less than two weeks later, the first sightings of the Mothman began to surface, and over time links between the two entities have invariably been made. Not only that, but many UFOs and strange lights were witnessed in and around the town at the time the encounters were going on. Some residents even reported paranormal activity in their homes, which gradually abated after the sightings themselves had ceased. Even the famed men in black were said to have made an appearance on a few occasions.

Whoever or whatever the Mothman was, there is no doubt that something strange was going on in that small city on the banks of the Ohio river during the latter half of the 1960s. Whether people were seeing a genuine cryptid or nothing more than a figment of someone's extraordinary imagination, we have to ask ourselves which is the more bizarre; a species yet to be discovered, of earthly origin or otherwise, or the lengths some people might go to in order to save their town.

In closing, this picture was taken near Point Pleasant on 20th November 2016, almost fifty years to the day after the first Mothman sighting occurred. And whilst this could be nothing more than a bird of prey clutching a snake in its talons, the question must be asked; could the Mothman have finally returned to Point Pleasant after all this time?

Fig. 16 - *Has the Mothman returned to Point Pleasant? Or is this nothing more than a bird with a snake in its talons?*

9
THE MANDELA EFFECT

Is the very essence of our reality changing in ways we don't understand? Could there really be a universal phenomenon occurring all around us, affecting everyone and everything, morphing the very fabric of space and time? Have you ever heard of The Mandela Effect?

Like all beginnings, it started with an end, an end to a life; a global phenomenon born in the wake of one man's death. On a warm, South African summer evening in 2013, a family stood grieving around a home hospital bed, looking down upon the body of a man who had just breathed his last breath. To many, he had been a great man, a revered man, adored and respected throughout his country and much of the world. The date was the 5th December, and the body belonged to none other than Nelson Mandela. The next day, as news of his passing was being broadcast around the globe, an entire nation found itself in the grip of mourning. But elsewhere in the world, a palpable feeling of surprise was brewing over these reports.

Mandela's death had not been unexpected. He was in his 95th year and had been ill for some time, but the news of his death still came as quite a shock for many people. Because as far as they were concerned, he had already been dead for almost thirty years, apparently having passed away some time in the mid-1980s whilst he had been in prison. As the days and weeks passed by, more and more people expressed this same feeling of surprise, not just in their hundreds, but in their thousands. The world suddenly found itself polarised between those who believed Mandela had died in December 2013, as reported, and those who remembered him dying many decades earlier. How and why did this discrepancy arise? It was not the first time such an inconsistency in the details of a historical event had been noticed, but it was by far the most prominent example to date.

Before Mandela's death, there had been no name for this alleged phenomenon. But due to the high-profile nature of this one occurrence, people began referring to any disagreements over how things are remembered and the subsequent feelings of confusion as "The Mandela Effect". And so, the phenomenon was born. Yet the truly strange thing is that there has been no shortage of other apparent anomalies throughout history. Shortly after the phenomenon had made itself known and had been christened in honour of the great man himself, many other examples began to surface.

For instance, there are a whole host of people who absolutely believe, beyond a shadow of a doubt, that the space shuttle Challenger disaster did not occur in 1986, but three years earlier in 1983. That Tank Man, the youngster who stood up to a column of armoured vehicles in Tiananmen Square in 1989, was actually run over and killed by the lead tank, not spirited away by the police as was seen on film. And that Mother Teresa had already been canonised as a saint before her death in 1997, as opposed to September 2016. No saint has ever been canonised whilst still alive and many people remember, rather vividly, the resulting controversy surrounding this almost sacrilegious breaking of convention.

These apparent anomalies are not just limited to major events, they also occur in more subtle ways. In fact, one of the most famous examples of The Mandela Effect is that of the alleged misspelling of The Berenstain Bears, a much-loved series of children's books which originated in America during the 1960s. Many long-time fans of the series were confused—and some even outraged—to find that the titles of these books had changed from "Berenstein" to "Berenstain", which is not how they remembered or even pronounced the name growing up. However, when they investigated the series' history, they couldn't find any record whatsoever of the books ever having been published under the Berenstein name. Understandably, their initial confusion and outrage turned to shock.

Similarly, many other less significant changes have occurred, most notably in the scripts of films. For instance, in Disney's *Snow White*, millions of people will remember the evil queen's famous line "Mirror, mirror on the wall", but in fact it is, and apparently always has been, "Magic mirror on the wall".

In *Forrest Gump*, many would agree that the titular character's quote, "My mom always said life is like a box of chocolates" just doesn't sound right when said as, "My mom always said life *was* like a box of chocolates", but apparently, the latter version is how it has always been said.

And we all know that the original *Star Wars* trilogy has been edited, almost to its detriment, over the years, but the line "Luke, I am your father" has been quoted and used on merchandise ever since the release of *The Empire Strikes Back*. Why, then, does Darth Vader actually say "*No*, I am your father"? Even in a documentary on the making of Star Wars, James Earl Jones quotes the line as "Luke, I am your father," during an interview.

Considering all of the above, why do so many people remember things differently? What is The Mandela Effect and why is it happening, if it is even happening at all? As you can imagine, speculation is rife and has ranged from the insipid to the outright bizarre.

One of the more unusual explanations refers to M Theory. M Theory postulates that there are an infinite number of universes all stacked close together, much like a loaf of bread, where each slice represents a different reality. The closer one slice, or reality, is to the next, the more alike those realities are. The proposed theory is that our universe has moved so close to a neighbouring universe that it has created a bridge of sorts, whereby people cross over from one reality to the next and are not even aware that they are doing so. In our neighbouring universe, Nelson Mandela may well have died in the 1980's, so people crossing over from that reality would carry with them different memories to the people in this reality, where he died in 2013. This would in turn cause a disagreement between these individuals, thereby giving rise to The Mandela Effect. Prominent physicists have stated that, if there is any truth to M Theory, this is most definitely plausible. And there are even documented cases throughout history of supposed visitors from other realities, such as The Man from Taured. But for the time being, at least, it is something we can neither prove nor disprove.

One of the more exotic suspects is time travel. Of course, we have always been told that time travel is impossible and, at least for those of us inhabiting the macroscopic world, that is an imperishable truth. We know, however, that once we enter the quantum realm the laws of causality are not so strict regarding certain subatomic particles. Whilst the sub-atomic world his highly unstable, the macroscopic world is the complete opposite, and some have gone so far as to suggest that this lack of unification between the two may create glitches, which go on to cause so-called time slips.

There are also those who believe that secret government projects have cracked the puzzle of time travel and that we are, in fact, capable of travelling through time. Or at least some of us are. Many people throughout history have reported unwittingly slipping through time, travelling both backwards and forwards. The experience usually only lasts for a few seconds, sometimes minutes, but on rare occasions witnesses have described episodes where they have been trapped in another time for hours, even days.

Whether deliberate or accidental, could time travel be causing these anomalies or branching timelines in the universe at large? It is doubtful. Any changes to events in our past would result in everyone's memories of those events being altered at the same time, and no one would be any the wiser.

Other theories include the possibility that we are all wired up to a huge super-computer, as illustrated in the 1999 film *The Matrix*, and that these anomalies are simply glitches brought on by intrinsic updates to its source code. Others purport that experiments at CERN, the Large Hadron Collider on the France-Switzerland border, are responsible, though they seem unable to clarify in what way, exactly.

On the other hand, leaving the pseudoscience behind for a moment, maybe the explanation lies more in the mundane ways in which our brains work.

It has been proven many times over that each time we recall an event, we embellish upon it in some way, adding or subtracting details. We cement and reinforce these details as time moves on and, as the recollection begins to fade, we convince ourselves that a particular thing did or did not happen, even if the opposite is true. So, is The Mandela Effect nothing more than a side effect of the complex processes involved in the storing and recalling of memories?

Again, there is no clear answer. Whilst our memories are certainly fallible, this mostly only applies to things which we have seen, heard, or experienced only once. When you have grown up knowing that something exists in a very specific way and have seen it in that very specific way for most of your life, only to find that one day it suddenly and inexplicably changes, can we really put it down to the fickle and impressionable nature of human memory? Especially when so many other people out there also remember it in that same specific way you did and then experience the same confusion and alarm when they also realise something has changed? It's an interesting question. Whatever is responsible for The Mandela Effect, whether it is neighbouring realities, clandestine time travellers, glitches in the source code or just our brains playing tricks on us, it is no less of a phenomenon. And it looks like it is here to stay.

10
WHO ARE THE MEN IN BLACK?

Government agents of suppression? Or extra-terrestrial visitors in disguise? Who are the Men in Black? And could recent CCTV footage finally provide proof of their existence?

Back in 1968, when the Condon Committee was sampling public attitudes towards UFOs, they gave the following statement to a cross-section of the American public: "A government agency maintains a Top-Secret file on UFO reports that are deliberately withheld from the public." The respondents were then asked to answer TRUE or FALSE. A substantial majority, almost two thirds of all people surveyed, agreed with this assertion. Amongst teenagers, the gap was even wider, with almost 75% of them believing the statement to be true. If that same survey was carried out today, it is believed that the percentage of those in agreement would be even higher.

This is hardly surprising, considering that we now live in an age of free-flowing information, or disinformation, depending on who you ask. Especially since the advent of the internet, it has become almost a normality to question and make accusations against those in power. But little over half a century ago, this lack of trust in government was nowhere near as prevalent as it is today. And one could argue that it all started back in the late 1940s, in the wake of what is now known as The Roswell Incident. This one event, whether there is any truth to it, brought into the mainstream the very notion of government conspiracies and cover-ups.

Throughout the 1950s, when the concept of flying saucers and visitors from outer space was still in its infancy, UFO witnesses and investigators alike were apparently being harassed, threatened, and ordered into maintaining silence by mysterious individuals known as the "men in black". These strange men were often described as wearing black suits with dark hats and that they travelled around in black cars, usually of the classic American variety. At the time, it was believed that these individuals worked for a secret government organisation, tasked with suppressing any mention of UFOs or extra-terrestrials within the public domain. But over the years, this assumption has evolved, and advocates of the MIB's existence now consider the possibility that these supposed government agents themselves might in fact be extra-terrestrial in nature. The 1997 film of the same name made light of the MIB conspiracy and did so to disarming comic effect. But for the people who have apparently been visited by these mysterious entities, it is no laughing matter, and what follows is but a small selection of accounts regarding such encounters.

In 1952, a former US Air Force serviceman turned author and amateur ufologist by the name of Albert K. Bender set up an organisation called the International Flying Saucers Bureau to investigate and report upon the strange UFO activity being witnessed all over the world at that time. The organisation was initially a success, publishing a weekly newsletter, which was distributed to its small, but dedicated audience of around 2000 people worldwide. However, in early 1953, Bender suddenly and mysteriously shut down his operation and ceased all publication, leaving in the newsletter's final issue a rather ominous message.

> "We advise those engaged in saucer work to please be very cautious".

Colleagues reported his odd demeanour at the time, stating that he seemed agitated and nervous, as if someone or something had scared him out of his wits. Bender did not eat or sleep properly for weeks after he closed the bureau and was said to have suffered with unbearable headaches during that time. When questioned about his sudden and inexplicable decision, he refused to elaborate and maintained this silence for many years afterwards. Almost a decade later, in 1962, Bender finally explained his actions, saying that he had been visited by three men dressed in black suits who had appeared out of thin air and warned him not to continue his work on UFOs.

Some years later in 1976, a well-known and highly respected family physician, Dr. Herbert Hopkins reported a very chilling encounter. Hopkins was home alone at his residence in Old Orchard Beach, Maine, on the night of 11th September. He was studying a UFO incident which had occurred some months prior when the phone rang. Hopkins answered and a man's voice was heard on the other end, identifying himself as a representative of the New Jersey UFO Organisation (something which later turned out to be fictitious). The caller asked Hopkins if he was alone and whether he could visit him to talk about the UFO case he was investigating. Hopkins agreed and the man hung up after telling him that he would "be there shortly."

The moment he put the phone down, the good doctor went to the front door to turn on his porch light and noticed that the man was already coming up the steps in front of his house. He recalled feeling a little unnerved by this, because even if the man had called from his neighbour's house, there was no way he could have reached the front door in the time it had taken Hopkins to walk from the phone over to the light switch. And bear in mind that this was before the advent of mobile phones. Nevertheless, he was still keen to hear what this man had to say and upon inviting him in, Hopkins was struck by the stranger's appearance.

He was a tall, skinny man, who wore a dark, ill-fitting suit and had a black derby on his head. His skin was smooth and deathly pale, and when he sat down and removed his hat, Hopkins noticed that he was completely bald. He had no hair whatsoever; he was devoid of any stubble, eyebrows, or eyelashes. His lips were a brilliant, ruby red and he spoke in an expressionless voice. There was no intonation or inflection in his delivery and all his words were evenly spaced.

Throughout their conversation, he sat motionless, his mouth being the only thing that moved. As if that was not disturbing enough, on one of the few occasions that the stranger did move another part of his body besides his lips, he happened to wipe his mouth with the back of his hand, which left a red smear across his cheeks. It was at this point that Hopkins realised the stranger was wearing lipstick and then further noticed that his mouth was a perfectly straight slit; he did not even have a pair of lips.

Hopkins became very frightened at this point and when the visitor asked him to remove the copper coin that sat in his pocket, he complied immediately. How this strange man even knew that he had a copper coin in his pocket is a mystery, but throughout the conversation the doctor had a distinct feeling that the visitor was somehow reading his mind. Hopkins held the coin the palm of his hand as instructed, and the visitor simply told him to "observe". As he watched, it slowly began to change colour from copper to silver, then became blurry, almost as if it was going out of focus, before disappearing right in front of his eyes. The visitor told the utterly bewildered doctor in no uncertain terms that if he did not destroy all the information he had collected on the UFO case, he himself would suffer the same fate as the coin.

As the visitor spoke these last words, Hopkins stated how his speech seemed to slow down, like a vinyl record playing at slow speed, and that his words had become slurred. The strange man suddenly told him that his energy was running low and that he needed to leave. The doctor showed him to the door and watched as he walked down the steps, holding onto the railing, almost as if he was crippled. He then hobbled around the corner and out of sight, at which point there was a huge, bright flash and then… silence. Hopkins was deeply disturbed by this experience. His family came home later that evening to find him sitting in the living room staring into space, with every light in the house turned on.

There have been many accounts over the last fifty or sixty years regarding men in black and many—especially those as fantastical as the Herbert Hopkins encounter—have been met with cynicism and sometimes even outright derision from the wider community. Their existence is extremely difficult to prove and more often than not, belief boils down to the credibility of the witness. And that just isn't enough for most sceptics.

However, in 2012, some very interesting footage surfaced on the internet. The video was recorded four years earlier in 2008 and was taken from a CCTV camera situated in the lobby of a hotel, near Niagara Falls in Ontario, Canada. Two weeks prior to its recording, one of the employees at the hotel had witnessed strange UFO activity over the Niagara River in the early hours of the morning and had mentioned the incident to friends and colleagues. This resulted in an unexpected visit from two strange men dressed in black. The camera captured these two individuals entering the hotel reception, walking in exactly the same way as each other, wearing exactly the same clothes and even appearing to look exactly the same in both facial structure and build. Witnesses reported that they were very tall and thin, and that they looked like identical twins.

Hotel guests and employees alike were profoundly disturbed by their presence, not just because of their threatening behaviour, but because of their appearance in general. The descriptions given were very similar to the stranger who had visited Hopkins; tall, thin, utterly devoid of hair and failing to exhibit any kind of emotion or facial expression. They both had identical icy blue eyes, which were described as being almost hypnotic. They never blinked once. They were said to have a determined, inquisitive nature and once again, the people who encountered them reported that they felt exposed, as if their innermost thoughts were somehow being read.

These strangers kept asking to speak to the young man who had witnessed the UFO activity two weeks earlier, but fortunately for him, he was not at work that day. When they failed in their attempts to locate him, the strange men apparently began asking staff members about other UFO sightings and conspiracy theories. They appeared neither satisfied nor dissatisfied with any of the answers given to them, they simply logged the information and moved on, leaving as abruptly as they had arrived, never to be seen or heard from again. This encounter is very similar in description to many other accounts and it would seem to suggest that the men in black are not quite of this world. Other accounts have been much less fanciful, with witnesses of those encounters reporting no such odd appearance or behaviour from the men who visited them.

Taking all of this into consideration, what are we to believe? Are the men in black human or non-human? Or are they a combination of the two; humans and extra-terrestrials working together towards the same goal? Do they even exist at all?

There is very little evidence that would suggest so, and even the CCTV footage recorded at the hotel in Ontario is questionable. It was, coincidentally, released on the internet at around the same time that the third *Men in Black* film was being heavily promoted, which has led many sceptics to believe it was nothing more than a viral marketing campaign. But this doesn't explain the 2008 timestamp or the numerous witness accounts. In general, sceptics have pointed out that the men in black phenomenon is largely limited to North America, that it has become an ingrained facet of American folklore and is above all, relatively recent. They state that the height of its notoriety occurred during the 1950s, at a time when paranoia over unidentified flying objects was at its peak. Finally, they argue that it all began with one man—Albert Bender—and that every other account since then is the result of copycats and opportunists wishing to further inflate the legend.

However, this is not strictly accurate. Reports of men in black are not just limited to the United States, many encounters have occurred in Europe, Australia, and elsewhere around the globe. And whilst the modern descriptions of these individuals can mostly be traced back to Bender's account, the phenomenon is not all that recent and predates the 1950s era by hundreds of years. During the Middle Ages people would often report encountering men dressed in black robes, wearing dark hats; malevolent entities who possessed inhuman capabilities and were odd in both appearance and behaviour. Descriptions of these strange men were nearly always the same, leading many to believe that they were all manifestations of the same being, and that that being was the devil.

Could these individuals be paranormal as opposed to supernatural?

It has been suggested by some that the men in black are in fact demonic in nature and links to supposed "shadow people" have been made, particularly the ominous character known as "the hat man", for obvious reasons. Relationships with the black-eyed children have also been reported, with some witnesses seeing both men in black and black-eyed children travelling around in the same vehicles.

Regardless of these theories, it is largely assumed and accepted by the fringe community that MIBs are fundamentally linked to extra-terrestrials. It is difficult to dispute the correlation between UFO sightings and the subsequent appearances of these entities. Some even believe that the reasons the men in black look so odd is either because they are extra-terrestrials disguised as humans or are, rather chillingly, reanimated corpses controlled remotely by these higher intelligences. Their motives are believed to be the infiltration and subversion of various governments around the world. Worse still, some believe that those governments are aware of their presence and are, in fact, complicit in their schemes. To what end is anyone's guess.

Whoever the men in black are, it is clear that they are rather sinister and that no good ever comes of their presence. Witnesses often feel intimidated, threatened, and disturbed after encountering them. Whether they are government agents, extra-terrestrial beings, paranormal entities, or nothing more than a figment of the imagination, the thought of coming face to face with them is no less terrifying. If you are ever lucky enough to see a UFO or witness some other supernatural event, only to hear a gentle knocking at your door in the dead of night, we advise you not to answer it.

11
THE PECULIAR DEATH OF CHRISTOPHER CASE

In April 1991, a man was found dead in his apartment after a week of telling friends that something was trying to kill him. Did he literally scare himself to death? Or was his passing the result of a terrifying curse?

Whenever the notion of curses arises, it invariably invites ridicule and derision, and the not-so-in-depth scrutiny of a victim's mental state. It is far too easy to dismiss such afflictions as the product of paranoia and delusion. But if you were to ask yourself—as a sane and rational human being—if you were to become so utterly convinced that something beyond your understanding was out to get you, would you be as quick to dismiss your own experiences in the same off-hand manner? It just so happens that the following story centres around an otherwise down-to-Earth, rational and, more to the point, non-religious individual who became so wedded to the belief that he was being stalked by supernatural entities that it changed the course of his life. A change, of course, which unfortunately led to his untimely death.

Christopher Case was a small-town radio DJ who had grown up in Richmond, Virginia. He was a well-rounded individual; intelligent, sophisticated, and an absolute fitness zealot. He took vitamin supplements daily and exercised religiously. In his early thirties he decided to move out west to Seattle in Washington State, to start a new career as a music executive. He worked for the Muzak Holdings company, producing the soft music heard in lifts and waiting rooms all over the world. Chris was a popular young man. He had made good friends in his new role and still managed to keep in regular contact with old friends back in Richmond, but despite this he was a bit of a loner and had been a bachelor for many years.

This is not strange in itself; his job required him to travel all over the United States and he had a real passion for music, particularly compositions of the ancient world. Chris's idea of a good time was sitting at home listening to his favourite tracks rather than going out to socialise of an evening. He found solace in the arrangements of notes and harmonies rather than in the company of others. He did not want for much. He did not bother other people and in return other people did not bother him. And it is for this reason that nobody who knew him has ever been able to understand the week in the spring of 1991 which would ultimately end in tragedy.

On the morning of Thursday 18th April, Chris was found dead in his apartment. There was no sign of a struggle having taken place or of forced entry. His body was discovered fully clothed, sitting inside his empty bathtub, in a kneeling position with his head resting against the wall. It appeared as though he had simply fallen asleep and passed away. But when police officers searched the residence, they found a multitude of crucifixes, books on the occult, and noted that salt had been poured at the entrance to his home and along every single skirting board inside his apartment. They also heard religious music playing quietly in several rooms. At the scene, the coroner was able to determine that Chris had died of heart failure. He was just 35 years old.

Whilst the circumstances surrounding his death and the state in which his apartment had been found were odd to say the least, the story which transpired over the following months of the investigation read like something straight out of a paranormal thriller. Shortly after his passing, friends reported that in the days leading up to his death, Chris had called them in a panic on numerous occasions, saying that something was after him and that he feared for his life. He had told them that he was certain he would be dead before the end of the week. This baffled authorities, and what was originally thought to have been a death by natural causes would take on a much more sinister twist. After weeks of looking into the case, investigators discovered a very chilling side to this story.

As it turned out, on the 11th April, seven days before his death, Chris had embarked on a business trip to San Francisco, meeting with other executives within the music industry. At some point during his visit, he had been introduced to an older woman who shared his passion for music of the ancient world, particularly that of Egypt and other Mediterranean civilisations. They seemed to have a lot in common and as their conversation progressed, it became clear to Chris that this woman wished to pursue a romantic relationship with him. She made no secret of her feelings and asked him to take her home on more than one occasion, but he politely declined these requests. Although she was an attractive lady, her intensity had unnerved the young executive. This, coupled with the fact that she was at least twenty years his senior, led Chris to suggest that they call it a night and go their separate ways, but this only seemed to anger her.

She felt the full force of his rejection and then said something strange. She told him that she was a witch, that she would put a curse on him and that he would be sorry. She then told him that he would be dead within a week. Chris, who thought of himself as a rational individual, simply shrugged this off. He did not believe in the paranormal or supernatural and he was not religious in any sense of the word, so he disregarded her threats and travelled back to Seattle the next day. He would relate this tale to his friend, Sammy Sauder, upon his return, who would also dismiss it with the same supposed rationality. And certainly, at least for the first few days after his return home, he completely forgot about the entire incident.

However, on the morning of 14th April, Chris called Sammy in a panic, saying that he had been kept awake all night by the sound of whispering voices coming from somewhere inside his home, though he could not find the source. He had also seen shadows moving around his apartment, even though he was the only one there and that he felt like he was being watched during the night. This conversation would be the first of three frantic telephone calls that Chris would make to Sammy over the next few days.

On the 16th, he called to tell her that something had attacked him during the night. He had woken to find himself paralysed, being throttled by unseen hands. The attack was particularly intense and violent, the force of it lifting him off his mattress before releasing him and throwing him back on to his bed. Afterwards he had noticed tiny cuts on the ends of each one of his fingers and that his bed sheets were stained with his blood.

This would prove to be too much, and the morning after, he visited a religious bookstore called Evangel Incorporated. The store manager, Rodney Higucci, described how Chris had entered the store, walked over to one of the displays and picked up a handful of crucifixes. Mr. Higucci asked how he intended to use them, and Chris responded by telling him what he believed to be the truth of the matter; that he was being attacked by paranormal entities and that he needed to defend himself. Rodney assisted as best he could and recommended a few books on the subject of fighting witchcraft.

Between his visits to the bookstore and his calls to concerned friends, Chris had begun a determined effort to fend off whatever mysterious forces had been tormenting him and by the afternoon of the 16th the battle lines had been drawn. He had placed several crucifixes around his home, which were interspersed with candles, and he had poured lines of salt along the extremities of each room, leaving small piles in each corner. He had also written many notes on methods of combating evil spirits, which were scattered throughout his apartment. It had been less than a week since his meeting with the strange woman, but Chris was a changed man, barely recognisable as the confident, rational young executive he had been only days beforehand.

This was an obsessed individual, determined to the point of it being detrimental to his health. He wasn't sleeping and he had not shown up for work in two days. He called other friends besides Sammy and they would describe how they could hear in his voice how utterly afraid he was. And unfortunately for Chris, the evening of the 16th would be his most harrowing experience to date. It is not exactly clear what happened during the night, but something frightened him so much that he left his home during the early hours of the morning and stayed at a hotel.

Because of this, Sammy could not get through to him the next morning. Her only recourse was to call a local police department and ask them to do a welfare check on Chris' property. Upon arrival, they found the premises locked and were unable to gain access. They left the scene and reported their findings back to his concerned friend. Living on the other side of the country, she felt distraught and helpless as to what else she could do. She had no other choice but to wait to hear from Chris.

That evening, Sammy came home to find a message stored on her answering machine. Little did she know that this would be the last time she ever heard from her friend. To her surprise, there was an eerie calm to the young man's voice, almost as if he had resigned himself to his fate. In the message, he spoke about how "they" had almost got him the night before and that he believed this would be his last night on Earth. Sammy would not be the only person to hear from Chris that day. He had also visited a Catholic priest in the afternoon, and later he had returned to Evangel Incorporated. On this occasion Rodney Higucci described how Chris had looked exhausted but desperate, and that he had asked for more advice on how to defend himself.

Despite Chris' best efforts, he would lose his life on the night of 17th April 1991. Myocarditis was listed as the official cause of death in the coroner's report, inflammation of the heart.

Did Christopher Case somehow manage to convince himself that he had been cursed and then literally scare himself to death? Or was there something far more mysterious and sinister at work? The jury is still out, even after all this time.

Myocarditis is a rare, but potentially deadly disease affecting 1 in every 100,000 people. It is not hereditary and therefore not based on genetics. It can affect anyone at any time, but most commonly occurs in people between the ages of twenty and forty. It is not unheard of for Myocarditis to afflict young men and women who are otherwise fit and healthy. It has been the cause of many sudden deaths in young athletes around the world. Some medical experts have also suggested that there is a link between the disease and man-made supplements, such as vitamins or steroids, which they believe could aggravate an existing condition. It is important to remember that Christopher Case was a fitness enthusiast; he went to the gym to exercise daily. He also took vitamin supplements. And at the age of 35, he was well within the scope of being affected by this disease.

However, close friends and relatives of Chris are not so quick to just accept the possibility that he died of natural causes. There are a variety of other symptoms which usually manifest in sufferers of Myocarditis, such as chest pain, difficulty breathing and general fatigue. Furthermore, before a fatal attack, the sufferer will usually display flu-like symptoms in the weeks leading up to their death. Chris experienced none of these things. He was an otherwise fit and healthy young man with a top-notch immune system.

We should also consider Chris' mental state during those last five or six days. As we have already established, he was a stable individual and not prone to such flights of fancy regarding the paranormal. So why did he suddenly and inexplicably change? Is it possible for someone to go from being a sane, rational individual one day, only to change to a desperate and obsessed wreck of a man the next? Mental breakdowns of this nature usually develop over weeks or even months, so this doesn't seem to make much sense.

Finally, we are faced with the fact that Chris knew he was going to die. He predicted it with alarming accuracy, saying to his friend Sammy on the 17th that he knew he would not last the night. What are the chances of an otherwise fit, healthy, and mentally stable young man dying of natural causes after a week of saying to friends that he feared for his life? One must wonder whether there is more to this than meets the eye. Whatever happened during that week back in April of 1991, Chris truly believed that he was being haunted—and ultimately hunted—by something sinister and horrific enough to literally scare him to death. After days of being tormented and tortured at the hands of who knows what, he finally succumbed to his fears, leaving behind a perplexing mystery, which will probably never be solved.

You may be wondering why the police never followed up on the identity of the woman who supposedly put this curse on him, but his death was never seen as suspicious and so it did not warrant that kind of investigation. Besides, Chris took her name with him to the grave. Whether he died of a terrifying curse or whether it was simply all in his head, this case is no less heart-breaking for those who were close to Chris, and we can only hope that he rests in peace.

12
THE MYSTERIOUS MURDERS OF HINTERKAIFECK

In 1922, six people were killed at a remote German farmstead. They were bludgeoned in their bedclothes, but were their deaths the result of a manic serial killing, out-of-control family feud, or even politically motivated?

Since the advent of DNA testing and thanks to the immense strides taken in forensic science, we now live in a time where relatively few violent crimes and murders go unsolved. But a hundred years ago, investigations into such offences were an entirely different affair. As we will see in the following story, there were often significant delays in the reporting of incidents to the police, and when officers did attend crime scenes, they had very little to assist them other than their instincts and the most rudimentary of forensic techniques. This particularly harrowing case also raises a key question. When you have no clear motive for such a crime, how do you then go on to identify a suspect?

It was the afternoon of Friday 31st March 1922. Snow covered the farmers' fields of Kaifeck, a remote hamlet bordering the small town of

Wangen, South Germany. Being mainly pastoral, Hinterkaifeck farm had good local trading links and was largely self-sufficient, with foods of all kinds readily available, despite the adverse weather conditions. The farmstead was comprised of one main house and a number of outbuildings, and this looked picturesque against the snowy white backdrop.

On this fateful Friday, farmer Andreas Gruber was at home with his wife Cäzillia, their daughter Viktoria Gabriel, and her two children—a young girl also named Cäzillia, aged seven, and a young boy named Josef who was just two years old. They also had a live-in maid by the name of Maria Baumgartner. With the duties done for the day, all should have been well. However, Andreas was still troubled by the events of the previous week. The farmstead was bordered at the rear by thick woodland, and he had found a strange set of footprints in the snow leading from the edge of the forest right up to the back of the house. He knew that none of the family had ventured out that way, and more concerning was that there were no footprints leading away. As one might imagine, the thought of a possible intruder, who had seemingly vanished without trace would have left him puzzled, anxious, and fearing for the safety of his family.

Andreas had reportedly been plagued by other strange goings on around the farm during that time. He confided to a neighbour about strange noises coming from the attic, items being moved around, and an unfamiliar newspaper arriving in the mailbox. Other reported worries included a set of keys disappearing, heightening existing concerns about a possible unknown presence at the farm. Nonetheless, he refused the offer of a gun for protection. Despite these warning signs, as they prepared for bed, the Grubers couldn't have known how cruelly they, along with their maid, would be slain in cold blood later that night.

The murders were extremely brutal, but an initial delay in even reporting the incident would hamper the investigation, and ultimately mean that an accurate time for the deaths could never be established. Four whole days passed before neighbours discovered the bodies. They were found on 4th April, concealed under a pile of straw in the barn, stripped and soaked in each other's blood. They had been piled one on top of the other. A messenger was sent to notify the Mayor of Wangen, and on 5th April, authorities were finally able to collect their evidence. Co-ordinating police efforts was an Inspector Georg Reingruber, who arrived by train from Munich.

The on-site autopsy was conducted by Dr Johanne Baptist Aümeller, who sent the heads of the deceased away for specialist examination, but ultimately this garnered no significant results. Evidence at the scene suggested that the killings were carried out in a quick and precise manner. Each victim suffered appalling skull, head, or facial wounds. In the cases of wife Cäzillia and of elder daughter Viktoria, strangulation was also noted as a factor. This suggested that either something had not gone as planned with the murders, that there could have been 'more than one' killer, or that the perpetrator was driven by more personal motives linked directly to the females in the house. It is believed that the youngest child, Josef, was killed in his bassinette, whilst the rest of the family were somehow led to the barn outside before being killed therein. The Gruber family's maid, Maria Baumgartner, may have been spared in other circumstances, but like Josef, she too was killed in her bed.

After the attack, all the bodies were then hidden from view under the straw. Rather chillingly, there are reports to suggest that one of the children was still alive at this time. Viktoria's daughter, Cäzillia, is believed to have lain bleeding under the straw next to the corpses of her family, and records show how she had pulled clumps of her own hair out before death, probably through pain, confusion, and grief. The full horrors experienced by each member of the family are revealed within police reports, which detail multiple horrific injuries to each victim. To this day nobody has been brought to justice for the Hinterkaifeck murders. Despite carrying out such slaughter, one has to wonder why the killer, or killers, were never caught by police.

Upon arriving at Hinterkaifeck, Inspector Reingruber and his detectives discovered the scene itself had been compromised. At the farmstead house, objects had been moved and several visitors had come and gone during the four days since the harrowing discovery. Nonetheless, in their quest for clues, the police were still able to record and collect some valuable evidence from the house. Large sums of money were discovered, so they were soon able to rule out robbery as the primary motive, and due to a lack of food in the Gruber household, Reingruber wondered whether the killer may have been eating meals there. The police could not be certain regarding this possibility due to the number of other people who had visited the farm in the intervening days. There was evidence of recent disturbance and possible habitation in the attic space, though it was not clear whether items had been moved by the Grubers themselves, or by another party.

The police discovered that the cows had been milked and other animals had been well-fed since the time of the murders, suggesting that somebody had been staying in the house afterwards, maybe intending to take over the farm. Accounts given to police by neighbours support this idea; they had reported seeing smoke rising from the chimney in the days since the incident. The investigation also revealed evidence of an incestuous relationship between Andreas and his eldest daughter Viktoria. The scandal was already well-known to the local community and, in fact, both had been jailed for incestuous offences some years before. The Gruber family, and particularly Andreas, were disliked by some of the locals, for the shame that the incest had brought upon the community. Mr. Gruber was apparently very outspoken on this matter, and though Inspector Reingruber could not draw upon a suspect based on speculation alone, Andreas clearly had more enemies than friends.

Despite an extensive search, police initially failed in their efforts to locate and identify a murder weapon. It has been suggested that investigators were inefficient in these early stages, though it could be argued that farms are full of tools and blades which might be used as potential weapons and, taking this into consideration, it is understandable that police found themselves at a loss. Even canine sniffer dogs could not pick up the required scent. It was only when the site was being cleared more than a year after the murders, that a farmhand by the name of George Siegl identified the weapon as a mattock, a type of long handled pickaxe, and one that Andreas Gruber had made himself. Siegl told police that this was normally kept with Gruber's other tools locked away in a shed. The mattock had been used to make precision cuts on each of the bodies and Siegl pointed out that it would require reasonable experience of agricultural tools to use in this way.

Georg Reingruber was yet to realise it, but he would work tirelessly on this case throughout the rest of his career. He was said to have been haunted by the murders, especially those of the children, though this only made him more determined to catch those responsible. He and his detectives questioned over a hundred people in relation to the murders, but still, no one was charged. Reingruber discovered that visitors to the farm in the days after the incident included a postman, who visited on 1st and 3rd April, and a mechanic who had come to repair a feeding machine in the barn on the 4th. Through his interviews, Reingruber also gathered useful information from the neighbours about the Gruber family and the maid, in order to build up a profile and consider who would target them and why.

He was surprised to hear rumours regarding paranormal activity and discovered that even the Gruber family's former maid had left six months earlier, complaining that the farm was haunted. On this particular point, it is an especially sad twist in the tale that the new maid, Maria Baumgartner, had only arrived at the farm the day before, and was killed just hours later. In the years that followed, stories told of how the Devil himself had visited the family on that cold night and had left his footprints to prove it. But did something far more human have a vendetta against the Grubers?

Reingruber questioned a broad spectrum of people, from vagrants and travellers to people in neighbouring villages. With robbery ruled out as a motive, he began to narrow down his options and identify his prime suspects. One of Reingruber's first interviewees—and later to become a significant suspect himself—was neighbour Lorenz Schlittenbauer. The only reason we know about the footprints in the snow and the noises in the attic is because of Sclittenbauer's account. It was his recollection that was reported to police and we must treat his story with some scrutiny for a number of reasons, but mainly because it was not corroborated by any other witness. Whilst it is possible that Andreas confided in Schlittenbauer, he did not report these concerns to the police personally.

It is also known that both men had had some bitter neighbourly disagreements. Schlittenbauer wished to marry Andreas' daughter, Viktoria, but he had been refused point blank. Viktoria had admitted to sleeping with Schlittenbauer on five occasions and he truly believed young Josef was his son. That was until the incest allegations resurfaced. Despite this, Schlittenbauer was asked to pay maintenance even though he was denied access to the child. Some believed this betrayal and continued sexual relations between the father and daughter provides a real motive, whilst others feel it was the bitterness over having to pay child support which is a factor. After all, Schlittenbauer had a wife and child of his own by this time. He therefore had more than one reason to be rid of the Grubers once and for all, and as a neighbour, he would have known Hinterkaifeck well, including where Andreas kept his tools.

During the interview process, Schlittenbauer could have cleverly used fabrication to divert attention away from his negative relationship with Andreas and, instead, cast further doubt on Andreas' integrity. He was also one of the first neighbours to arrive at Hinterkaifeck to greet police and had apparently been part of the group that discovered the bodies. Some reports even suggest that a dog (tied by its lead) at the farmstead barked and growled angrily at Schlittenbauer each time he passed.

Another suspect lies in Viktoria's own husband, Karl Gabriel. Though it is thought Karl was killed by a mine in December 1914 whilst away at war, his body was never recovered. With tests confirming that Andreas was also the biological father of her young son, this adulterous betrayal could have provided a motive for Karl to return unannounced and kill his father-in-law, his wife, and possibly even young Josef. So, did he go on to become the Hinterkaifeck killer? Or is there yet more to this mystery?

It is a possibility (albeit not widely reported) that there were political motivations behind the murders. The residents of Bavaria were traditionally Catholic, and conservative politically. However, the Anif Declaration of 1918 had led to a period of constitutional instability and some extremist groups favoured Bavaria as a hotbed for growth. Andreas Gruber was a Nazi sympathiser longing to bring about change to the status quo.

Unafraid to openly air his views, Gruber stood out for his political differences, especially within a small community of more liberal voters.

In 1922, the town of Wangen was due for local and mayoral elections, and its population stood at around 5,000. Some now wonder whether the Grubers were murdered in an attempt to thwart the growth of extremism in the region and ensure that votes went to mainstream candidates. A man by the name of Adolf Gump was listed as a suspect as early as 9th April due to concerns over his political activities with the Freikorps Oberland. The Freikorps Oberland was a group initially intent on rooting out Communist and Polish insurgents, but many of its members, including Gump, began to switch their attention to The Nazis. Unfortunately, Gump could not be traced. Despite a deathbed confession to a priest 22 years after the murders, by relative Kreszentia Meyer, claiming that Adolf Gump may have acted with his brother Anton to carry out the Hinterkaifeck killings, neither was sentenced for the crime.

Conversely, another theory suggests that the Nazis themselves attacked Hinterkaifeck. Extremist groups might have recognised that the farmstead had value as an obscure, remote hideaway. Similar rural Nazi hideouts have been discovered all over Germany, with many found in the Bavarian province. But why should a minority party in government choose to eliminate a family of their own supporters? Why not simply choose another location nearby? If the Nazis had a strong interest in the Hinterkaifeck property, the murders would have been planned in detail, and it is likely they found little interest or value in the Gruber family themselves. Initially, Andreas may have been an asset, but any resistance from himself or members of his family would have brought about swift retribution and they would have been shown little mercy.

This theory is also consistent with the belief that there was more than one killer at Hinterkaifeck. After dealing with the messy business of ending the lives of six people, the perpetrators would have looked after the farm animals, and taken meals, with the intention of discreetly taking over the property; perhaps even telling locals that the family had moved away.

Nonetheless, aside from any vengeful or tactical murderous plots, it is possible that the Grubers were just in the wrong place at the wrong time. A man by the name of Joseph Bärtle had escaped from a hospital in Günzburg in 1921 where he was being treated for a mental illness. He is thought to have been in the area at the time of the murders and is believed to have been capable of mass homicide. That said, the Hinterkaifeck murders have also been linked to the notorious Friedrich Harmann who was prolific during the 1920s with his vampyrous sensibilities. Whilst he generally targeted male prostitutes, his potential involvement simply makes the task of solving this mystery yet more complicated.

So alas, despite the many suspects and plausible explanations, we are still left piecing together the puzzle of exactly what happened at Hinterkaifeck. This was not something Inspector Reingruber could achieve in his lifetime. In fact, despite him working on the case for many years and even with subsequent re-investigations, the trail has gone completely cold. The latest police investigation in 2007 concluded that vital evidence was missing or not properly collected to begin with. They deemed it highly unlikely that the case will ever be solved. It does seem that Andreas may have been closer than he realised with his concerns regarding something in the attic. It's possible that the killer or killers could have used this space to hide out and listen in on the daily lives of the family, just waiting for his or their moment to strike. We are left with many possible perpetrators, but the ultimate failure to catch the killer rests on the shortcomings of the original investigation and lack of developments in the years following the murders.

For instance, the decision to only send the decapitated heads for analysis has become the subject of criticism, with concerns that important evidence may have been left on the victims' torsos. The method used was quite primitive, medically speaking, though we should allow for the fact that the crime was in a rural area, and decapitation was still occasionally used in wider medical practices of the 1920s. Even more tragic is the fact that the heads of these victims were lost. Whilst the official narrative is that they were presumed destroyed following the outbreak of war, individuals investigating the case wonder whether this may have simply been the result of negligence. In any case, the family was laid to rest, headless.

As the Grubers left no legal will, the buildings at the scene of the incident were demolished and redeveloped in the years that followed.

A drawing commissioned by a family member, just one police photograph, and one police sketch is all that was on file before they were torn down. This has made it difficult for new researchers to look at the original farm's size and scale and would limit any new forensic or archaeological findings. Since 1971, even the town of Wangen is but a memory. This now places the murder site within the larger town of Waidhofen (43 miles north of Munich) within the modern-day Neuburg-Schobenhausen district. A little-known memorial does, however, remain. The English translation of the inscription is as follows:

> *"Memorial for Hinterkaifeck in the immediate vicinity of the crime. Godless hand, the family Gabriel-Gruber fell victim here on 31 March 1922."*

This is followed by the names and years of birth of the victims.

Various books and songs released even in the past twenty years continue to pay tribute to the lost souls. With continued interest in the mystery and the speculation surrounding Hinterkaifeck, the events have also been dramatised in three films to-date: released in 1981, 1991 and 2009. We're now around a century on, and the awful truth is that we may never know who murdered those six people on that fateful night. Whether an escaped mental patient, a jealous husband seeking revenge, or even an early mass murder carried out by the Nazis. As we have seen, 'Hinterkaifeck', literally translated as 'behind Kaifeck', has long-since been erased from the map. We can only hope that someone will invest their time and energy into reinvestigating this challenging case before the Hinterkaifeck Murders, and more importantly the murderers themselves, fade into obscurity.

13
THE BODY ON THE RESERVOIR

In 1988, the mutilated body of a middle-aged man was found on the banks of an artificial lake in Brazil. Listed as one of the most disturbing deaths of a human being ever recorded, the question is who or what left the body on the reservoir?

Cattle mutilations are relatively commonplace across the globe. From the USA to the UK, and even as far afield as Australia, many farmers and ranchers have reported the often bizarre and inexplicable mutilations of their livestock. Many of these harrowing cases are dismissed simply as attacks by predators. However, the farmers, ranchers, and even veterinarians who attend upon these strange occurrences have their own suspicions regarding possible culprits. They often cite what appears to be precision cuts, a distinct lack of blood and, particularly in the UK, a lack of predators as reasons for thinking that something else may be responsible. But as disturbing as these cases are, what are we to make of similar mutilations which appear to have been carried out on human beings?

It was the afternoon of 29th September 1988. As the sun shined high in the skies over Sao Paulo, it bathed the huge sprawling city in a warmth that seemed to endorse the promise of the hot Brazilian Summer to come. To the south, the vast surface of the Billings Reservoir shimmered with an inviting serenity; offering a respite from the humid air, an escape from the worries and tedium of life, but belying a risk all too many people are willing to take. For the Billings Reservoir is not as peaceful as it may at first seem. Many deaths have occurred in and around those waters. Not a year goes by without at least one drowning and it has also been used as a dumping ground for the bodies of many a gangland killing on the streets of Sao Paulo. But occasionally, another kind of cadaver shows up. One which is not so easy to explain. One which scares the locals more than any other.

And so, it was on that beautiful spring day back in 1988 that a young boy was walking alone along the banks of the reservoir, holding a sling at his side. He had set out after school that afternoon with the intention of hunting birds and other small creatures inhabiting the long grass and woodlands surrounding the vast waterways. And he must have thought he was in luck when he spotted a large group of vultures on the opposite bank, not too far from where he was. They were all gathered around what looked like a large animal carcass, but there were too many of them to see what kind of animal it was. Only when he dispersed the birds by catapulting a stone into their midst was the full horror of what lay beneath them revealed. It was the badly mutilated corpse of a man.

He quickly made his way to the nearest village and breathlessly told the residents what he had seen. The police were called and a fire truck, along with two officers from the Santo Amaro Police Department, arrived on the scene shortly afterwards. After a quick assessment, they all agreed that the situation was beyond any of them, and by late afternoon, the area had been cordoned off and was crawling with police officers and medical personnel. As many rumours circulated over the next few hours, and as much as people in the surrounding villages talked about the discovery amongst themselves, nothing was reported on the news or in the tabloids that evening. The body and the investigators attending the scene quietly slipped away sometime during the night.

The next morning, all that remained at the location were discarded strands of police tape scattered here and there, and signs that the long grass on the banks of the reservoir had been trampled by many pairs of shoes. The victim's family were notified, but nothing else was heard of the case again and the incident began to slip from the minds of the locals and pass inexorably into legend. And that's how it would have remained, possibly forevermore, if not for a twist of fate six years later in 1994.

The coroner's report and accompanying photographs were somehow leaked to the press and low-key reports appeared in various newspapers and publications over the next few weeks. Someone, possibly working in government, had thought this case so disturbing that they had broken their silence and pushed the information out into the public domain. The details regarding the state in which the body was found are not for the faint of heart. And as we will discover, it comes as no surprise that those details had authorities questioning exactly who could have done this to another human, and whether it was even possible for another person to have inflicted such injuries at all.

The identity of this unfortunate individual was determined by dental records but was not widely divulged out of respect for the victim's family. All that was known at the time was that he had been subjected to a horrible mutilation, the likes of which had never been seen before and has never been seen since. At least not in the public sphere. According to the autopsy report, the eyes had been extracted and eyelids cut away, the tongue had been removed, the left ear had been sliced off, the lips and flesh around the mandibles and neck had been excised, and a significant piece of the jawbone was missing.

Examining the rest of the body, investigators found that the armpits had each been punctured by a single hole approximately 1.5 inches in diameter. Similar holes were found elsewhere on the legs and arms, where it was discovered that flesh, including entire muscles, had been extracted. These apertures were all uniform in terms of size and the way in which they had been inflicted. In instances where there were two holes on opposite sides of the body—such as those located in the armpits and limbs—these were found to be symmetrically aligned with each other.

When the coroner attempted to inspect the state of the victim's internal organs, he was shocked to find that these had been removed too. The liver, kidneys, stomach, large and small intestines, and pancreas were all missing, and the chest and lower abdominal cavity had shrunk and sunken inwards as a result. However, there was no incision in the abdomen besides another small hole where the navel should have been, similar in size to the others. This left the coroner with no choice but to conclude that the organs, along with the muscle tissues, had been sucked out via these orifices, an unusual and completely unnatural method of extraction.

The victim's colon had also been cored out, leaving a huge hole where the rectum should have been. He had also been castrated and, moreover, every single drop of blood had been drained from his body. When trying to determine which instruments had been used to inflict such injuries, investigators found that the holes made in the limbs and torso, the extraction of the rectum and scrotum, and the cuts made to the facial features all had a surgical quality to them. This indicated that they had been made with speed and precision. All wounds showed a distinct lack of bleeding, either attributed to the fact that blood was being extracted at the same time the incisions were being made or because the wounds themselves had been cauterised. Rigor mortis had not set in, despite the death having occurred more than 24 hours beforehand, and the corpse did not emit the usual cadaverous odours. Even though the body had been covered with vultures when it was first discovered, there were no signs to indicate that they had fed on the flesh or entrails.

By far the most disturbing aspect of this case was the fact that the toxicology reports showed no signs of anaesthesia, or an accompanying paralysing agent having been administered at the time these injuries were inflicted. This was extremely odd, because there were also no signs of any kind of restraint found anywhere on the victim's body. This determined that the individual had been fully conscious during the entire procedure and must have been paralysed by some other means. It is unlikely that he was able to move freely due to the immaculate nature of the cuts.

Indeed, when the cranial cavity was opened, the coroner's report listed two items; an unimpaired skull cap (meaning the cranium was otherwise undamaged) and signs of a cerebral oedema. The presence of a cerebral oedema without accompanying trauma to the skull is indicative of an agonising death. The autopsy lists the cause of death as follows:

> "...acute haemorrhage in multiple traumatisms. There is a component of causa mortis by vagus stimulation."

Roughly translated, this means that the victim died of cardio-respiratory arrest brought on by extreme pain. The report also states that there was an element of torture with regards to the death of this individual.

The victim's name is known in smaller circles, but out of respect for his family, we will not divulge it here. What we will say is that he was a 53-year-old man, who suffered with both epilepsy and alcoholism. He frequently visited the reservoir to fish, and he had been reported missing three days prior to his body being discovered. Police found his clothes hidden in the woods on the opposite bank, suggesting that he had removed them before swimming eighty metres to the other side for a more lucrative fishing spot. Family members confirmed that this was a usual habit of his. He had been taking Gadernal for the epilepsy, and authorities initially believed that he had mixed alcohol with this medication and that this had resulted in him experiencing a strong reaction, collapsing, and dying after such a strenuous swim. They believed that his body was then preyed upon by scavengers such as rats, insects, and vultures and that his injuries were a combination of decomposition and animal predation post-mortem.

However, it was quickly established that this was unlikely due to other findings in the coroner's report. The victim had not been dead long enough for natural decomposition of the suggested magnitude to have taken place. Nor had enough time passed for animals to have eaten the amount of flesh and organs that were now missing. Add to this the fact that there were no signs of predation even having occurred. There were no bite marks, or tell-tale signs that are usually left by the beaks of carrion birds. All incisions were of an unnatural, possibly man-made origin.

Despite the seemingly overwhelming evidence to suggest that foul play had occurred, investigators quickly closed the case and dismissed it as an unfortunate tragedy. Stating that the man had died of natural causes attributed to his illness and lifestyle choices. For this reason, the case is not widely known outside of Brazil, and even within Brazil's borders, you would be hard pressed to find someone who was familiar with the specifics. Authorities have been accused of covering up the wider details regarding this death and there is, in fact, evidence to support this claim. The fact that the case only came to light six years after the fact, via an internal leak, speaks volumes about a possible desire to keep it out of the mainstream press.

Furthermore, in almost every single article regarding this story, the location where the body was found is almost always incorrectly reported as Guarapiranga Reservoir; this is a falsehood. The body was actually discovered on the banks of the much larger Billings Reservoir, a few miles to the east. Although, geographically speaking, the two waterways are close to one another, the body was nowhere near Guarapiranga. This has led many researchers to believe that some of the details were incorrectly reported to further throw the public off the scent. But why do this if it was believed to have been a natural death? Why the secrecy to begin with? Theories regarding what happened to this unfortunate individual have been varied to say the least, but ultimately it comes down to just four possibilities, two of which require an open mind.

If we are to do our due diligence, we must question the official explanation as, at first glance, it does not appear to stand up to scrutiny when we consider the details of the coroner's report. As we have said, the presence of a cerebral oedema suggests that this man died a very painful death. And whilst it is true that sufferers of epilepsy do not feel any pain during a seizure, there is no denying that the body itself goes through a variety of trauma, of which a cerebral oedema is a rare, but possible outcome. A particularly bad seizure will cut off oxygen supply to the brain, which will cause varying degrees of damage, if not outright death.

That being said, the autopsy clearly states that the victim had died from cardiac arrest. Whilst it is also very rare for an epileptic fit to cause such complications, seizures do increase a sufferer's heart rate considerably during an episode and, if violent enough, could cease heart function if particular variables regarding the person's lifestyle are met. As we have already learned, this individual was middle-aged and an alcoholic and therefore could have had a compromised cardio-respiratory system under those circumstances. Although very unlikely, it is not beyond all possibility that both the cerebral oedema and heart failure were brought on by an epileptic seizure.

This still leaves the question of how the injuries inflicted to the rest of the body had occurred. Some have speculated that the apertures were caused by some form of burrowing animal, which preyed upon the body after death and consumed the flesh and internal organs from within. Also, the vultures seen on and around the body at the time it was discovered are notorious for targeting the soft tissues of a carcass and for tearing small holes in the skin, which they then poke their heads into in order to access the organs and flesh. But the uniformity of these holes and the fact that they had a surgical quality to them invites a degree of scrutiny upon this theory, particularly because of the cauterisation of some of the wounds, which is wholly unnatural to say the least. As already determined by the coroner himself, it is highly unlikely that these abrasions were caused by predation or decomposition, given the time frames involved.

Given the lack of evidence to suggest a natural death, the question must be asked; could this individual have instead been murdered? And, if so, who could have inflicted such injuries upon another human being, and perhaps more importantly, why would they kill somebody in this way? What was their motive if they even had a motive at all? Murder was ruled out fairly quickly during the investigation due to a lack of evidence suggesting another party's involvement. There was no indication of restraint or signs of any kind of struggle between the victim and a would-be attacker. There were also no other tracks, besides the victim's, at the site where the body was discovered.

Authorities also questioned whether it was even possible for another human to have inflicted such injuries, unless they were a highly skilled surgeon and even then, it would have been exceptionally difficult without some form of anaesthetic or paralysing agent. Extraction of organs via suction devices is used in some medical procedures, but it nearly always damages the organ being removed during the process, so what would have been the purpose of doing this besides abject torture? Although it is not an impossibility, homicide by another human being is perhaps more unlikely than a death by natural causes. What we are left with, then, is the possibility of this being a natural death, in which nearly every single variable somehow aligned in an extremely unlikely way to present the image of an *unnatural* death. Otherwise, the death was so unnatural, that it begins to enter the realms of the supernatural.

There are those who believe that he could have been attacked by an unknown cryptid stalking the woodlands around the reservoirs. Indeed, people from the surrounding villages have reported all sorts of strange goings on over the years, and this is not the first or last mutilation to have occurred in the area, but it is certainly the worst. Unfortunately, it is difficult to attribute this case to local legends when there is little to no evidence to support the existence of such a cryptid.

Elsewhere, similarities have inevitably been drawn between this case and the multitude of animal mutilations recorded all over the world. These mutilations have often been attributed to UFO activity and possible extra-terrestrial experimentation on various species of mammals, particularly those of the bovine, ovine, and porcine varieties. Indeed, when the coroner was shown images of these animal mutilations in the years following the investigation, he was shocked at how similar the incisions were to those found on the body of this unfortunate individual. In particular, the way in which the eyes and skin around the jawbone had been removed was of a striking resemblance, as were the apertures through which internal organs had been extracted, all indicative of the same modus operandi.

So, could extra-terrestrials have abducted this man? Could they have subjected him to a swift but extremely brutal procedure in which he met his end? If so, one would have to question the motives of these beings and express a deep concern over their complete disregard for human life. After all, if we recall the coroner's report, this man was subjected to the most harrowing experience imaginable. Having his skin peeled from his face, eyes gouged out, tongue removed, organs sucked from his body, blood completely drained, and both rectum and scrotum cored out and dismembered all in the same instance, whilst fully conscious, without anaesthetic and completely paralysed.

They clearly had no sympathy or consideration regarding the utter pain and suffering this man must have gone through. They then discarded his remains like rubbish with no apparent attempt to hide his body. For that reason, this theory should give anyone pause for thought and we would be reluctant in considering it a possibility, if not just for the disturbing connotations it puts in one's mind regarding how extra-terrestrials might view humanity.

This case is now well over a quarter of a century old, and whilst authorities consider the investigation closed, whether they believe their official line or not, it is still very much unsolved in many peoples' eyes. And although some aspects of this story might seem unbelievable, the details are all there in the coroner's report and in photographs which are all widely available to the public. The images are far too disturbing to show here. A quick search on Google for the Guarapiranga Reservoir mutilation will garner results if you so wish to research this further, but be warned, the images are extremely graphic and unsettling. If you are brave enough, we urge you to investigate this case yourself and make up your own mind. Our hearts go out to the family of this poor man and may peace be upon his soul.

14
DOPPELGÄNGERS AND THE STRANGE CASE OF EMILIE SAGÉE

In 1845, a school in Latvia became the scene of some disturbing paranormal activity as a newly employed teacher began to appear in two places at the same time. We now recount the strange tale of Emilie Sagée, and ask the question; could we all have a doppelganger?

What is the difference between a doppelgänger and a dead ringer? People often confuse the two, but they are, in fact, very different. A dead ringer is the living double of an individual. Two unrelated people who are very similar in appearance, but who lead very different lives and, in all likelihood, have probably never met. The experience of running into your double, whose existence you were otherwise completely unaware of, would of course be rather breath-taking. But the fact is that every one of us probably has at least one look-alike out there in the wider world, and it is even more likely that we each have several.

After all, there are more than seven billion people on this planet, and whilst there is an immense variety of features and characteristics amongst human beings, those same features and characteristics can only arrange themselves in a finite number of ways, and so combinations of such will eventually repeat. There is nothing particularly strange about dead ringers. Interesting? Yes. But the fact remains they are nothing more than coincidental.

Doppelgängers, on the other hand, are something else entirely. Literally translated, doppelgänger means "double walker" and these entities are not just mere lookalikes. They are not just similar to an individual in terms of appearance, they are exactly the same. A carbon copy. In fact, they are the person they are emulating, or at least a ghostly reflection of them. Seeing your own doppelgänger is like looking into a mirror and catching a glimpse of an alternate reality. But you had better hope that never happens, for seeing your doppelgänger is considered an extremely ill omen. A sign of your impending doom. Throughout history, there have been many people who apparently saw their own doppelgängers and died shortly afterwards.

One such story—and perhaps the most famous doppelgänger case on record—centred around a young teacher from France known as Emilie Sagée. 32-year-old Emilie had taught at many schools in her native country, but in 1845 she travelled to Latvia to begin teaching at an exclusive girls' school called Pensionat von Neuwelcke. She was popular with the students there, but the school board was somewhat concerned about her employment history. She had moved around quite a lot, having taught at nineteen different schools over the course of just 16 years. Good teachers were hard to come by, so naturally they feared that she would move on somewhere else at the earliest opportunity and leave them with yet another vacancy to fill.

However, just weeks after she commenced teaching at the school, the answer as to why she could not stay in one place for too long would present itself in shocking fashion and it did not take long for them to realise the unfortunate truth of the matter. As it turned out, no one would have her, for Emilie was at the centre of some very strange goings on. And although she never saw her doppelgänger, everyone else did.

The first time Emilie's ghostly twin appeared she was teaching a class of thirteen students. She had her back to the room, writing on the chalk board when all of a sudden, another Emilie appeared right beside her and mirrored her movements exactly. It seemed to have no unique awareness of its surroundings or of what was going on. Students described that it simply copied the real Emilie, the same way a mirror image would, only not reversed. This instance was bewildering enough for those who witnessed it, but nobody would believe them. Not at first anyway. The second time it happened, Emilie was sitting in the school hall eating lunch. It was relatively empty at the time, but the few people who were present were alarmed to see the ghostly apparition blink into existence behind her yet again and start copying her movements as she ate. Whilst Emilie was sitting down, the doppelgänger stood. No food could be seen in its hands.

Sagée herself was completely unaware of her doppelgänger's presence, but she would often say that she felt tired and drained whenever it materialised. As time went on, the appearances became more frequent and her ghostly double would begin to wander beyond the real Emilie's immediate vicinity. More importantly, it began to appear as though it had a mind of its own, as its actions and interactions would diverge away from those of the young teacher.

On another occasion Emilie asked a colleague to watch her class whilst she helped other students with the gardening. At some point during the lesson, Emilie walked back into the classroom and the stand-in teacher left. The students at their desks thought nothing of this until they looked out of the window and could see the real Emilie still working in the garden. Her doppelgänger simply sat in its seat, silently watching them. Although Emilie confirmed she had been outside the whole time, school officials documented in their notes that at the exact time of the sighting, she had wished she was indoors teaching her sewing class instead of working in the garden. Several brave students did eventually find the courage to approach the apparition. They reported that when they reached out to touch it, their hands were met with a strange resistance, the air immediately surrounding the figure was like a thick fabric.

The doppelgänger eventually became a permanent fixture at the school, but unfortunately for Emilie, it had a habit of not only confusing people, but absolutely terrifying the students. A number of parents complained, and Miss Sagée was asked to leave.

As fantastical as this case may sound, this phenomenon is not unique and has in fact affected some of the most famous people in history. For instance, Abraham Lincoln was said to have seen his doppelgänger shortly after being elected to his first term in office. He lay down on a couch one evening to rest and just happened to glance over towards a mirror, when he saw not one, but two faces staring back at him. Whilst he was certain that both faces were his, the second one looked gaunt and deathly pale. Upon telling his wife, she became deeply troubled. She interpreted the vision as a premonition, stating that her husband would be elected president twice, but would die during his second term. Sure enough, Lincoln was assassinated shortly after being elected for a second time in 1865.

Catherine the Great, the Russian Empress, was awoken one night in 1796 by worried servants who reported that they had just seen her entering the throne room. This intrigued her as she had not left her quarters since retiring for the evening three hours earlier. She decided to see this for herself and upon entering the room, Catherine saw her doppelgänger sitting calmly on the throne. She immediately ordered her sentries to shoot at the ghostly apparition, but their muskets had no effect. The doppelgänger eventually faded from sight and the Empress died shortly afterwards.

Johann Wolfgang von Goethe was a famous German writer, poet, and politician. On a summer's day in 1775, he happened to be riding along a path when he saw a mysterious stranger riding towards him. As they passed, Goethe was startled to discover that the other man was him, or at least someone who looked exactly like him, but they were wearing different clothes. Eight years later, he happened to be riding down the same path in the opposite direction when he suddenly recalled that this was where he had seen his double. It was then that he realised he was now wearing the exact same clothes that the mysterious stranger had worn all those years before.

There are many more cases involving doppelgängers, which unfortunately we don't have time to explore, but suffice it to say that their appearance is not as rare as one may think. There are a multitude of high-profile cases involving celebrities and other well-known individuals that have been recorded throughout the ages, and there are also many everyday occurrences. You may well have seen someone else's doppelgänger or even interacted with one and not even realised it at the time. But the most pressing question is, of course, who or what are they?

Unfortunately, there is no definitive answer. Doppelgängers are yet another addition to the list of other unexplained phenomena witnessed throughout this strange and beautiful world. And just like any other unexplained phenomena, doppelgängers have been met with much speculation and, indeed, outright scepticism. Most prominent among theories is that these mysterious entities are astral projections, an embodiment of one's thoughts and wishes which are so powerful that they manifest in the real world. This would certainly appear to correlate with the experiences surrounding Emilie Sagée, whose doppelgänger always seemed to act out exactly what she was thinking at the time. But could there be multiple explanations?

Goethe's experience seemed to suggest a crossover of realities and timelines, and many people have reported similar occurrences, especially in recent times. The Mandela Effect has been referenced as a possible culprit, with some individuals postulating that the appearance of these apparitions may be the result of "glitches in the Matrix" or that we are seeing a glimpse of another reality altogether. Accounts vary regarding the level of interactivity with these beings. Some people report that they have been able to converse with their doppelgänger, whilst others say that they seem to display no awareness of other people or their surroundings at all. In demonology, there are said to be certain parasitic spirits, which can impersonate anyone, including their host. For this reason, others have suggested that some doppelgängers—particularly those that display a level of intelligence and can interact with the world around them—might in fact be demons. On the other hand, they could also be the embodiment of one's higher self, here to guide and advise.

The number of cases where individuals have died shortly after seeing their doppelgänger is more common than most and there is, in fact, scientific research which may support this. A study on a number of test subjects found that when certain areas of the brain were stimulated, the participants felt an outward presence of themselves standing in the same room. It is theorised that natural stimulation of certain areas of the brain through injury, illness, or chemical imbalance could cause someone to hallucinate and see their doppelgänger. These illnesses or injuries could then go on to cause the death of these individuals, hence why the sense of impending doom surrounding the appearance of these apparitions exists.

With so many accounts of doppelgängers recorded over the years, it is difficult to simply dismiss their existence altogether. Conversely, given that there are so many differences between these experiences regarding what the apparition did or did not do at the time of its manifestation, it is hard to pin down exactly what their nature or purpose is. In any case, when you go to brush your teeth before bedtime tonight, after you have rinsed your mouth out with cold water, and as you stand to look in the mirror a final time, you'd better hope you only see one of yourself staring back at you

15
THE BLACK-EYED CHILDREN

Over the past twenty years, the number of online testimonies describing encounters with phantom children have increased exponentially. Who are these nocturnal visitors? And what exactly is it that they want from those whom they unexpectedly approach? In this chapter, we examine the phenomenon of the Black-Eyed Children.

The snow had been falling steadily for several days and had totally blanketed the sleepy corner of Vermont where the elderly couple lived. The moon shone in a clear black sky, its borrowed light spilling onto the fields below, amplified by the reflective nature of the flawless, crisp white snow. It somehow gave the impression that dawn was close at hand, but that was not the case. It was nearly 2am when the husband was unexpectedly awoken by the sound of persistent knocking, emanating from downstairs at the front of his property. Having arisen, he moved across to the window and looked outside to see who might be calling at this ungodly hour. There was no vehicle parked outside or tracks of any kind imprinted in the virgin snow covering the path in front of his house.

Shrugging his shoulders, he slowly made his way downstairs as his wife got out of bed behind him. Reaching the hallway, he opened the front door, and standing on the porch, seemingly unperturbed by the freezing temperatures outside, were two children, a boy and a girl. Both were dressed in old-fashioned clothing with traditional haircuts, and neither seemed to want to make eye contact with him. Speaking in a slow and deliberate manner, the boy simply stated that their parents were coming to collect them and asked if they could come in and shelter from the freezing cold weather. Their account was vague, but despite the old man's misgivings, his wife was quick to usher the two youngsters past him and into the front living room.

The pair settled themselves on a sofa, and both immediately become unresponsive, failing to reply to any of the couple's questions. There was something deeply unsettling about these children, which, for some time, the elderly man could not quite figure out. That was until he noticed that their eyes were entirely black, with no discernible pupil or iris. In an instant, the man was overcome by a crippling feeling of dizziness and unease. As he collapsed backwards into an armchair, his wife gasped upon seeing blood pouring from his nose. She ran to the kitchen to grab a towel, and as she tried to staunch the flow, all the lights in the house suddenly flickered and went out.

A sing-song voice then pierced the darkness, as the little girl announced that their parents had arrived. The two small shapes rose from the sofa, making their way to the front door and out of the premises. Waiting outside was a black, classic American car, with two men in dark suits standing beside it. They all left together. The couple remained huddled in the dark, terrified by what had just happened, until the lights mysteriously came back on about half an hour later. But the wider effects of this sinister visitation would take far longer to conclude. Both husband and wife continued to suffer from dizzy spells and nosebleeds in the months following the incident. In addition to this, the old man was diagnosed with skin cancer, despite having never spent any significant time out in the sun. And of the couple's four house cats, one would be found lying dead from a haemorrhage, on the sofa where the children had sat, and the other three ultimately vanished without trace.

The mysterious, and deeply unsettling, phenomenon of the Black-Eyed Children—who are also described as Black-Eyed Kids or BEK's—was largely unheard of until the mid-1990's. It was at this time that stories involving these strange entities began to circulate online, prompting more and more internet users to come forward and share their experiences. But examples of people receiving unwanted visitations from BEK's stretch back far beyond this period.

One of the earliest recorded examples of such an encounter dates back to 1950, when a sixteen-year-old boy living in rural Virginia returned home to his parents in a panicked state. Sobbing uncontrollably, young Harold Whittaker had explained to his father that he had been walking home from school, when he had noticed a boy of similar age, leaning up against a nearby gatepost. This other boy had stepped out in front of him and said, "I want to go to your house. You will walk me to your house."

Harold told his father that the youth's eyes had been pitch black, and that he was suddenly overcome with a feeling of absolute fear and apprehension. He also remembered having the distinct impression that the other boy was somehow reading his thoughts. The black-eyed adolescent moved to block his path and ordered the terrified teen not to run, again demanding that he show him the way to his house. Harold related how he had suddenly become light-headed and unable to think clearly. An uncomfortable suggestion began to form in his mind, urging him to comply, but he suddenly panicked and made a run for it. The last thing that Harold heard, was an animal-like howl echoing behind him.

The story that first brought the concept of BEK's into the public consciousness was posted online in 1996 by a man named Brian Bethel. A resident of Abilene in Texas, he had written about his experience earlier that year. According to Brian, he was seated in his car on North First Street and had been writing out a cheque when there was an unexpected knock at the driver's side window. When Bethel had looked up, he was surprised to see two boys standing alongside the vehicle, whom he guessed were aged about nine and twelve. When he wound the window down to talk to them, he was suddenly struck by their penetrating jet-black eyes, which seemed to pierce his very soul when they came to rest upon him.

Speaking in a monotone and emotionless manner, the eldest of the two informed Bethel that they had no money and needed a lift home. Utterly disturbed by their demonic appearance, Bethel made his excuses and told the boys he couldn't help them. They seemed to become visibly angry at this and urged him to let them into his car. Suddenly, Bethel noticed that his own arm was now reaching for the door handle, very much against his will. Intimidated by their intense gaze, he instead wound up his window, locked the car doors and drove off into the night. As he had accelerated away, Bethel had looked in his rear-view mirror, only to realise that the two boys had completely disappeared, as if they had never been there at all.

Another, more recent encounter took place in the English county of Staffordshire in 2004. On the morning of the 13th September, a husband and wife were walking their dog across the Cannock Chase nature reserve. They were proceeding along the main path near to Stile Cop, when they heard the unmistakable sound of a small child giggling, hidden within the confines of a treeline they were passing. The couple stopped and were stood peering into the dark undergrowth looking for the source of the laughter when it abruptly stopped. After a time, they turned to resume their walk, but almost jumped out of their skin when they saw that a young girl was now standing a short distance away, blocking their path. She was dressed in an old-fashioned white dress, but it was her emotionless and unblinking black eyes that held their attention.

The girl stood motionless, regarding them with a somewhat unsettling smile on her face. She did not respond or move at all when they tried to speak to her. She simply stood stock still and stared back at them. It was only when the couple's dog cautiously ventured towards her that she turned and ran back into the tree line, laughing to herself. When describing the haunting encounter to a local newspaper, the husband stated that, throughout the incident, the girl had seemed to have her head cocked to one side. The angle it had been resting at looked uncomfortable and unnatural, almost as if she had been hanged with a rope or cord of some kind. The husband and wife are only two of many witnesses who have encountered this apparition at Cannock Chase, and the repeated sightings of the black-eyed girl have given rise to a number of theories about who these mysterious children are.

During the mid-1960's, a series of brutal killings took place along the route of the A34 road, and they would later become known as the Cannock Chase Murders. The bodies of six-year-old Margaret Reynolds and five-year-old Diana Tift were found half-hidden in a ditch at Mansty Gully in January 1966. Both girls had been abducted from different parts of the West Midlands whilst travelling to and from school, several months before. The following year, another body would be found less than a mile away, that of seven-year-old Christine Darby. The local constabulary would put hundreds of man hours into trying to identify the killer, but it would not be until November of 1968 that the case finally received a breakthrough. Witnesses to the attempted abduction of a ten-year-old girl from a street in Walsall provided police with a car registration number, resulting in the arrest of a man named Raymond Leslie Morris.

Morris was well known to the authorities for his obsession with young girls and he had been one of the suspects interviewed in the disappearance of Christine Darby. Whilst he was being held in custody for the abduction, his wife admitted to officers that Morris had coerced her into providing him with a false alibi for the day of Darby's disappearance. He was eventually convicted for her murder and died in prison in 2014, becoming one of England's longest serving prisoners. Despite never being convicted of the murders of Reynolds and Tift, it was long believed that Morris had been responsible for their deaths too and the reports of a ghostly girl in and around Cannock Chase started to appear soon after his incarceration. Local residents believe that the black-eyed girl is the ghost of one of these victims, her young spirit unable to move on.

The idea that Black Eyed Children may be the spirits of children does seem an obvious one and some of the persuasive or repetitive behaviours of these so-called apparitions are similar to those associated with phantom hitchhikers. But the majority of cases involving Black Eyed Kids are either too isolated or bizarre in nature to trace back to a local ghost story. Some believe that rather than being confused or misguided spirits, these individuals are in fact possessed by a far more malevolent and divisive entity. To the ancient Celtic tribes of the United Kingdom, children with black eyes were believed to be otherworldly demons, who walked our plane of existence in search of blood rituals and sacrifices.

Across the ocean, in many Native American cultures, black-eyed people were thought to be similar to the Wendigo, in that they were the unfortunate victims of an evil entity with hostile intentions. The Iroquois referred to this spirit as the Otkon, a malevolent being whose goal was to infect key members of a tribe and gradually turn them all against one another, starting with the most vulnerable prey; the children.

As recently as 2017, the inhabitants of a native Oglala reservation located at Pine Ridge in South Dakota asked for a shaman to visit and bless their encampment, after having reported a series of encounters with BEK's. Over a period of weeks, strange children with haunting black eyes had approached the borders of their camp and tried to encourage the Sioux youngsters to play with them. Unsurprisingly, the camp's children refused to do so, finding the eyes of the newcomers soulless and terrifying. The strangers then focused on the adults of the reservation, asking for food and shelter in dull, monotone voices. When this was also refused, one of the children asked the horrified residents if they had any blood to spare, before they disappeared back into the trees. In the weeks afterwards, a number of pets went missing from the community, until the Shaman's blessing seemed to end the matter altogether.

In a significant number of encounters describing BEKs, such as the one in Vermont, witnesses have described seeing the children meeting up with what are believed to be men in black. Sometimes these mysterious and intimidating individuals are seen driving the children around in their cars. In other situations, MiBs have either ushered the black-eyed children away or visited their victims in the aftermath of an encounter. This has naturally given rise to the theory that the children may be extra-terrestrial in origin, or human children who have been abducted and assimilated in some way. The fact that they appear to possess some level of psychic persuasion, and the ability to harm the people they encounter, suggest to some commentators that they are either participants in or escapees from a sinister government test programme.

Given the lack of overt hostility displayed during most encounters, and the fact that the phenomenon is quite recent in nature, there is also the possibility that it is little more than an urban legend or creepypasta. A certain percentage of the testimonies which have been published online is almost certainly little more than creative writing on the part of the author. On the other hand, it is relatively easy these days to purchase sclera contact lenses that completely cover the exposed areas of the eye. Many horror movies utilise them to terrifying effect. There are also numerous forms of medication where a widely expanded pupil is a common side effect. It is entirely possible that environmental conditions such as street lighting may give the impression that someone's eyes are completely black during an encounter.

What is perhaps surprising about the phenomenon of the black-eyed children, is the widespread absence of photographic or video evidence. Their legend has been precipitated in an age of smartphones and surveillance cameras, and yet alleged witnesses do not seem to be able to capture even fleeting footage of them, despite being in possession of recording equipment at the time.

A common feature of stories and accounts involving the supernatural make reference to the eyes of the creatures and entities involved being somehow different to those of a normal person. The overwhelming number of ghosts, aliens and monsters who have been described throughout the ages possess eyes that are devoid of a pupil or iris and consist of only one colour. These are usually red or black in appearance, colours most commonly associated with evil and malevolence. This means that stories involving children with black eyes can traverse different genres, such as ghost stories or alien abductions, and it is entirely possible that, rather than being an isolated phenomenon, the concept of BEK's is simply a common horror trope, that commentators are choosing to view in isolation. Regardless of this, the stories continue to come thick and fast, with these strange intruders displaying ever more bizarre and unsettling behaviour. All we can say is, remember to keep your doors and windows closed, and your camera phone handy, should an insistent knocking suddenly occur in the early hours of the morning.

16
THE DISAPPEARANCE OF KENNY VEACH

In November 2014, an adventurer by the name of Kenny Veach went missing after finding a strange cave out in the Mojave Desert, which seemed to have supernatural properties. Did he stumble upon something he was never meant to find? Or were there more personal reasons behind his disappearance?

The Mojave Desert, also known as The High Desert, is the hottest, driest place in North America. At nearly 48,000 square miles, it is home to a wide variety of landscapes, from picturesque vistas to barren wastelands. From high mountains to deep valleys, from places where nothing lives, to sprawling communities buzzing with activity. Cities such as Las Vegas, San Bernardino and Lancaster sit at its peripheries, though the larger area of the desert itself is sparsely populated. Its rich scenery and regions such as Death Valley, which regularly records temperatures as high as 134 degrees Fahrenheit (58 degrees Celsius) are amongst the most popular tourist attractions. The desert's mountains, endless networks of caves and its myriad of abandoned mines also pull in adventurers from all over the world, though this terrain is by no means for the inexperienced; many who go trekking across the Mojave never return alive.

Kenny Veach was one such adventurer and, at the age of 47, was an avid and highly experienced hiker. He had a passion for the outdoors and had spent many years exploring the Mojave and Great Basin deserts of North America. Sometimes he would take his girlfriend along with him, but most of his hikes were solo and many of them involved camping over a number of days. On 10th November 2014, he packed his bag for an overnight trip, kissed his girlfriend goodbye and set out for the southern Mojave Desert on what would be his last ever hike. He was never seen again. And were it not for some very intriguing comments made by Kenny and other users on YouTube in the months prior to his disappearance, this case would have passed us by with barely a mention anywhere outside of his local community. Instead, it includes a captivating twist, which would ultimately garner worldwide interest and become one of the biggest internet mysteries of the decade.

Kenny had been an active user on YouTube, not so much in terms of producing content—he only ever uploaded five videos—but he did take a keen interest in hiking vlogs and would often comment on these videos. In June of that year, he had left a comment on a video entitled "Son of an Area 51 Technician". He described how he had stumbled upon a strange cave whilst hiking in the Nevada Desert out near Nellis Air Force Base. This cave was apparently shaped like a perfect uppercase "M" and as he approached It, his whole body began to vibrate. He said that the closer he got, the more intense this vibration became. Suddenly he was overwhelmed with fear and abandoned his attempt to enter the cave altogether, despite that, as an adventurer, he usually made a habit of entering every cave he discovered. In this case, it was just too much.

This comment would spark a four-month long online conversation between Kenny and other users, who challenged him to embark upon a second hike to the same area in order to locate this strange cave once again. They asked him to take a video camera with him, to document his findings and upload the video to YouTube. Kenny did, in fact, revisit the region in October and made a vlog of his experiences during the hike. However, he was unable to locate the cave on this occasion, but the video is available to watch online and can be found by searching for "M Cave Hike".

Kenny's failure to locate it a second time did not deter him. In another post on YouTube, he stated his intentions to return to the area once more, and that this time he was absolutely determined to find this strange cave. Whilst this generated encouragement from the YouTube community, there was one comment which stood out from the rest and was rather ominous in nature. It was left by user 'Lemi Killmister' and it read:

> *"No! Do not go back there. If you find that cave entrance, do not go in, if you do, you won't get out."*

Kenny did respond to this comment asking, "What makes you say that?", but he did not receive a reply, and nothing has been heard from this user since.

Veach left for his third tour of the area on Monday 10th November and by the 14th he had still not returned. His girlfriend reported him missing later that day. After a week and still no sign of Kenny, authorities began to search the region. Large search parties were formed, and a helicopter was deployed to the area. They found his mobile phone resting on the ground outside an entrance to a mine. This led many to believe that he had probably fallen into the deep mineshaft within and had died from the fall, but when cameras were sent down to investigate, there was no sign of a dead body or that the pit had been disturbed in any way, by someone falling in or otherwise. There was little in the way of tracks and nothing else was found of Kenny's belongings. Members of his local community assisted in the search and the extra manpower meant that a much larger area could be covered, but it was all to no avail. It was as if he had vanished from the face of the Earth.

The first anyone in the online community heard of his disappearance was a month later, on 10th December 2014, when Kenny's girlfriend left a comment stating that he had not returned from his trip and that he was now listed as a missing person. Despite subsequent and continued searches by enthusiastic YouTube vloggers wishing to investigate further, Kenny's body has never been recovered. This has left behind a thought-provoking mystery which has grown into something of an internet sensation, not least because of its connections to something which could possibly be described as Fortean. Unsurprisingly, there have been many ideas regarding what happened to Kenny.

First and foremost is the theory that he died of natural causes and that his remains are still somewhere out there in the wilderness. Although Kenny was an experienced hiker, it has been noted that he took monumental risks, refusing to take basic navigational aids along with him on his hikes. Kenny was known to have something of a cavalier attitude towards hiking, saying that maps and compasses were for amateurs, a point of view which the great American wilderness will readily subjugate if given the opportunity. Many speculate that Kenny either became disorientated and lost his way or that he ran out of supplies, collapsed from a combination of exhaustion, and dehydration and succumbed to the elements. However, either scenario is unlikely as Kenny was hiking in a very specific area and a death by natural causes would have resulted in a higher probability of his body being found or at least the discovery of some clues to indicate this outcome.

Other less plausible theories suggest that he may have been bitten by a rattlesnake or attacked by a mountain lion, but this is doubtful as Kenny had taken his gun with him and signs of such an attack would have been obvious. No blood was found on his phone, for instance, and there was nothing to indicate animal predation in the location where it was discovered. There are those who postulate that he may have witnessed something he shouldn't have, such as a gangland killing, a drug deal, or even a classified military exercise and that he had been "silenced". Once again, there were no signs whatsoever to indicate that something like this had taken place.

A less popular explanation is that Kenny faked his own death. It is known that he had quit his job to start a new business about a year before he disappeared. That business was not doing as well as he had hoped and in one of his videos, he talked about selling his home because he was running out of capital. Although there is no evidence to suggest that he owed money to any particular individual or organisation, this has led many to believe that he staged his disappearance in order to avoid paying his debts.

That being said, there are many problems with this theory. First of all, faking one's death to start a new life is no easy feat. It is an immense undertaking, requiring a huge amount of planning, financial investment and an outright acceptance of personal loss. Kenny had a girlfriend and many others dear to his heart and it is hard to believe that he could have left all these people behind and not once felt the need to see them again. Secondly, the amount of attention which has been drawn to this case since his disappearance would have made faking his death all the more difficult, so once more, this scenario is highly unlikely.

This now leads us to address the elephant in the room; Kenny's comments regarding this so-called M-shaped cave. The question over exactly what this cave was (if it even existed at all) has been prominent in the mystery surrounding his disappearance. An obvious theory regarding his fate is that he did, in fact, manage to locate and enter this cave on his third and final attempt and that he was either killed, abducted, or fell victim to some sort of accident, and died therein. The comment left by the user 'Lemi Killmister' only makes this possibility even more chilling.

So, if Kenny did indeed find this cave, what was its purpose? Nevada is home to a number of US air bases, including Nellis, Creech and, of course, the infamous Area 51 facility at Groom Lake. There are those that believe the cave was an entrance to a Deep Underground Military Base, otherwise known as a D.U.M.B. There are also many conspiracy theories surrounding such installations and possibly the most famous example is that of Dulce in New Mexico, where all sorts of horrors such as experimentation on human subjects are said to take place. The strange vibration and subsequent feelings of fear experienced by Kenny as he approached this cave could have been the effects of what is known as an Access Denial System. This may sound like science fiction, but these devices have actually been developed and tested by the US military in various applications, though they usually use heat as a deterrent and work in much the same way as a microwave does, only not as destructive.

Investigators have theorised that the device used in this cave could instead have been based on infrasound. Infrasound is a relatively new discovery of ultra-low-frequency sound waves, which have significant effects on human beings when exposed to them. People are said to experience strange vibrations, auditory and visual hallucinations and intense feelings of fear when subjected to such low frequencies. They occur naturally and their existence has been put forward as a possible explanation for a variety of phenomena, including hauntings and even alien abductions. These sound waves can be recreated under the right circumstances and could be used in a military capacity. It should be noted, however, that the M-shaped cave could have been a completely natural formation and may have, in fact, generated its own infrasound waves.

Some of the more fringe theories suggest the involvement of extra-terrestrials. Of course, Nevada is no stranger to UFOs and odd goings on. An ex-US Airman by the name of Charles James Hall wrote a book about his experiences working out in the Nevada Desert, where he interacted with an alien race known as the Tall Whites. In his book, *Millennial Hospitality*, he describes how the Tall Whites had supposedly entered into an agreement with the US government whereby they were given secret underground bases in and around the Mojave. Could the M-shaped cave have been the entrance to one of their facilities? And could Kenny have been killed or abducted for stumbling upon something he was never supposed to find?

The fact of the matter is we may never know.

In any case, Kenny's girlfriend left a heart-breaking comment on his channel in 2016, which seemed to suggest something of an unexpected possibility regarding his fate. It was made in response to a question from an amateur investigator on YouTube. In the message, she says that she believes Kenny took his own life, as she had noticed a significant change for the worse in terms of his depression, due to increasing money issues. As already stated, he had quit his job of seventeen years to pursue starting up his own business, but this had been something of a failure and he was essentially living on his retirement money.

She mentioned that Kenny had opened up and talked to her about his suicidal thoughts, thoughts he had had for most of his adult life. His father had committed suicide when Kenny was in his early twenties, and he had always said that if he was ever going to take his own life, he would not do it at home, but out in the wilderness where no one would ever find him. She believed he said this because of the painful memories he had endured after finding his father's body at home.

When Search and Rescue were given the go ahead to examine Kenny's residence, they apparently found articles on suicide in his internet search history and that he had written the words "help me" several times. Kenny's girlfriend doesn't know whether he left that morning with the intention of taking his own life or whether he decided to do it whilst on the hike. He had left his video camera at home, which raises the question of whether he had any desire to find the M-shaped cave on this occasion, or whether he had more pressing things on his mind. She believes his body could be in any one of the thousands of caves or mines dotted all over the Nevada Desert and that it would be very difficult to find him if he is there.

If true, her post speaks loud and clear about Kenny's state of mind at the time of his final hike. Whatever the explanation for his disappearance, as time rolls on, the sad truth is that he is more than likely no longer amongst us. Our thoughts are with Kenny's loved ones and if they are never again to see this man—who by all accounts was a lovable, genuine individual with a huge heart—we can only hope that they find solace in the fact that he died doing what he loved. Our hearts go out to those who knew him and no matter how slim the possibility, until his body is found, we hope for his safe return.

17
THE GHOSTS OF STOCKSBRIDGE BYPASS

In 1988 a new section of road was laid across the Peak District in Northern England to divert heavy traffic away from a small town. Shortly after building work commenced, reports of strange happenings began to surface and the road soon became notorious, not only for its paranormal activity, but for the amount of lives it would claim.

It was 17th November 1991, the sun had long since sunk beyond the horizon and the rolling hills of the Yorkshire countryside were bathed in a tepid darkness. A glow appeared over the treeline, the distant headlights of a car, cutting their way through the endless black. It was driven by a young woman, travelling home after a long shift at the hospital where she worked. The clock on the car's dash read 2:51am. The high beams danced over a road sign, revealing a combination of numbers and letters which read A616 Stocksbridge. The young woman yawned and looked in her rear-view mirror and immediately wondered why she had bothered; the road receding behind her was pitch black. There was nothing to see. The darkness made her feel very alone and in that instant the air seemed to turn cold. An unborn fear, not yet realised, lurked somewhere in the pit of her stomach yet she had no idea why.

Regardless, she decided to turn on the radio to ease her nerves. When she flicked the switch, only static poured from the speakers. The sound of this alone sent a chill up her spine. Suddenly, she felt compelled to look to her side. The passenger seat was empty, but for some unknown reason she felt a presence there. Another look in the rear-view mirror revealed nothing. It was a momentary lapse of concentration, for when she glanced back towards the road, her heart skipped a beat.

She slammed both feet on the brake pedal. The tyres began to screech as the car swerved from side to side, succumbing to the road's icy surface. She was now travelling sideways. There was an almighty thump and suddenly the car was rolling down an embankment before it came to a crashing halt. The last thing to cross the woman's mind before everything turned black was the lone figure that she seen standing in the middle of the road right before her accident. A figure which had now vanished without trace, as if it had never even been there. The headlights of the car died as her vision faded to darkness, the smell of burnt rubber hanging in the air. It was not the first crash to have occurred on this road... and it would not be the last.

☠

Twenty-five years later in October of 2016, the local radio station was advising drivers on their morning commute to avoid the bypass, as it had once again been closed off by the police, in order to assist them in dealing with an ongoing incident. It would transpire that this was a head-on collision involving a van and a heavy goods vehicle, resulting in serious injuries to both drivers. That accident was one of hundreds to have occurred on the road since its construction back in 1988, with over 25 people having lost their lives. This average of one fatality per year, all along the same innocuous length of carriageway, has earned the Stocksbridge Bypass the somewhat unwanted reputation as one of the most haunted sections of highway in the world.

This particular stretch of road itself is only five miles long but makes up part of a lengthier 38-mile thoroughfare, that connects the industrial cities of Sheffield and Manchester. It allows quick and easy access through the counties of Nottinghamshire and Derbyshire, but even before it had opened, reports were circulating that something mysterious and terrifying was already stalking the route.

One evening in September of 1987, whilst the road was still under construction, two security guards named David Goldthorpe and Steven Brooke were out patrolling the work site near Pea Royd Bridge. The men had already begun to experience the unnerving feeling that someone or something was out there in the darkness, watching them, when they suddenly heard the unmistakable sound of children singing a short way off in the distance. They had earlier ensured that the building works had been locked down and secured for the evening and were a long way from the nearest town or habitation, and so the two guards set off to investigate. After a short walk, they spotted a small group of youngsters about a hundred metres away, playfully singing and dancing in a circle underneath an electricity pylon.

Both men were struck by the medieval style clothing they were wearing, and assuming this was some sort of re-enactment, they walked over to see what was going on, especially as it was late and there appeared to be no adults present. But when they were only a few metres away, the singing and dancing suddenly ceased, and the children instantly disappeared right before their eyes. For a few short moments, the only audible sounds were the whistling of the wind, and the uncontrollable racing of the two men's hearts, before they caught sight of further movement over by the nearby steelworks. Unnerved, but determined to find out what was going on, the two men went back to their Land Rover and headed up the road in that direction.

They had not travelled far when Brooke caught sight of a solitary figure. It was stood watching them from the top one of the recently constructed bridge sections. When Goldthorpe drove the vehicle up an embankment and onto the new section of road, its headlights illuminated a mysterious hooded form, just standing there silently regarding them. It seemed almost as if the headlights were passing directly through the figure, perfectly illuminating the concrete behind it. But as Brooke opened the passenger door to exit the vehicle, the figure immediately vanished into thin air. This was more than enough to terrify the two men. Their nerve broken, they turned and drove away at speed from the site, heading for the nearby town of Stocksbridge.

The following morning, Constable Dick Ellis arrived at work to find the two ashen-faced security guards sat quietly waiting in the front office of the police station. He listened impassively as they described their encounters with the phantom children and the sinister hooded apparition. After he had sent them on their way, he shared the story with a colleague, PC John Beet, who jokingly suggested they should have instead consulted the parish priest. A short time later the station phone rang, and PC Ellis found himself speaking to the rector of Stocksbridge Church. The cleric informed him that the two security guards had come to see him straight after they had left the police station and had remained there for some time as they were too terrified to go anywhere else. In calm and rational tones, he urged the officers to investigate the men's story, for the sake of the whole community.

On Friday 11th September, three nights after the security guards' sightings, Police Constables Beet and Ellis arrived on site at Pea Royd Bridge to follow up on the suspicious activity. It was midnight and they were sat in their car with a somewhat blasé attitude to this assignment. They were not expecting to witness anything of interest. However, within ten minutes Ellis was certain he could see shadows moving around on the overpass. He got out of the car and, wary of intruders, climbed the fixed ladder up to the bridge. In the darkness, he could hear a flapping sound and with the beam of his torch, he soon identified a piece of plastic sheeting blowing in the wind. After securing it in place with a brick, he returned to the car, where he and his colleague joked about the fact that the security guards had been spooked by nothing more than a piece of loose polythene.

Unfortunately for them, their amusement did not last long.

Ellis had been staring out of the driver's side window, at nothing in particular, when he turned back to look across at his partner and suddenly cried out in alarm. Immediately behind where the unsuspecting Beet was seated, the unmistakable outline of a man's upper torso was now pressed up against the glass of the passenger side window. As soon as the cry had escaped his lips, the stranger disappeared, only to immediately rematerialise on the opposite side of the car, now pressing up against the driver's side window. Both men stared in horror, as they realised that the intruder had no head or face; its torso ended just beneath where the neck should have been.

The figure was dressed in a dark coloured robe, tied off at the waist by what appeared to be a length of rough rope, and its presence caused both men a great deal of anxiety. After a few seconds, it had vanished again, and when the two officers got out to investigate, they could find no footprints, or hear any sound of someone fleeing the scene. There was no sign that anyone other than themselves had been there. When they clambered back into the police car to leave, Ellis found it would not start, and it was another anxious few minutes before it finally fired into life. As the vehicle pulled off, it was suddenly hammered by a series of mysterious blows, as if someone was violently striking it from behind, before the police officers gunned the engine and escaped into the night, believing full well that they had just seen a ghost.

Reports of ghostly sightings and encounters only increased in frequency after the bypass was eventually opened to the general public. Commuters travelling along the road have reported all sorts of strange phenomena, from thumping sounds to apparitions which appear either in or beside the road and sometimes even in the passenger seats of their cars.

One morning in July 1990, David and Judy Simpson were driving to work along one of the thoroughfare's minor tributaries, the B6088. They were passing the village of Wortley, when David caught sight of what he thought was a jogger up ahead. As their car closed in on the moving figure, both occupants gasped. The individual's outline was ill-defined and dark in appearance, making it impossible to tell who, or what, it was. Even more disturbing was that it appeared to be running in mid-air, with a full three-foot clearance between it and the ground beneath. At the last second, the apparition suddenly hurled itself into the road, directly in front of the oncoming car, before disappearing completely.

This incident is eerily similar to one which was experienced by Graham Brooke and his son Nigel, who were out one evening running in the fields not far from Wortley. The two men were training for a marathon and had been jogging for about an hour when they were stopped in their tracks by a truly bizarre encounter. As they had gone to cross a field, they had suddenly come face to face with a strange individual moving towards them from the other direction. The newcomer was human in appearance but seemed to be walking with his lower half completely submerged below the surface of the field. Its face was concealed by a dark-coloured hood of some kind, and as it had passed the father and son, both had been overwhelmed by a musty and unpleasant odour. The figure disappeared when it reached the entrance to the field, leaving no physical trace behind it.

Far more concerning was a report made to the police by a young couple on New Year's Eve in 1997, in which they described nearly crashing due to the actions of a ghostly spectre. The male party stated that he and his partner had been travelling along the bypass, when a cloaked figure had come looming out of the darkness, directly in front of them. It seemed to have been hovering above the road's surface. Had there been any other traffic on the road at the time, the driver was certain he would not have been able to swerve around the figure without colliding with another vehicle.

As the above examples demonstrate, most witness testimonies pertaining to Stocksbridge Bypass and the surrounding area, describe encounters with a combination of phantom children and monks. So, are there any clues as to the identities of these unearthly and mischievous manifestations? The earliest efforts to build a thoroughfare in the region came during the early 18th century, when a local businessman named John Stocks resolved to build a wooden bridge over the nearby Little Don River. Gradually, more and more road traffic was drawn to use this crossing, which inevitably became known as Stocksbridge. Tragically, a few years after its construction, it was the scene of a horrific stagecoach crash, which resulted in several fatalities. For decades after the tragedy, local residents reported hearing the sounds of horse's hooves travelling along the approaches to the bridge, despite there being no traffic on the road. On occasion, some people would also report seeing a driverless black carriage, hurtling towards the crossing at full pelt, only to disappear as it reached the edge of the river.

The ghostly hooded figure which stalks the highways is believed by locals to be the spirit of a trainee novice from Hunshelf Priory, who had become disillusioned with his faith and left the order to work at nearby Underbank Hall. There are conflicting opinions regarding why he has returned to haunt the bypass, either because he ended up being buried on non-consecrated ground, or because the building work somehow disturbed his remains. In relation to the groups of ghostly children who have been sighted along the route, no definitive explanation exists. Some commentators believe that they were the victims of blood sacrifices going back as far as the Bronze Age. Others argue that they may instead be the spirits of children who died working in the various pits and mines that are scattered about the surrounding area.

The Stocksbridge Bypass is far from unique in being a stretch of allegedly haunted highway, and many more roads around the world are believed to be focal points for hauntings and other paranormal phenomena. Clinton Road, in New Jersey is plagued by reports of cryptids and witches, as well as the pale-faced ghost of a young boy who apparently fell into a river off one of the local bridges and drowned. Sweet Hollow Road, which is located in Huntingdon, New York, is a similarly supernatural location. In addition to spirits of patients killed in a fire at the local asylum, the road is also haunted by the ghost of a police patrolman who was murdered there. He will reportedly pull motorists over, only for them to realise that the back of his head is missing, at which point both he and his vehicle immediately disappear.

So, are we to believe that the 25 drivers who have lost their lives travelling along this small section of rural road did so because of vengeful and malicious ghosts? This is certainly the view of many of the residents and commuters who utilise the bypass. It is also the main reason that some drivers choose to avoid the route altogether, fearing that the road itself may somehow be cursed. As compelling as these reports are, as is the history behind them, it is still important to be rational and objective in our approach to such a subject. All roads possess the capacity to be dangerous, dependant on the various factors that can influence one's journey. A significant number of the Stocksbridge fatalities will have occurred either during the hours of darkness, or in adverse weather conditions, and it would be disingenuous to blame the majority of them on so-called murderous spirits.

It may be that existing knowledge of the stories and legends surrounding the Stocksbridge ghosts ensures that some drivers are overly susceptible to suggestion, their heightened levels of fear and apprehension leading them to misinterpret shadows or reflections as something far more sinister. Or perhaps it is this anxiety that empowers whatever force resides there, providing it with a conduit to the living world. Whether it is the apparitions that are contributing to the traffic accidents, or the traffic accidents that are creating the apparitions, there is no doubt that there is something very wrong with this otherwise inconspicuous highway. Our thoughts are with the friends and loved ones of those who have lost their lives along this stretch of road.

18
THE CURSE OF CARL PRUITT'S GRAVE

In 1938, a man killed his adulterous wife and then took his own life shortly afterwards. After his death, his spirit was said to haunt the cemetery where he was buried and may even have been responsible for much worse.

Stretching back thousands of years, the concept of curses is nothing new. Afflicting a broad range of mediums, from places to people, and even various objects, history is littered with stories of the misfortunes which befall those who touch or disturb something they shouldn't have. From the tombs of Egypt to the accounts surrounding the death of Christopher Case, with so many examples of such phenomena, one has to question whether there could, in fact, be any truth to these tales or whether they are all just products of susceptible imaginations. It is a subject we will revisit many times, and in fact, it is a subject we have broached a number of times already, but here we address one of the creepiest and possibly one of the most famous stories in recent times. Whether it is true or not remains to be seen.

Carl Pruitt was a carpenter from Pulaski County, Kentucky. To most he was known as Mr. Pruitt, to his friends, he was simply Carl, but through a strange sequence of events which occurred even after his death, he will forever be remembered by the rest of us as the "Chain Strangler". Mr Pruitt would never be allowed to rest in peace, and many now wonder whether his spirit was responsible for the deaths of several people, who apparently interacted with his gravestone.

In June 1938, so the story goes, Carl arrived home from work expecting to find his dutiful wife in the kitchen cooking his evening meal; instead, he found her in bed with another man. He was known to have something of a vile temper and this betrayal caused him to fly into an uncontrollable rage. Whilst his wife's lover managed to escape by jumping out of the window, Carl took the full force of his retribution out on his significant other. In his fury, he wrapped a piece of chain around her neck and garrotted her. Seeing his wife's lifeless body lying before him, he became so overwhelmed with grief and remorse that he grabbed his pistol and took his own life shortly afterwards.

In the aftermath of such a vicious murder-suicide, his wife's family were heartbroken, and adamant that Carl Pruitt's body be buried in a separate cemetery. Whilst Carl's final resting place has never been identified, his initial burial site, before its relocation, was situated in a graveyard a few towns away from that of his spouse. Bizarrely, after only a few weeks of his body being committed to the Earth, grass started to grow around his gravestone in chain shaped circular patches. Others noticed a strange discolouration on the headstone itself. The anomaly seemed to be growing in size, forming into links like a chain, which reached out towards other gravestones in the vicinity. But despite requests from the locals to remove and destroy the grave on account that it may be cursed, authorities refused to take these concerns seriously.

The following month, James Collins, a teenager riding his bike along with a group of friends went to the graveyard, perhaps to show his peers that there was no substance to the tales of Carl Pruitt's ghost. He was of the opinion that perhaps the chains appearing around and on the grave were merely naturally occurring patterns, combined with credulous imaginations running amok. After he threw a stone directly at Pruitt's headstone, taking a chip off the top edge in the process, the boys quickly left the scene for fear of getting into trouble with the groundskeeper. As Collins cycled away, his bike inexplicably picked up speed and veered off the path, colliding with a nearby tree. Somehow his chain came loose, wrapped around his neck, and strangled him to death. When his friends went to look at the gravestone later, it was undamaged, despite the fact they had clearly witnessed James defacing it.

This story began making the rounds, with further insinuations of curses, vengeful spirits, and black magic, until everyone was linking Collins' death to Pruitt's grave. Some weeks later, seeking her own form of revenge, Collins' mother attempted to destroy the headstone with an axe. Eyewitnesses state that she broke it into at least a dozen pieces. After she had not been seen for a number of days, her friends became concerned. They later found her strangulated body hanging from the clothesline in her back yard. Reportedly, the gravestone was found to be completely intact just a few days later. This only served to escalate the legend further.

By this time, people from all over the country were coming to see Carl Pruitt's supposedly tainted resting place, much to the annoyance of the locals in the area. In an act of frustration and possibly bravado, a farmer riding past the cemetery in a wagon with three of his family members shot at the gravestone with his revolver. The sound of this gunshot made the horse bolt around a corner and veer off the road. Whilst his family managed to jump free, the farmer himself was thrown from the carriage and got caught in one of the trace chains, snapping his neck.

Shortly after this incident, and at the request of a local congressman, two police officers were sent to investigate the burial site. During their assignment, the officers were said to have mocked the supposed possibility of a curse and took photos of themselves in various degrading poses in front of the headstone. Though they saw nothing untoward at the graveyard itself, the officers were distracted upon leaving by a ball of light which was said to have emanated from Carl Pruitt's grave. It followed their car and after speeding up and swerving sharply to try and avoid it, one policeman was thrown from the vehicle and suffered only minor injuries, whilst the other crashed the car into a nearby fence. One of the chains between the fence posts struck the driver in the neck and almost completely severed his head from his body, killing him instantly.

After this fourth death, stories about a vengeful spirit haunting the gravestone were becoming rife. It reached such a culmination amongst locals that a man by the name of Arthur Lewis took it upon himself to prove once and for all that the grave was not cursed and that there was nothing haunting the burial site. His wife wished him luck as an anxious crowd of locals gathered outside the churchyard. Arthur had armed himself with a large hammer and chisel and soon began to systematically destroy the headstone. Despite his bravery, anticipation soon turned to anguish when an almighty scream split the night sky. By the time rescuers reached him, Arthur was dead, having somehow been strangled by the large chain which had previously been hung across the entrance gates. Up to fifteen people could vouch for either seeing or hearing Arthur Lewis splinter Pruitt's tombstone, yet once again, it was found to be fully intact.

Despite yet another death, authorities refused to admit—at least publicly—that there was anything sinister at the grave site. Fearing for their own safety, many of those who had loved ones buried at the cemetery made the difficult decision to exhume the remains of their family members and have them moved to another resting place. Concerns about Pruitt's ghost continued in the years that followed, until the graveyard was completely redeveloped in 1958 to make way for strip-mining. Common belief was that the reign of the murderous phantom ended forever when Carl's remains were concealed under the new concrete structure.

However, no more deaths attributed to Carl Pruitt's grave occurred after the end of the 1930s, meaning that there was a period of almost twenty years where his spirit must have remained dormant and undisturbed. This has added to speculation that Carl's body was perhaps moved to an undisclosed location many years before the redevelopment took place. If this is the case, it is possible that the ghost of Carl Pruitt is simply waiting for the next time his grave is disturbed, whenever and wherever that may be.

This supposed paranormal killing spree has been recounted various times in recent years, in books and on internet forums. Although, as with many events, certain details differ between accounts. Some suggest the discoloured links on the gravestone formed a cross rather than a circle, and others state that Mrs. Collins' washing line was apparently made of chain instead of wire or rope. Whilst this is intriguing, it does add weight to the possibility of embellishment and that the real truths have, perhaps, been lost over the passage of time. Though we should not disregard the possibility of the paranormal, some of the events in the Pruitt story seem highly implausible. Aside from the notion of a spirit killing a living human being, people have also pointedly asked, amongst other things, why a farmer, experienced in the handling of horses, would risk shooting at a supposedly cursed gravestone. Especially whilst he was in control of a carriage which was carrying his family and knowing full-well that the horse would likely bolt at the sound of a gunshot.

At the same time, important details, including Mrs. Pruitt's first name, the name of her lover, and the name of the farmer all seem to be unavailable. These may have been kept confidential out of respect for living relatives, though some suggest a larger scale cover-up, with the search of public data for the recorded deaths, burials, or exhumations of Kentucky Pruitt's at this time also drawing a blank. Based on the evidence we do have available (or lack thereof) we are obligated to question whether Carl Pruitt existed at all, and whether this entire story is nothing more than an urban legend. On the other hand, if there is any truth to this tale, then whatever the cause of the killings, there remains the possibility at least that Carl Pruitt now lies in an unmarked spot, untended and undisclosed. His spirit may still be at large, sitting at the fringes of our reality, waiting to exact revenge on anyone who dares disturb his final resting place.

The memory of the Chain Strangler lives on.

19
THE DYATLOV PASS INCIDENT

In February 1959, a group of hikers died in mysterious circumstances on the slopes of a then unnamed mountain. Now one of the most famous mysteries of the 20th Century, are we any closer to understanding what exactly caused the Dyatlov Pass Incident?

The sun was beginning to set over the western rise as the two men crested the hill. A combination of exhaustion and the biting cold of the late Russian Winter had slowed their progress to a crawl, but it had not dampened their determination. They plodded on through the deep snow with only one thing on their minds. They were students of the Ural Polytechnical Institute, and they were out searching for theirs friends who had failed to return from a hiking trip two weeks prior. The dying light unfortunately meant that they would soon have to call it a day. They did not relish the prospect of finding their way back to camp in the dark, especially through such unforgiving terrain, but despite those dangers, they could not help but appreciate the allure of their surroundings. This wilderness had a calming, almost serene beauty and they could only hope that it had been kind to their friends. Although their hearts remained resolute, after so many days searching, that hope was fading as quickly as the setting sun.

Ahead of them were the rising slopes of Kholat Syakhl, translated from the Mansi phrase meaning "Dead Mountain", so named by the local Mansi tribes due to the fact that nothing ever grew there. For this reason, the vision that greeted the two men in that late afternoon was an immense, perfectly smooth hillock, blanketed with pure white snow. They would have turned back at that point, if not for the fact that something had caught their attention. In the midst of all that brilliant white, they could make out a singular dark spot about halfway up the side of the mountain, sticking out like a sore thumb, completely at odds with its surroundings. It would take them another half hour to reach, but as they got closer, they could make out the vague outline of a large tent.

They knew immediately that it belonged to their missing friends and upon inspection; they found that, besides a large hole in the side canvas, everything else was in order. The sides of the tent had been insulated with coats and empty backpacks, ski boots were lined up neatly near the entrance, padded coats and blankets lined the floor, and elsewhere they found personal items stowed away along with a wood axe at the far end of the roughly eight square metre shelter. The two rescuers breathed a sigh of relief as they noticed that there were no bodies. They cautiously celebrated as they permitted themselves a ration of belief that their comrades were not dead, but they could still not shake the feeling that something about the scene before them seemed a little off.

They did not know it at the time, but this was only the beginning of an enduring mystery, one which remains unsolved to this day. A mystery that would go on to become one of the most famous and strangest cases, not just in Russia, but in the history of the entire world. Over the next few days, they would begin finding the bodies of their friends, but nothing about their deaths seemed to add up. There would be no satisfactory conclusion, and all investigation would quickly cease, not to be talked of again for quite some time. In the 1990s, after being buried in top secret archives for more than 30 years, the Russian government finally released the details of the incident to the general public. It was not largely known about outside Russia, but it would gain international attention throughout the late Noughties thanks to creepypasta websites and, of course, YouTube.

This is a story you may have no doubt heard countless times already but we'll take the liberty of telling it one last time. We will present only the facts and try to cut out any embellishment. We will run through the timeline of events and the precise details of the journey leading up to the incident itself. We will address every theory in turn and pick them apart one by one, and by a process of elimination, we will try to deliver a clearer picture. But the fact of the matter is that we may never know exactly what happened on that freezing cold night back in February of 1959.

What we do know is that a month prior, in January of that year, nine students of the Ural Polytechnical Institute in Sverdlovsk and an older, former military companion set out to hike across the Siberian wilderness. There were ten group members in total and they were all experienced hikers, each being rated at Grade II in their capabilities by the Institute itself. Their aim was to reach Gora Otorten, a mountain in the Northern Urals. It was a trek which would take them across nearly 300 miles of terrain in the depths of a harsh Russian Winter. They were led by Igor Dyatlov, an accomplished radio engineer and a natural-born leader, respected by many of his peers. Everyone aspired to take part in one of his hikes and it was considered a high honour to do so. It was after him that the mountain pass, where the incident occurred, would later be renamed.

Making such a difficult journey would ultimately garner a Grade III certification in hiking for all participants: the most prestigious hiking qualification in the country at that time. An achievement which required all group members to cover at least 186 miles of ground, a third of which had to be in challenging terrain. The minimum duration of the trip had to be sixteen days, with no fewer than eight of those days spent in uninhabited regions, and with at least six nights spent in a tent. It was a tough assignment, but in completing this task, the certification would allow each member to teach their craft as Masters of Sports, a distinction that everyone in the team was desperate to attain.

And so, a mixture of excitement and determination was in the air as the ten companions stood on the platform at Sverdlovsk train station, stooped under the weight of their packs. Not once did the thought ever cross their minds that this would be their last trip, one that would ultimately end in disaster. Nine of the ten members would never return alive. As fate would have it, the tenth member, Yuri Yudin, would cut his trip short halfway through the hike due to ill health. It is thanks to him that we have a detailed account of the group's movements up until 28th January. Everything after this point has been pieced together from journal entries and photographs taken by the group. Their arduous journey would play out as follows.

On the evening of 23rd January, they caught the 9:05pm train from Sverdlovsk, which would take them over 200 miles north to Serov. The journey was roughly eleven hours in length and would see them arriving at their destination at 7:39am the next morning. Whilst in Serov, they caught up on some much-needed sleep and then spent the afternoon entertaining the children of a local school. In the evening, they boarded another train, which would take them a hundred miles further north to Ivdel, arriving there at around midnight. This left them with a six-hour wait before they caught a bus at 6am out to Vizhay on the 25th January. The next day, they travelled further north to an area known simply as Sector 41, and there they would spend the evening. At 4pm on the 27th they travelled up the frozen Lovza River, in the dead of night, and would arrive at an abandoned geological site in the early hours of the next morning.

It was at this point that Yuri Yudin—hindered by rheumatism and other ongoing illnesses—was forced to turn back. After saying their farewells, the rest of the group continued travelling north towards their objective. Yudin would look over his shoulder one last time to see his friends skiing away in the opposite direction, his heart heavy with disappointment, oblivious to the quiet irony that his illnesses had just saved his life. This was the last time he ever saw his friends alive.

It was on this day, the 29th January, that the group's hiking adventure would commence proper. After having travelled mostly by road and rail, it was now time for the hard work to begin, as they made the rest of their way towards Otorten on foot. They continued skiing north along the frozen Lovza River into the late evening, before setting up camp for the night. On the 30th, they would head west following the Auspiya River, one of the Lovza's tributaries, all the way up to the base of an unnamed mountain, marked on maps simply as Height 1079. In the years that followed, this peak would come to be officially recognised by its Mansi name of Kholat Syakhl, The Dead Mountain.

It was here that they would set up camp and build a cache to store any excess supplies in an effort to lighten their loads. This was in preparation for the ascent of Otorten. The 1st February would see progress slow to a crawl as the harsh weather began to set in. The low visibility would contribute to the group's straying off course and in the last hours of daylight, they would find themselves halfway up the slopes of Height 1079. Igor made the decision to set up camp here for the night, perhaps due to a combination of not wanting to lose the ground they had already covered and the fact that the daylight was fading fast. He also more than likely wanted to practice camping on a mountain slope as an extra challenge for himself and the group.

In any case, it is known that the hikers were settled into their tent by around 5:30pm. They worked on a mock paper together, The Evening Otorten, which was a humorous report on the group's activities over the last few days, and also served as a team building exercise. Photographs had also been taken whilst they were making camp, and everyone seemed to be in good spirits. However, whatever took place there over the next few hours is highly mysterious and would go on to become what is now known as the Dyatlov Pass Incident. Nobody knows for sure exactly what happened, but from collected evidence, authorities were able to ascertain that at some point during the night of 1st February, something spooked the hikers so much that they would cut their way out of the tent and run out into the freezing cold night, barefooted, and in little more than their underwear.

All nine group members perished; most of them from hypothermia, but some from horrific injuries, of which nobody has ever been able to satisfactorily explain. The entire event remains steeped in mystery, even after all this time. Although a few theories have come close to presenting a plausible explanation of what exactly took place, none of them are without their problems.

The first sign of anything amiss came about midway through

February. Igor and his companions had been due to return to Sverdlovsk on the 13th, but nothing had been seen or heard of them. This was no immediate cause for concern; delays were normal and at the start of the trip, Dyatlov himself had told Yuri Yudin—the young man who had abandoned the hike early due to ill health—that he expected the return journey to take longer. By the 15th, families were beginning to feel a little concerned. They reasoned that at least a telegram or some other form of communication informing them of the delay should have been received by now, but they had heard nothing. Five days later, on the 20th, with still no word, the group's families demanded that a rescue operation be mounted in order to locate their loved ones.

The search parties were initially assembled of volunteers such as family members, fellow pupils, and teachers from the university. On 26th February, a student by the name of Mikhail Sharavin, accompanied by a close friend of Dyatlov's, found the abandoned tent on the gentle, 30-degree incline slopes of Kholat Syakhl at an altitude of 800 meters. It had collapsed and appeared to be badly damaged, with a large slit in the side canvas. It had been partially covered with snow and they found many of the group's belongings inside, but they could see nothing of the hikers themselves. The fading light meant that the search would have to be called off for the day. The rescuers made camp in a more optimistic mood than they had started out with. They firmly believed that the group were out there somewhere, alive, and possibly braving the cold in a snow cave or abandoned house. They could not have known that the bodies of their friends were lying beneath the snow, lifeless and silent, not too far from their own camp. It was only a matter of time before the full horror of the Dyatlov Pass Incident would begin to unfold.

On the morning of 27th February, the search and rescue party made an early start, keen to determine the group's direction of travel away from their abandoned tent. They were soon joined by a larger group of volunteers, as well as members of the Russian military. Leading away from the campsite, the rescuers discovered at least eight sets of footprints, possibly nine, heading down the slope towards the edge of a wood at the very base of the mountain.

Bizarrely, most of the tracks looked as if they had been made by people wearing only socks and even barefooted in some cases. They disappeared after about 500 metres, apparently covered by snowfall. The woods were situated almost a mile downhill on the opposite side of the pass. At the edge of the tree line, underneath a large cedar tree, they found the remnants of a small fire. They also noticed that the cedar tree's branches had been broken, or snapped off completely, up to five meters above the ground, suggesting that someone had climbed it. This at first looked promising, but any hopes of finding the hikers alive would be short-lived.

Early on the morning of 27th February, they found the body of Yuri Doroshenko underneath the cedar tree, close to where the fire pit was situated. At 180cm tall, Doroshenko was the group's tallest and most well-built member. He was described as impulsive and brave by those who knew him. On a previous expedition, he had apparently chased away a bear that had wandered too close to camp. Doroshenko had minor cuts and bruises all over his body. His nose, lips and one of his ears were covered in dried blood. His upper lip was swollen as if he had been hit in the mouth. A grey, foam like substance was also found on his cheeks suggesting he had suffered from a pulmonary oedema. His right temple and one of his feet had been burned. Despite all these factors, the cause of death was listed as hypothermia.

Yuri Krivonishchenko's body was found lying right next to Doroshenko and was discovered at roughly the same time. Krivonishchenko had been the group's joker and musician and had something of a reputation for being a master storyteller. He had been studying construction and hydraulics at the university. As with Doroshenko, minor bruises and abrasions were found on his abdomen and various limbs. The tip of his nose was missing, possibly eaten by animals after death. A chunk of flesh had been torn off the knuckle on the back of his left hand, which was later found to be in his mouth, suggesting that he had bitten himself, possibly as a way of staying awake or—if he had been hiding—in order to stifle a cry. Both of his hands had suffered burns. The cause of death was also listed as hypothermia.

The next body to be discovered was that of Igor Dyatlov, the group's leader. Highly intelligent and meticulous in preparation, Igor was well respected amongst his peers. His knowledge of radio systems was said to be encyclopaedic, having crafted a few wireless devices using household items. His body was found later the same day further up the slope, 300m from the cedar tree, as if he had died whilst heading back towards the tent. He was found face up and covered with snow. Both his hands were clasped together in front of him, with his arms tight against his chest. His watch had stopped at 5:31am. Like the others he had minor abrasions and bruises. Blood was found on his lips and his lower jaw was missing an incisor. The coroner reported that injuries to his hands were consistent with those which occur during a fist fight. As with the other two bodies, Dyatlov had also died from exposure.

The last hiker to be found that day was Zinaida Kolmogorova. Zinaida, or Zina, was regarded as lively and bright by her friends. She had a natural warmth, and her outgoing personality was very welcoming. She was highly attractive and many of her male companions privately admitted to having had a crush on her. Her body was discovered face down 630m away from the cedar tree. Like Dyatlov, it seemed that she had died whilst struggling to make her way back to the tent. She had also apparently died from hypothermia, but her body was in a similar state to the others. However, she had a fresh, foot-long bruise in her lower right lumbar region. It appeared as though she had been hit with a blunt object, such as a baton or the butt of a rifle. The coroner also found that she was not sexually active. This was investigated in order to determine relationships within the group and whether this could have been a cause for any kind of friction between the male members.

Rustem Slobodin's body was not discovered until 5th March 1959. Slobodin was the group's second musician, and he always carried a mandolin with him on every single hike. He was the son of affluent university professors and had already earned a degree in mechanical engineering. Rustem was found face down 480m from the cedar tree, somewhere between Igor and Zina. Like them, he also appeared to have been trying to make his way back to camp. He was one of the few hikers to be found wearing footwear, although he only had on one felt boot on his right foot. Like the others, he had minor wounds all over his body, but somewhere along the line he had fractured his skull. Despite such an appalling injury, it was not serious enough to have caused his death. Slobodin also died from exposure.

Dyatlov, Doroshenko, and Krivonishchenko had all been lightly dressed. Their bodies were found wearing little more than their underwear and long-Johns. Kolmogorova, and particularly Slobodin, on the other hand, were better dressed than the other three, although the clothing they had on was nowhere near sufficient enough to withstand such low temperatures. With the exception of Dyatlov, it was discovered that the other bodies had been moved in some way after death; most were found face down even though they had died on their backs.

The bodies of the last four hikers were not discovered until two months later when the snows began to melt. A Mansi native by the name of Kurikov noticed cut branches, forming a trail, which receded 75 metres further back into the woods behind the cedar tree. This led to a six-metre-deep ravine where a pair of black cotton pants was found. The ravine was still half filled with snow, but on 5th May, rescuers worked tirelessly to dig it out. The remaining four bodies were located inside, buried under four metres of snowfall. All of them were better dressed than the previous victims—it was later discovered that only one of them had died from hypothermia—and it was assumed that these four had taken clothes from the other dead bodies found near to the cedar tree. Along with the hikers, they also found two hastily constructed dens, which suggested they had survived for some time whilst in the ravine.

Alexander Kolevatov was a student of nuclear physics, a methodical young man with an imposing physique. He was a very private person and enjoyed smoking a pipe. Kolevatov was the only member found in the ravine who had apparently died of hypothermia. Despite this, he had a broken nose, a deformed neck, and was missing his eyes and the soft tissues around them. There was also a large open wound behind his left ear and portions of his clothing were found to be slightly radioactive.

Rescuers found Alexander Zolotaryov's body right next to Kolevatov's. They were embraced back-to-breast. At 37, Zolotaryov was the oldest and most experienced member of the group. He had seen military action on the Russian Front during World War II and was something of a stranger to his companions. Nobody really knew him;

he had joined the hike at the last minute, but the others had warmed to his personable nature rather quickly. He had already achieved his Grade III certification in hiking, and they respected his expertise. His birthday was on 2nd February, and it is a particularly sad twist that he either died on or just before his thirty-eighth birthday. Zolotaryov had not died from hypothermia, but from a crushing injury to his chest. All bones in the top half of his right rib cage had been fractured. He had a large open wound on the right side of his head, a cut so deep that the skull bone had been exposed. He was also missing his eyes and eyelids and was found with a pen in his right hand and a piece of paper in his left but had died before he could write anything down.

Nikolai Thibeaux-Brignolles was found just two metres away from the other two. Brignolles had already graduated from the university, earning his degree in Industrial Civil Construction. Though serious and extremely well-read, he was the most humorous member of the group. Brignolles had died from a massive impact to the skull, with multiple fractures to the temporal bone. This sort of injury would have left him unable to move. It should be noted that Zolotaryov and Brignolles were the best dressed members of the group, both were found wearing footwear, which has led many to believe that they might have been outside of the tent at the time the incident took place.

Finally, Lyudmila Dubinina's body was discovered only a metre away from the other three. Lyudmila was the youngest member of the party and was a fervent Communist. She had a reputation as an outspoken and highly principled student and although serious on the surface, she had a razor-sharp wit, which often kept her companions in high spirits. Unfortunately, of all the group members her body was found in the worst state. Like Zolotaryov, she had also suffered a crushing injury to her chest; all but eight of her ribs had been broken. Her eyes, tongue and the soft tissues around the mouth and eyelids were missing. The coroner found a significant amount of blood in her stomach, which suggested her tongue could have been removed whilst she was still alive. Animal predation shortly after death was also listed as a possibility.

The injuries to Dubinina, Zolotaryov, and Brignolles were of particular interest. The coroner reported that they did not exhibit the blunt force trauma associated with any kind of attack using melee weapons. Instead, they were the sort of injuries only seen in car accidents or explosions. They were inflicted at high-speed and caused by a huge amount of pressure.

Needless to say, authorities were initially baffled. They could have accepted one or two hikers having lost their lives, but the deaths of nine highly experienced individuals seemed incomprehensible. The campsite was examined and re-examined countless times, and from the evidence gathered, investigators were able to piece together a rough idea of what happened. Forensic examination of fibres in the tent material determined that the cuts had been made from the inside. The main entrance was still buttoned up, suggesting that none of the group had left the tent in this way, they had all exited through the large hole in the side canvas. Many of their belongings were left behind, things that would have otherwise saved their lives, including layers of protective clothing.

Footprints leading away from the tent indicated a haphazard and panicked flight. The tracks initially diverged on different routes of escape but regrouped about a hundred meters further down the slope. It was determined at this point that the hikers were no longer running, but taking calm, methodical steps. They walked almost in single file. Upon reaching the tree line at the bottom of the slope, it is assumed that Doroshenko and Krivonishchenko, the least well dressed, quickly began to suffer from hypothermia. They all huddled around a hastily lit fire in order to keep themselves warm, but it was most likely not sufficient enough.

They could not see the tent from their position, and it is assumed that somebody climbed the large cedar tree in order to survey the scene and ascertain whether it was safe to return. Investigators believe that three members of the group, freezing and already in the initial stages of hypothermia, decided to brave the elements and make their way back to the tent. The remaining four members stayed behind to look after Doroshenko and Krivonishchenko, hoping the other three would return with provisions. Little did they know it, but Dyatlov, Slobodin, and Kolmogorova would expire at various stages of their ascent.

After the deaths of Doroshenko and Krivonishchenko, and with still no sign of the other three, the remaining four members decided to head into the woods for better protection from the weather. Stumbling through the darkness, three of them fell from a height of six metres into the ravine and suffered appalling injuries. An alternative to this theory is that they all made it to the bottom of the ravine but were crushed under a massive collapse of ice and snow from above. All members of the group now lay dead or dying as the snow and wind howled across the slopes of Kholat Syakhl.

Authorities were fairly confident that this is what happened, or some variation of it, at least. But the question on everybody's lips was, what on Earth compelled these individuals to leave the safety of their tent in such a panicked and distressed state? Something must have taken place at the campsite which disturbed them so much that they prioritised fleeing the scene over the structural integrity of their only shelter and of protecting themselves against the sub-zero temperatures. And this is the crux of the entire mystery: what was that event?

There have been several theories over the years. Most prominent amongst them—and the explanation almost everyone uses to try and rationalise the incident—is that an avalanche was responsible. It is theorised that during the night, the hikers heard a rumble heading towards their camp and fled in fear for their lives. However, this possibility does not stand up to scrutiny.

The 30-degree incline of the mountain slope was just not steep enough to pose any threat from an avalanche and if Dyatlov or even Zolotaryov had suspected such a danger, they would never have made camp where they did. Secondly, an avalanche would have completely covered the campsite, including the footprints that were found leading away. The tent was only partially covered with snow and was still standing when found. Finally, the hikers would never have been able to outrun an avalanche over such a distance. This is not to say that one did not occur elsewhere on the mountain. The hikers may well have heard a rumble echoing through the valley and believed that an avalanche was bearing down on their camp, when in fact it was occurring elsewhere. But surely they would have realised their mistake long before they reached the trees, which were situated a mile downhill.

In keeping with the more mundane explanations, an idea that

seems to be gaining a lot of traction suggests that a fire broke out in the tent. The Dyatlov group carried with them a small wood-burning stove, which they set up inside their shelter. This would serve two purposes; to cook food and provide an extra heat source, a welcome addition in the depths of a harsh Russian winter. The stove was usually set up every single night without fail and, in fact, it became something of a competition between the hikers to see who could assemble it in the quickest time.

It is proposed that during the night, the stove caught fire inside the tent and that the hikers panicked and cut their way out. Whilst, on the surface, it is a reasonably sound theory, it unfortunately falls apart under further examination. Firstly, investigators found no smoke or fire damage to the tent canvas. Secondly, when rescuers discovered the abandoned shelter on 26th February, they found that the stove had not even been assembled. It was still neatly packed away in one of the hiker's backpacks. Finally, even if a small fire did break out, how realistic a reaction would it have been for the hikers to run a whole mile from their only shelter, without looking back even once to confirm that it was indeed a total loss?

Another theory is that the Russian military had been carrying out weapons tests in the area. The air force was known to deploy floating mines over parts of the Ural Mountains, which were explosive devices attached to parachutes. They would usually detonate about a metre above the ground and it is possible that one could have exploded near to the tent, injuring some of the hikers in the process and causing the rest to flee. That being said, there would have been distinctive tell-tale signs, none of which were found despite the area being combed extensively during the search and rescue operation.

Some people suspect that the group may have been attacked or coerced into leaving the tent by a third party, whether that third party was Russian Special Forces, members of local Mansi tribes, or other people wishing to do them harm. This theory is supported in some way by the fact that, whether major or minor, nearly every single member of the group had suffered some form of injury, which alluded to the possibility of a struggle having taken place. Could the calm, measured paces further down the mountain slope suggest that they were being ordered to walk away at gunpoint? Again, this is highly unlikely. No other tracks were found in the area besides those of the hikers themselves and it is difficult to pinpoint a motive for anyone to do such a thing. After all, none of the group's belongings were taken, not even their money, which decisively rules out a robbery.

Interestingly, Yuri Yudin believes that his friends stumbled upon something they were never supposed to see and were killed by Russian Special Forces. One of the lead investigators attested that the Russian military had in fact found the abandoned camp site two weeks before the search and rescue team, and that the discovery of other tracks in the area was covered up. This theory is not beyond all possibility. After all, how can we be certain about the extent of footprints in the area—or lack thereof—when the entire scene had been compromised by people walking all over the region immediately after the camp had been discovered?

Some suggest that there was internal conflict within the group, but this seems even more implausible. Why would a fight amongst certain members cause all of them to leave the safety of their camp? Espionage was also suspected, with some people theorising that the entire hike was a ruse so that certain individuals in the group could meet up with western agents and exchange information. It is thought that not all of them were aware of this and that a struggle broke out when the true intentions of the trip were uncovered. But again, this does little to explain the mass exodus of the tent.

A photo taken by Brignolles on 30th January—the now infamous Frame No. 17—depicts what many believe to be a Sasquatch or Yeti stalking the group. The local Mansi tribes tell of many legends about such creatures and absolutely believe that they inhabit the Siberian wilderness. The hikers also wrote a small article about the Yeti in their mock newspaper. This has led some people to put forward the possibility that the group were either spooked by one of these beings coming too close to camp or were indeed attacked by one or even several for encroaching upon their habitat. However, this brings us back to the issue that, although wildlife tracks were found in the area, there was nothing significant enough to match a Bigfoot or even a bear for that matter. Not only that, but even cryptozoologists examined Frame No.

17 and supposedly determined that the proportions match those of a human being rather than those of a Sasquatch.

Fig. 17 - *The infamous Frame 17 captured by Brignolles, which some believe depicts a yeti*

Carrying on with paranormal or supernatural themes, the number nine is said to have been quite significant in this case. According to local Mansi legends, nine hunters died on the same slopes hundreds of years before in horrifying and mysterious circumstances. In 1991, an aircraft carrying nine people crashed in the same area killing all aboard. This has led some to suggest that Kholat Syakhl is cursed, or even haunted by evil spirits. Did one of these spirits manifest in the middle of the hiker's tent on the night in question? Or was it something more alien?

Perhaps the most prominent fringe theory suggests that UFOs were involved. Although this may sound far-fetched, there may be some weight to this idea. Another hiking team, just a few miles away from the Dyatlov group, reported seeing lights in the sky over Kholat Syakhl on the night of 1st February. This was corroborated by several locals who also reported seeing orb like shapes in the sky over the same area. Mansi tribesman would also say that this sort of phenomenon is fairly common in the Ural Mountains. A rather chilling photograph on

Krivonishchenko's camera—the final shot he ever took—shows what looks like an odd light anomaly in the night sky. Zolotaryov's second camera seems to show more images in a similar vein, although the film was damaged, and it is hard to say exactly what they depict. Moreover, lead investigator Lev Ivanov stated many years later that the Soviet government had pressured him to keep anything to do with supposed extra-terrestrial involvement out of his reports.

Of note are the burn marks he found on trees at the bottom of the slope, particularly the tops of some of the pines, which were singed black. Ivanov was of the belief that these trees, or someone hiding within them, had been shot at indiscriminately with heat-based weapons. The state of some of the bodies was also consistent with cattle mutilations found all over the globe, although this could have been down to a combination of animal predation and putrefaction post-mortem. The coroner also reported that the bone fractures were caused by a high-pressure force, the same kinds of injuries which are seen in car crashes, particularly when an unfortunate victim has been run over. They were not caused by blows to the body using fists or hard-edged weapons.

Finally, the radiation found on one of the group's clothing is also a point of contention. It is a common factor seen in so many cases which allegedly involve extra-terrestrials, but in all likelihood, this probably had more to do with the fact that Kolevatov was a nuclear physics major. The contamination could have occurred in one of the labs at the institute where he studied, before the trip even began.

Perhaps the most convincing theory of all was put forward by Donnie Eichar in his 2013 book *Dead Mountain*. Eichar believes that the group were affected by a naturally occurring phenomenon known as infrasound. As mentioned in another chapter regarding the mystifying disappearance of Kenny Veach, infrasound is an ultra-low frequency soundwave which is said to have extremely negative effects on humans and animals, causing them to feel nausea, fear, dread and even hallucinate in some cases. Eichar postulates that the group became convinced of an impending doom about to befall them and left the tent without any consideration for how they were going to survive in the aftermath. All they could think about was escape. When they finally realised the folly in what they had done, it was far too late. Experts in infrasound phenomena have examined the contours of Kholat Syakhl and have stated that, if the conditions were just right, the smooth slopes would be perfect conductors for such soundwaves to manifest.

So, is this what caused the hikers to leave the safety of their tent in the middle of that freezing cold night, inadequately dressed and ill-equipped in most other aspects? There are a few issues with this explanation, of course. Infrasound affects different people in different ways, so why would they all react in the same way? Surely, at least one of them would have seen reason. Not only that, but would the effects of infrasound really be strong enough to affect a whole group of people continuously over the course of a mile? The jury is still well and truly out.

After all these years, we are still no closer to understanding what kind of incident could drive so many people to act so recklessly, and unfortunately, we may never know the truth. It seems the secrets of Dyatlov Pass died on the slopes of Kholat Syakhl, along with the young men and women who undertook such a difficult assignment. Whatever happened, it was such a tragic waste of life. Truly, our hearts are with their loved ones and these once vibrant and talented individuals should never be forgotten. If we are to have any hope of solving this case, we should never stray from the curiosity we all feel regarding their final moments. The sounds of their toil, laughter, and even their horror will forever echo through the lonely mountain pass where they spent their final days. May their brave souls live on forevermore.

20
JAMES DEAN'S LITTLE BASTARD

Amidst the Hollywood glamour, Fifties film star James Dean enjoyed a passion for fast cars and track racing. We look at how he played out this obsession in theatrical roles and reveal some surprising premonitions about the actor's death, as well as his supposedly 'cursed' vehicle dubbed Little Bastard.

The tales of both Christopher Case and Carl Pruitt share a common theme in that they centred around a curse, which manifested some form of paranormal entity. One featured a scorned witch who stalked, tormented, and eventually killed the man who had rejected her. The other, a vengeful spirit of a murderer, which brought retribution upon those who desecrated his gravestone. In either case, the antagonist was marginally personified, and we had a feeling of who—or what—was responsible. But the following story involves a curse which is somewhat different; brought about by an inanimate object rather than a clear, sentient intelligence. In this story, the killer is somewhat faceless, inherently soulless and, for that reason, far more terrifying.

Renowned artist of both screen and stage, James Dean, was born on 8th February 1931. In his early years, he lived in Marion, Indiana, but moved to Los Angeles at the age of five and spent much of his younger years on his uncle's farm. Though James took part in school play productions, it was not until he attended college that he decided to focus his attention on the acting career that would one day make him a household name. By this time, the 17-year-old Dean had developed a great personal interest in sports-car racing and had become a regular spectator down at the local track. A move to New York in 1951 saw him appear in a number of TV shows and many expected his interest in motorsport to subside. During this period, Dean was also awarded a part in the long-running Broadway show *See the Jaguar*, the title a reference to the wild cat rather than the vehicle manufacturer.

However, in 1953, as soon as he turned 21, Dean sought to emulate his racing idols with the purchase of his first car, a 356 Porsche Super Speedster. Though keen to compete, this eye-catching model was undoubtedly a significant investment for the young man, not least because it was some time before his acting roles were bringing in a reliable income. He once said, "Racing is the only time I feel whole," and thus made a committed decision to try and further both his acting and racing ambitions. James Dean would go on to become a popular name on the amateur racing circuit, running alongside his stage and film work over the next couple of years.

Things began to unravel for Dean in 1954 when Warner Brothers—for whom he had made the movie, *Giant*—attempted to ban him from racing altogether, resulting in some tough choices. Spurred on by a powerful sense of adventure, Dean was adamant that he wanted to race competitively, and there was no question that he was an adept and confident amateur racing driver. Nevertheless, some of his closest friends and advisors were worried about the dangers posed by driving at such high speeds and the ever-present risk that an injurious accident would affect his acting career. This left him in a serious dilemma, but rather than heeding these warnings, Dean made a defiant choice and continued to expand his vehicle collection, initially with the purchase of a Triumph Tiger T110 in 1954. He then went on to race at Palm Springs in March 1955 and in May the same year, he partook in road races at Minter Field, Bakersfield, and Santa Barbara.

Having achieved modest success, Dean enrolled for the road race at Salinas. He traded in his two-year-old Speedster, upgrading to a Porsche Spyder 550, which was capable of speeds of over 140mph. It came with custom fibreglass panelling, was silver in colour and had the number 130 proudly displayed on the front, sides, and engine cover. The words 'Little Bastard' were also painted on the rear cowling. This was applied at Dean's request by pin-striper Dean Jeffries. Bill Hickman, who had worked with Dean as a stuntman and dialogue coach on *Giant* had jokingly called Dean himself a 'little bastard' and this was to become a running joke, now attributed to the vehicle.

The self-confessed thrill seeker had gotten himself a newer, faster racing car, one of only ninety in this range ever made. He hoped that this would be enough to give him an edge come race day. However, it was to come as a great shock to friends and fans alike when James Dean suffered a devastating car crash not on the racetrack, but on the road. A collision in which he would tragically lose his life. Motoring accidents were relatively common, even in the Fifties, though there were far fewer fatalities than there are today. He would be mourned by millions in the weeks and months that followed.

The tragedy itself occurred on 30th September 1955, as Dean was test driving his new Porsche Spyder, accompanied by his mechanic Rudolf (Rolf) Wütherich, who was in the passenger seat. Bill Hickman was driving a Ford station wagon close behind and the route had been carefully planned to incorporate quiet roads, which would allow the Spyder to reach similar speeds to what it could achieve on track. At around 5:45pm, Dean was heading in the direction of California Polytechnic at an estimated speed of 85mph when a black and white Ford Tudor coupé came out from the adjoining intersection on Route 46/41 near Cholame. The two vehicles collided, flipping Dean's car into the air. The Tudor, meanwhile, skidded nearly 12 metres upon impact. It is still hotly debated to this day whether Dean was speeding at the time of the accident or whether he had, in fact, slowed down. Either way there is no concrete evidence to support either claim.

In any case, Dean suffered multiple broken bones and internal bleeding, striking the steering wheel with his head, which caused the actor's neck to snap violently. Whilst ambulance crews attended the scene quickly, there was unfortunately little they could do. He was taken to the Paso Robles War Memorial Hospital and pronounced dead within the hour. His mechanic, meanwhile, had not worn his seatbelt. He had been thrown from the vehicle but escaped with his life, albeit with serious injuries including a broken hip and jaw. The driver of the coupé, a 23year-old student by the name of Donald Turnupseed, was relatively unharmed but bruised and in shock.

An inquest was held into Dean's death by the San Luis Obispo Court and Turnupseed was asked to give evidence. The Court suggested that the low profile of the coupé, combined with high speeds were key contributing factors, but attributed no blame to either driver. A verdict was returned of accidental death without criminal intent. Dean himself may not have been entirely surprised that he died in a car crash; he is quoted as saying, "What better way to die? It's fast and clean and you go out in a blaze of glory." That said, he could not have known that he would crash the Spyder within nine days of having purchased it. Multiple sources, including contemporaries, have commented on Dean apparently having problems with his car in the time leading up to his death. Given the Spyder's unfortunate accident, some believe the vehicle was evil and cursed with bad luck. Chillingly, various accounts corroborate that anybody directly associated with the car was at risk of being affected, potentially even harmed by "The curse of Little Bastard."

One example of this can be attested by crash survivor, Rolf Wütherich, Dean's mechanic. He successfully went on to work with the Porsche Rally team, yet he too would be involved in a crash in his own vehicle some years later. Meanwhile, a sequence of events involving the car's wreckage are somewhat chilling to say the least. Car designer, George Barris, later known for designing the Batmobile, bought Dean's car to sell for parts. But as soon as his team entered the garage, the car's engine slipped, breaking the legs of one of the mechanics.

Physician Troy McHenry bought the engine of the car from Barris on 26th October 1956, though he fared no better with it. When racing a vehicle, which housed the Spyder's engine, at the Pomona Fair grounds it spun wildly out of control and hit a tree, killing McHenry in the process. Moreover, another racer at Pomona, William Eschrid, who had coincidentally purchased the transmission from Dean's car, had his vehicle flipped over in a similar manner to Dean's fatal accident. Thankfully, Eschrid survived, but again, not without sustaining serious injuries.

In light of all these events, Barris became uncomfortable with the Little Bastard wreckage, though he proceeded to sell the tyres to an interested buyer from New York. The curse was said to strike again when those tyres, now fitted to another vehicle, all blew at the same time whilst driving, almost causing another collision in the process. In another incident, a plucky adolescent slipped and gashed his arm when trying to steal the steering wheel. With little else to lose, Barris decided to loan the car out to the Californian Highway Patrol to use for their training exercises. To his disbelief, the CHP later reported that their garage had been burned down just a week later.

But despite the devastating fire, Little Bastard had strangely remained intact. At this point, Barris wanted little more to do with the vehicle. It had caused at least six injuries and two deaths by that time, and he thought it best to take Little Bastard out of commission for good. It was taken to an exhibition at Sacramento, but whilst on display, the car suddenly slipped off the exhibition stand, breaking the hip of a teenage visitor. Lorry driver, George Barhius, became the haunted vehicle's next unfortunate victim. He was tasked with transporting the Porsche, when it suddenly fell from his flatbed truck, crushing and killing him inside the cab.

Traders and automobile enthusiasts talked about how James died too young and how the car didn't seem to "want" to go to another owner. The mishaps and accidents continued until 1960 when the car mysteriously vanished after Barris had requested that it be transported back to Los Angeles. However, when the transporter reached its destination, Barris opened the back of the trailer to find that it was empty. A reward of $1million was offered for its return but nothing came of it. Apparently, a few parts are with Dean's relatives and, more recently, a part was apparently sold on eBay, but its authenticity is yet to be proved.

The stupefying events concerning the wreckage of Little Bastard now sit alongside the tragedy of the star's early death. Strangely, it would not be the only car to apparently inflict upon its owner some kind of hex. Ever since the motorcar was invented, there have been many accounts of haunted or cursed vehicles. Not least among them was a golden 1964 Dodge 330, dubbed the "Golden Eagle". A car which was not only suspected of being responsible for several vicious murder-suicides at the hands of its various owners, but one which also inspired the Stephen King novel, *Christine*. But that is a story for another time.

With Dean being such an experienced driver, the nature of his death still divides opinion to this day. The question of whether the accident could have been prevented has been raised countless times and there are a number of plausible theories which argue in favour of this. Firstly, and perhaps the most blatant example of any kind of warning, is the fact that both Dean and Hickman were issued with speeding tickets on the day of his death at around 3:30pm. Despite this stern cautioning from the law, Dean persisted in pushing the new Spyder to the limit.

It has also come to light that Dean had actually intended to purchase a Lotus MK10 instead of the Spyder. The MK10s were less curvaceous, and perhaps more typical in appearance to something seen today at Le Mans. More important is the fact that it incorporated a unique disc-braking system, and some believe this may have made a difference, even at high speeds. Dean would have had to import the Lotus from the UK, a lengthy process, which meant he would miss certain events on the racing calendar. This was a dealbreaker for the young star and so the Spyder was purchased as his second choice. Aside from the vehicle mechanics involved, various anecdotes from other film stars have surfaced—likely prompted by the strange events surrounding Little Bastard after James Dean's death—in which they claimed to have warned him about the ill-fated vehicle.

Ursula Andress, Dean's own girlfriend, refused to get in the car, saying that it had an evil presence. Fellow actress Eartha Kitt apparently once told Dean, whilst the two were out for a drive in it, "James, I don't like this car. It's going to kill you." On 23rd September 1955, just seven days before Dean's death, he shared dinner in Hollywood with fellow actor Alec Guinness who gave the younger man a stark warning. He said: "It's now 10 o'clock, Friday 23rd September 1955. If you get in that car, you will be found dead in it by this time next week." Though Dean laughed this off, time would go on to suggest how a serious message had been ignored.

Andress is also known to have been dating Marlon Brando at the same time. By bizarre coincidence, back in 1947, Brando performed a screen test for an early Warner Brothers' script based on a then little-known novel, *Rebel Without a Cause*. Researchers have also noted a few strange coincidences in Dean's lifetime. These include curses and events such as the re-enactment of car crashes, that some believe to be significant or even ominous. One of Dean's first recorded stage roles was in Shakespeare's *Macbeth*. Many actors involved with this play have died or become injured with the belief that real witches' spells were used by Shakespeare in his script, and that the play is in fact cursed. Chosen from over 350 auditioning actors, Dean played the role of Malcolm during his time at UCLA.

When filming *East of Eden*, he couldn't have known he would go on to win a posthumous Golden Globe and be nominated for an Academy Award. Moreover, when production finished in the Salinas Valley, the very same haunting landscapes would provide the setting for his unfortunate end just months later.

Dealing with tough themes such as juvenile delinquency, the film release of *Rebel Without a Cause* was an 'X'-rated release in Britain, which had various scenes cut. Dean's character gets involved in vehicle crime with disastrous consequences. He races a fellow competitor and sees his rival's vehicle plummet over a cliff, bursting into flames. This was the last film to be made during Dean's lifetime, one which is still highly regarded to this day. The young star would be immortalised in his role as Jim Spark, becoming somewhat affectionately known as 'Jimmy Dean'. In one final twist of fate, Dean's last known stage performance also includes an echo of his impending demise. He performed as a character called Jeffrey Latham in a play called *The Unlighted Road* and, once again, the plot includes a car crash scene. In the play, Dean causes another vehicle to swerve off the road, killing the driver.

So, is there any truth to the curse of Little Bastard? Or was it all just a series of coincidental and unfortunate events? Either possibility, when taken in context and compared to Dean's lifestyle and role-playing choices, is no less chilling. It seems Dean was a truly gifted actor, but whether this is a case of life imitating art, or art being a spookily accurate representation of life, his time with us surely ended prematurely. His memory lives on, through his work and even via recent reports of strange visions in Bakersfield of a lone man with obscure features, driving along the highways in a silver Porsche Spyder.

In closing, we leave you with the words of The Eagles:

Little James Dean up on the screen
Wonderin' who he might be.
Along came a Spyder, picked up a rider
Took him down the road to eternity
James Dean, James Dean, you bought it sight unseen
You were too fast to live, too young to die, bye-bye

21
THE WRAITH OF TRENCH POOL

Whilst cycling to work early one morning, a young man had a chilling face to face encounter with a ghostly apparition, but the terror would not end there. The entity would go on to stalk him for weeks afterwards, leaving him with a terrifying vision of The Wraith of Trench Pool.

The switch clicked back into position as the kettle came to the boil. Steam rose as its contents were poured into a waiting mug, the rich, flowing burble of water whispering through the air. The smell of coffee filled the room, seeping into every corner, almost as overpowering as the darkness smothering the further recesses of the kitchen. The bulb had blown the night before and Reece Matthews was preparing his drink by the light of the adjacent hallway, which wasn't particularly bright. But that was the nature of energy saving bulbs; just luminous enough to get by.

Taking a sip from his mug, he regarded the scene in front of him. The world outside his window was cold, dark, and wet. It was late October in 2015, and the reputation of the British Winter weather had preceded itself. A sideways drizzle was scoring the landscape of the cobbled roads and town houses inhabiting his street. *Jesus!* He thought to himself. *I should get a taxi.* But a quick glance at the clock put paid to that idea. It was 4:30am and the taxi firms were still charging double time. It was a thought that occurred to him every single morning, but the outcome was always the same; he just didn't have the money to waste on cabs. The buses weren't running at that time in the morning either, so his only option was and always had been to cycle to work.

Reece lived in the town of Telford in Shropshire, England. Famed as one of the birth places of industry, and home to the world-renowned Ironbridge, Telford is a thriving municipality of around 170,000 people, one of the fastest growing towns in the UK. For this reason, the routes of transportation are excellent and cycle paths compliment most busy roads throughout the town itself. This was of at least some comfort to Reece, who had to brave the quieter traffic of the early morning every single day. Quieter traffic, of course, often led to more reckless driving by some, so the cycle paths were a welcome alternative to the roads themselves. Parts of his route, however, would take him off the beaten track, along dark paths, where no streetlamps shone. But that was the last thing on his mind as he finished his coffee, slipped on his waterproof coat, and mounted his bike, ready for his daily five-mile journey to the manufacturing plant where he worked.

The world was still submerged in darkness when he left, it was just coming up to 5am and sunrise at that time of year wasn't until after six. The going was easy. There weren't too many hills and if there were, the inclines were gentle. The rain, on the other hand, was more troublesome. There was no avoiding it, it pierced the exposed skin of his face like a thousand icy shards. In some small way, it felt invigorating, in most others it was an incorrigible nuisance, but never did it pose any kind of threat in stopping him. He cycled on through rows of dark houses and shops. Every now and then a vehicle of some description would come tearing past, taking advantage of the empty roads. But for the most part, the world was silent and peaceful. This close to the depths of Winter, most birds had already flown south, so not even they made a sound. Reece often used this time for reflection, his route was so routine by now that he could often navigate on auto pilot, leaving him free to think on things.

At the midpoint of his journey, he turned off the main highway and began to cycle down an old gravel path, which would take him past Trench Pool. Trench Pool is a large body of water, used mainly as a balancing lake, but is often fished by the locals. The pathway was confined on both sides, with the pool to its left and a thick brush to the right, the other side of which was a busy dual carriageway. There were no streetlamps adorning this part of the route. It was a long straight path, running at least 250 metres in length and would have otherwise been hidden in darkness if not for Reece's high-powered bicycle lamp. It shone so brightly that he could see all the way to the end of the track in front of him.

He began to pick up the pace as he noticed that the route ahead was clear. With his head down, he switched into a lower gear and began to pump the pedals with all the power his leg muscles could muster. He was now travelling at speed, but something—he didn't know what—made him look up from the path immediately in front of him.

No more than three metres away stood a figure. He was moving at such a velocity that he was sure he was going to collide with whoever it was, and in that instant, time slowed to a crawl, as is often the case in such circumstances. Everything happened in slow motion and for this reason, Reece was able to take in every single detail. The figure was that of a woman, dressed in formal office-wear and holding a handbag tightly at her shoulder with one hand. She stood with her legs together and she wore high-heeled shoes. Of her features, he could see nothing; she was looking down at the floor and her drenched, black locks hung down over her face. As he closed in on her, she did not move. She did not cry out in panic. She did not even flinch. She did not react in any way, shape, or form. She simply stood there, stock still and deathly silent.

At the last moment, Reece adjusted his handlebars just enough to go sailing past, missing her by mere inches, but still she stood there, unmoving. He immediately slammed on his brakes, skidding sideways in the wet gravel and almost fell off his bike. He turned back towards her to apologise, but there was no one there.

Confused, he looked from left to right and back again, but the woman was nowhere to be seen. Once he realised the truth of the matter—that there was nowhere else she could possibly have gone—every single hair on his entire body stood on end. Stunned, he turned back around and continued cycling along the path, not once looking back for fear of what he might see. He was fully convinced that he had just seen a ghost. He spent most of that day at work in near silence, only opening his mouth to speak when he needed to, walking in trance-like disbelief. Colleagues noticed this change in him, but he told them nothing of what he had seen. On the way home he took a different route and would, in fact, steer clear of cycling along Trench Pool for months afterwards. But as much as he tried to avoid bumping into whatever he had seen that morning, that choice, it would seem, would not be his.

About a week after his sighting, Reece was walking to his local shop to buy some beer. It was late evening, around 10pm, and the sun had long since set. He was on a path next to a main road, with houses on either side, but the streets were empty. A car would pass every now and then, but for the most part, he walked in silence underneath fluorescent orange streetlamps. What happened at Trench Pool the week before had weighed heavily on his thoughts in the time since, but he had resolved to put it down to tiredness and the possibility that his mind was playing tricks on him. He wasn't even thinking about the incident at the time; his thoughts were on other things, such as video games or TV shows he had been watching. But out of nowhere came the sound of high-heeled shoes walking behind him, echoing off the faces of the houses lining the road.

He did not turn. In fact, he thought little of it until the footsteps started getting louder and closer. Whoever was walking behind him were obviously going at a faster pace than he was and so he decided to stop and let them past as the path was too narrow to overtake. As he slowed, he turned his head to indicate his intention, but to his complete and utter shock, the pathway was empty, and the sound of footsteps abruptly stopped. There would be many more instances like this whenever he was walking alone, either during the day or late at night, and it would never fail to chill him to the bone. He also suffered from episodes of sleep paralysis during this time and whenever it occurred, he swore he could feel a presence somewhere in the room with him, watching.

On other occasions, he would be standing, minding his own business when he would suddenly get the unshakeable feeling that someone was stood right at his shoulder, so close it felt as though they were trying to whisper something in his ear, but they never said a word. This continued for some time and just as Reece felt as if he was beginning to lose his mind, the activity began to abate. Life would return to normal for him, but it would be months before he dared cycle anywhere near Trench Pool again. Only when the sun began to rise earlier, as Winter gave way to Spring, did he feel brave enough to take the gravelled pathway running past the lake.

He would always wonder what it was that he had seen in that cold, dreary October and he would go on to tell close friends of his experience. Through them, he would come to learn that he was not the only person to have experienced something strange in that area. There were stories of fishermen who had seen figures standing on the gravel pathway, which wouldn't have been anything out of the ordinary if not for the fact that these figures were often faceless and sometimes even hovering a few feet above the ground. The sound of ghostly footsteps had also been heard walking along the wooden jetties at either end of the pool. And in another chilling account, a man walking along the same gravel pathway had heard a low, guttural growl—like nothing he had ever heard before—coming from the brush running next to the walkway. It seems the lake is no stranger to paranormal activity and there are perhaps some valid reasons for this.

In mid-2017, one of Reece's friends happened to overhear an interesting conversation about Trench Pool. It included comments from an amateur diving instructor, who one morning many years before, had received a phone call from an officer at Malinsgate Police Station in Telford Town Centre. Reece's friend learned that there had been an altercation between a group of teenagers on the banks of the lake and one of them had fallen in and was suspected to have drowned. The police had called for his assistance as their own diving team was training on the other side of the country at the time. Under a thickening air of apprehension, he and another amateur diver had had to suit up and swim out into the murky water, which went down to a depth of about 20ft. That morning they retrieved the body of an 18-year-old man from the lake, and it would not be the first or last time that someone had lost their lives in those waters.

As mentioned previously, there is a busy dual carriageway on the opposite side of the tall, dense treeline, running alongside the gravel path. Several lives have been claimed in tragic car accidents, which have seen vehicles plough through the brush and end up in the lake. Other times, people have stumbled out of the nearby pub late at night, heavily inebriated and decided to go for a swim, drowning in the process. There is no question that there have been several tragic deaths in and around the pool, but who was the young woman that Reece saw on that gravel pathway in the early hours of that morning? Could she have been the ghost of someone involved in some sort of accident? Or maybe the victim of something more sinister, something as yet unknown?

Reece is unsure, but amidst all the chilling experiences which occurred in the aftermath of his sighting, he sometimes got the feeling that the presence was trying to communicate with him in some way. Whoever, or whatever, it was, it had obviously noticed that he had seen it, and maybe that is ultimately the reason why he was "followed". It has been nearly two years since his experience and Reece still cycles to work. He has resumed his route alongside the lake and although he has not seen anything since, the image of what he encountered is not so easy to forget. Indeed, there is never a time goes by where he doesn't feel a moment's hesitation before turning off down that gravel pathway. And although he may have laid his fears to rest, he feels the same cannot be said for whatever it is that haunts Trench Pool.

22
SECRETS OF CELLE NEUES RATHAUS; A NAZI OCCULT TALE?

During the cold war, soldiers stationed on an army base in Germany found themselves at the mercy of sinister and terrifying paranormal activity. Events were said to be so frightening that some of the men apparently committed suicide. Was there a dark history surrounding the base and could it reveal the secrets of Celle Neues Rathaus?

By April 1945, the forces of Wehrmacht, under the command of Adolf Hitler, were in a full-scale retreat across Germany as the Western Allies pushed east into the Fatherland. German soldiers were surrendering in their thousands, a humiliating end for a military machine which had once outgunned and outmatched the forces of any other nation. On 10th April, the US 84th Infantry division crossed the Weser River and captured Hanover. A city which had been bombed almost into oblivion by allied air raids, resulting in 90% of the city centre being reduced to rubble, so there was little to no resistance when US ground forces finally arrived. The war had been long, its end overdue, and the over-extended, under-resourced German soldiers had had enough. Their morale had collapsed along with the buildings around them. The surrounding townships soon followed suit, raising the white flag as soon as allied armour rolled into view.

One of these towns, sitting 20 miles north-east of Hanover, was Celle, a comparatively small, unassuming community of around 40,000 people. It was well known for housing one of the largest free-standing brick-built structures in Europe at the time; its Neues Rathaus. Neues Rathaus simply translates to "New Town Hall" and nearly every single German town and city has one. There is nothing special or unusual about its name, but there *is* something special and *definitely* unusual about this Rathaus in particular. And whilst this story is famous amongst the British and German soldiers who once took up residence there during the cold war, it is relatively unknown to the wider world.

The town of Celle surrendered on 12th April 1945. As with Hanover, there was no resistance from German forces and certainly not from any of the civilians residing in the bombed-out buildings. The town hall had miraculously escaped the bombing campaign relatively unscathed and, being the gargantuan structure that it was, seemed the perfect place to house occupying troops and form some sort of temporary administration. It had, after all, served as a barracks for German troops and had even housed an SS battalion. The building itself had five floors above ground and five floors below, but what US forces quickly realised, after taking control of the Rathaus, was that they could not access the lower levels. They had been completely flooded with water. This immediately piqued the interest of the commanding officer as he could see no reason for the SS to have gone to such an effort unless they were trying to hide something.

Over the next few days, he would make a determined effort to ascertain exactly what the Germans had attempted to cover up. And the events that followed would become known in military circles as the legend of Celle Neues Rathaus.

On the 15th April, three US Navy divers arrived in Celle with orders to reconnoitre the submerged depths of the building. It was a daunting prospect for any diver, let alone these men, who were some of the best trained in the world. Swimming down into a maze of confined rooms and corridors in pitch black darkness would be enough to unnerve even the hardiest of men. Due to the obvious dangers, each diver was tethered by a line to the surface and sent down at different entry points. What took place over the next half hour is not fully understood, but what is known is that two of the divers never made it back to the surface. Their tethers were retrieved, but not their bodies. The third diver, however, did resurface, apparently raving like a lunatic. When he finally came to his senses after a couple of hours, he reported seeing strange symbols and pentagrams etched into the walls and floors of some of the rooms on the first two levels.

On the third level down, he said that, in the darkness, he had seen mutilated corpses strapped into chairs. He reported that they were in a horrifying state; some had their abdomens split wide open or all of their limbs removed, and others had goat's heads attached to their bodies in place of their own. Whilst this was terrifying enough, he spoke in whispered tones about how he had seen them moving, as if they were still alive. This had caused him to panic and swim back to the surface. On his return, he reported that a dark, cloudy mass had chased him through the water.

By all accounts, this man was never the same again and was discharged from the Navy shortly afterwards. The commanding officer was reluctant to investigate further as he did not wish to put more lives at risk. In any case, time was running short as Celle was in the British Zone of Occupation and British forces would soon be arriving to relieve the Americans. The building was handed over to the British Army on 21st April and the basements were sealed over with concrete shortly thereafter.

During the Cold War, Celle became a very important garrison town, staging a sizeable contingent of NATO forces. The town hall was converted into a permanent army barracks and housed regiments from the British and German militaries. The stories regarding the flooded lower levels, and the fate of the US Navy divers, were rife during this period and many believed them to be nothing more than urban legends. But no one could get away from the fact that access to the basement floors was indeed restricted. It was obvious that most stairwells leading down into the lower levels had been hastily filled in with concrete, as the tops of bannisters or handrails could be seen protruding from the floor. The question was why?

Paranormal phenomena in and around the barracks were commonplace. An infantryman by the name of Stephen Daily reported that, on his first night in the building as a new recruit, he saw silhouettes of people walking back and forth outside his window. He didn't think much of this at the time, as soldiers would have been on patrol, until he realised the next morning that his window was, in fact, seven feet above the ground on the exterior of the building. Daily served four years in Celle during the 1980s and he experienced all kinds of strange goings-on, such as hearing jackboots marching on the parade grounds and through hallways even though half of the camp was on leave and no parades were taking place. There were instances of people hearing voices conversing in German behind the doors of otherwise locked and empty rooms. A sergeant-major was utterly stupefied in the early hours of one morning when he witnessed a column of German Panzer tanks pass him by in complete and utter silence.

The strangeness didn't end there. A young private by the name of Martin Fox woke one night to find that the ceiling of his bedroom was only inches away from his face. At first, he thought it was his roommates playing a prank, but when he realised his bed was floating several feet above the floor, he screamed out and both he and the bed came crashing down, waking his sleeping comrades. Other soldiers reported having their rooms vandalised, even though they had been locked and secured in intervening times, and no one else had been in there. Some even saw dark shadowy figures standing at the ends of their beds and in hallways.

Most unsettling was the unusually high rate of suicides amongst the men stationed at the Rathaus. There were certain rooms on the upper levels, which were said to have had pentagrams etched into the floors and walls, and legend has it that many recruits ended up taking their own lives shortly after spending the night in them on a dare. A large number of soldiers were also discharged on medical grounds after undergoing psychological evaluations. Many of them had become deeply depressed during their tour of duty and officials felt they might be a danger to themselves and others if they remained on active service.

The general feeling throughout the ranks inhabiting the base was that a dark, oppressive atmosphere hung over the town in general. After all, Bergen is a suburb of Celle and this is, of course, where the infamous Belsen concentration camp was situated. In fact, many Jewish prisoners were transported by rail into the town centre before being despatched to Belsen thereafter. And although Celle was captured during the war without a single bullet being fired, it was no less a scene of unwavering tragedy; a place where thousands upon thousands of innocent people lost their lives in an untimely and barbaric manner. Could the very knowledge of this have had a negative effect on the men's moods and behaviours? And if so, why did this dark cloud seem to hang specifically over the Rathaus?

The rumours around camp were intriguing, to say the least. It is no secret that the Nazi Regime and in particular, Heinrich Himmler, had a deep-seated interest in the occult. It is thought that the Third Reich was looking to harness untold powers in order to tip the fortunes of war in their favour. For instance, there are tales of German troops making expeditions to Antarctica to locate hidden entrances to the so-called Hollow Earth, which would supposedly lead them to a dormant race of giants. Other rumours suggest that the Spear of Destiny was stolen from a museum in Vienna to aid in the summoning of dark forces and that German Naval commanders employed the use of dowsing in an attempt to locate British submarines and merchant vessels. Hitler himself was no stranger to paranormal experiences as he had recorded such instances in his private journals many times. But what does all this have to do with the Rathaus in Celle?

The study of witchcraft was high up on the agenda for the German elite and the Rathaus was said to be one of many sites across the country where the SS carried out such research and even experimentation on human subjects. In this case, those subjects were Jewish prisoners from Belsen. There were rumours that the SS were summoning dark and sinister forces in the rooms situated on the lower levels and that prisoners were being horribly mutilated in order for their bodies to become more accepting of demonic possession. The building itself is said to have occult symbolism running all the way through it, from the way it is laid out to the very smallest of details, such as the shapes of concrete tie rods and decorative architecture. Many believe the Rathaus served as an antenna or gateway, which amplified the effects of such practices.

A German soldier who had been stationed there during the cold war years had an interesting, and somewhat bizarre, story to tell. Posting anonymously on an internet forum back in 2009, he recalled how his father had told him that the SS had been attempting to bring soldiers back from the dead, allowing demonic entities to possess the deceased and use their bodies as vessels. His father went on to describe how attempts in doing this had been successful, but that these reanimated corpses apparently had no sense of honour or loyalty and that research in this area was abruptly halted.

Connections to the occult are further reinforced by the supposed etchings of pentagrams and particularly the accounts of the third diver who reported seeing people with goat's heads strapped into chairs whilst exploring the basements. That is, of course, if the story regarding the US Navy divers is to be believed. One would have to question exactly what was down there in those cold, dark depths and what had been responsible for taking the lives of two of the men. Could it have been something paranormal or even supernatural? Or was it something altogether more rational, such as the fact that it was a dangerous assignment to begin with, that two of the divers became trapped and that the third worked himself up into a panic as a result of the dark and confined spaces?

Of course, we must also ask whether the diving incident even happened at all. Reading this story back, one must admit that it has all the hallmarks of an urban legend, all the clichés of fabrication, perhaps concocted to frighten new recruits. There is no doubt that the Rathaus in Celle does have floors below ground which are inaccessible and have been covered over with concrete. Whether they are—or were—flooded is another matter. After all, how practical would it have been to fill the equivalent volume of a football stadium with water? Surely gutting the building with fire would have been a far quicker and easier method of destroying any evidence of whatever had been going on there? Unless the SS were not trying to hide evidence, but instead to quarantine whatever abominations they had created. The likelihood is that we'll never know for sure.

What is less easy to explain is the sheer amount of paranormal activity that soldiers experienced whilst on the base. There are far too many accounts—even from senior ranks—to dismiss altogether. If you are lucky enough to speak to any British or German soldier stationed here during the cold war, you'll more than likely find that they believe there was definitely something evil and twisted about the Rathaus. This likely supports the idea that something sinister was going on in the maze of dark halls and rooms of its lower levels at some point during its history. Whether it had connections to the occult or otherwise is up for debate.

In any case, British and German forces vacated the premises entirely in 2012 and the building was re-purposed as originally intended; to embody the seat of local government. Parts of it have also been converted into a hotel, which has seen glowing reviews from visitors on various travel websites. That said, guests still report, even to this day, strange goings on and the ever-present sound of jackboots echoing through the halls. It seems the secrets of Celle Neues Rathause will endure.

23
THERE IS SOMETHING IN THE WOODS

David Paulides, an ex-police office turned author believes something strange is going on in and around North American national parks. After cataloguing thousands of mystifying deaths and disappearances, we join him in asking whether there is something in the woods, that is stalking and hunting human beings.

The national parks of North America are some of the most haunting and beautiful places on Earth. From Yosemite and Yellowstone in the US to Yoho and Jasper in Canada. All offer something stunning and unique, whether that be snow tipped mountain ranges, serene lakes, endless grasslands which stretch as far as the eye can see, or forests that seemingly never end. These parks attract millions upon millions of tourists from all over the world. Their landscapes are truly a sight to behold and it's no wonder that so many visitors flock to these areas of outstanding natural beauty year after year. But it should also come as no surprise that many people get lost whilst hiking or hunting in these regions. And although most of them are located by dedicated search and rescue efforts within 48 hours, some vanish, often in mysterious and inexplicable circumstances, never to be seen again.

Magnificent and unforgettable these places may be, but in amongst all that splendour there appears to be a dark and sinister truth that authorities seem reluctant to address. Oftentimes described in the US as "the nation's silent mass disaster", people have been disappearing from national parks in their thousands over the last few centuries. The exact number is not known because, astonishingly, the US National Park Service has only recently begun to compile a database on these missing persons. This was a fact stumbled upon by David Paulides, a former police officer turned author, investigating the high strangeness in which these people seem to vanish. Paulides has catalogued over a thousand of these bizarre disappearances in a series of books titled *The Missing 411*. Although his investigations are comprehensive, the picture he paints is by no means complete; he fears there could be many more cases that are not known to the public and probably never will be.

Paulides apparently began working on this project shortly after visiting a national park, where he was approached by a ranger. This ranger told him that he was part of the search and rescue effort on a couple of recent unexplained disappearances and that he believed something bigger was going on. Being an accomplished outdoorsman himself, Paulides was intrigued by the notion of experienced hikers and hunters going missing in terrain which they themselves were highly familiar with and promised to investigate it. Little did he know it at the time, but he had just embarked on an almost insurmountable task involving years of research and investigation, which would culminate in an extensive body of work and bring these mysteries well and truly into the spotlight.

He began by filtering out certain factors so that he could focus solely on incidents which defied conventional explanation, logic, or behaviour. He excluded cases that explicitly involved foul-play, mental illness (and therefore the possibility of suicide), clear signs of animal attack, the possibility of missing persons drowning or being washed away and—at least to begin with—cases in and around urban areas.

Over time, he noticed that these disappearances formed into clusters, congregating specifically around North American national parks and the great lakes. Paulides concludes that something strange is going on. Something as indefinable as it is elusive, as unsettling as it is mysterious. He believes there could be an unknown quantity behind these disappearances. One which is intelligent and patient. Predatory and unseen. What follows is a select few of the strangest vanishings ever recorded in US and Canadian national parks. And one must bear in mind, when considering these cases, that conventional explanations have either been ruled out completely or are extremely unlikely.

Possibly the most famous example of someone vanishing without trace in a national park is that of Dennis Martin, a six-year-old boy who had set out with his father, grandfather, and nine-year-old brother on 14th July 1969, to hike up to an area known as Spence Field. At around 4pm, Dennis, his brother, and a couple of other young boys they had befriended decided to play a game of hide and seek. As the game ended, all of the boys came out from their hiding places except for Dennis. He was nowhere to be seen. The last time anyone saw him, he was running towards a bush on the edge of the field, behind which there was thick woodland. His father, William Martin, became increasingly concerned and proceeded to run two miles up the Appalachian Trail in the hopes of locating his son, but found nothing.

Over the next two weeks, more than 1500 searchers, covering an area of 56 square miles, and with the aid of helicopters and sniffer dogs, searched in vain for the missing child, but he was never seen again. Even a crack team of Green Beret's joined the effort, although they worked alone and refused to engage with anyone outside of their group, which many people saw as strange in and of itself. Typically, the Green Beret's would only be called out in matters concerning National Security.

On the day that Dennis disappeared, the Key family, hiking up towards Rowans Creek, about 4kms away from Spence Field (as the crow flies) heard an almighty scream at around 5:30pm. This was about an hour and a half after Dennis was last seen. When they looked in the direction the scream had come from, they saw what they described as a bear crossed with a man carrying a small child over its shoulder, scurrying off into the dense forest. The FBI dismissed this, saying that the time frames involved were too narrow and that no one could have hiked that distance over rough terrain in such a short amount of time. However, a ranger involved in the search by the name of Dwight McCarter proved this assertion to be false when he hiked the same journey in just over an hour.

Trenny Gibson was a high school student from Knoxville who visited the Great Smokey Mountains whilst on a field trip in October 1976. She was with 40 of her classmates and they were hiking from a parking area to a spot called Andrew's Bald. As the afternoon wore on, the students broke up into smaller and smaller groups, each determined by their respective walking speeds. Trenny was about 20 metres ahead of her group when she was seen to suddenly stop in the middle of the path. Friends later reported that she was looking off to one side, almost as if she had spotted something off in the bush. She then stepped off the trail in the direction she was looking and disappeared. Police did not initially believe her friends when they indicated where she had left the path as it was a steep, almost sheer drop, followed by hundreds of metres of dense woodland. It would have been impassable without the use of heavy-duty equipment. Despite massive search efforts, Trenny Gibson was never seen again.

In July 2010, a man by the name of Eric Lewis was climbing Mount Rainier with two of his associates. They were all tethered together by the same piece of rope and were spaced about 20-30 metres apart. The lead climber, Don Storm Jr., stopped at 14,000 feet and waited for his two companions, hoping they could summit the mountain together. He was joined shortly afterwards by the second climber, Trevor Lane, and they both waited for Eric to arrive. He never did.

After reeling in the rope, they discovered he was not attached to the other end, even though they had caught glimpses of him behind them only moments before. Bad weather had been rolling in and they assumed that he had detached himself in order to take a rest, something which would have been highly irresponsible, but not unheard of. Heading back down the mountain side, they saw no sign of him whatsoever, and discovered that his tracks seemed to just stop in the middle of nowhere. Helicopters scoured the slopes but found nothing. Search and rescue discovered his backpack, climbing harness, and snow shovel at 13,600 feet, but Eric himself was never found.

Stephanie Stewart was a seventy-year-old wildfire spotter, working for Jasper National Park in Alberta, Canada. On the night of 26th August 2006, she happened to be working at the very remote Athabasca lookout tower, situated 25 miles northwest of Hinton. She had a very important job, looking out for any sign of bush fires during the day and sleeping at the tower during the night. On the morning of the 27th August, she failed to carry out a routine radio check-in with her supervisor, a task which was required at least three times a day. Another fire spotter was sent to the tower to check on her but found that she was gone.

All that was missing from the cabin was her blanket. There were no signs of a struggle or of forced entry having taken place. The stove had been lit and a pot of water had been placed on the hob, but the contents had long since boiled away. Her truck was still outside, and authorities found no tracks leading in or out of the area other than those left by her own vehicle. She was of a sound mind and had a loving family. It seems unlikely that she would have just left in the middle of the night for no apparent reason. Stephanie was never seen again, and her disappearance caused the provincial government to change the way lookout towers operate throughout the region.

Charles McCullar was a nineteen-year-old amateur photographer from Virginia. In December of 1974, he hitchhiked out to the west coast on an extended vacation, photographing scenery along the way. In January the following year, he found himself staying with a friend in Oregon. He planned a short excursion out to Crater Lake, to photograph the beautiful Winter landscapes there, and then to return to his friend's house two days later. However, he was never seen alive again. Massive search and rescue efforts were launched, but nothing was found. No tracks, no scents, and no eyewitnesses. A year later, a couple of hikers located a backpack twelve miles off the trail head and after being examined by authorities it was determined that it belonged to Charles. Park rangers got a horse patrol out to the same area within hours and shortly afterwards, they found McCullar's body. Or what remained of it.

The scene was strange to say the least. All they found of him was his jeans, unbuttoned, sitting on a log in the middle of nowhere, frozen in position as if an invisible man was sat inside them. His socks were sticking out of the legs at the bottom as one might expect, and inside them, they found small foot-bones. Twelve feet away they found the top of his skull. His shirt, coat, boots, and all his other belongings were nowhere to be seen and they never found the rest of his body. Most perplexing of all was how he had even got to this location to begin with. On the day he vanished, there was seven and a half feet of new snow on the ground, making it impossible to travel there at that time, even if he had used a snowmobile.

A similar case occurred in Canada's Yukon Territory in 2004. 49-year-old Bart Schleyer was—according to everyone who knew him—the greatest outdoors man you never heard of. He was smart, strong, unbelievably fit, and had been hiking and hunting the wilds of North America since his pre-teen years. There was no doubting his experience. In September of 2004, he chartered a pilot to fly him into a remote region 175 miles north of Whitehorse, with the intention of hunting moose, alone. He was well equipped, taking along three crates of supplies, which carried his food, camping equipment, and hunting gear. The pilot dropped him off and arranged to return three weeks later to pick him up. That was the last anyone ever saw of him. When the pilot did return, he found Bart's camp set up and well stocked, but could see no sign of the man himself.

The RCMP mounted an extended search of the area and eventually found a few of his teeth and shards of bone on the ground about 60 feet from his camp. Not too far away from these remains they found his dry bag on the ground—indented as if he had been sitting on it— and his hunting bow propped up against a tree. Examination of bear and wolf scat in the area ruled out the possibility that he had been eaten by a larger animal. And friends are quick to dismiss this in any case saying that he was far too canny an outdoors man to have been surprised by a bear or some other large predator. Aside from this, there was no disturbed ground or snapped branches indicating any signs of a struggle and authorities queried—if he had in fact been taken unawares by a bear or wolf—why had the supplies at his camp had not been raided.

Another strange case which occurred two years earlier in 2002 centred around a 20-year-old surveyor from Ellerslie, Georgia. Christopher Thompkins was working as part of a four-man crew near dense woodland in Harris County. At the end of the day, the team headed back to their vehicle and was walking along Warm Springs Road, a straight highway, which is bordered by woodland on both sides. Each crew member was walking roughly 50 feet apart and Christopher was last in line. Within a few seconds, he had vanished. His colleagues went back to the point he was last seen and found around 12 cents in coins on the ground. They also discovered one of his work boots snagged on the barbed wire fence lining the road, as well as fibres from his work trousers. Despite a wide-ranging search involving hundreds of people, Christopher was never found. Several months later, his other boot was located by the property owner, near a swamp, 900 yards from where he vanished. The fact that they found the contents of his pockets on the road suggests that he had been turned upside down.

Todd Geib was a 22-year-old man from Casnovia, Michigan. On the night of 11th June 2005, he attended a keg party with his cousin, but left at around 12:30am because he was feeling tired. He hadn't drunk much but decided to walk home as he preferred not to take the risk of driving whilst under the influence. At around 12:51am, he called a friend and was heard to say, "I'm in a field" before the phone suddenly cut off. The friend called him back but heard only heavy breathing and/or rushing wind before the call cut off again. Todd then tried to call his friend back two more times, the last attempt being at 12:57am, but nothing else was heard from him that night. The next day he failed to show for a family gathering, which was completely out of character for the young man, and when it was discovered that no one else had seen him after the party, his concerned parents reported him missing.

A huge search took place involving over 1500 volunteers and helicopters equipped with infrared. Lakes and swamps in the area were dragged and dived, but nothing was found. It was as if Todd had simply dropped off the face of the Earth. Three weeks later, on the 2nd

July, a couple walking along the shore of Obenhall Lake saw something out in the water. It looked like a man standing upright, his head and shoulders bobbing on the surface of the lake. It turned out to be the body of Todd Geib. The location where he was found shocked everyone as the lake had been searched multiple times in the intervening weeks and it was in completely the opposite direction to where he had been heading. The cause of death was listed as drowning whilst under the influence of alcohol, but no water was found in his lungs and his blood alcohol limit was relatively low.

So, who or what is responsible for these killings and/or disappearances? Paulides is reluctant to single out any particular culprit or cause, but he has indirectly hinted at several possibilities, and the tone of his books is highly suggestive of something out of the ordinary. Sceptics have largely disparaged Paulides' work, arguing that, oftentimes, he deliberately omits certain details which do not fit his narrative, and that there are rational explanations for every single one of these cases. Their reasoning includes:

- Animal attacks
- A serial killer or possibly even several people becoming disorientated or injured
- People having a desire to intentionally disappear or commit suicide
- Drug dealers or drug manufacturers conducting business out in the wilds and killing those who stumble upon their operations
- Quick or sudden death due to illness or exposure

Animal attacks will always leave tell-tale signs which include blood, pieces of flesh, torn clothing, tracks, scents, and signs of a struggle having taken place such as snapped branches or disturbed ground. None of the cases Paulides presents show any evidence of this and he therefore rules this out as a possibility. The same can be said for potential serial killers; it is highly unlikely that they would fail to leave any trace of having been there. Becoming lost and disorientated is indeed plausible, but many people who disappear are highly familiar with their surroundings and have either hiked or hunted in those locations' countless times before. And even if they do get lost, why do organised search parties, sniffer dogs and helicopters with forward looking infrared still fail to find them?

In all of these cases, the individuals were of a sound mind as far as their friends, families, and colleagues knew, so this makes suicide an unlikely cause, although not an implausible one. Disappearing intentionally to start a new life, on the other hand, could be a possibility, but doing so would be an immense undertaking, would take months of planning and cost a great deal of money, something which would be difficult to hide from friends or loved ones. In either of these cases, this does not explain why search and rescue parties are unable to locate any trace of them whatsoever.

Drug manufacturers operating in remote regions is not unheard of. After all, anyone who has ever watched the TV series, *Narcos*, will know that Pablo Escobar used the Colombian jungles to conceal his production operations. That being said, the national parks of North America seem like an unlikely place for such practices given the number of annual visitors. Drug dealers would know that killing someone would only invite more unwanted attention to the region in the form of the National Park Service, search and rescue parties, and police officers.

Finally, succumbing to some underlying illness or injury sustained whilst hiking is probably the most likely cause of these disappearances. Paulides even notes that many of these individuals had some form of disability or condition or reported feeling unwell before they vanished. However, it is very odd that search and rescue attempts still fail to locate their bodies. One would think that an individual who was feeling ill would not stray too far off established trails, if at all. Depending on the nature of an injury, accident victims would not be too difficult to locate either, especially with the help of sniffer dogs and search helicopters equipped with infrared.

So, when all of these explanations have been exhausted, what are we left with? Paulides is mystified by the apparent commonalities between each case, such as the fact that in instances where dead bodies are found, they rarely find the victims shoes or boots, or they are in a state of undress and a satisfactory cause of death is rarely established.

Of course, some people have suggested that these disappearances are the result of something paranormal or supernatural. Theories have ranged from woodland spirits to large cryptids such as Bigfoot or the Dogman, alien abductions, people slipping through inter-dimensional portals, and even certain plant-life activating some form of defence against human presence.

And as unbelievable as these suggestions may sound, there have, in fact, been instances where people experienced such things whilst in national parks and lived to tell the tale. There is a bizarre phenomenon, which countless people have reported whilst hiking, known simply as *The Silence*. Usually, whenever a large predator is nearby, the woods tend to go quiet, but this phenomenon is entirely different. Not only does all wildlife fall silent, but the breeze rustling through the leaves dies down completely and the air seems to thicken, almost as if time itself has frozen. By all accounts it is an incredibly unnerving experience; people often report feeling as if they are being watched or stalked by something during this time.

Jan Maccabee—wife of renowned optical physicist Bruce Maccabee—experienced this deathly quiet whilst she was bow hunting in Ohio in 2010. It was around 6:30pm and she was in a tree-hide approximately 15 feet off the ground. She reported that everything suddenly went quiet and within minutes she noticed an odd distortion moving through the branches about 20 feet from her position. She described it as a humanoid figure and that it appeared to be "cloaked". She managed to take one picture before it moved off and the sounds of nature returned. The image shows what looks like the edge of a face, with hair sticking out from behind it, backlit by the sun.

A compelling piece of footage, uploaded in 2016 by YouTuber Scott Carpenter appears to show what looks like a bigfoot peeping out from behind a tree, perfectly camouflaged by its surroundings. And although this could be nothing more than a case of pareidolia, it is interesting, nonetheless. Whatever is responsible for these disappearances, whether it is paranormal, supernatural, or something altogether more ordinary, the prospect of losing your way in such vast and often inhospitable terrain is no less frightening. Truly, these places are wonderful examples of just how beautiful our world can be, and this story should not deter you from visiting them if you are lucky enough to have the opportunity. But we would urge you to be vigilant, make all the necessary preparations and take all the necessary precautions. And finally; expect the unexpected.

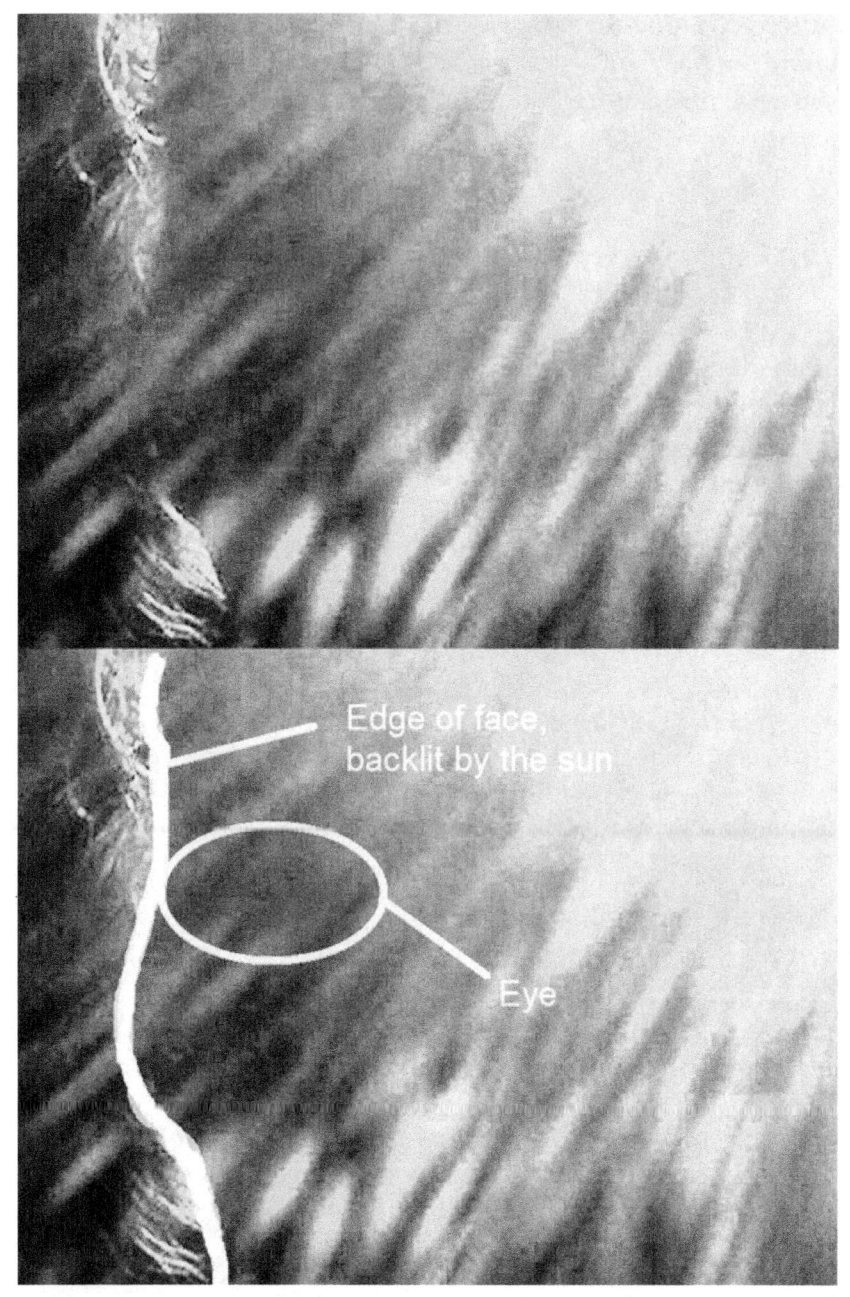

Fig. 18 - *The strange anomaly photographed by Jan Maccabee in Ohio, 2010*

Fig. 19 - *Did this photographer capture a Bigfoot camouflaged in the trees? Or is it just a case of pareidolia?*

24
THE ALIEN OF VARGINHA

In 1996, a small Brazilian town surrounded by countryside would play host to a string of supernatural events. Was it all just a ploy to increase tourism? Or is there any truth to this tale; The Alien of Varginha.

Brazil appears to be a land steeped in legends of UFOs and extra-terrestrial visitation, second only to the US for its record of bizarre occurrences. God-fearing, and somewhat superstitious, her people may be, they take accounts of "little green men" far more seriously than most. Events of this nature seem brazenly frequent and, more often than not, downright terrifying. What follows is perhaps one of the most famous cases on record, not just in Brazil, but throughout the entire world. There are many instances of people witnessing UFOs. Seeing the occupants of those UFOs, on the other hand, is far less common.

It was January of 1996 and the mood amongst the residents of the small town of Varginha was upbeat. The recent New Year's celebrations had been a success and plans for The Carnaval were well underway, an event which traditionally takes place in February, and is something of a highlight on the Brazilian calendar for many people. Back in the mid 90's, Varginha was little more than a promise of the thriving city of culture and commerce it would eventually become. Located in the south-eastern state of Minas Gerais, it was very much an up and coming town. The coffee trade was significant for local employment. Many commuted to nearby cities for work, though some multi-national companies had also begun to invest in the region. With its rapid growth and steady stream of exterior income, the residents of Varginha didn't want for much. Compared to the sprawling cityscapes of Sao Paulo and Rio de Janeiro, it was nothing more than a sleepy backwater town where nothing much happened. But on Saturday 20th January a series of events occurred which were to shake this community to its core.

It all started in the early hours of the morning at a farm situated on the outskirts of town. Eurico Rodrigues, who lived and worked as a farmhand along with his partner Oralina Augusta, was awoken at around 1:30am by the unsettling sounds of panicked bleating and mooing from their livestock. Initially, they considered that one of the animals may have escaped, or that maybe there was a thief or predator on the prowl. They were absolutely dumbstruck when they looked out of the window and saw what appeared to be a UFO that was troubling the animals. The description given for the strange craft was a grey submarine-like object in the sky, about the size of a small bus. It was said to have been completely silent with no lights whatsoever. The cows and sheep were in a disorientated state and it is believed the craft was visible for around five minutes before it disappeared from view.

Despite their encounter, Eurico and Oralina decided not to report their sighting to the authorities for fear of being ridiculed or labelled as hoaxers. Unknown to them at the time, the ramifications of what they had just witnessed would not hit home until a few days later, when they read reports in the local press of possible UFO activity, and even humanoid sightings in and around the town. One of these accounts would stand out amongst all others and came from a pair of sisters who lived with their mother in the hilly suburban outskirts of Varginha.

The Silva family resided in the Santana district and though aged only 14 and 16 years, Valquíria and Liliane Silva were beginning to mature into responsible and reliable young women. Later that same day, hours after the sighting at the farm, the teenagers had met with their older friend Katia Xavier, who worked as a cleaner in the nearby Jardim Andere district. The three of them regularly walked home together. It was a case of safety in numbers and they just so happened to enjoy each other's company. On that fateful day, the group decided to take a shortcut home through the small woods that separated their two neighbourhoods. After walking through a section of woodland in Jardim Andere, they arrived at a fallow, but were suddenly startled by a strange looking entity five to ten metres in front of them.

There was something crouching down near a wall, which they initially thought was some kind of animal, but its grotesque appearance and odd behaviour unnerved them. As they approached, the creature turned its head in their direction and stared directly at them with terrifying bright red eyes. What it did or where it went after that point is not known as—needless to say—the girls immediately fled the scene in horror. Upon arriving back home, the Silva sisters were said to have burst in through the front door in floods of tears. Even after some comforting, the youngest, Liliane, was inconsolable for some time. When their mother asked them what they had seen to upset them to such an extent, they simply replied "the Devil".

It wasn't long before the local press got wind of the story and by the following day, Brazil's most-watched Sunday TV show, *Fantastico*, sensationally announced the news that an extra-terrestrial being had been spotted in Varginha. However, rumours were rife amongst the locals that there had, in fact, been multiple sightings of aliens roaming the streets during the previous day. The feeling in the town was one of confusion and concern, with most residents simply trying to piece together exactly what had happened. Katia Xavier later gave a description of the creature they saw, saying it was a small, emaciated, non-human, non-animal being, with brown skin, an oily appearance and an overly-large head with three rounded extrusions (or possibly even horns) adorning the top of its skull.

People came forward to say that they too had witnessed further alien or UFO activity. According to some reports, as many as 200 residents have given accounts in the time since the event; bearing witness to the fact that they saw extra-terrestrials, with many descriptions matching that given by Katia. Despite being sworn to secrecy, even some military and government personnel came forward and give their versions of events, though their identities have remained anonymous for obvious reasons.

There was a military base very close to the farm at Tres Coracoes, about 16km outside Varginha itself, and it is presumed that this is where some of the information may have been leaked from. One source revealed how he believed the aliens were rounded up and captured like animals by military firefighters, before being transported out of the town through the woods under the cover of darkness. Upon capture, the aliens were said to make some kind of buzzing sound, similar to the drone of a beehive. It is even suggested that the military transported the creatures by road to Brasilia and were then secretly dispatched to the US by air, where they were killed and dissected.

Another interesting, yet unconfirmed, claim involving the US suggests that the North American Aerospace Defence Command actually issued a warning to their Brazilian counterparts at CINDACTA about an hour before the sighting at the farm. Apparently, the US had intelligence about a possible UFO landing somewhere in the state of Minas Gerais, and they tried to pre-warn the Brazilian authorities. If correct, it somewhat supports the Rodrigues and Augusta UFO sighting near Tres Coracoes and adds weight to the claim that aliens may have been sent back to America. Though never validated by the farmhands, a government source has even said that a cigar-shaped UFO crash-landed in a field just outside Tres Coracoes, and that he was part of a clean-up operation to remove the debris. A crash certainly seems a more plausible explanation as to why extra-terrestrials were apparently seen roaming the countryside rather than for a UFO to have simply dropped them off and left them behind.

Of course, most of these reports are unconfirmed and it is difficult to discern between what is true and what is fabricated. After all, many eyewitnesses only came forward *after* the televised report of the sighting by the three women. Were they all simply jumping on the bandwagon for financial gain? Or did a UFO land or possibly even crash in Varginha during the night? Perhaps best placed to answer this question, is Señor Ubirajara Rodrigues, resident of Varginha in 1996 and, coincidentally, a part-time ufologist. He has worked hard on this case looking for new leads and visiting suspected hotspots across the city. Some witnesses have come forward anonymously to provide information specifically for his investigation. Working with Vitorio Paccaccini from nearby Belo Horizante, the pair have garnered valuable insight from key witnesses including Katia Xavier and the Silva family.

It transpires that in February of 1996, a couple of weeks after the alien sighting, the Silva family received an unexpected visit from four men in dark suits. The girls' mother Luiza arrived home to find the men already at the property and in conversation with her daughters. They asked the girls if they were willing to deny their sighting of the alien. The men offered a large cash sum but left without identifying themselves. When revisiting the area of woodland with Rodrigues in 2003, the women were said to be visually upset. Could the famed men in black have been involved in this case? It would certainly seem so if Luiza's story is to be believed, but given their somewhat fleeting and relatively unnoticed appearance, what was their role and just how deep did their involvement in this case go? Were they even part of the government investigation? Or something far more sinister?

Much of Rodrigues' early work questions how the aliens were able to travel around the city, how they were then captured by the military and disposed of without there being a public outcry. His conclusions are that whilst many people saw aliens and others saw the military presence, they did not see any interactions between the two. Indeed, some criticism has been levelled at Rodrigues' work. He previously claimed that the alien autopsies were carried out by Dr Badan Palhares. Palhares himself publicly denied any involvement in the affair in 2012.

As for some people testifying that they had seen firemen assisting in the capture of the aliens, it is important to consider that, like many countries, both the fire service and the police in Brazil are an extension of the military. Specially trained firefighters may have been used. However, despite compelling testimony from Varginha's residents, a wealth of international attention, and even endorsement from the city council, the Brazilian Government maintains that it did not facilitate the capture of extra-terrestrial entities. But then, of course it would, given the potential ramifications of admitting such a thing.

With this in mind, if no supernatural incident took place and this is all merely a product of hysteria, hearsay, and conjecture, what was it that the girls saw in the woods that day? Katia and the Silva sisters have remained steadfast in their recollection of events and it must be said that their account seems genuine, with the manner in which they tell it being very convincing. But if the official reports are to be believed, the creature they saw was nothing more than a case of mistaken identity. It may sound callous, but the theory goes that the young women were simply spooked by a deformed and malnourished homeless man. The disproportionately thin body given to the description of the alien tallies well with this notion, and it is thought that the brown skin may be explained by the individual either being covered in mud or receiving too much exposure to UV rays. Internet sources vary greatly in providing the homeless man's name—from Little Luis in some cases to Mudinho in others—with some investigators even claiming to have photographs of this man.

For some, questions remain as to what extent it is by design, rather than default, that the city of Varginha has been able to benefit so greatly from the supposed arrival of otherworldly beings. The event has assisted in the city's sustained growth and prosperity, helping a small town become a vibrant commercial and cultural centre. And it is easy to see why many people view the events of 20th January 1996 with such scepticism, purporting that they were well orchestrated hoaxes, engineered towards that end. Thanks to widespread media coverage, the small town of Varginha has received international notoriety and an influx of alien related tourism. In fact, since events in 1996, the city has remained very much in the supernatural spotlight.

For instance, 2001 saw the construction of a 20ft high water tower, the Nave Espacial de Varginha, a disc-shaped monument to commemorate the event. This has become widely known as the "ET Spaceship" and lights up during evening hours. In 2004, the town was also host to ufologists and researchers from across the globe when it held the UFO Congress of Varginha. That being said, an influx of tourism as a result of this event should not automatically de-legitimise claims long held by the residents of the city. There are examples of other towns which have succeeded following supposed supernatural activity such as Point Pleasant and, of course, Roswell.

The simple truth is that so many people believe that something out of the ordinary did occur in that small town back in January of 1996. Whilst it is possible that some eyewitness accounts were fabricated, surely not all of them were? With all things considered, we are no more qualified than anyone else to say what did or did not happen. Only Katia, Valquíria, and Liliane know for sure what they saw that day and, unfortunately for them, it will forever haunt their nightmares. For the rest of us, at least, it will forever pique our curiosity.

25

THE CROSSWADE INTERLOPERS

In the Spring of 2013, what seemed to be a straightforward emergency call out for two police officers would turn out to be anything but. Not only would this experience chill them to the core, but it would have them questioning their own sanity for years afterwards as they tried to solve the riddle that was the CrossWade interlopers.

The pitch of the engine soared as the vehicle picked up speed, racing along dark country roads that would have been as black as pitch if not for the high beams illuminating the trees and hedgerows around them. James Havilland, who was sat in the front passenger seat, had briefly considered switching on the blues and blaring the sirens, but decided there was little point. The roads were empty and there wasn't another vehicle for miles around.

It was 2:21am on 31st March 2013 and James and his on-duty partner, Chris Braddock, who was driving, had just received a call from the CCR—Contact and Control Room—about a possible break-in at a remote facility out in the countryside. They were in a rural area on the outskirts of Whitehaven, a town situated in the Copeland district of Cumbria, England, about three miles from their intended destination. They would be on the scene within minutes, although neither man could have known, at that moment, that this call would challenge their very understanding of reality and change their lives forever.

The facility they were heading towards was owned by CrossWade Enterprises and was known locally as something of an oddity; its modern architecture stood out like a sore thumb against the otherwise beautiful and unspoiled English countryside which surrounded it. The amount of technology it boasted was also at odds with its rural setting; a highly advanced security framework, remote access and lighting control, and the latest building management systems and head-end software suites all housed within, what is otherwise known in the industry, as a "Smart" building. It's quiet and remote location was the last place you would expect to see such a thing.

Nevertheless, the building stood in silence as they arrived, shrouded in an eerie darkness which made it seem even more out of place. The facility looked deserted. No internal lights were switched on and there was certainly no sign of a break-in. The call had come through stating that the alarm had been going off intermittently and that some of the PIR (passive infrared) sensors had picked up on heat signatures within the building itself. This information had been provided by the Facilities Manager who was off-site but had remote access to the building's security systems. Even so, the relative calm of the scene in front of them made Chris and James feel hesitant.

They parked across the road and sat in silence for a moment, observant, waiting for any kind of movement or indication of criminal activity. At one point, James thought he saw a flash of light through one of the ground-floor windows but reasoned that it could have been a sensor or smoke alarm or, indeed, just his imagination. Over the next few minutes, nothing at all happened. They could hear the muffled sound of wind blowing around the exterior of the vehicle and the leaves rustling in the breeze, which was somehow both peaceful and slightly unsettling all at the same time, but there was no sign of anything untoward.

However, their attention was soon drawn to the lobby when he and Chris both witnessed the light flicker on and illuminate the space inside. Suddenly, the automatic doors at the front of the building opened and shut of their own accord before the alarm began to sound, piercing the air with a high pitched, undulating screech. Although startled, both men believed that they had the measure of the situation; that the access system was malfunctioning and that the opening and closing of the doors was breaking the live circuit and setting off the alarm. But just as they were about to radio back to the CCR, a figure emerged from the front entrance, then appeared to look over towards their police car before jogging off to the right around to the rear of the building. Just seconds later, another much taller figure emerged, but headed round to the left instead.

In normal circumstances, James and Chris would have jumped out of their vehicle and scrambled after the two men, but something had given them pause. Although the figures had been distant and only silhouettes cast against the light coming from the lobby, there was no mistaking what they were. They could tell by the shapes of the caps and bulky stab vests that these two figures had, in fact, been police officers. Chris scanned the scene for another police vehicle, whilst James radioed back to Dispatch asking if there was another unit on the scene. The reply came back negative; Chris and James were apparently the only ones there. The only other explanation was that the other two men were security guards, but the two police officers had been under the impression that the facility had no on-site security. After all, it was in the middle of nowhere. Something was obviously wrong with this picture and whilst the situation was becoming confusing, things were about to turn extremely weird.

Just as James finished using the radio, both figures walked back around to the front of the building and stood outside the entrance looking confused. The taller one of the two appeared to kick a pebble on the ground, which might have seemed like an insignificant action at the time but would later prove to be pivotal in realising the truth of the matter. There was something oddly familiar about these two men and both Chris and James were sure that they must have known them. Something about the way they moved and carried themselves reminded them of someone they knew, but they could not put their finger on exactly who it was. Suddenly, both figures looked over towards the police car and, surprisingly, began to run towards it. Chris and James stepped out of their vehicle and donned their caps ready to greet them, but when they looked up, the security guards or police officers or whatever they were had disappeared.

All that stood before Chris and James was the dark CrossWade building, the lights had all turned off again and the alarm was no longer sounding. Both police officers looked left and right. They were in a wide-open car park. There was nowhere else these two other men could have gone. They had simply vanished into thin air. They looked at each other in stunned silence, neither man willing to speak first about what they had just witnessed. Time seemed to stand still. The wind was no longer blowing, the leaves no longer rustling. The air had become thick and heavy as if muffled and weighted down by an inevitability which neither man was aware of at that moment in time.

After their initial shock had subsided, James was the first to speak, suggesting that they go over and take a look at the building. Chris agreed, but there was no denying that both men felt a stab of apprehension as they made their way over the road. They noticed as they approached the front entrance that it was completely locked down; they had to relay a request to the Facilities Manager in order to gain access. As they entered the lobby, Chris went up the flight of stairs to the first floor, whilst James remained on the ground floor and began checking through the dark offices as the lighting system had still not activated. He found nothing out of the ordinary but couldn't help feeling a little spooked about what had happened only moments before.

As he was walking back towards the lobby, he noticed the entrance light flicker on. Then he heard the hiss of the automatic doors as they opened and closed before the silence was suddenly shattered once again by the sound of the alarm. He picked up the pace and noticed Chris coming down the stairs as he exited the building, fully believing that an intruder had just slipped past them. He looked over towards their vehicle and quickly scanned the car park for anyone running away, but there was no one there. His instincts told him to run around to the left of the building as it was the quickest way for someone to get out of sight. However, as he made his way around to the rear, he was confronted with a refuse area, which was surrounded by high brick walls. He checked the bins inside and out and even tried to scale the wall itself, but it was just too high. There was no chance someone could have escaped this way.

Returning to the front of the building, he noticed Chris walking back from around the other side and they met up in front of the entrance. Not for the first time that night, they were completely baffled by what had just happened. They contemplated radioing back to the CCR to tell them that the access and alarm systems were malfunctioning and would need to be checked over. They were reluctant to put it all down to a false alarm as they knew they had witnessed two other people on the scene, although they would have had trouble in explaining in their reports exactly who those people were or, indeed where they had gone. It was only when Chris, James' well built, 6ft 6 tall partner, casually kicked a pebble on the ground in front of the building whilst discussing their options that the reality of the situation came crashing down.

But it couldn't be... Surely?

They looked back towards their vehicle and sure enough, they saw two faces staring out at them from behind the windscreen, the dash lights reflecting off their skin. And they knew in that instant, that those two faces were their own. They ran back towards their car and saw the doors open. But no one stepped out. The two men inside had vanished.

James has spent the last four years pondering exactly what happened in the early hours of that morning. Before this, he had never experienced anything he would describe as paranormal or supernatural. He was an ardent sceptic, and in most cases, still is, but he has no rational explanation for what occurred. He has researched online and has spoken to many so-called experts, but usually finds that they have more questions than answers. Neither he nor Chris are certain what they experienced, whether they saw their own doppelgangers or whether it was a glitch in reality, where the universe slipped time and allowed them a brief glimpse into their own futures. Or maybe even that they both temporarily lost their minds.

They are well aware of how unbelievable this sounds and for this reason, they did not write it up in any of their reports. Names and details have had to be changed in order for us to share this story with you. There is no such company as CrossWade Enterprises, but somewhere out in the wilds of Cumbria, there is a building which stands alone and in stark contrast to its surroundings. A building which sends a very real chill up the spines of at least two police officers whenever they think back on the events of that early morning all those years ago.

26
THE BABY ALESHENKA

Walking in the woods one night on the outskirts of her town, an elderly lady found what she believed to be an abandoned baby lying on the ground. She would take it home with her and decide to raise it herself, but an unfortunate sequence of events would leave her community asking whether the baby Aleshenka was even human.

Life in the rural areas of the vast Siberian wilderness might seem like a harsh existence to outsiders who inhabit a more conventional world, with its elaborate technologies and innovations. But to the Russian people, the existence they face in these cold and remote environments is not so different. At its most fundamental, living in the Ural Mountains involves the ever-frequent routine of waking, eating, working, and sleeping, albeit in a manner which conformist society would surely find all too foreign. Especially those not accustomed to bare-bones social conditions. This perception is only heightened by the sheer isolation and lack of outside contact the native peoples are otherwise completely comfortable with.

Although modern luxuries such as radio and television are available, this way of life has been hard to abandon for these people, since it is very much the same way their forefathers and ancestors eked out their existence. But from time to time, moments occur which break up the monotony of everyday life. When that one strange occurrence or sighting in these remote regions catches the attention of the entire world and brings an unwelcome stir of controversy to an otherwise insignificant and unassuming populace.

Such was the case in 1996, when a shocking discovery would lead the inhabitants of a small, rural town into an overbearing scrutiny by the international community. The incident took place in the territorial district of Kyshtym, a town located on the fringe of Chelyabinsk Oblast, at the southern toe of the Ural Mountains. The territory was once the site of the Chelyabinsk fortress during the time of the Tsars and was the epicentre of the Soviet Union's economic push during the Great Patriotic War to expel the Nazi invaders. The site grew to house key production facilities, which produced tanks and armaments, and boasted a population of almost a million, but the area's primary notoriety stems from its proximity to the nuclear research facilities that the Soviets erected during the Cold War. In 1957 the Mayak nuclear fuel reprocessing plant in Kyshtym exploded, releasing a cloud of radioactive dust which covered an estimated twenty thousand kilometres and contaminated the nearby Techa River.

Remarkably, the town of Chelyabinsk was spared due to its distance from the site, but in the years that followed, dumping of radioactive residue in the river led to an environmental catastrophe. This caused some ecologists to claim that pollution in this region was responsible for numerous birth defects in the years after the disaster and perhaps it was this incident that indirectly put the town of Kyshtym back on the map. Because ultimately, it may have led to another scandal, which would turn the collective scientific community on its head.

As the story goes, one dark and eerily quiet night in May 1996, an elderly woman, Tamara Vasilievna Prosvirina, was out walking in the woods just outside the town of Kaolinovvy when she heard an odd sound in the near distance. She headed towards it, thinking it could be a trapped animal, though it sounded more like the wailed cries of an injured child. As she got closer, she looked down and found what she described as a baby lying in the debris of the town's rubbish dump.

Without a moment's hesitation, she scooped it up and wrapped it in a blanket, then took it back to her apartment where she determined she would raise the child herself.

Two days later, she was visited by her daughter-in-law, also named Tamara. For the entirety of her stay, nothing seemed out of the ordinary, but just as the younger woman was getting up to leave, Tamara senior suddenly asked if she would like to help her feed the baby. This surprised young Tamara, as her mother-in-law had not mentioned anything about the infant up until that point. Upon entering the elderly woman's bedroom, sure enough, she spotted a crib and walked over to investigate. What she saw inside went beyond her comprehension. Tamara Junior stated that the infant looked far too small for a new-born baby, but what she found most alarming was its general appearance. Its head was twice as big as the rest of its body and it had hard, elongated features, which seemed as if they were built into its skull.

Its eyes, darting back and forth at a startling rate, appeared much larger than a normal infant's and the pupils could widen and elongate in a similar fashion to cat's eyes. It appeared to have long arms and fingers, with no visible genitalia or eyelids. What shocked her most was the way it consumed food, for it had no movable jaw as far as she could tell, only a small hole for a mouth. When it fed, it appeared to suck the food in rather than eat it. Although the creature had two sharp teeth in its mouth, she noted that it did not appear to be able to chew, yet somehow ate the food rather quickly. Tamara Junior would later go on to claim that the baby "was not of this planet". When she asked Tamara Senior what the baby's name was, she replied that she had named him Aleshenka, or "Little Alexey", apparently after one of her deceased grandsons.

In the days that followed, Tamara Senior's strange behaviour was noted by the neighbours in her apartment block, as she went about cheerily claiming she had a new baby, which they obviously doubted. They had described her as behaving erratically and at times evasive, especially when asked to give further details about the child. One night, a neighbour heard the older woman banging on her door. She claimed that she was frightened because her baby was ill, and she had no medicine to give him. This resulted in local police being summoned to her apartment. However, they came not to help her, but to take her to a nearby hospital for medical evaluation, where she would remain in their protective custody.

Other reports insist that she was discovered by neighbours after becoming severely ill and that this is how she arrived in hospital. Whatever the case, she was taken away against her will, saying she had a baby in her room and could not be away from him, but the locals and the medical orderlies did not take her claims seriously. This stemmed from the belief that she was suffering from the early stages of a mental illness, a view her neighbours and others who knew her shared due to her actions in recent years. They claimed that she displayed odd behaviour at times and was known to frequent the local cemetery to steal flowers from graves, using them to decorate her house. What no one at the time seemed to realise was that with Tamara Senior in custody, little Aleshenka was left alone in the apartment.

From this point onwards, events are unconfirmed and there is speculation as to the veracity of what exactly happened. But from what has been pieced together, it appears that subsequent events pit a policeman named Vladimir Bendlin at the centre of this mystery. Bendlin had supposedly arrived at the police station in the nearby town of Novogorny to question a man named Vladimir Nurdinov. Nurdinov was a known petty thief and criminal who had been detained in relation to an incident regarding stolen power cables. As the interrogation progressed, the policeman was dismayed when Nurdinov told him that he had in his possession a dead baby that he wanted to give to him, as he had no use for such a thing and no idea what else to do with it.

Bendlin agreed to go back to Nurdinov's apartment and take a look at the supposed dead infant, and it was there that he found what he could only describe as the dried up, mummified remains of a small child. But what was odd about the tiny cadaver was how it looked so much like an unborn foetus, malformed and emaciated. The body was greyish and lacked any trace of hair, its head splotched with darkened spots and it barely measured ten inches in height. From his account, Bendlin asked Nurdinov how it came to be in his possession.

The story goes that Nurdinov had spent time in the apartment of Tamara Senior and was present whenever she fed Aleshenka. Unfortunately, he was out of town when she was detained for medical evaluation and when he returned, he found the child had died of thirst and hunger and took it back to his home. Other sources state that Tamara Junior herself called Nurdinov to come and help check on the baby, as it tended to frighten her when she was alone. Upon finding Aleshenka deceased, the grief-stricken Tamara handed the body to Nurdinov in order to give it a proper burial, something he had apparently never gotten around to.

What is certain is that Bendlin took the body away from Nurdinov and immediately set about having its DNA analysed, perhaps in the hopes of finding someone who might have been a relative. Or, on the other hand, to ascertain whether it was a hoax which could simply be written off. Instead, he was in for a surprise.

Forensic analyst and clinical expert, Doctor Lyubov Romanowa, stated that tests concluded the infant's body and skin were not those of a regular human child, but something altogether "alien". She described numerous features which were impossible for a child to have, even in severe cases of deformity or birth defects. Romanowa related how the skull was composed of only four bones and that its shape indicated an unnatural elongation. The fingers were long and pointed, the body far too short to naturally support the head, and that the shape of the head cavity was especially sharp and pointed, a feature which no malformed infant she had ever come across had exhibited before. To her—and she put it mildly—the baby was not of human origin and could not have been a human child to begin with.

Soon afterwards, Tamara's neighbours began spreading rumours that she had been raising an alien baby and word soon reached the attention of the local press. A local television broadcaster caught wind of the story and contacted Bendlin for information on the creature. This prompted the police officer to record footage of himself inspecting the remains. It shows the body and its size in relation to Bendlin's hand as he moves and turns it over, and from the manner it is observed it is clear that no one present had an exact idea of what this small entity was. These initial reports eventually generated increased media attention as television reporters and newspaper journalists began to visit Kaolinovvy to find out more about the "Kyshtym Alien".

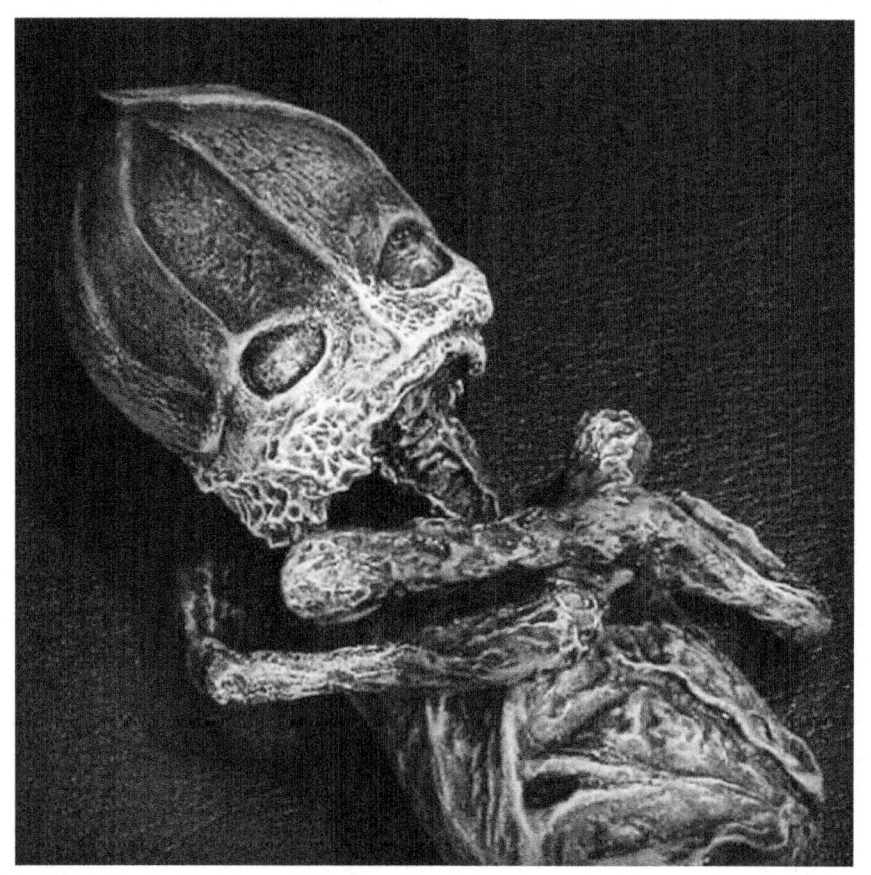

Fig. 20 - *The remains of an alleged alien baby, Aleshenka.*

There are reports of locals corroborating or selling any information they had for a good price and many journalists were all too willing to pay them. Even the Japanese broadcasting corporations MTV Japan and Asahi TV did an editorial on Aleshenka and, in the words of one journalist, threw money at anyone who could tell them about the alien. Many locals even went as far as accusing Tamara Junior and Nurdinov of orchestrating the whole thing, claiming it was all a hoax which they had concocted for fame and fortune. But the fact was that neither Tamara Junior nor Nurdinov of orchestrating the whole thing, claiming it was all a hoax which they had concocted for fame and fortune. But the fact was that neither Tamara Junior nor Nurdinov went forward to sell information for monetary gain at all, thus seemingly contradicting these statements.

Perhaps unsurprisingly, the arrival of numerous journalists and TV reporters brought an increased number of UFO experts hoping to get a glimpse of the baby Aleshenka. What no one knew at the time was that the baby was no longer in Kyshtym. Bendlin had handed it over to a UFO research academy, headed by the noted ufologist Boris Zolotov who claimed he wanted to conduct further testing on the body. Bendlin's hopes for a definitive answer started to dwindle as the weeks turned into months and no word came back on the results. When Zolotov was finally located, he gave a bizarre media interview regarding baby Aleshenka's fate.

According to him, he had asked one of his assistants to transport the body by car to a lab in another town when, out of nowhere, a large metallic craft landed in the middle of the road, blocking the vehicle's path. The assistant stated that the craft's occupants had stepped out and, wordlessly, asked her to hand the body over to them. The assistant complied and the craft flew away, but when asked to identify the area where this encounter took place, Zolotov could not trace the location and refused to discuss the matter any further.

If this was indeed the case, then it would seem that Aleshenka was taken back by his own people and the matter would have been closed for good if not for the lack of credence given to those who told this story. Some researchers theorise that Zolotov was intercepted by government agents and ordered to turn the body over to them. A purported eyewitness even claimed to have been visited by an investigative team of an unknown group who urged them to sign confidentiality papers and speak nothing more of the body. There is also the supposition that Zolotov was, in fact, approached by an eccentric collector interested in purchasing Aleshenka and readily sold it to him for a significant sum. But this is all speculation, which cannot be confirmed. The only thing we know for certain is that Aleshenka's body was never seen again.

With that, Bendlin thought he had heard the last of the case. But then in 1997, a woman approached him claiming she had taken the original shawl which Tamara Senior had used to wrap the baby in and kept it hidden throughout the media frenzy. She told him she would hand it over to him for a full DNA examination on the condition that he would investigate the matter seriously, a condition he was only too eager to agree to after everything that had happened. Bendlin took the shawl to Tamara Junior and had her confirm that it was the exact same one her mother-in-law had used to cover Aleshenka with. With her consent, he then took it to the Vavilov Institute of General Genetics in Moscow.

What followed were several years of constant research and testing, and waiting, before eventually the results came back inconclusive. To the disappointment of some, the tests found no residue indicating extra-terrestrial origin, but they did discover several particles of organic material mixed in with human DNA and flecks of female blood, suggesting a miscarriage or abortion. Trace amounts of alcohol were also found, hinting that the baby had been washed or doused with the substance just prior to being handed over to Bendlin. Although the body itself was missing, this circumstantial evidence led the researchers to conclude that it could not have been anything more than an undeveloped foetus.

In April 2004, Doctor Irina Yermolaeva, one of the initial researchers who had studied the body first-hand, recanted her original 1997 statement and declared that there was nothing alien about the baby. To her the creature "was no hoax, but a genuine mummified body that was once living tissue". She found that the state of the body corroborated with numerous cases of miscarried foetuses often found within twenty to twenty-five weeks of development. She claimed that she had counted a complete rib cage, an ample shoulder girth as well as wrist bones. And whilst the head was indeed the strangest aspect of all, she explained that it might have only partially formed during development. In her expert opinion, Dr. Yermolaeva stated that the body was deformed as the result of radioactive fallout which had enormously affected the area of Kyshtym following the nuclear disaster in 1957. She believed the infant had been born prematurely, or was likely miscarried, and that the distraught mother had then abandoned it in the forest for Tamara Senior to find.

On the other hand, Bendlin's clinical assistant, Lyubov Romanowa, did not agree with this finding. According to her, deformities and premature birth defects were nothing compared to what she had seen in the infant's body. She described that Aleshenka was simply "not of human origin" and could note at least twenty different features, which she stated were not commonly found in deformed children. There were many differences in the head and there were a lot of sharp edges in the cavity, something not found in children's skulls. She insisted that human foetuses could not live more than a few hours once exposed. Aleshenka had apparently lived for a few weeks before passing away. And whilst experts insist that Aleshenka was nothing more than an underdeveloped foetus, there is still the testament from Tamara Junior claiming that the baby was alive and able to consume food, an impossibility for a human child of that age.

Despite this, it must be said that Aleshenka did bear a striking resemblance to the "Atacama Alien", which was discovered in a deserted Chilean town in 2003. The two specimens shared many similar features, with neither of them resembling a distinctly human form. However, further tests were carried out on the "Atacama Alien" in early 2018 and the results were conclusive; the bones most definitely belonged to a malformed human foetus, which somewhat supports the idea that baby Aleshenka may also have been completely human.

Even so, the "Kyshtym Alien" was still making headlines in 1999 when Tamara Senior attempted to flee the institution where she was being treated for mental health issues. One night in September she was seen on a road outside the facility. Attempts to hail her went unanswered, when suddenly out of the darkness came a speeding car, running down and killing the elderly woman in what had looked to be a deliberate hit-and-run. Some conspiracy theorists suggest there was more to this death, due to reports that she was going to be placed under hypnosis to recount the entire experience. Could she have been silenced?

Again, we are left with more questions than answers, and although the case may be closed there is a newfound appreciation for the story, which appears to grow with each recounting. What was Aleshenka? Was he truly an underdeveloped foetus, the tragic result of a radioactive disaster? Or was he an alien who lay dying before being discovered in a swampy marsh? Did the Russian government attempt to cover it up, to the point of threatening people and even silencing the old woman as a final measure? Or are we simply reading too much into an otherwise mundane story?

Aleshenka's origin cannot be determined even to this day, despite a great deal of media coverage and continued interest in his story. Since its publication it has been met with plenty of scepticism and an equal amount of credibility at the same time. No one denies that something was found in the forest outside of Kyshtym and that whatever it was briefly touched the life of an elderly woman who selflessly accepted it as though it were her own child. Though it is sad that we find no happy resolution to this case, we can always take comfort in the knowledge that, at least in this instance, we saw a rare and brief display of warm-hearted humanity; an elderly woman willing to take in and care for what most others would have rejected, regardless of whether Aleshenka was alien or entirely human. If indeed he was of extra-terrestrial origin and was taken back by his own people, and if there is something that passes for an afterlife in that community, then it is our heartfelt hope that he found peace amongst the stars.

27
WHAT KILLED OLIVIA MABEL?

> *One afternoon in 1994, a series of silent 911 calls from a remote Texas property would result in several police officers descending upon the scene. What they found after breaking in through the front entrance, would shock them to the core and leave them questioning what killed Olivia Mabel.*

The death of a child is one of the greatest pains any loving parent could possibly bear. To lose something so special, which brings so much joy to one's life would be every mother and father's worst nightmare. A journey far too agonising to take; one which would leave them feeling desolate and alone, and on the verge of self-destruction. The tragedy of burying one's own child often results in ongoing, lifelong depression and, in many cases, suicide for those bearing the brunt of this kind of heartbreak. They end up living in a world of memories, which they can no longer recreate, torturing themselves within a prison from which they cannot escape.

Back in March of 1990, this very misfortune descended upon a household located in Celina, Texas. The Footlights Ranch, a 13-acre property situated about an hour north of Dallas, was owned by Travis and Olivia Mabel. They had relocated there in 1983, shortly after

Olivia had given birth to their son, Aiden. As a happily married couple they hoped that in purchasing a larger home, they might extend their small family, although during those first years, they doted heavily on their only child.

On the afternoon of 13th March, a seven-year-old Aiden had asked his mother if he could go off and play in the grounds surrounding the property. She had, of course, agreed, as she did so every day on the proviso that he was back in time for his dinner. Aiden had whooped and cheered as he set off on yet another boyhood adventure. Olivia didn't see him for the rest of the afternoon. By 5:30pm that evening, however, he had still not returned even though his dinner was sitting on the table going cold. Both parents set out to look for him, thinking he was probably having too much fun and that he had simply lost track of time, but the reality was tragically very different. Not too far from the household, they found their son floating face down in a pond. He had fallen in and drowned.

Travis and Olivia were beside themselves with grief over the death of their child and, unfortunately for them, their relationship just wasn't strong enough to withstand the pain and heartache they both felt. They blamed themselves. They blamed each other. Both of them were wracked with a guilt that would never cease to weigh them down. Olivia withdrew into herself. She did not return to work, rarely left the house, ceased attending her local church and began to shut out her friends, family and, eventually, even her husband. The couple divorced the following year and Travis moved east to make a fresh start.

Olivia, on the other hand, chose to remain at the house, living alone and in seclusion, surrounded by the memories of her lost child. No one ever saw or heard from her again, save for a brief sighting by a neighbour late in 1991. Phone calls and letters went unanswered, visitors to the house were ignored, except for the groceries which she had delivered. But for all other intents and purposes she was completely closed off from the rest of the world. Years went by without so much as a peep from her and people began to wonder whether she even lived at the property anymore. That was until 27th February 1994, when the police department in Celina received a 911 call from an unknown source. The operator who answered heard only silence on the other end before the line eventually cut off after a couple of minutes. As procedure dictated, the police department began to trace the call, but before long, the phone rang a second time, and the operator was again met with the same eerie silence.

In all, three calls were made from the same number, all of them silent and all of them traced to the same address: The Footlights Ranch, the home of Olivia Mabel. A patrol car was sent to check on the house, but the police officers found that it was completely locked down. They couldn't see in through any of the windows, which were white-washed, and the front door had not been used in so long that it had swelled and bowed outwards into the door frame so that it was jammed shut.

Thinking that someone could be in distress, the police officers forced open the front entrance and entered the stricken home, and what they found defied all logic. The interior of the house was in a serious state of neglect, with layers of dust piled up on the furniture and cobwebs infesting every crack, corner, and crevice. Each room looked as though it had not been touched in years, let alone lived in, and this was the same scene that greeted the officers as they explored the rest of the household. That was until they reached what had once been Aiden's room.

Inside, they found all his clothing and toys stored neatly away in drawers and cupboards, everything was pristine and tidy. No dust. No cobwebs. It had all been perfectly well kept. In the centre of the room, they found Olivia Mabel in a nightgown and slippers, sitting in a rocking chair, deceased. Clutched in her hands was a small doll made in her son's image, wrapped in pieces of his clothing. Officers reported that it looked as though she had been dead for a couple of months. In front of her was a makeshift altar made in Aiden's honour, decorated with candles, fresh flowers, and her late son's possessions, as well as photographs and drawings of him. Amongst his toys they found heart-breaking letters, written by a grieving mother to her lost son. Needless to say, it was quite upsetting for those present, but there was one question, which hung over the whole scene: who had made the 911 call?

Francesca Santiago was one of the first officers on the scene, and she described what they found that day. She reported that there was no sign of forced entry, other than the main entrance which had been forcefully opened by police. All doors and windows were locked from the inside and even the phone exhibited a layer of dust, showing no indication of having been lifted in order to make a call. And as if that wasn't strange enough, things took an even more bizarre turn when an officer examined one of the letters, which had obviously been written by Olivia. The exact wording was as follows:

> *"My Aiden, I'm sorry. I am so sorry. I should have never let it get like this. I'm leaving. I will not let you keep me you ViLE, EViL CREATURE. Mommy's coming for you, Aiden, my sweet Aiden. Mommy loves you."*

The thing that both mystified and disturbed investigators about this letter was that it was dated 27th February 1994, the day the police had entered the home and discovered her body. Other worrying signs pointed to the possibility that Olivia had been dabbling in occult practices. Adorning the makeshift altar dedicated to Aiden, there were a number of characters written in Sanskrit, which when translated, were found to spell "construct" or "to build". It is believed that Olivia had been trying to construct a Tulpa, or thoughtform. Given the altar, Sanskrit, isolation, obsession, and finally the doll, which was found clutched in her hand, this could be seen as a fair assumption. Olivia might have been channelling her boundless grief into manifesting an entity in her son's image.

Tibetan Buddhism sheds some light on this practice, saying that a being can be created through sheer spiritual or mental discipline and powerful concentration of thought. Considering her desperation and powerful emotional state, could Olivia have constructed a being of pure thought? And based on her letter dated 27th February, could this being have slipped the shackles of her control and turned against her? Perhaps taking her life in the process?

Francesca, in particular, notes that she and other officers felt a strong, angry presence looming over the household when they arrived. And it is difficult to explain certain aspects of the case without considering the paranormal. The current owner, Christopher Hagen, has been unable to sell the property and it has remained empty for almost three decades. Prospective buyers are apparently put off by the oppressive atmosphere they feel upon entering the home. Christopher himself reported multiple paranormal occurrences during renovation work and beyond.

In 2005, he invited Austin based paranormal investigator, Drew Navarro, to visit the property. Navarro claimed that out of the hundreds of locations he has studied, he has never felt such an imposing force and went on to report how he could not breathe upon entering the home. He described feeling a constant, shifting energy, which behaved erratically, like a jealous child throwing a tantrum, and that at no point did it feel inviting. He finished by saying that the house should be avoided, and a serious intervention is needed, as he didn't quite know what he was dealing with.

So, what killed Olivia Mabel? Did she die of a broken heart? Or was there something far more sinister at work? Before we make any assumptions, allow us to consider the alternatives. It is, of course, possible that someone entered the home, wrote the letter, and placed the call to the police, but as there was no sign of forced entry and coupled with the fact that the phone and house in general had not been disturbed in months, this seems unlikely. Our minds are drawn, then, to question whether this whole incident even took place at all.

Whilst a death certificate does exist for seven-year-old Aiden Mabel, which determines a death by misadventure and lists both Travis and Olivia as his parents, amateur investigators have found no such death certificate for his mother. Secondly, there is no coroner's report detailing the cause of Olivia's death. Also noted is the complete absence of any online news articles regarding the bizarre circumstances in which her body was found. One would think that local press, at the very least, would have jumped on such a strange story, as they did with Christopher Case back in 1991, which raises yet another red flag. Finally, as far as we can tell, reports of this strange case only started to surface a couple of years ago. This was roughly around the same time that a Kickstarter campaign was initiated in order to fund a movie entitled *Thoughtform*, based upon the events surrounding Olivia Mabel's death. Many sceptics point to this as a clear sign of viral marketing, something many film studios employ in this wonderful, modern age of the internet.

But as dubious as all this sounds, none of it is clear-cut proof of a hoax. Just because a death certificate for Olivia Mabel has not been found does not mean it doesn't exist. Relatives may have wished to keep her death out of the press. And finally, a couple of opportunistic filmmakers, who stumbled upon an intriguing story and decided to make a film out of it, does not mean the whole affair is part of a shrewd marketing campaign. When all is said and done, this story is out there and whether it is true or not, it's sad enough to bring a tear to the eye and creepy enough to send a chill up the spine. If it is fictional, then it has done its job as a piece of art in making the viewer, listener, or reader feel at least *something*.

If it is indeed true, however, then we can only hope that Olivia has finally been reunited with her beloved Aiden and that they both rest in everlasting peace, together.

28
THERE IS SOMETHING IN THE WATER

What lies beneath the rippling surfaces of our lakes, rivers, and oceans? Could prehistoric predators, long thought extinct still roam? Or huge, perhaps deep dwelling creatures that are as elusive as they are mysterious? We know less about our oceans than we do about our solar system. Truly, there is something in the water. The question is, what?

The seas, lakes and rivers of our world are as fascinating as they are enigmatic. Mankind has long held an affinity towards these vast bodies of water. They are the life blood of this planet and we, as human beings, seem to have an inveterate curiosity of the depths beneath those rippling surfaces. It's an interest that seeds our wildest dreams and fuels our darkest nightmares. We have seen but a glimpse of this mysterious realm and, in fact, more people have visited the Moon than have visited the deepest parts of our oceans. Despite covering more than two thirds of the Earth's surface, 95% of our seas and oceans remain unexplored. And of the tens of thousands of new species which are catalogued each year, a huge number of them are aquatic. The truth, it seems, is an ominous one. There are potentially millions upon millions of water-borne species still undiscovered, which raises the question; what else could be lurking in those depths?

For centuries, sailors have reported horrifying encounters with various sea monsters, with perhaps the most recognisable amongst them being the dreaded Kraken. In modern times, these stories have largely been dismissed as tall tales of the sea, told to frighten fresh naval recruits and to deter piracy. But it may surprise you to learn that sightings of so-called sea, river, and lake monsters are as prevalent today as they were all those years ago. Interest in the subject saw a huge resurgence in the late 90's when an ultra-low-frequency sound was detected underwater by the US National Oceanic and Atmospheric Administration (NOAA) in 1997.

It was said to have been so loud and so powerful that it was picked up by multiple sensors more than 3000 miles away. It was referred to simply as "Bloop" and scientists initially suspected that it must have been made by some huge, as yet undiscovered marine animal, larger than anything on record. By 2012, however, investigations had revealed that it was nothing more than sea ice, scraping against the ocean floor. Nevertheless, imaginations had been captivated and people had already begun to take stories involving sea monsters more seriously.

The legend of the Kraken stretches back thousands of years. Homer's *The Odyssey* mentions a very similar beast, but it was Norwegian writer, Erik Pontoppidan's 1755 book *The Natural History of Norway* which first described one in detail. Pontoppidan wrote, that according to fisherman, it was so huge it could easily pull a 5000-tonne vessel into the murky depths and that its tentacles were long enough to pluck sailors from the deck of a ship and drown them. These tales were often taken with a pinch of salt and no naturalist of any repute regarded them with any seriousness.

But the legend began to move from fiction to scientific fact in 1857 when a Danish naturalist by the name of Japetus Steenstrup examined a large squid beak, which had washed up on a local beach. It was three inches wide, far larger than any found in known specimens. He could only make estimations as to the animal's full size, but when he was later handed two large tentacles, which had appeared on a beach in the Bahamas, he famously declared that the Kraken was indeed real.

In more recent times, giant and even colossal squids have been described, growing up to 15 metres in length and some estimations have even suggested that that range can extend to 20 metres. Unbelievably, live specimens of these huge animals were only filmed and photographed as recently as 2004. But could they really be responsible for the famous stories of old? It is unlikely, as giant squids have never been seen at the surface. They tend to stay at depths of between 800 and 1600 metres. And whilst they may look fearsome, they are relatively gentle creatures, which prey on much smaller animals. It would seem that the Kraken was possibly nothing more than an exaggeration of their size and ferocity. But who knows what else is down there? After all, the legend of the Kraken existed long before we were even aware that giant or colossal squids existed, so one might question what exactly seeded this legend.

In 2004 a GPS tag, which had been attached to a nine-foot Great White Shark was discovered on a beach in Australia, just four miles from where it was originally tagged. Wildlife conservationists analysed the data contained within the device and discovered something strange. During those first four months, this female shark had been habitually hunting the coastal waters, rarely exceeding a depth of 600 feet. At 4am on 24th December, she was seen to suddenly plunge over the edge of the continental shelf to a depth of 1900 feet in just under two minutes, a speed greater than she was capable of.

The initial belief was that the tag had simply detached from her body, but this was quickly ruled out. If the shark could not swim as fast as the tag had descended, then it certainly couldn't have sunk as fast. More importantly, during the descent, the temperature was recorded at a constant 78 degrees Fahrenheit, much warmer than the 46 degrees that was recorded when it was attached to the shark's fin. Coupled with the fact that it was sinking into much deeper—and therefore much colder—water, the tag should have experienced a sudden drop in temperature if it had simply detached, but this was not the case. When the device was examined, investigators discovered what appeared to be stomach acid lining its exterior casing. This clue suggested that the shark had almost certainly been killed and eaten by something bigger. The question was, what?

Some theorised that she had been attacked by a Killer Whale. Orcas have been known to hunt sharks and they are certainly big and powerful enough to do so, growing to lengths of up to 32 feet. The issue with this explanation is the depth. The deepest a Killer Whale has ever been observed is a mere 850 feet, less than half the depth seen in this instance. Ten years later in 2014, marine biologists believed they had cracked the case, stating that the culprit was "obviously" another, much larger Great White Shark, acting either through extreme hunger or the result of a territorial dispute.

However, this theory is not without its problems. First of all, it is extremely rare for Great Whites to resort to cannibalism, especially in waters that are as abundant as those around Australia. If it was a territorial dispute then, again, this goes against everything we have learned about these huge predators. Being the extremely intelligent animals they are, they usually settle these disputes non-violently through various gestures and interactions. Finally, the temperature recorded by the tag as it descended did not align with this explanation. At 78 degrees Fahrenheit, it was 14 degrees warmer than the highest possible temperature of a Great White's stomach, which is 64 degrees

These inconsistencies have led some people to believe that a Megalodon was responsible, possibly the largest, most powerful fish to have ever existed at an estimated 60 feet in length. Despite the scientific community being largely in agreement that the Megalodon went extinct about 2.6 million years ago, people have contested this belief, with numerous eye-witness accounts of "massive" sharks from all over the globe. Whilst most of these sightings are simply written off as mistaken identity, with Whale and Basking Sharks being the most likely candidates, this has not deterred people from believing that the Megalodon is alive and well and is still prowling the depths of our oceans. After all, in 1875 a drag net from British ship HMS Challenger pulled up a Megalodon tooth. When this tooth was dated, using a method which measures the build-up of manganese dioxide, it was found to be only 11,000 years old.

The Megalodon isn't the only extinct species thought to still roam our oceans. In 1915, a German submarine, U-28, had a terrifying encounter with a huge marine reptile. Commander Freiherr George G von Frostner reported in the vessel's logbook exactly what happened:

> "On July 30th, 1915, our U-28 torpedoed the British steamer Iberian, which was carrying a rich cargo across the North Atlantic. The steamer sank so swiftly that its bow stuck up almost vertically into the air. Moments later the hull of the Iberian disappeared. The wreckage remained beneath the water for approximately twenty-five seconds, at a depth that was clearly impossible to assess, when suddenly there was a violent explosion, which shot pieces of debris—among them a gigantic aquatic animal—out of the water to a height of approximately 80-feet.
>
> At that moment I had with me in the conning tower six of my officers of the watch, including the chief engineer, the navigator, and the helmsman. Simultaneously we all drew one another's attention to this wonder of the seas, which was writhing and struggling among the debris. We were unable to identify the creature, but all of us agreed that it resembled an aquatic crocodile, which was about 60-feet long, with four limbs resembling large, webbed feet, a long, pointed tail and a head which also tapered to a point. Unfortunately, we were not able to take a photograph, for the animal sank out of sight after ten or fifteen seconds."

If the commander's report—which was also verified by his crew—is to be believed, then what he describes sounds very much like a Mosasaur. Mosasaurs were huge marine reptiles, which could grow up to 60 feet in length. They are thought to have gone extinct hundreds of millions of years ago, but these creatures have apparently been sighted off the coast of New Zealand as recently as 2013 and in other parts of the world over the past 300 years. The scientific community once again rules out these sightings as merely the misidentification of Saltwater Crocodiles. But this seems to convenient for most eyewitnesses, who have reported lengths of more than 50 feet. The largest Saltwater Crocodile on record is just under 20 feet long.

But these alleged monsters of the deep are not just limited to prehistoric animalia. Towards the end of the 20th century, a Japanese whale research vessel, working in the Pacific, reported seeing a huge creature breaking upon the surface of the water. It was approximately 90 feet in length, white in colour, much like an albino whale. But it had a humanoid shape with a round head and tendril like "arms" or fins, which were as long as its whole body. It had no legs or feet, but instead the lower half of its body tapered into a mermaid like tail.

Because of its oddly human-like shape, the research crew named it "Ningen", the Japanese word for human. It has been sighted many times since, most commonly in the southern Antarctic Ocean, leading many to believe that it dwells in colder climates. Photographic and even video evidence does exist, but the quality of the footage leaves much to be desired, leading many to speculate that this colossal creature is nothing more than a hoax. If the Ningen does exist, however, some have suggested that it could be an undiscovered species of whale.

Of course, such sightings do not just occur on the high seas. There are many lakes and rivers throughout the world which are thought to hide exotic or ancient creatures, with possibly the oldest and most well-known example being the Loch Ness Monster. Sightings of Nessie date back as far as the 6th century, but the majority of eyewitness accounts only began to appear after the 1930s. There is a multitude of compelling photographs taken around Loch Ness and even video evidence showing strange disturbances out on the surface of the lake. Many of these sightings conjure up the image of a plesiosaur, a large aquatic reptile thought to have gone extinct around 66 million years ago. There are several theories which attempt to explain how a large group of plesiosaurs might have survived the mass extinction event millions of years ago and continued to eke out an existence in the lakes of the Scottish Highlands.

Unfortunately, the legend seems to wane somewhat with each passing year, as hoax after hoax is exposed, and we are left wondering whether Nessie was ever real to begin with. Loch Ness is only one of many large bodies of water thought to be home to a plesiosaur.

Sightings of similar creatures in deep lakes are reported all over the world and they have even been seen in the ocean. In 1977, a Japanese trawler fishing off the coast of New Zealand pulled up a large carcass, thought to be the rotting remains of a plesiosaur. The photographs are compelling to say the least, a long neck and a set of fins are clearly visible and whilst many scientists insisted that it was not a fish, whale, or other mammal, analysis later indicated that it was more than likely the heavily deteriorated remains of a basking shark.

Fig. 21 - *Are these the remains of a plesiosaur? Or simply a Basking Shark?*

More recently, attention has very much been focused on the River Thames, with speculation that this ancient river, snaking its way through the city of London, is home to its very own Loch Ness type monster. In 2016, a video was uploaded to YouTube, which seems to depict a large dark mass swimming upriver close to the O2 Arena. Two humps are seen to briefly break the surface, before submerging again and disappearing for good. A week later, another piece of footage, filmed near the Thames barrier was uploaded, which showed a very similar dark mass, again breaking the surface of the river, this time for a much longer period. The person filming did not notice the anomaly until after he reviewed the footage. Unbelievably, a third piece of film was captured during the same week over by the docklands. Once again, it shows another large, dark mass swimming beneath the surface. Wildlife experts were mystified by these videos. Although seals, dolphins, and porpoises have been known to swim up the Thames, nothing this large has even been seen before or, for that matter, since.

So, what are we to make of all these sea, river, and lake monsters? Is there any truth to these sightings or are we to dismiss them all as nothing more than exaggeration? There simply isn't enough compelling evidence to conclude that any of these creatures exist, but on the flipside, the depths of the Earth's waters are so opaque, mysterious, and inaccessible that they might as well be in some far-flung region of the solar system. We simply do not know what is down there. We cannot deny that the possible existence of oversized, predatory, or rarely seen creatures in our waters has captivated our imaginations for centuries. It seems we have plenty left to discover and, possibly, plenty more to fear. The next time you go paddling in a lake, river, or sea, you might want to take a moment to consider what might be lurking beneath your feet.

29
THE DEVIL MADE ME DO IT

In the early 70's, a young man by the name of Michael Taylor committed one of the most gruesome murders in England's history. He was arrested shortly afterwards and when asked why he had committed such a horrendous deed, he simply replied "The devil made me do it."

One of the most terrifying prospects for any advocate of the paranormal is the possibility of being possessed by an evil or demonic entity. The age-old fear of demonic possession, especially by the Devil, has lived with man for as long as anyone can remember. Early civilizations told tales of demons of the night who could seize hold of a person and force them to commit vile and cruel deeds against their will. Hebraic and Sumerian folklore spoke of Lillith, the purported first wife of Adam who gave herself to evil spirits and visited men in their dreams to steal their essence. The Old Testament related how King Saul was invaded by demonic entities and underwent severe depression before young David cast them out, whilst Jesus Christ is said to have expelled seven demons from Mary Magdalene during one of his many miracles.

Islamic culture told tales of the djinn, a magical demon capable of granting wishes, whilst also seizing control of an individual, and Hindu belief warned of *rakhshas*, entities which could drive men to harm themselves and others. Over the course of history, we hear stories of the Devil possessing people without warning and of the efforts to combat these demons in holy rituals called exorcisms. Yet what was once viewed as a genuine battle between good and evil has now come to be seen as hysteria, borne out of primitive societies' ignorance to scientific and rational explanation, and in some cases even farce and entertainment.

The wider world is largely unaware of the 1949 case of Robbie Mannheim—a Baltimore boy who was possessed by demons and underwent an excruciating exorcism—but is more familiar with the piece of fiction it inspired, William Blatty's novel *The Exorcist* and its 1973 film adaptation. Perhaps that is why the most notorious cases of such instances are lesser known, since there are times when these struggles have not always turned out favourably. One tragic example is the 1974 case of Anneliese Michel, a teenage German girl who was allegedly possessed and died during the exorcism, a case which loosely inspired the 2005 film, *The Exorcism of Emily Rose*. And perhaps it is also no coincidence that in the same year, one man in England fell victim to what many felt was a clear case of demonic possession and committed one of the most gruesome crimes in English history.

It was a crisp and calm autumn morning on Sunday 6th October 1974, in the quiet little village of Ossett, near West Yorkshire. For the devout Anglican villagers, the highlight of the day was the regular trip to morning mass, a traditional practice by the pious folk, which had taken place there since antiquity. For one woman, however, the thought of heading out to church that morning must have been the furthest thing on her mind as she picked up the telephone to contact emergency services. Just outside her window, she watched as a tall man ran stark naked past her front gate, yelling something incoherent about "Satan". He was apparently covered in what she described as red paint. As she urged the operator to send an officer to the scene of the disturbance, little did she—or in fact, anyone in the quiet town—realise that the biggest scandal ever to rock their conservative community was just about to unfold.

31-year-old Michael Taylor was often described by neighbours as being a gentle and kind man, a loving husband, and a wonderful father of five. He was born and lived his whole life in the small village with his family and, although he made a modest living during a time of increasingly high unemployment in the country, he was generally a happy and affable man. Several friends even noted that they often heard laughter coming from his home, for he loved to tell jokes and often tickled his children to no end.

Things, however, took a sudden change in April 1974, when he suffered a back injury after falling from the rafters of a home whilst attempting repairs. Although the injury was minor, he suffered chronic back pain, causing him to resign from his occupation. As he struggled to find a new line of work, he began experiencing severe bouts of depression. In June, he eventually settled into a job as a butcher and, although it brought in a low wage, he cheerfully did his best to live a decent lifestyle.

But that all appeared to change after Michael began to express discontent with his meagre salary and behaved rather coldly towards friends and co-workers. He also experienced mood swings, often becoming confrontational over minor things, a trait he had never exhibited before. His wife, Christine, supported him during this troubled time but became concerned by his sudden change in behaviour and confided to neighbours that she was concerned about his mental state. Her worries prompted a family friend, Barbara Wardman, to talk Michael into turning to a local religious gathering, the Christian Fellowship Group, so that they could help him in his time of need.

Even in the early 1970s, Ossett was a very devout village, with much of the populace attending church regularly on Sundays. Wardman felt the Word of God was the answer. She attributed Michael's change in mood to his religious indifference, opining that his lack of faith was leading to his employment difficulties and struggles at home, so it was with good intentions that she brought Michael to the group's meeting house on Saturday 12th September. And it was through her that he met the group's 21-year-old faith leader, Marie Robinson. It was a meeting that was to have massive repercussions.

Claiming to be able to communicate with God, Marie Robinson

easily accepted Michael into the group, and he fell almost immediately under their influence. Marie described her denomination as being a "vital front line in God's battle against evil" and even claimed to possess miraculous powers, which allowed her to exorcise demons from individuals. The group also practiced speaking in tongues, prayed long hours into the night, and some reports even alleged Marie could summon the Holy Spirit during exorcisms. As her charm and favour towards Michael became more obvious, so too did his infatuation with her.

Almost immediately after joining the group, he started to spend a great deal of time sequestered in private with Marie, supposedly praying for hours on end. But behind the scenes several of her followers suspected her of engaging in a torrid affair with Michael. Some reports at the time claimed that he would even set out just after dinner to go to the congregation. Even on nights when the group did not meet, he joined Marie in prayer against the full moon, which she believed weakened her special powers. The more time Michael spent in her company, the more the rumours continued to run rampant that they were becoming far too inseparable for anyone's liking.

Christine bravely put up with much of the gossip, but by October 1974 she too had had enough. At home, Michael's attitude towards her and the family dramatically worsened. His mood swings turned violent, and only when he was around Marie did he appear to regain some of his former cheerfulness. On the evening of 1st October 1974, Christine joined her husband for what was to become an unforgettable night with the group. Unforgettable for all the wrong reasons. Almost as soon as she arrived, Christine immediately accused Michael of having an extramarital affair and demanded him to confess his sin before the group. Instead, he suddenly rose and began to scream wildly and without warning, lunged out to attack Marie. Several group members helped to subdue him, but the look on his face was one of unbridled rage and, as Marie later described, "bestial fury".

Marie started screaming in tongues and chanting "Jesus, Jesus" in an effort to calm him, and after nearly an hour of being restrained, Michael eventually succumb. The following day, his mood had completely changed, and he claimed to remember nothing of the incident. Although wary, Marie forgave and absolved him, and reluctantly allowed him to remain in the group. In truth, the experience had made the young woman fear for her life and several of the members closely monitored Michael to ensure he did not repeat this violent attack.

But his attitude at home did not change as he continued to act aggressively towards his wife and family. Neighbours and friends noticed this and alerted the Vicar of Ossett. After some observation, the Vicar concluded that Michael was desperately in need of divine intervention. He requested help from the Anglican Church of England for permission to perform an exorcism. For this endeavour, the Church sent Anglican pastor Father Peter Vincent and Methodist minister Reverend Raymond Smith to meet with Michael, and they came to the same conclusion that an exorcism was indeed necessary. They set the date of the session for Saturday 5th October 1974 and would hold it at the Church of St. Thames in Barnsley. They would be in for one long night.

At 10pm the exorcism commenced, and right away Michael's behaviour became evidently violent. Shouting in tongues and writhing about in almost inhuman convulsions. He exhibited all the commonly described signs of demonic possession: scratching, biting, spitting, and uncontrollable fits of rage. His conduct towards the two priests became so dangerous that he was forcibly tied to the floor whilst they continued to do battle with the demons inside him. By their count, Vincent and Smith claimed that at least forty demons lay buried deep in Michael's mind and each one was going to be difficult to remove. They named the demons of carnal sin, those of blasphemy, bestiality, incest, and even masochism. For more than eight exhausting hours they battled their way through his psyche, to the point of near collapse, before finally declaring most of the demons expelled the following morning.

Although he appeared cured, Michael was warned by the priests that three terrible demons remained in his head and that he had to be careful. Michael appeared thankful and then asked if he could return home. Fathers Vincent and Smith reluctantly released him from their charge and watched as he headed home with Christine, unaware that in just several hours' time, they would come to regret this decision.

That same afternoon, just after 12pm, Police Constable Ian Walker responded to a phone call concerning a man creating a disturbance near the street where the Taylor residence was located. Upon arriving he found a naked man crouched in the foetal position, giggling maniacally, and covered in what he thought was red paint. Walker then recognised the man as Michael Taylor and noted a faint, odd smell coming from him. Upon closer inspection, he realised—to his horror—that he was covered not in paint, but in blood. Human blood. Michael appeared to be in a dazed state, as though he had awoken from some terrible dream and, when asked, he professed that he had no idea where the blood had come from, but he feared he had harmed someone. Walker then requested reinforcements and, after authorities arrived on the scene, they entered the Taylor home, thoroughly unprepared for what they were about to find.

In what could only be described as a scene from a horror film, the police found Christine Taylor lying dead in the living room in a pool of her own blood. They found she had been strangled and that her face had been horribly mutilated afterwards. Her eyes had been gouged out, her tongue had been ripped from her mouth and the flesh on her face was clawed, with chunks of her skin lying scattered around. The police also found the tattered remains of the Taylor family's poodle, having also been strangled and then mutilated in a similar fashion to Christine, with its limbs ripped out of their sockets. When the coroner took a closer look at the body, he found there was blood in Christine's oesophagus and stomach, indicating she had choked on her own blood as she lay dying.

It did not take long for the police to conclude that Michael had committed the deed, surmising that after killing his wife and their dog, he had then removed his clothing and bathed in their blood, after which he left the house. Several neighbours and witnesses claimed he ran around chanting, "It's the blood of Satan!" Michael appeared to remember nothing of murdering his wife, despite admitting the blood was surely hers, but made no challenge as they placed him under arrest. Once word of the gruesome murder leaked, the shocked townsfolk of Ossett found themselves at a loss for words. Several of the Taylor's friends and neighbours could hardly believe someone so close could do such a thing and, as the story rocked their town, reporters began flocking to Ossett to learn what they could of the crime.

When news correspondents learned that the murder had taken place the day after Michael had undergone an exorcism, the story took on an even more macabre tone. Newspapers called it "the Devil's work" and claimed that Mr. Taylor had been possessed by a demon and had murdered his wife at its whim. The coroner had even listed the time of Christine's death to be 10am that morning; a mere two hours after they had left the St. Thames Church. Michael was sent to the Broadmoor Secure Hospital for the Criminally Insane to have his sanity evaluated, but whilst he was detained, several people in Ossett began to point their fingers.

Many blamed the Christian Fellowship Group, accusing them of being little better than a fanatical cult which used brainwashing techniques to influence Michael's already agitated mental condition. An equal amount of criticism was aimed at Marie Robinson. Some believed she had been using the group to convince Michael he harboured demons and filled his head with paranoid thoughts. Allegations of their supposed affair disgraced her even further. But then another group came under fire as the case began its hearings, the priests Peter Vincent and Raymond Smith. The media believed that the incomplete exorcism and their inability to completely drive out all of Michael's demons had led to Christine's untimely death.

Reverend Smith's own wife, Margaret, who was present at the exorcism had even warned that something terrible would happen to Christine once she had left the church, but even then, the exhausted priests had allowed them to leave together. Journalists criticised them as being inept and felt they had used the exorcism to further warp Michael into a frenzied delirium, which resulted in the murder. As the trial began on 17th February 1975, prosecuting barrister Geoffrey Baker called the case so bizarre, it would be "rather difficult not to believe one was back in the Middle Ages". The prosecution wasted no time in presenting the gruesome evidence to the jury, stating that Michael had been held against his will and was forced to undergo a harrowing religious frenzy. During the course of this ritual, he had reached breaking point and, in his exhausted state from the exorcism, was driven to kill his wife in a fit of extreme rage.

The defence in turn stated that the guilty parties, not present at the trial (the Christian Fellowship Group, Marie Robinson, and the priests), had merely used Michael for their own ends, experimenting on him and making him believe that he harboured demons. They ventured that the exorcism was another deliberate attempt to keep him under their control. The defence attorney famously laid the blame on the cult and religion as a whole, and public opinion soon turned against the Church for filling Michael's head with paranoid thoughts. The backlash from the trial made many uncomfortable with the thought of exorcisms, and the resulting public outcry forced the Anglican Church of England to act. They released an official statement that no further exorcisms would ever be conducted by any member of the church again, and to this day, that has remained the case.

Perhaps ironically, the prosecution's attempts to paint Michael Taylor as a neurotic, mentally unstable man at the time of the murder worked to save him. In March 1975, the jury returned a not guilty verdict by reason of insanity, meaning that Michael would not be sent to prison for his crime. Instead, he was sentenced to two years of medical observation at Broadmoor Hospital, to be released only upon a final evaluation of his mental state. Four years of medical treatment would follow the trial before he was released in July 1979 to an understandably wary Ossett community. Granted only minor visitation rights, Michael was never able to reconnect with his children and his mental state began to suffer drastically. In 1981, he was hospitalised for the first of what would be four suicide attempts, brought about by severe depression and the unenviable infamy of being the victim of demonic possession.

His name was back in the headlines in England when in July 2005, Michael was arrested for making unwanted sexual advances towards an underage girl. He was found guilty for this misdemeanour and once again was admitted to hospital for three years of psychiatric evaluation and treatment. When his second trial took place, old memories of his demonic deed resurfaced and made a new generation of Ossett's citizens wary of his presence.

In reviewing this case we are left with several unanswered questions. What really happened that October morning in 1974? We know from reports what took place, but how could a man be driven to murder his wife in such a brutal manner? Was it all really the result of ongoing mental deterioration which had been brought about by fervent influence and mental conditioning by a religious cult? Or was it something far more sinister? Something unthinkable? Are there such things as demons and can they cause us to commit such acts of barbarity? And if this is the case, who amongst us is most vulnerable?

We are left with one final, haunting thought: Michael Taylor's remaining demons were apparently never excised from him. We are to question, then, whether they ever truly left him or whether they are simply lying dormant, waiting to come forth once again and remind us that we might each be carrying the devil inside.

30
THE MAN FROM TAURED

In 1954, a businessman arrived in Japan on an inbound flight from a country called Taured. It was a place that simply did not exist. After his subsequent and inexplicable disappearance, a new generation of investigators are questioning whether the man from Taured was an interdimensional traveller.

The Multiverse; a hypothetical state of infinite realities all existing together at the same time. It was a term first coined by American psychologist William James in 1895, albeit in an entirely different context to the one we know today. He referred to a moral multiverse rather than a physical one; something he called "a world of plasticity and indifference". It would take almost 60 years for his contribution to the English language to become mainstream and only after it was hijacked in 1952 by eminent Austrian physicist, Erwin Schrodinger, to describe the possibility of alternate universes.

Although as off-the-wall as it was ground-breaking, it was a concept Schrodinger—and other physicists, for that matter—had been toying with for many years. It was even lightly touched upon in his now famous thought experiment known as Schrodinger's Cat. He hypothesised that throughout a person's life, they may be faced with millions of different choices which could lead to millions of different outcomes. That each time one of these proverbial crossroads is arrived at, the universe splits into several possible branches based upon the decisions available to the individual at that moment in time. These branches then go on to co-exist as separate space-times.

Given the amount of life forms on this planet, let alone in the universe at large, this would result in the existence of an infinite number of alternate universes. The distance between these universes could be anything from a couple of nanometres to billions of light-years and would, in fact, be irrelevant as there is no way they could ever interact with each other anyway. Or is there? Whilst many physicists are still on the fence regarding this possibility and it is strictly a hypothetical concept, history is littered with accounts of people who have supposedly travelled to alternate realities or have arrived from them. And one of the most striking examples on record is a case known as The Man from Taured.

On a scorching summer's day in July 1954, so the story goes, a passenger airliner touched down at Haneda Airport in Tokyo, Japan, during the late afternoon. The sun was still high overhead as the passengers disembarked. They were mostly Japanese, perhaps returning from holidaying in other parts of the world, but some of them were European. They immediately set about collecting their luggage and made their way through to customs in that rushed and haphazard way only world-weary travellers seem to exhibit. As far as the airport officials were concerned, it was just another mundane day at the office. However, one passenger in particular had caught their attention.

He was a slender, well-dressed European man, carrying a leather-bound briefcase along with his luggage. His primary language was French, although he could also speak Japanese, as well as a few other languages, and he told the officials that he was visiting on business. They had no reason to doubt him, he certainly didn't look like a tourist, but when he handed over his passport, things began to take a somewhat bizarre turn. He presented to them an official looking document of impeccable condition, which had travel stamps from several other nations, including Japan. But what struck them as odd was his country of origin; proudly emblazoned on his passport in bold lettering was "Taured". None of the officials recognised this name and, whilst they didn't doubt that the document was genuine, they pulled him aside all the same in order to clarify the situation. They took him into a small room and asked to see other forms of identification, which he was only too happy to provide, and sure enough they established that he was, indeed, a citizen of a country called Taured.

He also presented currency; banknotes issued by his homeland, which did not look in any way counterfeit. Based on these findings, they then placed a map of the world on the table in front of him and asked him to pinpoint the exact location of his country. He proceeded with a smug expression on his face, but as it transpired, it would now be his turn to be confused. He pointed to an area, right on the border between France and Spain where the modern-day Principality of Andorra is, saying that this is where his homeland should have been. He declared that the Kingdom of Taured was nearly a thousand years old, so there was no way it could not have been on a standard world map. He also claimed that this was his third trip to Japan that year, that he had been making similar trips over the past five years and had never encountered a problem before. The travel stamps in his passport certainly seemed to corroborate this.

Nevertheless, when airport officials decided to drill down into the finer details of his story, they discovered that the company he claimed to be visiting had never heard of him, the company he claimed to work for did not exist either and the hotel he was supposed to be staying at had no reservations under his name. His confusion quickly turned to anger, accusing the staff of pulling a practical joke at his expense. Unsurprisingly, he demanded to see government officials at once so that they could clarify the matter. As it turned out, he would be in for a long wait and since they couldn't detain him in the customs room indefinitely, he was granted a suite on one of the top floors of the airport's hotel. His room was guarded by two immigration officers, who were under strict orders not to allow him to leave. He was served a meal and was said to have taken a nap, but when government officials arrived later that evening and knocked on his door, there was no response.

Upon entering the room, they found that he was nowhere to be seen; the man from Taured, along with all of his belongings, had simply vanished. The immigration officers on guard duty were firmly rebuked, although they maintained that they had been watching the room all day and that no one had been in or out except for room service. The only other exit was through a ledgeless window, six stories up. A fall from such a height would surely have killed anyone trying to escape this way. Whilst authorities were left baffled by this strange event, no one ever saw or heard from this man again, leaving the rest of us to question what happened to him.

Who was the man from Taured? Why was there such confusion over his country of origin? And how did he vanish from a guarded room on the sixth floor of a hotel? The pervading opinion amongst fringe theorists is that he was an unwitting inter-dimensional traveller who came from a reality very similar to our own, albeit with marked differences. During his flight from Taured to Japan, he somehow crossed a bridge into our reality, where his homeland did not even exist, all the while blissfully unaware that anything had changed. And here he stayed for several hours, before he was finally pulled back into his own reality at some point during the evening, disappearing from our universe altogether.

They surmise that he probably found himself waking up in a different hotel, perhaps the one he had booked before his trip, and looked back on this experience as some kind of strange dream, never quite sure whether it actually happened. He may have reported it at the time. And it may now sit on a few obscure websites in his own reality; just one of hundreds of other strange accounts lost in the ether, believed by advocates of the multiverse theory, but dismissed by sceptics; not too dissimilar from what happens in our own reality. For the case of The Man from Taured is not unique by any stretch of the imagination. It is apparently a well-travelled phenomenon, which has affected numerous individuals over the course of history.

For instance, in 1972, four girls travelling across the Utah-Nevada state line crashed their car into a creek bed after what they described as a terrifying drive through an otherworldly landscape, where they were apparently chased off the road by "humanoid beings driving egg-shaped vehicles". They relayed their story to an understandably dubious state trooper the next morning, but when authorities checked the scene of the accident, they found that the vehicle was 3km off the main highway, yet its tyre tracks started only 200 metres before the creek bed where they had crashed. How could they have travelled so far, over the soft sand of the desert floor and not made any tracks for much of that distance?

In another case, a woman by the name of Lerina Garcia awoke one morning in 2008 and noticed that subtle changes had been made to her bedroom during the night. Her bed sheets were not the same, her furniture was out of place and the pyjamas she had on were not the ones she remembered wearing the night before. As the day progressed, things got even weirder. After driving to work, she found that she did not recognise any of her co-workers, her department was not where it was supposed to be, and her job role was not the one she had been working in for the past 20 years. She returned home later that day to find that her partner was in fact a boyfriend that she had broken up with six months prior and her new love interest, whom she had been dating for a couple of months, was nowhere to be seen. Unfortunately for Lerina, she has been stuck here ever since.

So, what are we to make of these experiences? Could there really be multiple universes and, if so, do people unwittingly travel between them at random? It is a question we have asked before and is in fact one of the most prominent theories behind the so-called Mandela Effect; the possibility that our universe has become conjoined with another and that our respective histories are now merging in an altogether contradictory fashion.

But of course, no theory would be complete without a healthy dose of scepticism, and as far as the most doubtful amongst us are concerned, the man from Taured is nothing more than an urban legend. After all, nobody can trace the origin of the story. The earliest reference is believed to have been published in a 1981 book, *The Directory of Possibilities*, written by Paul Begg. Begg does not go into any detail regarding the story, it is simply a single line paragraph presented as a titbit of "truthful" information. In fact, the extended version of the story, relayed here, was only traced as far back as 2012, when it appeared on a website called *Before It's News*, written by Terrence Aym.

Sceptics take this as an obvious sign of fabrication and question why there are no newspaper articles from the same time period reporting on the incident. But then, one might question whether such an event was even newsworthy? It might have been kept out of the press in order to save both the airport and Japanese government any embarrassment. And as we have said numerous times before, you will probably find a kernel of truth in most—if not all—urban legends, buried in amongst the layers of embellishment. In either case, we simply do not know and the prospect of becoming an unwitting inter-dimensional traveller is no less harrowing. If true, it's a phenomenon that seems to occur at random, affecting anyone, anywhere, at any time, which raises the question; could you be next?

31
THE NIGHTMARE

During the late 1970's, a DC-10 passenger jet crashed shortly after take-off, killing all on board. Little did anyone know it at the time, but in the days leading up to the tragedy, one man's disturbing dream would turn out to be a nightmare premonition.

What are dreams? It surprises most people to know that even in this modern age of unrelenting discovery and innovation, we still don't fully understand what these brief moments of unconscious awareness are or why they occur. Some believe they are gateways into parallel universes, an alternate reality where everything is similar to our waking world, but not quite the same. Others view them with rationality and reason that they are part of an important brain function, the mind's way of deconstructing and deciphering everyday worries and stresses.

It is said that we experience many things when we dream and oftentimes, we find a realm populated by our most secret fantasies. We envision being the person we wish to be, whether through fame and fortune, winning the respect of our peers, or something as simple as finding love. Our deepest desires tend to manifest in many ways throughout this process. But so too do our darkest fears. It is safe to assume that everyone has suffered nightmares in some form or another during the course of their lives. More often than not, they are fleeting and rare, but unfortunately far more vivid and, at times, even dangerous.

Each year, thousands of people report their dreams taking a somewhat hazardous turn, resulting in cardiac arrest, unexpected seizures, or even physical injury. Borne out of the stress and anxiety of our circumstance, nightmares are usually a good indication of what's going on in our personal lives and some see them as a window into understanding how to fix whatever is wrong. On the other hand, they can take on a far more foreboding nature. And in the late 1970s, one man would come to learn just how deadly dreams can be.

David Booth, an office manager from Cincinnati, Ohio, lived a modest existence. He was married, earning a decent income, and raising two young children, and for most of his life he had experienced no major upheavals or problems. But all that would change in the early morning hours of Wednesday 16th May 1979, when he awoke in a nervous sweat and rushed to his bathroom. His wife awoke with him and noticed his state of distress. Concerned, she asked him what had happened and, reluctantly, he related to her what was to become the first in a series of recurring nightmares. David explained that in his dream, he was looking out to his right over a field, and there was a jet flying towards him, which wasn't making any sound. He said that it suddenly banked, with its right wing up in the air, turned over on to its back, so that it was flying inverted, and then flew straight into the ground and exploded.

He awoke just as the noise from the explosion was dying. Despite how vivid and yet surreal the dream seemed to be, David did not feel that it had any significance. The next night, however, he would experience the same dream again. He described the plane and its crash in the exact same way as before, with more striking detail and the impact of such a vision would leave him sobbing in his sleep. To his surprise and horror, he found himself having the same dream again a third night in a row. And then a fourth. And then a fifth. And for a full six nights up until 22nd May. The same dream, the same plane, the same disaster, all just as he had witnessed the very first time. And as he continued to dream, David worried that the event was going to happen sometime in the near future.

Without any clue as to when and where, he felt there was little he could do to prevent it from happening. Nevertheless, after the dream reoccurred on the seventh night, he decided to act. The key detail which stood out to him was an instinctual feeling that the plane was connected with the then iconic American Airlines, one of the busiest in the country. David managed to get into contact with Paul Williams, manager of the Federal Aviation Administration Office in Cincinnati and proceeded to tell him about his bizarre dream. Rather than dismissing the young man's fears out of hand, Williams took the warning seriously and asked David for any information he could give, but the only thing he was aware of was that it was an American Airlines flight. Williams asked him to go through his dream in more detail in the hopes that David could try to narrow down the possibilities of when and where the disaster might occur.

Through this effort, David was able to provide several more clues regarding the plane; stating that it bore three turbine engines altogether; one on the tail end and one on each wing. Using these details, Williams ascertained that the plane was a DC-10 jet aircraft, but unfortunately, nothing further could be determined. For David, the dream persisted for three more nights and with each occurrence he became overwhelmed by the trauma of experiencing the same tragedy night after night. Around the same time that he informed Williams of his visions, he also contacted a psychiatrist in the hopes of obtaining treatment for this ongoing trauma, which was beginning to cause him to question his sanity.

Williams, meanwhile, brought the information to a number of flight managers at several nearby airports, but because nothing useful could be gained from the apparent lack of details, no one was realistically in a position to do anything about it. The following night, on 25th May 1979, David envisioned the dream once again, but when he awoke, he had the distinct and unshakeable feeling that this was to be the last time. Resigning himself to this notion, he left work early that morning with mixed feelings. Deep within his soul, he somehow knew that his affliction was over and for that he felt relieved. Yet he also knew that somewhere out there, a tragedy was imminent. And for that he felt despair.

At 3:05pm that afternoon in Chicago, a DC-10 jet plane registered as Flight 191 took off from the runway at O'Hare International Airport, bound for Los Angeles. It took off normally and started its climb when, without warning, the plane rotated onto its side and flew out of control towards the ground. Despite attempts by the flight crew to correct its trajectory, they had completely lost control and, after only several minutes in the air, it came crashing down on the field to the left of O'Hare, almost precisely as David Booth had envisioned. A total of 258 passengers, its 13-man flight crew, and 2 persons on the ground were killed in the tragedy, resulting in the worst and deadliest aviation disaster to have occurred in the continental United States.

When the investigation was conducted, it was discovered that the engine on the left wing had separated mid-flight and had struck the rear of the jet, destabilising its course, and severing its hydraulic and electrical systems. This led to the slats on the left wing being jammed in position and resulted in the aircraft edging into an asymmetrical drag, which caused the right wing to lift higher than the left, ultimately inverting the plane and causing the loss of control. As if to heighten the mystery further, the last inspection recorded on 11th May—five days prior to David Booth's dreams—showed that there were no existing problems, but these records were somehow lost in the aftermath of the investigation.

The news hit David hard and he almost suffered a nervous breakdown. In his own mind, he blamed himself for not doing enough to prevent the disaster. Although Williams and many other aviation officials assured him he had nothing to feel responsible for, David believed the lives of hundreds of people were lost that day because of his inability to act. Several newspaper editors somehow learned of David's attempts to warn the FAA and of his dreams foretelling the crash, and in the days that followed they tried to contact him for his sensational story. He reluctantly gave a small number of interviews, which lasted only as long as the investigation into the crash. Afterwards he all but disappeared from the media spotlight. As far as we know, David Booth never had any dreams of a similar nature ever again.

Despite the horrific plane crash, O'Hare recovered from the disaster and continues to this day to be a major airport within the United States, but gone from existence is the DC-10 jet aircraft. The crash of Flight 191 sounded the death knell for the plane, which many felt was not all that surprising. Even before the disaster the DC-10 was viewed as structurally insecure and had fallen victim to a number of faults and accidents. Of particular note was the crash of Turkish Airlines Flight 981 in 1974, which killed 346 people. The jet was eventually decommissioned and phased out of service in 1983 following a lack of orders due to safety concerns, and in some ways, many feel David's dream actually foretold the end of the jet itself.

What makes the tragedy rather unique is the fact that David was not the only person to have an upsetting premonition about that particular flight. In recent years, the story surfaced that actress Lindsey Wagner, famous for her role in the TV series *The Bionic Woman*, had booked a ticket along with her mother for Flight 191 to Los Angeles. Before boarding the plane, however, she was overcome by nausea, which she took as a warning that the plane was dangerous. She managed to convince her mother not to board the flight and they stayed behind to witness the plane crash just moments later.

Noted author and former editor of Playboy Magazine, Judy Wax, and her husband unfortunately did board the aircraft and perished in the disaster. A few admirers of her work pointed out shortly after her death that her final book, *Starting in The Middle*, carried a line which expressed her fear of flying, on page 191, the same number as the doomed flight.

Were all these apparent premonitions merely a coincidence, or was something attempting to warn certain individuals that the plane was heading for tragedy? This brings us back to our original question: just what are dreams? It is possible that some dreams do attempt to warn us of future events and, whilst there is still heated debate as to the veracity of precognitive dreams, some historic examples do exist, which seem to support this idea. In 1858, Mark Twain reportedly had a dream in which he attended the funeral of his younger brother, Henry, two weeks prior to the latter's death in a steamboat explosion. President Abraham Lincoln famously told one of his aides that he had dreamt of walking into his own funeral three days before his assassination in 1865.

In 1898, writer Morgan Robertson published a novel about a brand-new transatlantic luxury liner named the Titan. Touted as unsinkable, the ship strikes an iceberg and sinks with a large loss of life in the month of April. This shares obvious and ominous parallels with the Titanic, which sunk after striking an iceberg a mere 14 years later. Some reports alleged that he had dreamed up the concept, and to add further weight to this theory, a number of passengers who survived the sinking of the Titanic in 1912 even claimed to have dreamed of the disaster days, or even hours, before it took place.

And finally, in October 1966, a little girl in the village of Aberfan, Wales, named Eryl Mai Jones related an experience where she dreamed "something black coming down" all over her school. The following day, a landslide of black, wet coal slurry came crashing down onto the Pantglas Junior School, trapping, and killing little Eryl Mai and 115 of her schoolmates. At least six other persons, in the surrounding towns and countryside, were also reported to have dreamed of the disaster just days before it took place. Most would argue that dreams and nightmares are not real to begin with and, whether pleasant or painful, rarely come true. Those that do are nothing more than mere coincidence.

However, a nightmare lasting at least ten days should be strong evidence to suggest otherwise. If the case of David Booth is anything to go by, it also stands to reason that we should not take these dreams too lightly. One could argue that the alarming accuracy of some premonitions is rather telling; something more is going on within these psychological processes.

Philosophers, psychologists, and even scientists have postulated that what we perceive as reality is nothing more than a construct of the mind, that it does not exist outside of the body, but is created within the brain itself. An internal existence rather than an external one. What if the thing you perceive as three-dimensional space is created solely within your mind? That everything you touch, taste, smell, see, and hear is simply an electrical impulse detected and deciphered by your brain to give you only the illusion that what you perceive is real? After all, if you were somehow able to alter your senses regarding a particular object, would not your perception of that object's reality also change?

And if we live by the rule that everything we perceive via our five senses—which, incidentally, are created and interpreted within the brain—is real, does this mean that our dreams, which are also created and interpreted within the brain via our five senses, are also real? Could they be glimpses into an unconscious reality where every possible outcome is perceived? And that sometimes, those outcomes manifest in our waking world? It is often said that life imitates art. But we would argue that art often imitates our dreams. Therefore, our dreams, and even our nightmares, are very much intertwined with our waking world. The question is, do our lives dictate the way we dream? Or do our dreams dictate the way we live?

32
THE EVIL WITHIN

When a thirteen-year-old boy living on a farmstead in Mexico partakes in what he believes is a harmless bit of fun with friends, he inadvertently invites something into his home, which goes beyond his understanding. Over the next few months, things go from bad to worse, as those around him try to expel the evil within.

The paranormal manifests in many ways and means many different things to many different people. For some it involves ghosts and hauntings, for others clairvoyance and other psychical gifts. For most, however, it means absolutely nothing and merely the mention of any bizarre experience will often invite upon the storyteller strange looks, most commonly of ridicule and disbelief. The world of the paranormal is a puzzling one. There are those who have seen and heard things they cannot explain yet remain sceptical. There are those who have seen and heard nothing at all yet believe implicitly. And then there are those who simply do not know, who sit on the fence and find the prospect of experiencing something paranormal far more interesting than they do terrifying.

This tale comes courtesy of one such person; a young man from the State of Hidalgo in Mexico named Lucas Villa. And for him, what started out as a game, a trifling venture into what he assumed was purely imaginary, would become all too real. Lucas is, by now, a young man of 23, leading a normal life in the city of Pachuca, where he grew up. He works long hours earning a steady income and nurtures the hope of one day settling down with his girlfriend Sofia, whom he describes as the love of his life. From the outside looking in, Lucas is a regular guy, hardworking, personable, and well-liked amongst his peers. But in truth he bears a decade old secret, which still troubles him during his quieter moments and haunts his dreams to this very day. Not even the passage of time has eased this burden.

For when Lucas was just 13 years old, he went through one of the most terrifying ordeals of his life. Nothing would allow him to forget the events that occurred back in the Summer of 2007. At the time, he and his family lived on an old farmstead on the outskirts of town. They didn't have much in the way of livestock, just a few goats and heifers which produced milk and cheese, and a few hens which laid eggs daily. What they did have was land. 150 hectares to be exact. And whilst the family wasn't particularly well off, they produced annual crops of wheat, corn, barley, and beans, which brought in a reasonable income.

Lucas spent most of his days either attending school or helping around the farm. On those occasions when he had time to himself, he would while away the hours playing video games or hanging out with friends from the surrounding countryside, getting up to the kinds of mischief that boys their age tend to do. In reality, Lucas was a good kid and displayed many of the traits that would define him in later life. He stuck to his studies, worked hard for his family and was popular with his friends. But an incident in May that year would begin to turn his life upside down.

At the beginning of that month, his parents came home one evening to find him and three of his companions gathered in the family room playing with a Ouija board. Whilst it was merely a bit of fun to him and his friends, his mother and father were Roman Catholics and were both deeply religious. They saw the act as an affront to God and after they had asked his friends to leave, they proceeded to burn the offending article and grounded their son for two weeks. His pleas of ignorance fell on deaf ears, his parents were superstitious to a fault and they were adamant that Lucas should understand the seriousness of what he had done.

He could not even begin to understand the reasoning behind what he thought was an irrational punishment. During his experience with the Ouija board a few strange things had occurred, but nothing he couldn't explain. He and his friends had heard knocking from other parts of the house and had seen the flames on the candles flare momentarily up to a foot in height, but Lucas had put this down to coincidence or his friends playing some very clever pranks. He just didn't share his parents' superstitions about the paranormal, but over the coming months, that would profoundly and irrevocably change.

The first couple of weeks passed by without incident. Lucas' ban on leaving the house for anything other than school or toil was over and he was once again free to enjoy his horseplay and spending time with his friends. But in June of that year, whilst he was clearing out one of the farmstead's disused outbuildings, he found—lodged beneath the piles of old farming equipment—another Ouija board. To his surprise, it looked exactly like the one he and his friends had used back in May, except it was tattered and covered in dust. Not wanting to incur the wrath of his parents a second time, he decided not to tell them and tossed it out with the other rubbish. Although the discovery had unnerved him, he soon forgot about it and continued with his work. That night, however, he awoke in pools of sweat and gasping for air. He'd had the most awful dream; something black had been leaning over him as he slept, getting closer and closer to his face, to the point where he felt he was being smothered and couldn't breathe.

Unfortunately for Lucas, this became a recurring nightmare, which called upon him every night for the next few weeks and began to affect his sleep. During the day, he found that he was snapping at and arguing with those closest to him, but lack of sleep was not the only reason for his irritable mood. He was beginning to find items which belonged to him in other parts of the house, in places where they never should have been. Sometimes these items went missing altogether and were never seen again. Other times, they returned to their original spot, even though he had searched those areas over and over.

Things continued like this for some time, but it would be the events of 22nd June, which would escalate the situation beyond his understanding. On this day, when he was in his room looking for his BB gun, he noticed an item jutting out from under his bed, which looked familiar. On closer inspection and to his utter disbelief, it turned out to be the Ouija board from the outbuilding, which he had discarded the week before. Surprisingly, he felt angered by this and marched downstairs and confronted his parents, accusing them of playing pranks on him. He suspected that they had not burned the Ouija board as they had originally said, but that they had planted it in the outbuilding and later under his bed for him to find and that they were moving his belongings around the house, all in the name of teaching him a lesson for using the Ouija board.

But his parents appeared genuine when they told him, in no uncertain terms, that they had no idea what he was talking about and when he stormed off, their confusion turned to deep-seated concern. Lucas had been acting out of character over the past few weeks, but this was highly irrational behaviour. He had not long turned a teenager and, at first, his mother had put this down to the fact his hormones were probably running amok. But this revelation about him finding the Ouija board a second and third time had alarmed her. That night, she prayed for her son, burning incense, and going from room to room reciting prayers to ward off evil spirits.

As the weeks rolled by, things gradually got worse for Lucas. He was beginning to experience other strange things around the house whenever he was home alone. On one terrifying occasion, he was sat watching TV when he heard slow, thudding footsteps walking towards him in the hall just outside the family room. At night he would hear knocking on his bedroom walls and his name being whispered, which sounded like it was coming from under his bed. In the morning, he would often find strange markings and scratches on his body and another time, he awoke in the middle of the night to see a dark figure standing in the corner of his room, unmoving and staring at him as he had slept. He kept these things to himself, for he didn't want to concern his parents and, whilst these occurrences frightened him, he reasoned that he could simply try to ignore them.

That was until the blackouts started.

The first one occurred in mid-July, when Lucas awoke in a thicket of trees more than a kilometre away from the house, with his skin baking in the hot afternoon sun. His body was tangled in foliage and covered in minor cuts and bruises. His head was unscathed and resting just outside of the thicket boundary. It was almost as if someone (or something) had tried to drag him through the brush into the darkness of the wood beyond, but his body had become entangled in the undergrowth. What seemed to him like just a few moments before, he had been turning over topsoil on the east side of the farm. Now he was all the way over on the west side. When he staggered in through the kitchen door back at the household, his shocked, but visibly relieved parents asked him where he had been all this time. More than three hours had passed.

The blackouts only seemed to occur whenever he was alone. Sometimes they would last minutes, other times hours, and he would always wake in odd places or lying in strange positions. Often, items of his clothing had been removed and he would have more marks and scratches on his skin. But the real horror would begin when he started to wake up in the middle of torturing animals. The most disturbing instance—the one that shook him to his very core—was when he awoke sitting upright, holding a knife in his hands, which was speckled with blood. A baby goat from the farm was pinned between his thighs, bleating wildly, with lacerations to its hindquarters and a look of unbridled terror in its eyes.

When Lucas came to his senses and realised what he was doing, he ran. He ran across the corn field in front of his house, onto the track leading away from the property and exited the gateway on to the main road. He ran along highways, past people, cars, and houses. He ran over more fields and through woods and down into creeks and across dry riverbeds, through brush and over rocks the size of vehicles. He ran until he had nothing left and collapsed, exhausted and sobbing.

When authorities finally caught up with him two days later, he had run almost 25 miles away from his home. In the hospital, where he was being treated for dehydration and exposure, Lucas finally came clean to his mother about what had been happening. She had had no idea as to the extent of his strife. Discussing this with her husband, Hector, they reasoned that there was no such medicine for this kind of affliction and contacted a local priest at the earliest opportunity.

Father Benito Jose Carita made several visits to the Villa residence in the month of August and determined that Lucas' body and mind was indeed playing host to a malevolent and parasitic entity. Approval was granted to perform an exorcism and at the beginning of September, the Villa family and several members of the church gathered around the boy in order to assist in banishing whatever it was that had taken hold him. He was tied to his bed, not just for his own safety, but for the safety of those present, for they knew they were in for a difficult night.

Lucas himself does not remember much of the ordeal. In fact, much of what he told us in his own account was pieced together from only fragments of memory and of what his mother and father told him in the years following. Of the exorcism he has almost no memory at all. Except for one thing. Right at the very end, when it was all over, he remembers hearing a clunk beneath the bed and the sound of scrabbling claws across a wooden floor and the panicked gasps of those around him as they jumped out of the way. He looked down just in time to see what he thought was the top half of a black, oily, inhuman body, with no legs, hurriedly pulling itself towards the door with its spindly arms.

This memory is a point of a contention for Lucas, as his parents don't recall anything of that nature taking place. He is not sure whether he imagined it in his exhausted state or whether his mother and father disregarded it in order to protect the sanity of their son. Either way, he doesn't want to know. Lucas slept for almost three days solid after the exorcism and seemed to return to normal. There were no more blackouts or strange happenings around the household and that tattered Ouija board was never seen again.

Ouija boards have been around in some form or another for centuries and, although originally marketed as a children's toy in the early 20th century, they have since taken on a far darker reputation. There are those who believe that they serve as gateways to another realm, where only pain, sadness, and torment persists and that anything that steps through that gateway is inherently malevolent. Whether you are a believer or not, many will argue that in using a Ouija board, you are marking yourself as a target for something else, something predatory, which sees your willingness to open that gateway as a desire to connect with them. Lucas is unsure of the exact details regarding such things. Although he still classes himself as an atheist, he has resolved to never again mess with anything of that nature for as long he lives.

Before father Benito left, he placed an item in the palm of Lucas' hand. It wasn't a crucifix as you might expect or any kind of religious symbol for that matter. It was simply a small wooden disc inscribed with the word "Proteger" or "Protect". Father Benito told him to never lose it and to always keep it with him, and to this day Lucas wears it around his neck. Not that he would ever admit to being superstitious, of course, but even now, there have been a couple of times when he did not take it to bed with him. Instead of placing it on his bedside table as he usually does, he has left it in his coat pocket or sitting on the kitchen table or hanging on the key rack next the door. And whenever he has done this, he has had a terrible dream of a face, leaning over his bed, suffocating him whilst he sleeps.

33
THE BOYS FROM YUBA CITY

On a cold evening in February, five young men inexplicably left the safety of their car and struck out into the woods in the dead of night. It would be months before their bodies were found. Known as America's own Dyatlov Pass Incident, we're left wondering what happened to the boys from Yuba City.

A nauseating smell hung in the air as the riders pulled off the main trail and entered the deserted camp. It was early June in 1978 and the late afternoon sun was bathing the stunning Californian wilderness in an iridescent light and warmth. The bikers had been travelling all day and had decided to pull over for a rest and to investigate the curious cluster of abodes, tucked away in a cul-de-sac just beyond the treeline adorning the mountain road. In front of them sat a large trailer which was surrounded by four smaller ones. It was a US Forest Service Station. Its location was not unusual; many more like it dotted the landscape in this part of the world, strategically placed to help the Forestry Service carry out their duties in all kinds of situations, such as search and rescue or fire spotting. Most of them are staffed, but in the more remote regions, many of them sit unmanned and are only used when needed, as was the case with this camp.

The scent was more pungent now that the riders had removed their helmets. A couple of them had recognised it immediately. It was the smell of death. They reasoned that maybe a dead animal was lying close by, rotting in the heat of the afternoon, and stinking out the whole area. It was enough to make one of them gag and they briefly considered leaving until one of the men noticed that a window in the larger trailer had been broken and decided to go and investigate. Looking in through the pane of broken glass, he could not see anything of interest, just a few cupboards and work surfaces, seemingly untouched.

Surprisingly, the door to the trailer was unlocked and after some deliberation, the rider decided to enter. Nothing could have prepared him for what he discovered inside. Lying on a bed at the rear, under eight winter blankets and a swarm of blow flies was a dead body. What none of the men present that day realised was that they had just stumbled upon what would become a truly heart-breaking enigma. One which you, the reader, have probably never heard of.

Authorities en route to the scene already had a hunch regarding the identity of the deceased individual and upon arrival, their worst fears were confirmed. It was the body of one of five young men who had gone missing earlier that year in February. But much of the evidence in front of them just didn't seem to add up. In fact, as the full story unfolded, it would turn out that hardly anything about this case made sense at all. And in time, what we would be left with, is a thought-provoking mystery which has come to be known as America's very own Dyatlov Pass Incident. With that in mind, we take you back to the very beginning; the early evening of Friday 24th February 1978.

The day had been chillier than usual for the residents of Oroville in Northern California. It was 5.30pm and 25-year-old Gary Dale Mathias was sitting at his kitchen table eating dinner. Between mouthfuls of his meat loaf, he looked out of the window at the empty street in front of his house with an eager expression. He must have felt tremendously excited about that night's prospects. For several days, he and a group of friends from the nearby town of Yuba City had been planning to watch a basketball game at the California State University in Chico. Even though a light snowfall had been forecast for that night, Mathias assured his mother and stepfather that he would not need his windbreaker, since he would be home once the game was over.

Earlier that same evening, 32-year-old Theodore Earl Weiher had come rushing downstairs for dinner, which he consumed at an alarming rate. A few minutes later he heard a car pull up outside and honk. Weiher instantly rushed out of the door after insisting to his grandmother, Imogen, that he too would not be needing his coat that night. In the driveway, he found Jack Antone Madruga, 29, sitting behind the wheel of a 1969 Mercury Montego. In the passenger seat sat his other friend, Jackie Charles Huett, who was 24, and sitting in the back was 27-year-old William Lee Sterling. Weiher jumped in the vehicle and he and his friends set out for Oroville where they picked up Gary Mathias. From there they headed out on a half-hour journey towards Chico on what promised to be an eventful evening of sports and cheerful exuberance.

Each of them was an avid basketball fan and they loved to watch both local and televised games whenever they got the chance. They even played as part of a team themselves—The Gateway Gators—and had a match set for the very next day, the latest in a series of regional tournaments which would qualify them for the upcoming Special Olympics. They were promised a free trip to Los Angeles if they won the game. An aspect which made this case especially poignant was the fact that all five men were either intellectually disabled or suffered from mental health issues. They attended the Yuba City Gateway Programme, a vocational rehabilitation centre, where they learned trades whilst also playing on the centre's basketball team.

Ted Weiher was the oldest yet had the mind of a child and a natural friendliness about him which he often shared with the deeply religious Bill Sterling. At his family's insistence, he had recently quit a job working at a snack bar, due to concerns that he was unable to handle the high-pressure workload.

Jack Huett, on the other hand, was the shortest of the group, standing at five feet nine inches. His head drooped slightly, and he found it difficult to respond clearly in social situations. But when comfortable, he had a natural cheerfulness and got along famously with his friends. Weiher and Huett were described as inseparable and went almost everywhere together; the older man took care of his younger friend and would often make phone calls on his behalf.

Jack Madruga had graduated high school and served in the Army in Vietnam but was discharged after a medical evaluation. Although not diagnosed as intellectually disabled, he was generally considered slow by his acquaintances. Despite this, Madruga was competent enough to possess a state driver's license and loved driving his cherished Montego almost as much as he loved playing basketball.

Like Madruga, Gary Mathias had also enlisted in the Army and had been stationed in West Germany, but following a drug-related breakdown in 1973, he was diagnosed with paranoid schizophrenia and honourably discharged. For this reason, he had been taking prescribed medication for nearly five years. In that time, his condition had improved greatly, and he had even managed to hold down a job working for his stepfather's landscape gardening service.

Finally, completing the group, was Bill Sterling. Like Ted, he also had the mind of a child and rarely left the house for anything other than church, basketball, or attending the Programme. Ted would often phone Bill to read him bizarre newspaper articles or repeat strange names found in the phonebook, which both of them found highly amusing. Sterling also devoted time to the local hospital reading Bible verses to patients on the wards.

During the ride, the five friends more than likely talked amongst themselves. It's easy to imagine that their conversation probably centred around their upcoming match. Their parents had laid out their kit on the evening of the 24th, ready for their big game the next day, and they were in a highly excitable mood. Sadly, though, they would never get to play it, for that night, a mysterious sequence of events would seal an inexorable fate in which none of them were ever seen alive again. When all five boys failed to return home that evening, their worried families contacted the police and each other for any word on their whereabouts. It was unheard of for the boys to vanish without saying anything. None of them were the outgoing type and would often spend their nights at home. Although Gary Mathias tended to stay out late with older friends, this was out of character, even for him.

When the police issued a bulletin for the missing boys, it was not long before the news arrived in Chico, where the first pieces of the puzzle began to come together. Several witnesses confirmed seeing them at the basketball game and one or two believed they had seen Madruga's Montego leaving the parking lot after its conclusion. A cashier at a local store reported seeing them come into his shop just before closing time. They purchased several snack items, bottles of milk and soda and then left almost as quickly as they had arrived, just as snow was beginning to fall.

Police immediately began a county-wide search headed by Yuba Police Lieutenant Lance Ayers. Ayers had known the boys for years, having gone to high school with Ted Weiher and his brothers, and felt personally connected to all five. He worked extensively to find any trace he could and instructed the search to broaden into the surrounding areas near the Feather River Mountain Range. This decision eventually paid off when the news filtered back that Madruga's Montego had been discovered. To Ayer's surprise, the car was located on a road in the Plumas National Forest, seventy miles away from Chico, on 28th February. Snow had fallen in the time since the disappearance which had almost buried the vehicle, but oddly enough they had found it had been left perfectly parked. Inside they discovered several snack bar wrappers strewn over the seats. There were also four maps folded neatly in the glove compartment.

The car itself was in good condition, but the keys were missing, forcing the officers to hot-wire the ignition and drive it back to nearby Oroville. Even the fuel tank was supposedly a quarter full, which allegedly confused the police as it was more than enough for the boys to have driven home on. It should be noted, however, that there are conflicting reports regarding the amount of fuel left in the vehicle. Some of those local to the area suggested that the tank was indeed empty and that it was misreported as being a quarter full simply because the police had to put some fuel in it in order to drive it back to town.

Aside from this, authorities also wondered if it had gotten stuck in the snow, but this turned out not to be the case. Further attempts to search the area were halted by another snowstorm later that night and the search was reluctantly delayed until the spring. For Ayers, the investigation became an obsession, and with each passing day and no word on the boys, he became increasingly determined to find them. To this end, he and their families pursued every angle they could, even offering rewards for information on their whereabouts.

Phone calls came in daily, but most were unconfirmed sightings by unsure citizens, ranging from as far as San Francisco, Arizona, Ontario, and one which even claimed the boys were spotted in Florida. With each frustrating phone call, Ayers was becoming convinced that no one would ever see them again. And just when that possibility seemed more and more likely, a breakthrough finally occurred on 4th June, when he received a phone call from the group of motorcyclists at the US Forest Service camp.

The body found inside the trailer was identified as that of Ted Weiher, who looked to have died from exposure despite having been wrapped in several layers of blankets. Initial reports also showed that Weiher's 200-pound frame had shed more than 80 pounds, tragically hinting that he may have starved to death. But when investigators took a closer look at the scene, they were baffled. Weiher's shoes were missing, and frostbite had ravaged his exposed feet. The length of his unkempt beard suggested that he had been alive for the better part of eight weeks, but for some reason had never once tried to leave the bed.

The officers found several empty packets of Army C-Rations scattered on the floor, which confirmed he had eaten at some point. They also found a metal cabinet in the same room containing dehydrated, easily prepared food sitting untouched; enough to feed a small group of people for a whole year. It was never clarified whether this metal cabinet was locked or unlocked, but even if it was secured, someone who was determined enough could have gotten into the food store. When Ayers examined the scene, he was stunned to find that no one had attempted to build a fire. There were boxes full of matches and plenty of paperback books and magazines which could have been used as fuel. Even more astonishing, the propane tank behind the trailer was in perfect working condition, yet no one had turned it on. This would have provided heat for a few weeks at the very least.

The following day, Plumas County Police found the body of Jack Madruga eleven miles from the trailer, near the road leading back in the direction of the car. All signs indicated he had died on the way and that his body had fallen victim to animal predation. He had been dragged almost ten feet to a nearby stream, with most of the flesh on his right arm gone, his hand clutching his favourite watch and his eyes and two fingers missing. On the other side of the road, in a thickly wooded area, police also found several bones scattered about which later analysis confirmed belonged to Bill Sterling. Sterling's body had also been eaten by forest animals and his remains were spread over an area of 50 square-feet. Several articles of clothing matching what he had worn the night he disappeared also verified his identity.

When word reached Yuba City that three of the five boys had been found dead, the news was devastating. Two days later, Jack Huett Sr. joined the search—despite Ayer's pleas not to—and tragically located a backbone and the same Levi jeans and shoes his son had been wearing the night he vanished. The following day, an assistant sheriff discovered Jack's skull and the family dentist confirmed his identity using the boy's dental records.

Throughout this, Gary Mathias's whereabouts remained unknown, and this worried investigators since he had been taking prescription medication for his schizophrenia. Four months had passed since the group's disappearance and if he was still alive, they couldn't begin to imagine what sort of state he was in. Mathias's shoes were discovered in the trailer, suggesting to police that he had been there with Weiher and had swapped them for his friend's much larger leather shoes once frostbite had swollen his feet. To this day, Mathias's body has never been found.

Police speculated that the boys had driven up the road but had become lost, and as the snowfall worsened, they abandoned the car and tried heading in a southerly direction back home. This meant they would have walked more than twenty miles over rocky, mountainous terrain in freezing cold weather, before arriving at the Service trailer. Police believe that, once inside, the boys might have tried searching for food and something to start a fire with, but in the end, could not get one started and had simply failed to locate the supplies in the locker. With no idea about the propane tank outside and with Weiher's worsening condition confining him to the bed, Huett, Madruga, and Sterling might have left to locate assistance, leaving Mathias behind to keep watch over their friend.

If they had left around the time the blizzard hit on 28th February, it would have been their last mistake, as none of them would have made it back alive. If Mathias had indeed stayed behind, with no word from the other three men, he might have set off at a later time. A quarter of a mile northwest of the trailer officers found three blankets and a rusted torch. They speculated that Mathias might have gone out to locate his friends and give them the blankets he was carrying, but instead got lost and succumbed to the elements, although there was nothing to substantiate this. Needless to say, the question on everyone's lips was why had they driven up that mountain road in the first place? It was not on the same road connecting Chico to Yuba City. None of the boys had ever travelled on that road before, nor would they have been familiar with the area, even though Weiher and Sterling had been on hunting trips to nearby trails as children. Just how had they ended up there of all places?

Madruga's mother would later claim that someone, or something, chased them up that mountain trail, but she couldn't fathom how anyone would have gotten the upper hand on them. Although they had their disabilities, they were five very strong, able bodied men who could more than handle themselves. Police questioned what had compelled them, in the first instance, to leave the relative safety of a perfectly operable car and trek twenty miles through a forest on a freezing cold night. They also wondered why, upon reaching the trailer, the boys had not tried to start a fire or ransack it for supplies? Unless they were trying to hide. But hide from who, or what?

Given their intellectual disabilities and mental health issues, it has been suggested that maybe they just didn't understand how to cope with the situation. But if Mathias and to an extent even Madruga— who had both served in the army—had been with them, then surely, they would have been more capable and should have known what to do. Others speculate further in this direction, opining that most of them had the minds of innocent children, having been taught that stealing was wrong and that they wouldn't have burned the books or taken the food for fear of getting into trouble. However, this, again, does not account for the fact that at least two of them were more adult in their thinking. After all, they had already broken the window to gain access to the trailer. Furthermore, survival instincts will always take precedence over fear of consequence, even in children.

Unsurprisingly, rumours of foul play surfaced around the time the bodies were discovered and one person might have been able to shed some light on the sequence of events leading up to their disappearance. On 2nd June 1978, Lieutenant Ayers spoke to a man named Joseph Shones, who reported that on the night of 24th February, he had been driving along the same road where the Mercury Montego was later discovered. Shones' Volkswagen Beetle had got stuck in the snow and he suffered a mild heart attack whilst trying to dislodge it. This forced him to spend the night in his car. As he convalesced, he awoke at around 2am to the sound of strange whistling nearby. He looked out of the window and reported seeing several men and a woman holding a baby, backlit by a pair of car headlights about 100 feet away.

Hoping to get assistance, Shones called out for help, but instead, the group of strangers rushed back towards their car and the lights vanished in an eerie silence. Later that same night, he was awoken again by lights at his window, and more whistling sounds, but didn't know who or what was responsible. At 5am, Shones' ran out of fuel and his car engine, which had been keeping him warm, cut out. He was forced to walk back to a lodge, eight miles down the trail, in the freezing cold. Along the way he noticed the Montego sitting quietly on the road but thought nothing of it at the time. Shones' story appeared to fit with several early reports of men allegedly confronting the five boys in the parking lot at Chico University. People at a nearby lodge in Brownsville believed they had seen the boys stop by to make phone calls, but without proper leads and no further information, Shones' testimony did not lead to anything further. There is speculation that not everything was as it seemed, and if we examine the evidence further, there is possibly a much more sinister twist to this story.

Posting on a blog in late 2017, a person claiming to be Huett's sister-in-law relayed several pieces of information, which were not reported in the press at the time. She believed that the five men had witnessed an altercation between a woman and another group of men at the basketball game. They had gone to her aid, which had led to a hostile confrontation. Consequently, she claimed, Gary Mathias was thrown off a bridge and died from the fall, whilst his friends panicked and fled for their lives, ultimately driving up the mountain trail and getting lost in the woods. Another small detail which was apparently left out of reports at the time was that shell casings were found at the entrance to the mountain road. Had someone shot a gun at the car as they fled? If so, how do we explain the fact that the boys had visited a store to buy snacks? This hardly seems like the actions of a group fleeing from an adversary, unless this happened before the alleged chase commenced.

Unfortunately, this possibility only raises more questions. There have been many theories regarding what happened that night, from Mathias having a mental breakdown and coercing his friends into going up that road to alien abduction or yetis attacking them in the dark of the forest. As mentioned previously, this case has come to be described as America's own Dyatlov Pass Incident, and it's easy to see why. There are striking similarities between the two; both occurred in the month of February and involved a group of people leaving the safety of a shelter, running off into the wilderness and becoming separated, before dying from exposure to the elements, and with no one in the aftermath understanding why.

The boys from Yuba city, although grown men, were anything but. With the exception of Mathias, and possibly Madruga, they had young, innocent minds and in many ways, were just children. What makes this case so terribly heart-breaking is that we cannot even begin to imagine what their families must have felt and must still be feeling to this day, especially as the events which led to their deaths remain unexplained. Our only hope is that they rest in ever lasting peace and that one day, their families get the answers they have desperately been searching for.

34

THE STRANGE DEATH OF GAURAV TIWARI?

In July 2016, a young ghost hunter died in mysterious circumstances after visiting a supposedly haunted property. Authorities hastily ruled it a suicide, but this was not a satisfactory answer for many people, including those closest to him, who are still trying to understand the strange death of Gaurav Tiwari.

Arya glanced up from the magazine she was reading and looked across the room at the clock on the opposite wall. It had been nearly an hour since her husband had finally risen from his bed and lumbered into the shower, but he had yet to make his way downstairs, where she was sat waiting with Uday, his father. That said, given the events of the previous evening, this was perhaps unsurprising. Despite having obtained his pilot's license whilst studying abroad in the US, and successfully auditioning for speaking roles in a few Bollywood movies, Gaurav Tiwari instead chose to spend his time chasing reports of ghostly manifestations and other paranormal encounters.

This was hardly a career choice that paid the family bills, and when he had returned home at 2am from yet another investigation, she had decided it was time to make her feelings known. The subsequent argument had lasted well into the morning and ended with Gaurav going to sleep on his own in another bedroom. On passing the door to the spare room at 10am, she had found her husband awake, perusing the new emails that +had arrived in his inbox during the previous evening. When Arya had asked him to come and join her downstairs, he had mumbled in reply that he would do so after he'd had a shower, before continuing to trawl through his correspondence.

As she sat on the sofa, dejectedly reflecting on the previous five or six months that the couple had been married, Arya suddenly heard a loud thud above her head. Concerned, she made her way upstairs, to find the spare room empty and the bathroom door closed. Assuming that Gaurav may have dropped something whilst in the shower, she proceeded to knock on the door and call out his name, but there was no reply. On finding that the door was apparently locked from the inside and realising that she could not hear the shower running, Arya had shouted downstairs to Gaurav's father. Moments later he had successfully forced the door open and, simultaneously, they both let out a cry of alarm.

Gaurav Tiwari was lying on his back, gasping for air, and sweating profusely. Arya watched in horror as he clawed desperately at his neck, his eyes bulging in their sockets. An ambulance was called, but the paramedics who arrived at the family home were unable to revive him. As Gaurav's lifeless body was later recovered from the floor, Arya had caught a glimpse of an inexplicable thin line of mysterious dark bruising, that ran around the front of his neck. Her husband had been killed in such a way that offered no reason or explanation for how the incident had occurred.

From an early age, Gaurav had been determined to carve his own path through life. Born in the Indian city of Patna in 1984, he was raised a strict Hindu and came from a wealthy family, with his father serving as the director of an international company. But despite assumptions that he would follow the family career path into big business, as a young boy he instead announced his intention to become a famous actor. As soon as his school years were finally behind him, the teenage Gaurav had immediately started to audition for speaking roles in a wide variety of both film and television productions. But after successfully appearing in a number of major cinematic releases, acting roles unfortunately began to dry up, and he was forced to consider alternative career paths.

He was deeply convinced that he was destined for great things and eventually made the decision to move to America, in order to train as a pilot. And it was whilst living in a shared apartment in Florida, that he had his first encounter with the supernatural. The young Indian student and his housemates began to find their personal possessions mysteriously moved from room to room within the accommodation. Even items that had been securely locked away in drawers and cupboards would somehow mysteriously find their way out into the communal areas. But this was only the start of a much more protracted and intimidating phenomenon.

Items of furniture began to move of their own accord. Doors were observed to open and close when nobody was near them and, at night, the students began to hear the whispering of disembodied voices. These incidents culminated in one of the apartment's inhabitants witnessing a ghostly apparition, apparently move across from one side of his bedroom to the other. But whilst these occurrences proved terrifying for his housemates, they had exactly the opposite effect on the young trainee pilot. Rather than being scared by what he was experiencing, he was instead filled with a burning desire to understand the mechanics of what was taking place. Alongside his flying lessons, he began to research any aspect of the supernatural or paranormal that he could find.

At the same time as he graduated from the MVP Aero Academy in Texas, Gaurav found himself being certified as a Lead Investigator for the US Paranexus Association, an organisation devoted to the research and understanding of unexplained phenomena. Immediately upon returning to his native homeland in 2009, he decided to found an equivalent national body, which he named the Indian Paranormal Society. Gaurav and his team soon found themselves being inundated with reports of inexplicable and terrifying events taking place all over India. At its peak, the organisation was flooded with in excess of 500 phone calls and over 250 emails per day. Far more than it could hope to effectively deal with. And as Gaurav began to tackle the mysteries that were being presented to him, he inadvertently found himself drawn back into a familiar career path.

As the work of the Indian Paranormal Society progressed, their exploits began to attract significant media attention, which then evolved into offers from various television networks, asking that film crews accompany them and record their findings. The team's assignments were soon being documented by the likes of MTV, who went on to broadcast them to a global audience. By 2014, Gaurav Tiwari was something of a household name in his homeland, and he had managed to achieve a prominent position in the field of paranormal analysis and evaluation. His investigations were now no longer limited to India, and he found himself appearing alongside other supernatural experts in television shows being filmed in America, the United Kingdom, and Australia.

One of the reasons that Gaurav proved so appealing to both TV producers and audiences alike was his overwhelming commitment to his craft. He would push himself beyond the boundaries of a normal investigator, trusting his instincts and taking risks that nobody else was prepared to. A perfect example of this was the hour he spent lying alone in a morgue chiller, whilst investigating an abandoned mental institution. Unfortunately, any successful entertainment format immediately spawns imitators, and the market soon became saturated with copycat material from across the globe. Despite successfully capturing a wealth of apparent poltergeist activity and ghostly apparitions on camera, the television appearances started to dry up. Gaurav now found himself returning to the Indian Paranormal Society and its day-to-day activities.

In truth, despite having quite enjoyed the fame and notoriety that his international work had achieved, the ghost-hunter was at his most passionate when pursing the mysteries of his native India. Rather than fully embracing the colourful legends and beliefs of his homeland, Gaurav instead approached each reported incident from a firmly grounded and critical standpoint. He would analyse each investigation to its full extent, exhausting all rational and scientific explanations, before agreeing to allow his team to conduct the religious rituals believed necessary to remove whatever troublesome spirit they had encountered. But in January of 2016, when he married his girlfriend Arya Kashyap, Gaurav soon began to find it difficult to balance his passion for the unexplained with that of his married life.

On the evening of 6th July 2016, he and his colleagues attended a residential property in the Janakpuri neighbourhood of West Delhi. The family who lived there explained to the team that their young daughter was being menaced by an invisible entity. The paranormal investigators spent most of the evening with the family, before blessing the house and leaving. When Gaurav arrived home in the early hours, he was confronted by his angry wife, who demanded that he give up ghost hunting for the sake of their marriage. They argued for two hours, before going to sleep in separate rooms. At 11am the following morning, there was a desperate phone call to the authorities describing how he had been found struggling to breathe in the bathroom, before passing away.

A tearful Arya explained to the attending officers how it was as if some unseen force was preventing her husband from breathing, his face filled with terror as he had fought to stay alive. Uday Tiwari provided an equally disturbing account, describing how his son had seemed worried and distant in the last few weeks of his life, confiding to him that an invisible and negative force was somehow pulling him towards it. The investigating officers were naturally sceptical of such stories and when some of Gaurav's friends and colleagues misguidedly took to social media to inform people that he had died of a heart attack, the police immediately started to suspect a more sinister reason behind his death. All family members living in the Tiwari household were questioned for an eight-hour period and the bathroom was forensically analysed for any signs of foul play.

These interrogations yielded a number of developments, which the police began to work through and evaluate. It became apparent that all was not well within the family, and that Gaurav's refusal to change his employment had resulted in a few aggressive confrontations with both his wife and his father in the weeks leading up to his demise. The cause of death was confirmed as asphyxiation, with the black line of bruising around the victim's neck indicating the use of a ligature of some kind, and yet none had been found either attached to the body or lying anywhere on the bathroom floor itself. In addition to this, Gaurav's colleagues testified that he had consumed his last meal at approximately 6pm on the previous evening. When that food was later found still undigested in his stomach, suspicions were raised that he may have died much earlier than the time his family had reported the incident.

Unable to compile enough evidence in building a prosecution, the police eventually announced that Gaurav had died as a result of suicide, having hanged himself from a cloth found on top of a nearby towel rail. Almost immediately, this verdict was met with suspicion and hostility. There was no known reason for Gaurav to have committed suicide. He had not left a note behind and the fact that he had been checking his emails mere minutes before he died seemed to contradict the idea that he had in any way planned to end his own life. With each year that has passed, new theories have continued to come to light about the truth behind his senseless death. Some commentators claim that a second mobile phone, which allegedly belonged to him, was discovered by the police when they were searching the house. Rumours persist that this was linked to an extra-marital affair which he had been pursuing, and that the family had killed him when they discovered this.

Another hypothesis is that the death was indeed self-inflicted, but that someone within the family had hidden the ligature that Gaurav had used. Suicide is still considered something of a disgrace within Hindu culture. It may have been that Gaurav's relatives were trying to cover up this fact, or that they had chosen to invent the story in order to gain some form of sensationalism, and to forever enshrine his name in the field of paranormal research. Others have pointed to the possibility of autoerotic asphyxiation. But underneath these very earthly explanations, far more sinister and disturbing explanations persist. Many believers in the paranormal have theorised that the malevolent spirit who was terrorising the little girl on the evening of Gaurav's death may have been responsible. Prevented from causing further harm to its intended target, this entity may have decided to pursue and punish Gaurav for possessing the temerity to intervene.

Others believe that Uday's comments indicate that some sinister force may have been stalking his son for a far more protracted period. In subsequent interviews, he alleged that over dinner, Gaurav had sometimes mentioned mysterious and unexplained bruising similar to that which was later found on his neck. He had also seemed jumpy and distracted during his final days, claiming to have witnessed shadowy figures stalking him around the residence.

Over the course of his ghost hunting career, Gaurav Tiwari had apparently visited the scenes of as many as six thousand alleged hauntings. Is it possible that as a result of his repeated encounters with the paranormal, some malevolent force may have taken an unhealthy interest in him? Did this entity's power or control over him somehow increase as time progressed, to a point where it was ultimately able to destroy the subject of its obsession?

In truth, we will likely never know the real cause of Gaurav's death. So much controversy and uncertainty has been generated by the haphazard investigation that it is now almost impossible to distinguish the fact from the fiction. For those who believe in the supernatural, no natural explanation will ever prove satisfactory. On the other hand, those who do not believe in evil spirits feel that the evidence that implicates the rest of the Tiwari family is overwhelming. The only immutable truth of the whole affair is that whatever people's private opinions of Gaurav Tiwari, there is no detracting from the obvious determination and passion that he displayed in his pursuit of the unexplained. He was deeply loved, not only by those closest to him, but also by the countless people he helped during the course of his journey into the unknown.

If there are any positives to be taken from the circumstances surrounding Gaurav's death, it's that it raised the profile of his chosen profession and potentially inspired a new generation of paranormal investigators. Just as we hope that he has found a place of peace since his demise, we also hope that more brave souls will step forward, to fill the void that he left behind.

35
THE MYSTERIOUS DISAPPEARANCE OF FLIGHT 19

In December 1945, five torpedo bombers on a routine patrol over the Bahamas vanished without trace. It was an incident that would kickstart the notoriety surrounding the infamous Bermuda Triangle and even now, more than 70 years later, we are still questioning what caused the mysterious disappearance of Flight 19.

At the western extremity of the Atlantic Ocean, flanked on three sides by the islands of Puerto Rico, Bermuda, and mainland Florida, there is a vast expanse of open water, which has allegedly provided the setting for many strange occurrences. The area, known as the Bermuda Triangle, spans half a million square miles and is home to some of the world's busiest ports and shipping lanes. But during the latter half of the 20th century, The Triangle gained notoriety, as it was increasingly reported that many ships and planes entering the region were mysteriously disappearing without a trace, never to be seen again.

Despite numerous investigations and an apparent rise in the number of reported cases within the last fifty years, it seems very few people have been able to provide a clear and definitive answer regarding these vanishings. Perhaps the most well-known disappearance—a case which singlehandedly kick-started more than half a century of foreboding surrounding the area—is that of Flight 19, a group of five torpedo bombers on a routine patrol flying out of Fort Lauderdale in Florida.

It is a tale which has been told countless times before, in many different incarnations, and unfortunately, like so many mysteries, it has not escaped the hand of embellishment. The sequence of events has become somewhat distorted over time, muddied by inaccuracies and omissions, to the point where it is no longer obvious which version is the truth. Our aim here is to retell it as it was officially reported, dispel any myths, and hopefully give a plausible explanation as to what happened, although we know in our heart of hearts, that this is a mystery which will probably never be solved.

Wednesday 5th December 1945 started out sunny and bright, a typical Florida morning for the ground staff of Naval Air Station Fort Lauderdale, and one which promised excellent flying conditions. A series of bombing exercises were scheduled for that day, to train new crews of student aviators, and command of one of these crews was given to 28-year-old Lieutenant Charles Carroll Taylor. Taylor was an experienced pilot who had served two tours of duty in the Pacific Theatre during World War II. He had accumulated more than two thousand hours flying time and had become a training instructor towards the end of the war.

Aside from four other veteran pilots, most of the airmen were inexperienced fliers, with an average of just twenty to thirty hours flying time a piece, so Taylor certainly had his work cut out. Nevertheless, he was confident they would get the hang of things quickly and by that afternoon they were ready to embark on their training exercise. Flight 19 took off at 2:10pm, comprised of five TBM Grumman Avengers, and made east for Hens and Chicken Shoals in the Bahamas. Their mission was to carry out a mock bombing run at a pre-designated area, then continue 90 degrees east for 73 miles, before turning 346 degrees north to head in that direction for another 73 miles. Finally, they would turn 241 degrees south-west for 120 miles, which would take them back to Fort Lauderdale; a total flight time of around two to three hours.

As the exercise progressed, things appeared to be going smoothly; the squadron arrived at the bombing area and dropped their torpedoes in short order without any issues, but by 3:40pm the first signs that something was amiss began to manifest. Several of the crewmen expressed feelings of discomfort and disorientation and as they made their final turn back towards base, they noticed that hardly anything looked familiar. At the same time, back at Fort Lauderdale, another Avenger Torpedo squadron was airborne and getting ready to head for the bombing range when their commander, Lieutenant Robert Cox, picked up an unnerving distress call from Flight 19.

As Cox later recounted, he overheard an airman desperately asking for a position check, but no one could give an accurate answer. Cox intercepted the transmission and asked what the problem was, and to his surprise, a pilot identifying himself as Lieutenant Taylor responded with an ominous communication that would forever be cemented in Bermuda Triangle lore. He stated:

> *"Both my compasses are out... and I am trying to find Fort Lauderdale, Florida. I'm over land but it is broken. I am sure I'm in The Keys, but I don't know how far down, and I don't know how to get back to Fort Lauderdale."*

Confused by this statement, Cox radioed back to base, which had also been tracking the radio transmissions and requested assistance for the beleaguered flight, then he advised Taylor to put the Sun on his port wing and fly north up the coast of Florida. Meanwhile, ground crew at Port Everglades also monitored transmissions and offered their assistance. Although it was a clear day, Taylor appeared unable to find the sun, but insisted the flight would turn northeast in order to avoid flying over the Gulf of Mexico. To complicate things further, none of the in-flight navigators could accurately place their position either.

Taylor was asked to switch radio frequencies because his signal was fading out, but for inexplicable reasons he insisted on maintaining his current channel, then changed course once more in the hopes of finding a recognisable landmark. By this time, numerous ground bases had been alerted to the squadron's apparent distress, but they could do little more than monitor radio transmissions and soffer course corrections, most of which went unacknowledged as Taylor's frequency faltered. To make matters worse, by 4:30pm the weather began to deteriorate, which meant the crew risked having to navigate in poor conditions, no mean feat for experienced navigators let alone raw recruits, especially during that era.

At 5:15pm, Taylor reported that the flight was going to turn west in order to reach what he assumed would be Florida, but by then Port Everglades had advised their fuel reserves would not hold out for much longer. This situation was confirmed when, five minutes later, Taylor made what would be his last communication to Fort Lauderdale:

> *"We'll continue to fly 270 degrees West until we hit landfall or run out of gas."*

Ground based communications could no longer contact the flight but could still monitor the crewmen conversing amongst themselves for over an hour. By 6:20pm they heard what would be Taylor's last order to his men:

> *"We'll have to ditch unless landfall… When the last plane drops below 10 gallons, we will all go down together."*

And with that, all communication with Flight 19 ended, forever. As the chilling reality struck ground staff a short time later, the full scale of the tragedy was yet to be realised. Even before the flight was registered lost, aircraft and crews from naval bases all over Florida took to the air to search for the missing planes. As the light began to fade, two PBM Martin Mariner aircraft were diverted from their own training flights to assist in the search. At 7pm they split off to cover wider ground, but about thirty minutes later, one of the Mariner's reported a radio check and then, almost immediately, it too went silent.

Naval authorities now had to search for a sixth plane, and for the next five days, hundreds of aircraft scoured the entire area for any sign of what had happened. By the time the search was called off on 10th December, more than 930 sorties had been flown in search of the lost squadron and the missing Mariner plane, but nothing was ever found, and for more than seventy years that has remained the case. Meanwhile, various news outlets had gotten wind of the tragedy and authorities were flooded with questions, which they had no hope of answering at that time. The Navy placed the blame squarely on the shoulders of Lieutenant Taylor, saying that pilot error had led to a miscalculation in navigation and ultimately doomed the flight to a watery grave.

Many refused to accept this, however, pointing out that Taylor and a least four of his crew were highly experienced pilots. They questioned how they could have lost their way so easily, especially on a bright and clear day. Why had Taylor largely ignored the advice given to him by ground crew? Why had his navigational instruments failed so readily and why had he not subsequently relied on the readings of his wingmen? Inevitably, in the years following the incident, many embellishments were added to the story. There were reports of Taylor and his crew expressing that the sea "didn't look as it should" and that "everything appeared strange". There was also an infamous line about them entering "white water" and even being chased by UFOs. The Navy denied that any of these transmissions ever took place, but strange events during that same era do seem to correspond with the notion of something untoward befalling the flight.

There are various reports to suggest that planes were encountering UFOs throughout the 1940s. During the Allied bombing campaign of 1943, Allied and German aircrews allegedly reported seeing strange, glowing craft hovering beside their planes and flying in erratic patterns. Two years after the Flight 19 case, in 1947, American pilot Kenneth Arnold dramatically declared he had encountered a flying saucer over Mount Rainier during a training exercise. Later that year, an unidentified craft supposedly crash-landed near the Roswell Air Base in New Mexico.

Although there is a broad range of theories regarding why disappearances occur in and around The Triangle, UFOs have always been high on the list of suspects, and it didn't take long for people to associate them with the disappearance of Flight 19. Could UFOs or some other strange phenomenon have been responsible for the squadron's vanishing? It is unlikely. None of the reported transmissions mentioned anything about unidentified flying objects or of strange phenomena occurring, but many staunch fringe theorists maintain that the original transmissions had been tampered with to remove any mention of alien craft. They claim that the supposed embellishments are in fact the real communications and that those reported officially are pure fabrication in order to cover up the truth.

Whatever the case, we may never know for sure, but it must be said; the official explanation seems far more grounded in reality. Sceptics have rationalised the actions of Taylor and his men, and presented a theory of what they believe happened, proposing that there really isn't a mystery at all. Many claim that the navigators were too young and inexperienced to properly guide the planes back home, and that others often overlook the fact that the exercise employed a strategic navigational technique called dead reckoning. Dead reckoning is a method in which a navigator uses the sun's position and the local time to establish their current position, and then calculates the location they will be in half an hour's time. In 1945, this technique was far from perfect, and for a rookie navigator, one can only guess how difficult it would have been.

The squadron was also hampered by the fact that none of the planes had timekeeping devices installed and whilst most of the men had their own watches, none of them could find the sun during the latter half of the exercise. Even though the day started out bright and clear, the weather deteriorated later on and, with darkness closing in, attempts to locate a recognisable landmark would have been next to impossible. Another issue that troubles some researchers is that Taylor reported both of his compasses failing without warning, as well as those of his crew. It has been suggested that the Bermuda Triangle possesses certain magnetic qualities which are known to interfere with compass readings, and that ships and planes have fallen victim to the Triangle due to this interference.

The being said, there is no evidence to support this, and what many people fail to realise is that compasses are not infallible. They will invariably give different readings over larger areas, especially one as large as the Bermuda Triangle. Personnel at Fort Lauderdale and Port Everglades triangulated Flight 19's last known position to approximately 80 miles off the coast of Florida, due east of Palm Bay. It is believed that after the squadron had finished the first leg of its mission, instead of turning 346 degrees north-northwest, they had in fact, turned 45 degrees to the northeast, which took them over Great Abaco Island instead of Grand Bahama.

From the air, Great Abaco Island would have looked very much like Grand Bahama and none of the crew would have been any the wiser about their mistake, especially if they believed their compasses were malfunctioning. After they had turned 241 degrees to the southwest, thinking they were now heading back to Fort Lauderdale, they would have instead flown over the outlying Abaco islands in the north, known as the Fish and Pensacola Cays, and this is where the confusion began.

The Cays are a long, outstretched chain of islands much like the Florida Keys and from the air, they look very similar. Taylor mentioned specifically in his communication that he thought he was over The Keys and at that point, must have believed his compass was so far out of sync that the flight had actually turned southwest after the bombing exercise, towards the Gulf of Mexico. How he accounted for the fact that they had arrived over The Keys in half the time it should have taken them is anyone's guess, but perhaps he assumed they had picked up a tail wind.

If Taylor did believe he was over the Keys, then this would explain why he briefly turned due west before heading northeast; he was hoping to hit mainland Florida, but in reality, was flying further out into the Atlantic Ocean. This is supported by the fact that Cox had begun to fly south in the hopes of locating the lost squadron but found that his communication with Taylor was deteriorating. This suggests that Flight 19 was flying in the opposite direction to him and was nowhere near The Keys. With Flight 19 now over open water, they made a number of course changes in the hopes of finding the mainland, but ultimately ran out of fuel and had to ditch in the ocean.

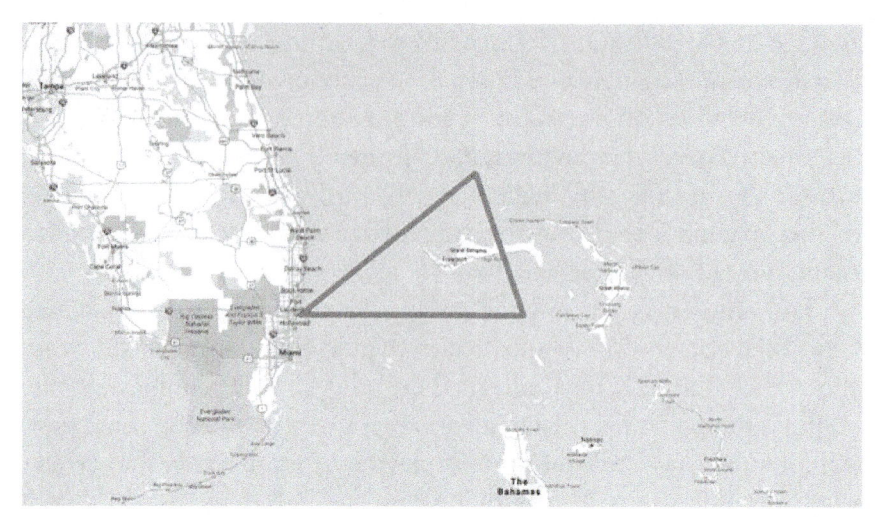

Fig. 22 - *The intended route of Flight 19*

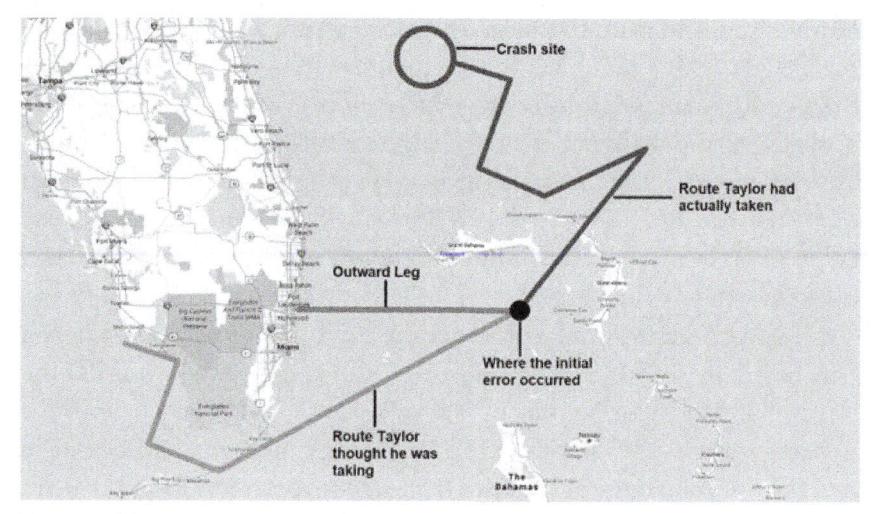

Fig. 23 - *The route Taylor thought he had taken by mistake vs. the route he had actually taken*

Several transmissions were heard in which frustrated junior aviators tried to get Taylor to head west, believing they were heading in the wrong direction to begin with, but he insisted they continue on their course. Many have questioned why they didn't simply change course themselves, but the crew had started to panic, and in their desperation, had probably turned to Taylor—the most seasoned and experienced pilot—to lead them back to land. This, coupled with their training and discipline, probably prevented them from going against his orders.

One of the biggest questions of all is why no trace of the doomed flight was ever found? A five-day search in all directions should have turned up at least something, rubber life rafts or the crew floating helplessly in the water, but there are those who suggest that once the planes had ditched in the ocean the men had likely perished on impact; the Avenger did not have the best record for landing on water. Perhaps the crews had escaped their planes, but then fell victim to sharks, injury, or even fatigue and slipped beneath the waves. As mentioned previously, The Triangle is said to encompass almost a half-million square miles of open water, and even for a case such as this, the chances of finding survivors—whilst not impossible—must have looked bleak at best.

However, debris was found in the area where the Mariner aircraft was last reported but was never confirmed to be part of that plane; it sank below the waves before it could be examined. It is worth mentioning that the PBM Martin Mariners were prone to fuel leaks, and a random spark could ignite the aircraft mid-flight. As a matter of fact, the crew of the tanker SS Gaines Mills reported an explosion in mid-air at the same time the plane fell off the radar and in exactly the same area it was last reported. This seems rather conclusive and although the cause of this aircraft's disappearance was not related to that of Flight 19's, it was nevertheless a tragic coincidence that they both vanished on the same day and over the same expanse of water.

Whilst we can only surmise the true cause of these disappearances, whether an unfortunate sequence of events or something more sinister and unexplained, it seems that the mystery surrounding this case and that of The Triangle itself are inextricably linked. As one gains in notoriety, so too does the other. Many believe that finding the missing squadron will somehow yield the key to solving, and thus understanding, why the Triangle has become such an enigma.

The TBM Avenger was responsible for sinking both Yamato Class Battleships of the Imperial Japanese Navy during the Pacific War, an amazing achievement in itself, but one which is unfortunately overshadowed by the infamy of this tragic incident. We must also take a moment to remember each of these men; young, confident American boys, who boldly took off from the tarmac at Fort Lauderdale and flew out into that vast shimmering horizon, seeking only to serve their country and honour their family name. They could never have known their fate, but perhaps one day, we will.

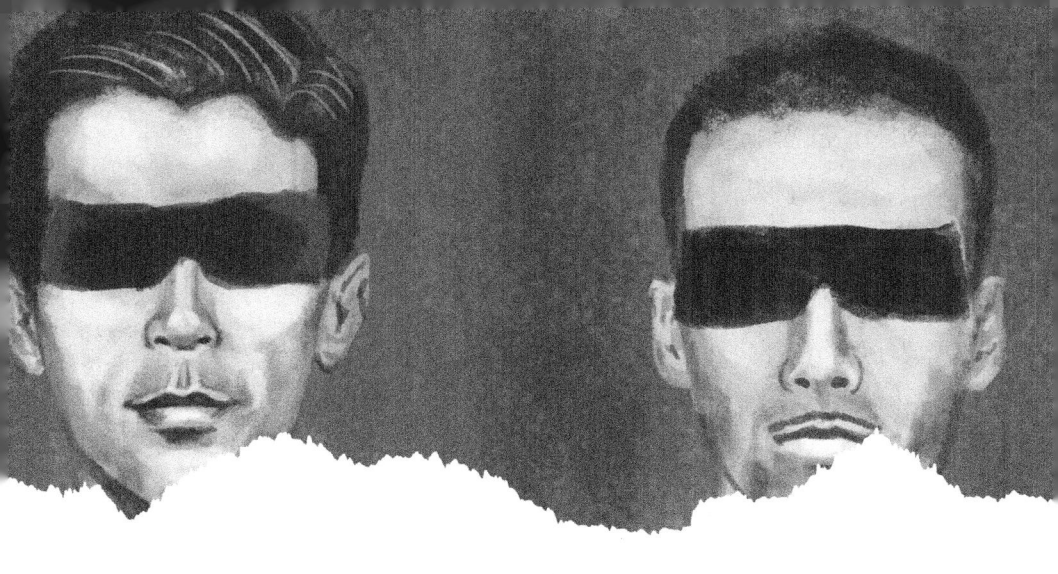

36
THE LEAD MASKS OF VINTÉM HILL

During August of 1966, the dead bodies of two men were found on a hillside in Brazil. Much of what was discovered at the scene would leave authorities baffled and has never been fully understood. What we are left with is a fifty-year-old mystery known as the lead masks of Vintém Hill.

Rio de Janeiro. Literally translated, it means "River of January". Except there is no such water source. When Portuguese explorer Gaspar de Lemos landed on the shores of Brazil in January of 1501, he mistook the huge natural harbour to be the mouth of an almighty river and named it after the month in which it was discovered. He did not come to realise his mistake until much later and yet the name stuck. Today, Rio de Janeiro is one of the most prominent states in the entire country and its very name evokes images of a lush tropical paradise, home to stunning beaches, vibrant blue seas and, of course, beautiful people.

Despite being one of the smallest of the 27 federative units of Brazil, it has the second largest economy, third largest population and is home to no fewer than 20 cities, the most notable of which is, of course, the state's namesake. But just off to the east of that sprawling metropolis lies Niterói, a thriving municipality in its own right. During the 60's, Niterói was barely recognisable compared to how it appears today. Back then it was an under-developed, poverty-stricken town, suffering all the drawbacks of rapid industrialisation, which would ultimately enable its growth into the important financial and commercial centre it has become. It was also the scene of one of the strangest and most enduring mysteries in Brazil's modern history; a case known internationally as The Lead Masks of Vintém Hill.

The late afternoon of Saturday 20th August 1966 was uncharacteristically hot considering it was mid-winter in the Southern Hemisphere. The skies had been clear with a heavy sun beating down after a long spell of torrential rain. As a result, the air in Niteroi had become still and humid as excess moisture evaporated into the atmosphere and with not even the gentlest of breezes to offer any kind of reprieve from the sticky heat. The high rise of Vintém Hill, on the other hand, was far removed from the streets below. Here, a young boy was flying his kite, running through the long grass, whooping and cheering with delight. At this altitude, the winds could be felt coming in off the bay, which were both cool and refreshing, and perfect for the kite's uplift.

As he traversed the slopes, tugging on the long string outstretched behind him, he noticed an odd depression in the grass, in which lay a dark heap that looked unnatural in amongst its surroundings. He decided to investigate and as he began to approach, he could make out various items of clothing. At first, he assumed that someone had dumped their unwanted garments on the hillside, but as he got closer, he found lying inside of those garments the decomposing bodies of two men, accompanied by the nauseating scent of death. Alarmed by his discovery, he rushed back home and told his parents, who wasted no time in notifying the local police station. Unfortunately, as it was now early evening, and due to the failing light and difficult terrain, authorities were not able to reach the bodies until the following day. Early on the morning of 21st August, several police officers and firemen arrived on the hillside, where they were greeted by an odd scene, to say the least.

The two bodies were found lying next to each other in a small depression and were partially covered by the long grass. They were dressed in formal suits, each wearing a raincoat, and next to them lay an empty water bottle and a package containing two wet towels. However, the strangest thing about them—and the very attribute that gave this case its name—was that both men were wearing small lead masks over their eyes, which appeared to have been crudely cut from sheet metal. In the pockets of the men's raincoats, police also found a few receipts and a notebook which contained what was believed to be a list of alphanumerical codes and a set of instructions. These instructions read:

> "16:30 be at the specified location. 18:30 ingest capsules, after the effect protect metals await signal mask"

Suffice it to say, authorities were mystified by these findings, but were soon able to identify the bodies as those of Manoel Pereira da Cruz and Miguel José Viana, two electrical technicians from Campos dos Goytacazes, a small town, 170 miles north-east of the city of Rio de Janeiro. There were no signs of violence or of a struggle, and the men carried very little on them in the way of money or valuables. Shortly after they were discovered, the bodies were sent to the local coroner's office for autopsy, but because the coroner was busy with other cases at the time, they were not examined until a number of weeks later. By that stage, their internal organs had decomposed to the point where it was impossible to determine how exactly the two men had died.

Authorities instead concentrated their efforts on trying to understand the movements and intentions of da Cruz and Viana, and they hoped that this would shed some light on the mystery. Police spoke to several witnesses in Niterói who claimed to have seen the two men in the days leading up to their deaths and from these accounts, they were able to piece together a timeline of events. It is believed that da Cruz and Viana travelled by bus from Campos to Niterói on the 17th August, carrying enough cash to purchase a used car. This information was ascertained from their business account, which showed a single withdrawal of a large sum of money. What they intended to do with this money is anyone's guess, but it is widely assumed that they were interested in purchasing electronic parts for their business.

Following this, they arrived in Niterói at 2:30pm that afternoon and the receipts found on their bodies indicated that they had purchased their raincoats from a local shop. Soon after, they walked to a bar further up the street, where one of them ordered a bottle of water. The waitress there stated that both men seemed agitated, particularly Viana whom she noticed glancing nervously around the establishment, checking his watch every few minutes. The last time they were seen alive, they were riding in the back of a jeep driven by two other men, heading to an unknown location, although authorities speculated that their intended destination would have been the foot of Vintém Hill.

What happened from that point onward is a complete and utter mystery, and for the last 50 years or so, that has remained the case. But the questions surrounding their deaths are still as prevalent today as they were all those years ago. Why had they travelled to Niterói? Who were they supposed to meet? Why had they donned those lead masks? And to what did those codes and instructions in the notebook pertain? As with any bizarre or unexplained death, there inevitably comes a torrent of speculation, especially from those within the Fortean community, and it was no different with this case. Brazil is a hotbed for strange events, so it comes as no surprise that a supernatural angle has been applied to this story.

The theory goes that da Cruz and Viana were not your average electronic repairmen. They were in fact highly trained technicians who had used their expertise to engineer a means of contacting extra-terrestrial beings and that they had arranged to meet these beings on Vintém Hill. Both men had been given a specific set of instructions and after this process had been followed, it is postulated that their physical bodies ceased to function and that their minds had been transported into some kind of extra-terrestrial afterlife, existing forevermore in a realm of infinite knowledge and consciousness. And as unbelievable as this sounds, investigators have found other elements of the story, which seem to corroborate connections with the supernatural.

At least two reputable newspapers reported at the time that a resident had seen a bright orange spheroid-shaped UFO hovering over

Vintém Hill on the same evening that da Cruz and Viana went up there. Secondly, a close friend of the two men, Elcio Gomes, stated that the three of them were all part of a local group calling themselves "Spiritual Scientists". He said that two months prior to their deaths, they had built a device in their backyard which they had apparently used to contact other-worldly beings, but that it exploded shortly afterwards. With this in mind, our attention is once again drawn to the writings in the notebook.

It was stated that there was a list of alphanumerical codes and some have theorised that these were encrypted messages received via their device, which translated into the given instructions. If we are to look at those instructions again, it doesn't require much of an imagination to see how such an extraordinary theory has been put forth.

> *"16:30 be at the specified location. 18:30 ingest capsules, after the effect protect metals await signal mask"*

This is exactly how the instructions were written down and, as it stands, the latter half of the sentence does not make a lot of sense. However, if we apply some speculative punctuation, the meaning becomes a little clearer:

> *"16:30 be at the specified location. 18:30 ingest capsules, after the effect, protect metals. Await signal. Mask."*

Exactly what the capsules were or how da Cruz and Viana had come by them is unknown. Nothing of the sort was found on their bodies and it seems obvious that the men must have ingested them as instructed. And as those capsules remain unidentified, it is difficult to determine what effect they were supposed to have. The "protect metals" line seems a little more cryptic, but as no valuables were found on either man, some have speculated that they were being instructed to remove their watches, rings, or any other kinds of jewellery and that perhaps these were to be wrapped in the towels found next to the bodies.

Finally, whatever signal they were supposed to look out for is also a mystery, but the word "mask" obviously refers the small lead cut-outs which covered their eyes. These masks had no functionality whatsoever; they were not see-through, and they had no stems to hook over the ears, so clearly, they were not meant to be worn for any extended period of time. Instead, their crude design points to the possibility that they were intended to briefly protect the eyes from an intense and blinding light source. And according to many a proponent of this theory, that light source would have been none other than a UFO.

But are we to accept this theory based solely on anecdotal and circumstantial evidence? It seems there are many more people who are sceptical about this version of events and believe that the deaths of these men have a far more rational and, indeed, earthly explanation. They believe that da Cruz and Viana were simply duped into coming to the hill where they were killed and robbed of their belongings. It has been suggested that they were targeted by a group of criminals, who saw them as naive and easy prey. This group probably cultivated da Cruz and Viana's trust over a period of weeks or months, promising to put them in contact with extra-terrestrials or to allow them to partake in some other form of spiritual enlightenment.

They then provided them with the capsules and a set of instructions just unusual enough to suggest that they were going to experience something extraordinary. Those capsules were more than likely a form of poison and once the two men had ingested them and died on the spot, someone from the group arrived to collect their money and valuables. It should be noted that all the cash the men had on them when they arrived in Niterói—at least 3 million cruzeiros—was never found. Neither were any of their belongings. And if we add to this the fact that another man—also an electronics technician—was found dead four years earlier on top of a different hill, wearing a similar lead mask, then suddenly this theory seems to gain more traction.

Again, much of this is pure speculation, and even if the evidence supporting the idea of a robbery is pretty damning, how could two men, who were intelligent, technically minded individuals be so naive as to fall for such an obvious ploy? And what about the codes also found in their notebook? Does their existence prove that the instructions were received via an encrypted transmission rather than face to face communication? It seems not, as those codes were later identified as part numbers of various electronic components and had no relation to anything else in the investigation.

Yet how do we explain the UFO seen above the hill on the night of the men's deaths? We should stress that this was witnessed by only one person. And if there is one thing we have learned during our research on many strange events, it is that UFOs are reported almost invariably in the aftermath of something unexplained. This is not to cast doubt on the individual's claim, but we feel we must be honest about the nature of such things. When all facts are considered, this case does seem to have foul play written all over it, although we shouldn't dismiss other theories out of hand. The assumption is often made that extra-terrestrials would have no interest in money or valuables, but who really knows for sure?

If some other eyewitness accounts are to be taken seriously, in which people have allegedly seen aliens posing as human beings, then surely, they would need such items in order to blend in. In any case, whether there was something more sinister going on and the truth has simply been covered up, or their deaths were the direct result of foul play, both possibilities are equally disturbing. Unfortunately, as intelligent as da Cruz and Viana may have been, their belonging to a group calling themselves "Spiritual Scientists" demonstrates that they had a desire to believe in something more. And as we are aware, beliefs are often strong enough to defy and override simple logic, making them difficult for an individual to let go of.

It could be that they were so enamoured with the idea of a higher intelligence and a never-ending pursuit of knowledge that they allowed themselves to suspend all cynicism and critical thought, which otherwise might have saved them. If the idea of robbery is to be accepted, then it is truly sad that two innocent men lost their lives over something as trivial as money. Gone from this world their physical bodies may be, but their spirits will forever rest on the slopes where they died, overlooking the city of Niterói, as a cool, lonely breeze rolls in off the bay of the "January River" and silently whispers through the long grass of Vintém Hill.

37
THE CURSE OF ATUK

Over the course of nearly two decades, seven celebrities lost their lives in tragic circumstances. The one thing they all had in common? Each of them had at one point or another, read the same film script. We question whether there is any substance to the ominous curse of Atuk.

Across the civilized world, the written word is one of the most prevalent of all forms of communication. It has been for thousands of years, and it will be for thousands more. From the writings of Homer, Aristotle, and Plato through to Shakespeare, Dostoevsky, and Tolkien, the written word has shaped our cultures, our societies, and philosophies. It has begun and ended wars, traversed space and time, and recorded our most cherished and reviled histories. The written word has taught us who we are, who we were, and who we will become. On average, each of us writes and consumes between ten and twenty thousand words per day, whether that be through writing posts, comments, texts, or emails, or reading books, newspapers, and online articles.

All too often, it seems we forget that the pen is far mightier than the sword. Screenwriter Tod Carroll was one man who would discover this in the strangest of ways. In 1977, he was commissioned by Canadian film director Norman Jewison to adapt a novel he had finished reading, Modercai Richler's *The Incomparable Atuk*. An accomplished writer himself, Carroll took on the project and immediately set to work drafting a film script, believing the story had the makings of a blockbuster film.

Titled simply *Atuk*, the story itself is a rather simple fish-out-of-water expository piece, filled with satire and scathing social commentary. In the story, Atuk is a young Inuit trapper and hunter who meets and follows a beautiful New York correspondent named Michelle Robinson. Michelle is on an assignment in his village to shoot several commercials for a real estate company. Atuk soon arrives in New York City where he rescues the son of a powerful but corrupt real estate mogul, who also happens to be Michelle's employer. The man then hires him to appear in a series of commercials aimed at convincing the public to back his latest idea, building a modern-day metropolis in the heart of the Alaskan wilderness. Atuk naively agrees to become part of the project after learning of Michelle's involvement, but when he discovers the venture's true purpose, which is to raze and destroy much of the ecosystem there, Atuk withdraws and informs the investors who are oblivious to the negative repercussions the venture could result in. Atuk's honesty and dedication wins over the executives, as well as Michelle, thus saving his village and getting the girl in the end.

By and large a typical coming of age story with no sinister implications, Carroll was exceptionally proud of his work. Yet he could never have known the havoc his screenplay would wreak upon those who became involved with it. After undergoing several rewrites, Carroll presented his final draft in 1979 and then sent word to actor-comedian John Belushi, a personal friend whom he'd had in mind from the outset to read the finished piece. Carroll had envisioned Belushi for the role of Atuk, and reportedly Belushi loved the concept. In late 1981 he agreed to play the main character in the film, but tragically, this would never come to pass.

On the morning of 5th March 1982, Belushi's friend and trainer, Bill Wallace, walked into his room at the Chateau Marmont Hotel in Hollywood to find the actor lying dead on the floor. After police were summoned and his body was taken to hospital, an autopsy was performed which found he had died from a combined overdose of cocaine and heroin. Belushi was just 33 years old. The investigation revealed that a groupie named Catherine Evelyn Smith had spent the night with him and had produced the lethal mixture, but she claimed she had given him a high dose purely by accident. In the years that followed there would be reason to suspect otherworldly entities were responsible.

Although Belushi's death would normally have ended the project altogether, in 1987 United Artists purchased the script and brought it to the attention of another actor-comedian named Sam Kinison. Kinison accepted the lead role and production started the following year, but very little was accomplished. Kinison's unreliability on the set, in addition to his extended alcoholism and argumentative nature, resulted in a clash with the film's financial executives, who immediately terminated the project after filming only one scene. Some accounts of the story say that Kinison had grown dissatisfied with the original script and had secretly commissioned an independent rewrite. It was even suggested that he appeared on the set with the new script in hand, and when executives learned of this, they reportedly fired him on the spot. Although he was no longer part of the film by the end of the decade, some believe that Kinison's insistence in deviating from the original work resulted in what followed next.

On 10th April 1992, Kinison and his entourage were driving along Interstate 95 towards Laughlin, Nevada, for a sold-out performance when a drunk driver drifted into his lane and collided head-on with Kinison's car. Although he was able to step out of the vehicle and walk around, he had sustained severe head and neck injuries which eventually proved fatal. As he lay dying in the arms of one of his friends on the scene, Kinison was heard to say, "I don't want to die, I don't want to die," as though he were pleading with someone only he could see. After a while, the invisible presence apparently responded, for Kinison was then heard to softly reply, "Okay, okay...okay..." and then quietly died. He was just 38 years old.

Once his death was made public, some people in the know came to believe the Atuk script had had something to do with his death, in the same manner as Belushi, but most did not give this thought any credence. That was until the screenplay fell into the hands of another iconic film star, John Candy. Candy learned of the project in 1993 and requested a copy of the script. Not long after receiving it, he agreed to become involved in the film and accepted the lead role. He then headed south to Mexico to complete what would be his final film, *Wagons East*, but on 4th March 1994, whilst on holiday from filming in Durango, Candy was found dead in his hotel room from apparent cardiac arrest. He was just 43.

It was from this point onwards that the "Curse of Atuk" was born, and students of the occult would later claim that Candy's untimely death was the result of his simply having the work in his hands. How it came into his hands has also become a matter of debate, as some believe he first learned of the project shortly after Kinison was released from the film, but the popular belief is that comedy writer Michael O'Donoghue gave him the script. O'Donoghue had allegedly been involved in the initial stages of the script's writing back when Tod Carroll had first worked on it and had supposedly delivered the script to Belushi in 1981. In 1994 he presented the script to Candy and discussed several changes he was considering, changes which Candy had apparently agreed to. This theory, however, cannot be proven, for eight months after Candy's death, O'Donoghue himself died of a brain haemorrhage on 8th November 1994, another purported victim of the curse. He was 54.

Then, in 1996, United Artists elected to begin a new project based on the Atuk screenplay. They approached comedian Chris Farley to play Atuk, and all indications suggested he was eager to become involved. Farley had been a lifelong fan of John Belushi and modelled his career on that of the late actor. Perhaps he learned that his idol had at one point been involved with the project and thought to honour him by playing the role he never got to perform, but whether this was the case or not will never be known.

Chris Farley had suffered from extreme obesity, took drugs, and drank excessively, and this had resulted in a sharp decline in his health. By early November 1997, it was clear that his condition had gotten out of control and attempts were made by friends and family to get him help. Farley's brother John took him to Chicago, to receive treatment at the John Hancock Centre, but it might have been too little too late. On the night of 18th December 1997 Farley had returned to his apartment accompanied by a call girl and spent the night drinking excessively and taking large amounts of drugs. At some point after 2am, Farley suddenly suffered a massive heart seizure and collapsed, begging his female companion to get him help, which she refused to do. He eventually succumbed to the heart attack and died.

When the coroner performed the autopsy the following day, he found that Farley had ingested a heavy dose of cocaine and heroin, but the autopsy also revealed a large build-up of atherosclerosis in his arteries, a condition which had been worsening for quite some time. Farley, much like his beloved idol Belushi, died at the age of 33. Sadly, it was not long before another victim came to be connected with the rumoured Curse of Atuk, and whilst the deaths mentioned already are tragic in their own right, by far and away the death of Phil Hartman is one of the most heart-breaking.

Hartman had worked extensively with Farley on the TV show *Saturday Night Live,* and it was Farley who had allegedly wanted them to work together on the Atuk project, telling Hartman that the role of Alexander McKuen, the film's villain, was a perfect fit for the actor. Hartman apparently read the script and expressed his interest. He suggested they start work in 1997—the year Farley died. In May 1998, Hartman's own end came about after he threatened to leave his wife Brynn after a series of heated arguments in response to her out of control drug abuse. The couple's marriage had been difficult for several years and whilst Brynn had been hooked on alcohol and drugs, she was also experiencing problems with controlling her anger. Despite these issues Hartman bravely attempted to keep the marriage from falling apart, but not even he was prepared for what happened next.

On the night of 28th May 1998, Hartman went to bed after another row with his wife, whom he had caught drinking after coming home from a late meeting. At three in the morning, she entered their bedroom, pulled out a handgun and shot him three times at point blank range as he slept, killing him instantly. He was 49. After fleeing to a neighbour's house, Brynn confessed to killing her husband and when they returned to the scene of the crime she was heard to declare: "I told you I did it! I told you I did! I killed him! I killed him and I don't know why I did it!" Her neighbour escorted the couple's children out of the house whilst she barricaded herself in the bedroom, and when police arrived on the scene, they heard her shouting these same words again before she turned the gun on herself.

With the news of Hartman and his wife's deaths, proponents of the script's curse were fully convinced that something otherworldly was at play, prompting them to make entreaties to have the script seized and secured. Although they continued to refute the claims of the supernatural, United Artists' executives quietly ordered a seizure of the script and hid it away in one of their main offices, even though several copies are allegedly available elsewhere.

So, what are we to take away from this story? Is the curse of Atuk simply an urban legend, or have we connected a set of dots that seem to indicate something foreboding? Is the Atuk script so truly cursed that anyone could die just from reading it? And if that is the case, what dark forces are at play and why would they go so far as to bring harm to others? When looking at the deaths of John Belushi, Sam Kinison, John Candy, Michael O'Donoghue, Chris Farley, and Phil Hartman, several things do stick out as coincidental and make us question whether a curse was really to blame.

Consider that each of these men were performers who dealt heavily with drug use and personal addictions. Both Belushi and Farley dabbled in cocaine and heroin, amongst other drugs, and lived painfully depressed lives in private. Candy and Farley each suffered from morbid obesity in the final years of their lives, whilst O'Donoghue spent the latter part of his career dealing with migraine headaches, which undoubtedly required him to rely on prescription medication. Sam Kinison was also known to be a heavy drinker throughout his career, and whilst Hartman himself took few if any drugs, his wife had a deadly relationship with cocaine which might have driven her to kill him. But these situations are not unique, nor are they the first of their kind.

Hollywood is, after all, a harsh environment to work in, and oftentimes the workload is excessive and can take a huge toll on an actor's health and wellbeing. Some will seek the comfort of drugs in order to cope with the stress and pain, so it stands to reason that these deaths, like others before them, were somewhat inevitable. If we follow this line of thought, then it can be argued that the Curse of Atuk is nothing more than an urban legend. And yet, evidence to the contrary is not so easy to ignore.

Some researchers have theorised that part of the reason for the curse taking hold was that they had each made suggestions to alter or change key details in the screenplay. No one knows exactly how many drafts Carroll's original script underwent, but it is well-known that both Kinison and O'Donoghue attempted to make changes to the final work, and in the case of Kinison he even had the entire script rewritten to better suit his role. Another argument in favour of a supernatural explanation is the fact that most of the victims died rather young. None of the actors lived past the age of sixty, and if this was the work of the curse, it suggests their deaths were somewhat preordained. Some were even unnatural, with Belushi and Farley dying from similar accidental overdoses, Kinison was killed in a car accident, and Hartman was murdered by his wife following a heated argument which turned violent.

Finally, the common thread that linked them all together was the fact that they all had, at one point or another, worked on the television show *Saturday Night Live*, appearing as guest stars or hosts. John Belushi and Michael O'Donoghue had even worked as original sketch writers for the series, whilst Farley died one month after his final appearance on the show in October 1997. Parallels have been drawn between the Atuk script and the infamous Hungarian song "Gloomy Sunday", which purportedly caused anyone who listened to it to commit suicide for almost no apparent reason. But some researchers theorise the song works on the human senses and stimulates certain vibrations within the brain.

Can a screenplay be capable of such a thing as well? If the Curse of Atuk did have something to do with these deaths, does that mean the script is dangerous? Tod Carroll, the screenwriter, denies such allegations to this day, and states that no one has died from reading his screenplay. Several known film executives are also in agreement, but if that is truly the case, why is the original script locked away? And if they truly believe there is no curse, why are none of them willing to resume the project?

Perhaps in this modern world, where Hollywood seems to have lost its creative spark and refuses to take risks, it could be that Atuk is no longer seen as a lucrative venture. It was written for a different audience of a different era and perhaps it would seem out of place in cinemas today. When all is said and done, the fact remains that, in all, seven people who were linked in one way or another to this script lost their lives and that in and of itself is tragic. Whatever the cause of their untimely deaths, we must spare a thought for them and their loved ones. May they each rest in everlasting peace.

38
THE WATERVALE RUNNER

Somewhere in South Australia, a small town holds a mystery in the palm of its hand. The disappearance of a young woman in October 2016 would turn the community upside-down and leave residents and local police questioning what happened to the Watervale Runner.

There is no denying that Australia is as stunningly beautiful as it is unique. From it's weird and wonderful wildlife to its rich and diverse landscapes unlike those of any other nation, the land down under is truly one of a kind. And yet such a huge landmass has such a relatively small population. The country's interior, known as The Outback, is a boiling, inhospitable desert, and so, more than 24 million people live their lives in the more forgiving climates near the coasts, which range from tropical to temperate. Many towns and cities are vast distances apart, divided across just six states. A truly fascinating place, Australia is also a bit of an enigma, much like the following tale, which comes to us courtesy of 26-year-old Jenny Roth.

The story takes place in Watervale, a small town situated in the Clare Valley of South Australia, a region famous for its vineyards and wine distilleries. With a climate not too dissimilar to Northern

California, the lush green valleys and quiet country roads seem like the last place you would expect to hear of any sinister happenings, but as we shall see, looks can be deceiving. What follows is a tale that defies belief and sends an ominous chill up the spine. And it all began on the evening of 29th September 2016.

Jenny had not lived in the area long, just a couple of months. She had moved from Adelaide with her girlfriend Abigail to be close to her partner's terminally ill father and, being a city girl since the day of her birth, the quietness of the countryside had been something of a shock to the system. The nights were dark. Darker than anything she had ever known. And life away from the hustle and bustle of a big city was not only an inconvenience, but also terribly boring. There were upsides to this relative isolation, however. The air was fresh and clean, the landscapes were beautiful, and there seemed to be a quiet harmony—a peacefulness—to everything. She had grinned from ear to ear the first time she heard the chorus of crickets after sunset.

The people were much friendlier too; she and Abigail had only been living there a few days before the neighbours arrived on the doorstep to say hello and welcome them to their small town. She had struck up something of a friendship with Marie from next door and they would often catch each other for a chat whenever Jenny went outside for a smoke. Marie, being the outdoorsy type, was nearly always pottering around in the garden, weeding, or digging, or cutting the lawn.

On this particular evening, Jenny stepped out onto the front porch for her customary post-dinner cigarette to find her neighbour getting ready to go for her customary evening run. They spoke casually for a few minutes and, as always, Marie invited Jenny to go along with her. As always, Jenny politely declined. It wasn't that she was averse to running as such, but as it was just after 6pm in late September, the sun would be setting in little over an hour and she already found the darkness and remoteness of the countryside unnerving as it was.

"Suit yourself," said Marie. "See you later." And with that she hopped off her porch and jogged away.

Jenny lit her cigarette and inhaled deeply as she watched her neighbour leave. She knew where Marie would be heading. Her route usually took her outside the small town of Watervale, along miles of dusty country roads surrounded by open fields, speckled with thickets of trees and small woodlands. Beyond all that, loomed a massive expanse of grassland and untamed bush, with only a few pockets of civilisation dotting the landscape, as wide open and stunning as it was intimidating.

Jenny could well appreciate why Marie insisted upon her evening runs and wondered briefly whether she could ever get used to living in a place like this. It was a nice change from what she and Abigail were used to, but something about this town made her feel exposed, both mentally and physically. In the end she decided no. Besides anything else, there wasn't enough in this small town to keep her occupied. Watervale was just one of those places where nothing ever happened. And with that thought still echoing somewhere in the recesses of her mind, she stubbed out the butt of her cigarette and headed indoors, completely unaware of just how wrong she would be.

The morning of 30th September started out bright and clear, and Jenny was pulling freshly laundered clothes out of the washing machine ready to hang out on the line in the backyard. She grabbed her cup of coffee along with the laundry basket and exited the house through the side door. She was surprised to see Marie sitting outside on the lawn, stock still and staring at the ground. It was rare for her neighbour to be up so early and it was even more unusual to see her sitting doing nothing in particular; she was usually always attending to some chore or another. Nevertheless, Jenny called out a greeting. But Marie appeared not to have heard her.

She called again, and this time her friend stirred and shook her head as if she had just been pulled from some deep trance. Marie apologised, saying she must have been miles away. But this was all she said before she slipped back into her reverie. Any attempts at idle chit-chat turned out to be in vain as Jenny quickly realised that her friend was far too preoccupied for conversation. So instead, she proceeded to hang out her washing, but every now and then she glanced over the fence at Marie, who continued to sit there in silence, frowning at the ground. Something was indeed troubling her. Before heading indoors, Jenny stopped and considered her neighbour for a moment, then asked if everything was okay.

"I'm fine," came the reply, but the tone of Marie's voice suggested otherwise. Needless to say, Jenny was not convinced and decided to push the boundaries of their newly formed friendship by probing what was on her mind. It took a little persuasion, but after a minute or two of gentle encouragement, Marie's shoulders finally drooped in resignation and she let out a soft, but audible sigh. "You won't believe me, but then Roger didn't either, so what the hell..."

Somewhat apprehensively, she began to relate what had happened. She told Jenny that whilst on her run the previous evening, she had been out a couple of miles west of Spring Gully as the sun was just touching upon the horizon, when she looked out across a wide-open field and saw three objects hovering close to the ground, about 300 metres away from where she was. She had stopped dead, mouth agape, just watching as they floated, still and silent. They stayed there for about two or three minutes before slowly moving off, disappearing over the treeline at the other side of the field.

Marie went on to say that they were unlike any aircraft she had seen before, they were each about 50 feet wide, metallic, and circular in shape, and that they didn't make any sound whatsoever, even as they moved. Even though she expressed that she didn't believe in aliens, she firmly believed that what she saw was not of this world. There was just something unnatural about the way they behaved, which had deeply affected her. Jenny did not doubt her friend's story. Not only was she open minded about the possibility of aliens and UFOs, having seen some strange things as a child, Marie had seemed sincere and genuinely disturbed by her experience. As a result, she held off running for a while afterwards and it would be a couple of weeks before she worked up the courage to head back out that way. But gradually, things did return to normal.

Marie's husband, Roger, on the other hand, didn't believe her, but that mattered little. Their relationship was strong enough for them to be open and honest with one another and, in any case, she didn't need other people to believe her; she knew what she had seen. Her only hope was that she would never see them again. And for a while at least, that much was true.

Then, at around 9.30pm on 21st October, Jenny and Abigail were sitting on the sofa watching television when they heard a knock at the door. It was Marie. She was bent forwards and gasping for air. Her husband, Roger, was stood behind her with a disapproving look on his face and when Jenny asked them what was wrong, he apologised for bothering them so late and then said, in a rather dismissive tone, that his wife had been hallucinating again. Breathlessly, Marie told him to shut up, then turned to Jenny and said, "They were there again!" It seemed the objects had returned.

According to Marie, she had been running next to the same field where she had seen them the first time, when they suddenly appeared out of nowhere. Quite literally; one minute there was nothing there, the next, a movement in the periphery of her vision made her look to her right and that's when she saw them again, hovering low to the ground over the field and moving slowly towards her. Again, she stopped dead in her tracks and was at first too stunned to move. But eventually, panic got the better of her and she ran to a nearby thicket of trees, dived into the brush and ducked out of sight. The objects continued to move in her direction, but as they reached the trees, they passed directly over her head and disappeared from view.

She waited for at least half an hour before leaving the small wood. Once she was sure that the coast was clear, she ran. And she didn't stop running until she reached the front door of her house, doubled over in agony and completely out of breath. At first, Roger had been concerned, but as soon as Marie had mentioned the UFOs, he had scoffed. They had gotten into an argument over his refusal to believe her, an argument which was now continuing on Jenny and Abigail's porch, much to the couple's embarrassment. Maybe it was just the adrenaline, but Jenny noticed that Marie didn't appear at all frightened by this second encounter, even though it was easily more disturbing than the first. If anything, she seemed emboldened by it and declared that she was going back there the next evening.

She challenged her husband to join her, which he wholeheartedly rejected, saying he was not prepared to indulge this nonsense any further and refused to entertain the idea of UFOs. With that, he apologised to his neighbours once more, then walked off the porch and went back indoors. Instead, Jenny offered to go along with Marie the next evening, whilst Abigail—who was pushing her mid-fifties and didn't relish the idea of a run—declined, chuckling to herself, as no doubt Roger had, at the prospect of space invaders.

And so, on the evening of 22nd October, Jenny left Abigail at home and headed out with her neighbour up to the field where she had seen the strange objects. It was about eight miles out of town and Marie had brought her phone along in the hopes of taking some pictures, but it was all to no avail. The UFOs did not appear. They did not appear the evening after, either. Or the evening after that. And after five days, Jenny—who had gone with Marie every night since—decided to throw in the towel. Although she believed her neighbour was telling the truth about what she had seen, her girlfriend was beginning to feel a little neglected and had asked her to stop spending so much time with their neighbour. Marie understood, of course, but was determined to prove her husband wrong and continued to run out to the field every night afterwards. It was a course of action that would end in tragedy.

In the early morning hours of 30th October—1:13am, as Jenny precisely recalled—she and Abigail were awoken by a loud thumping on the front door. It was Roger, and he looked utterly distressed.

"Is Marie here?" He had asked. Jenny shook her head, saying that she wasn't and, come to think of it, neither she nor Abigail had seen her all evening.

Roger told them that she had gone out for her usual run at 6pm, but she had not returned and that he didn't know where she was. He had waited up until just after 11pm, believing she must have dropped in to see a friend on her way back, but he had fallen asleep on the sofa. When he awoke again just after 1am and realised that she still hadn't returned, he panicked. At length, he said that he was going to drive the roads Marie had been running and, as he wasn't sure of the exact route she would have taken, he asked Jenny if she would go with him. Even though it was late, both she and Abigail agreed to help. It took them about an hour to reach the field where Marie previously said she had seen the objects, mostly because Roger had been driving at walking speed calling out her name and shining his torch into the fields and hedgerows. There was no sign of her whatsoever.

As it was getting on for 4am, they had to abandon the search and drove back to town, hoping against hope that they would find Marie at home safe and sound, but as they pulled up on the drive, they could see that the house was still dark and empty, just as they had left it. No one was in. Although Jenny tried to reassure Roger that there was probably some perfectly reasonable explanation as to why Marie had not come home, he stayed up all night worrying, and the next day Jenny and Abigail awoke to find a police car sitting outside their neighbour's house. Marie had still not returned and by 8pm that evening, a search was being coordinated comprising local police and volunteers from the town. This eventually grew into a state-wide search, involving hundreds of state police officers, helicopters, and sniffer dogs. Signs were attached to lamp posts and telephone poles in Watervale and in surrounding neighbourhoods, and local news put out bulletins asking anyone for information on Marie's whereabouts. But things remained eerily quiet.

The search parties found nothing. The helicopters and sniffer dogs found nothing. And although a few calls did come in from people who thought they saw Marie, these turned out to be cases of mistaken identity. Then, on 11th November, Police located a pair of running shoes, with the socks still inside them, sitting casually behind a hedgerow at the side of the road. They were found in such a fashion that suggested the person wearing them had simply been pulled right out of their shoes; the laces were still tied, and the socks were pushed inside them as if worn by an invisible pair of feet. Both Roger and Jenny identified them as Marie's and were shocked to hear that they were located not too far from the field where she had first seen the strange objects.

The search was formerly called off on 30th November 2016. No trace of Marie Gillingham was ever found, and she has not been seen or heard from since. Her disappearance hit Watervale hard. She was well known in the town and popular amongst other residents. They all said that it would have been highly unusual for her to just up and leave without so much as a goodbye. All of her belongings remained at home and still do to this day. She left for her run with only the clothes on her back and her mobile phone, which was also never found, and telephone records indicate no outgoing activity in the form of texts or calls since she vanished. Earlier attempts to triangulate her location using her phone also yielded nothing.

Taking all of this into consideration, Marie just didn't have the means to run away. She didn't work and had little money of her own and relied heavily on her husband's income. Roger, himself, was questioned over what kind of relationship he shared with his wife. Although they argued just like any other couple, they were still very much in love and had a strong marriage. He was ruled out as a suspect early on due to lack of any evidence or a motive suggesting he had been involved in her disappearance, and the fact that other people attested to his upstanding character and gentle nature.

The general consensus in the town is that Marie was kidnapped whilst on her run and possibly raped and murdered, and although police have not publicly stated this to be the case, it is by most accounts what they suspect. There is no evidence to suggest foul play, however. No signs of a struggle were found, no traces of blood or cadaver odours were picked up by the dogs and there were no suspect tyre tracks suggesting a vehicle had been in the area, other than Roger's of course, when he, Jenny and Abigail went to search for her. The investigation is still ongoing, and many believe that only time will tell.

Jenny, on the other hand, believes differently. She believes that no matter how much time passes, Marie or what possibly remains of her, will never be found. She has no doubt that her neighbour was abducted, but the question on her mind is not by who, but by what. She still lives in Watervale with her girlfriend. Abigail's father passed away in May 2017 and they now have no reason to stay. And yet something is keeping her there. Maybe it's guilt. Maybe it's that she feels duty bound to stay and support Roger in his moment of need. Or maybe she just misses her friend. She did not realise how close she and Marie had become until she was gone. And there is not an evening that goes by where she does not step out on to the porch and look across to her neighbour's house, hoping to see that familiar, smiling face looking back at her.

39
WHO IS THE GRINNING MAN?

Alien? Humanoid cryptid? Man in Black? Figment of the imagination? Or all of the above? This being who terrorises people in the dead of night is known by many names, but he needs only one. Who is The Grinning Man?

Cast your mind back to your childhood. A time when life was a curious mix of innocence, high-jinks, and promise. When each day was a new adventure. When there was no limit to your curiosity, energy, or imagination. When weekends brought you pocket money, scraped knees brought you tears, and darkness, all manner of foreboding. Just as surely as most children fear the dark, most also fear some kind of bogeyman. Was there a bogeyman in your town? Perhaps it was the village recluse, who lived in a decrepit old house at the end of the street. Maybe it was something unseen, watching from beyond the treeline of the woods behind your home. Or perhaps it is some unsightly creature, dwelling on a lonely, windswept moor, only venturing out during the night to feast on the blood of the young.

Whatever it was, your fear of it more than likely diminished with age. "There are no such things as monsters," your parents probably told you—drummed into you, even—and maybe you would believe them, maybe you wouldn't, but in time, as you got older, it became an accepted and imperishable truth. And yet even now, how can we be so sure? Every year across the globe, people report seeing what they describe as monsters. Aliens, ghosts, Bigfoot, the Wendigo, Skinwalkers, black-eyed children, the Chupacabra, Dogman, Mothman, Slenderman, Lizardman, pig-faced men, men in black. The list goes on and on and on.

And whilst encounters with such beings are said to be horrifying, by far and away one of the most frightening entities you could ever bump into on a cold, dark evening is said to be The Grinning Man. Not least because—unlike many of the others—he has been known to enter people's homes in the dead of night and watch them whilst they sleep. On the surface at least, The Grinning Man's appearance doesn't sound all too frightening. He doesn't have the large soulless, black eyes of an alien Gray, the huge, imposing girth of a Sasquatch, or the sharp teeth and claws of the Dogman, but there is something about him that disturbs eyewitnesses to their core.

Said to be about seven-foot-tall, with broad shoulders and a muscular physique, he is described as having small, beady eyes, which are set unnaturally wide apart, nestled either side of a shallow nose. His face and head are utterly devoid of hair and he is often seen wearing a tight-fitting one-piece suit, which is reflective, like tin foil. It is said that his facial expression would otherwise be docile, but for the fact that he consistently sports a wide, inhuman grin. And it is this grin which eyewitnesses find most disturbing, for it is not a grin of pleasure or even amusement; it is one of sheer menace. It is said that his mouth smiles, but his eyes do not. And aside from this disconcerting facial expression, witnesses have also reported a feeling of absolute dread when confronted by this being, almost as if they are staring death in the face. What follows is a select few of some of the most terrifying encounters with The Grinning Man.

The earliest recorded sighting occurred in Elizabeth, New Jersey, on 11th October 1966. It was 9:45pm and two boys by the names of Martin Munov and James Yanchitis were walking home from a movie theatre along New Jersey and 4th Street. After a while, they turned onto another road that ran adjacent to NJ and 4th and found themselves walking beneath the elevated New Jersey Turnpike. After dark, this area of town was certainly no place for two young boys and they must have felt uneasy as they walked through what was essentially a dark tunnel, with traffic pounding 30 feet over their heads and only a few pools of light emanating from the streetlamps on the road above. Lining their route was a high chain-link fence, the other side of which was a steep slope leading back up to the underside of the turnpike.

Earlier that evening, they had heard that a woman in town had been chased by a huge man wearing a green suit, but they tried to put this out of their minds as they walked through the darkness, chatting as nonchalantly as their nerves would allow. They had almost emerged from the other side of the turnpike when James noticed someone standing in the bushes on the opposite side of the chain-link fence. He nudged his friend and said, "Who's that?" Martin turned to look behind him and that's when both boys noticed how incredibly tall and well-built this figure was. He was wearing a green reflective suit and his attention seemed entirely fixed on a house across the street, situated some 200 metres away from where they were. He didn't even notice the two boys looking at him at first, but after a few seconds, he turned to face them. The boys later described him as "the weirdest looking guy" they had ever seen; his face didn't even look human. Needless to say, they panicked and ran, leaving the figure behind, grinning at their backs.

As fate would have it, famous author and ufologist John Keel was in the area shortly after the encounter, investigating a UFO which had been witnessed 40 miles north of Elizabeth. He got wind of the boys' story and set about interviewing them separately. They both gave the same description, and both indicated exactly the same spot where they had seen the strange entity. And because the aforementioned UFO sighting had occurred on the very same evening, it wouldn't be long before conclusions were drawn pertaining to the Grinning Man's otherworldly origins.

The second eyewitness account was to come less than three weeks later, some 500 miles to the west of Elizabeth in West Virginia. Woodrow Derenberger, a sewing machine salesman, was driving along Interstate 77 on the evening of 2nd November when he encountered a UFO, which dropped out of the sky in front of his car and stopped him dead in the road. A tall being with wide-set eyes and a huge grin stretched across its face exited the strange craft and approached his vehicle. Unlike the New Jersey Grinning Man, this one was said to be wearing a blue suit, but it had the same qualities in that it was a one-piece and was made of a reflective material.

To his surprise, the entity communicated with Derenberger telepathically, asking about the "strange glow" on the horizon, not realising it was the lights of a distant town. Derenberger reported that the individual referred to himself as Indrid Cold, a name which didn't mean anything to him at the time, but one which would gain much notoriety in the decades that followed. Cold proceeded to ask Derenberger many questions about the people and surrounding areas, then thanked him and left in his strange craft, but not before telling the startled salesman that he would be seeing him again. This encounter occurred just two weeks before the famed Mothman sightings began in nearby Point Pleasant, and people have often wondered whether there was any link between the two. Indeed, there was a sighting of The Grinning Man on the outskirts of Point Pleasant when the Mothman phenomenon was at its peak.

The Lilly family had been experiencing poltergeist activity in their home around this time, which had begun abruptly for no apparent reason. All of a sudden, things were being moved around the house of their own accord, objects were being thrown from shelves, doors were being slammed, and even lights were being seen in the sky above their house. It was a tumultuous time for the family, who were constantly bearing the brunt of this bizarre episode at all hours of the day and night. However, it would be the youngest daughter, Linda, who fared the worst and would experience the most terrifying instance of this strange activity.

At 1:45am on December 14th, 1966, Linda came running into her parents' bedroom screaming in terror. She told her mother and father that she had been awoken by an odd clicking sound and when she opened her eyes, she was horrified to see a figure standing at the foot of her bed.

"It was a man," she said. "A big man. Very tall. I couldn't see his face very well, but I could see that he was grinning at me. He walked around the bed and stood right over me. I screamed again and hid under the covers, when I looked again, he was gone."

Suffice it to say that Linda refused to sleep in her own room for weeks afterwards and by the time she did pluck up the courage to climb back into her own bed, the poltergeist activity in the home had abated and the Lilly family never experienced anything out of the ordinary from that point onwards. From late 1966 to early 1967, several people in Provincetown, Massachusetts, would have separate run-ins with a neighbourhood prowler, whom they described as very tall, muscular, and always wearing a fixed grin. The details of these reports do exist in old clippings from local newspapers, but unfortunately, they are yet to be published online.

Not all Grinning Man sightings have occurred in the US. A woman living in Scotland by the name of Mary Elizabeth McRae would have an extremely chilling encounter, which would trouble her for many years afterwards. Mary lived with her husband Alan on the outskirts of Dunkeld, a small village situated right on the cusp of the stunning Cairngorms National Park. The couple were in their mid-fifties and their children had long since left home, so for the most part it was just Mary and Alan living together in peaceful isolation. Their house was remote—their closest neighbour lived almost a mile away—but they enjoyed the relative privacy.

On the night of 23rd November 1972, Mary and Alan went to bed at around 9pm, as was usual for them, and they sat up reading for about an hour before turning off the lights and going to sleep. Mary reported that she was awoken in the early hours of the morning by an indistinct clicking sound and upon opening her eyes, she found herself lying on her front, completely paralysed, and struggling to breathe. Sleep paralysis was not fully understood or even identified as a disorder during the 1970's, so Mary, who had never experienced anything like this before, felt an inward and intensifying panic, but was unable to do anything about her situation. The clicking increased in volume, piercing her eardrums and then something suddenly dawned on her. She remembered that she had closed the curtains before getting into bed, it was something she always did every night without fail and yet now she could see that they were open.

All this time, she had had a distinct feeling of being watched and a very slight movement in the periphery of her vision drew her attention to the bottom left pane of the bedroom window. To her complete horror, she saw a face staring back at her. It had dark, beady eyes and was fixed with an awful, malevolent grin. As she stared back, she felt herself becoming transfixed, unable to avert her gaze. She then felt her whole body lift off the bed and slowly float towards the face in the window. In her panic she tried to scream out, but no sound came from her mouth and she was unable to move. She was not to know what happened next as she blacked out and when she awoke the next morning, she was suffering from a terrible headache, which did not ease for almost a week afterwards. She also noticed that the curtains were still open, a fact which cast doubt on any notion in later years that she had simply experienced a bout of sleep paralysis. Mary passed away in 2013 at the age of 94, but the memory of what she saw that night stayed with her until the day she died.

Taking all these accounts into consideration, what are we to make of this phenomenon? Just who on Earth is The Grinning Man? Or rather, what is he? Is there more than one of him? Or is he a single entity who chooses to terrorise unsuspecting individuals for no apparent reason? There are a few conflicting accounts regarding his identity, and whilst all eyewitnesses describe him in a similar fashion, the situations in which he has been seen vary significantly. For example, some people who have encountered the famed men in black have described them has having inhuman features as well as sporting malevolent grins.

Others who claim to have been abducted by aliens have also reported seeing a grinning man during their experience. Indeed, the clicking sounds heard in both the Linda Lilly and Mary McRae encounters are commonly reported in many alien abduction cases, and some abductees have even mentioned the name of Indrid Cold, the name given to Woodrow Derengerger during his experience. One such encounter occurred in Italy in December of 1979, when a man by the name of Pier Zanfretta—who allegedly had a history of being abducted by a race of reptilian aliens—claimed to have been contacted by a grinning man shortly before being taken aboard a UFO. He said that this man referred to himself as none other than Indrid Cold.

Throughout the late 60's and early 70's Woodrow Derenberger would go on to state that he was visited many more times by the same Indrid Cold he had met on that cold dark night back in 1966. He would also claim to have been visited by two other grinning men who went by the names of Demo Hassan and Karl Ardo. Even his wife testified to meeting these beings and she believed their agenda was evil. Sadly, she and Derenberger divorced shortly after these encounters. Finally, there is the connection with the Mothman, which many people believe was itself an extra-terrestrial being. Some fringe theorists have even presented the theory that The Grinning Man, Indrid Cold, and the Mothman were all one and the same, a member of a race of shape-shifting aliens who in fact walk amongst us and even pose as government officials in the form of MIBs.

But is this perhaps a stretch too far? After all, if we are to look at these accounts with a critical eye, we must point out that at least the first three reported sightings of The Grinning Man begin and end with John Keel. He was the first to write about them in his books and would have applied his own biases and taken his own artistic liberties. Even the Mothman sightings were further borne out and brought to international attention by him. Perhaps these encounters were embellished and made out to be more bizarre than they actually were, and it would therefore be reasonable to assume that any eyewitness accounts since then are purely copycat fabrications.

Of course, this is all speculation, and it is rather uncanny how all physical descriptions of this being are inherently similar, and interesting how these sightings always seem to occur around the same time of year; between Winter and Spring. Could it be that The Grinning Man, whomever he is, seems to prefer colder seasons? No pun intended, of course, on his alleged last name. The fact remains that, whether we believe it or not, the Grinning Man phenomenon is here to stay, with more and more encounters being reported with each passing year. And if you ever find yourself walking alone at night or even sleeping soundly in your own bed, pray you never come face to face with a tall man, who wears a fixed grin, and who calls himself Cold.

40
25 CROMWELL STREET

In February 1994, police searching a house in Gloucester, England, made a discovery that would lead to one of the most infamous and disturbing cases in British criminal history. From that point onwards, the property at 25 Cromwell Street would become known as "The House of Horrors".

The tale we are about to relate is not our usual Fortean fare. There are no unexplained happenings or bizarre creatures in this story, but it is just as horrific as anything we have covered in this book, if not more so. A tale so extensive, so complex, so disturbing, and utterly sickening in its depravity that it is difficult to know where to begin. It covers more than a quarter of a century of atrocities ranging from child abuse, molestation, and sexual perversion, to rape, torture, and finally cold-blooded murder. Nothing like it had ever been seen in Britain before and, thankfully, nothing quite like it has ever been seen since. But before we continue, please be aware that this chapter contains themes involving harm to children and young females, and discretion is advised.

On the afternoon of 1st January 1995, officers working at Winson

Green Prison in Birmingham, England opened the door of cell C4-01 to find Frederick Walter Stephen West slumped on his knees in the middle of the floor. His lifeless body was suspended in an upright position by a makeshift rope, which had been made out of torn up blankets and was tied between the door handle and the catchment of the window opposite. After coiling a loop around his neck, Frederick West had sunk to his knees and asphyxiated himself. His bowels and bladder had loosened after he had expired, and as prison officers stood surrounded by the fetid smell of faeces, urine, and death, watching as the doctor attempted to resuscitate him, they all must have secretly hoped that he was far beyond help. For the world was undoubtedly a better place without him.

The only real shame was that he had escaped the might of British justice. There would be no trial for him. No being left to rot in a prison cell for the rest of his life, wallowing in self-pity and despair. He had robbed those he had hurt of *that* pleasure and had taken the easy way out. The fact that he had been on strict suicide watch had made no difference whatsoever. "He was a practical man," his son would later declare. "And good with knots."

Good with knots. He would have to have been. Tying knots was just one of this despicable man's specialities. On the floor, in the corner of the cell lay a suicide note addressed to his wife, Rosemary Pauline West, his soulmate, his eternal love, his partner in crime. She was also in custody, awaiting her own trial, but unlike him she would not go on to fulfil the pact they had made between themselves; to end their lives if ever they were caught. Perhaps she blamed him. After all, it was his stupid, boastful mistake which had led to their arrest. A mistake which had come far too late, but a mistake we should all be thankful for, nonetheless. And it would all play out as follows.

Fred and Rosemary West lived at number 25 Cromwell Street in Gloucester, England. They were mother and father to eight children whom they regularly subjected to violence, sexual abuse, and in some cases even rape. In May of 1992, Fred forced himself upon his 13-year-old daughter, Louise, after asking her to help him move some empty bottles up to the first floor of their home. When the ordeal was over, she was found by her siblings, sobbing, bleeding, and writhing in pain. When Louise later confided to her mother what had happened, Rosemary was unsympathetic and simply replied, "Oh well, you were asking for it." That was the first time Fred had raped her. It would not be the last.

She was raped and even sodomised a further three times by her father during that week, and on at least one of those occasions, her mother was also present and even took part. After every instance, Fred warned his daughter that if she ever told anyone, she would end up buried beneath the patio "like her sister; Heather". Little did Fred know it at the time, but by issuing this threat, he had just opened up a crack in the slab that would crumble and deteriorate over the following months and collapse into a vast chasm, which led straight to hell.

As physically and emotionally damaged as Louise was by this experience, she did not take his warning seriously. Her father was always making this threat to his children whenever they misbehaved, and he almost always laughed it off as a joke immediately afterwards. And although she and her siblings had not seen or heard from Heather—their older sister—for several years, Fred and Rose always told them that she had run away to start a new job in Devon.

Finding no sympathy at home, Louise instead confided in a school friend about the abuse she had suffered at the hands of her parents. Her school friend then told her mother. Her school friend's mother then reported the incident to authorities and on 6th August 1992, the Wests home was searched by police on the pretext of looking for stolen goods. Although they discovered various items of sexual paraphernalia, including as many as 99 pornographic videos, they found nothing that could incriminate Fred in the rape of his daughter.

Nevertheless, Louise made a full statement through a specially trained solicitor, describing her father's actions and, as a result, all children in the household were immediately placed into foster care. Medical examinations of each of them indicated they had endured both physical and sexual abuse. They would each personally relate how they had suffered at the hands of their parents and how they had been threatened with beatings and even death if they ever spoke a word to anyone about what went on in the household. Police began a full investigation which would lead to Fred being charged with three counts of rape and one of buggery, whilst Rose was charged with child cruelty and as an accomplice to Fred's actions.

To make matters worse for them, their eldest daughter Anna Marie—who had long since left home—also came forward and gave details of the abuse she had suffered growing up, how Fred and Rose had raped her when she was just eight years old and prostituted her to much older men. She also told police that she had been trying to trace her sister, Heather, for many years, but had been unsuccessful. Unfortunately, the entire case against the Wests collapsed in June 1993, when both Louise and Anna Marie about-faced and refused to testify against their parents. Both Fred and Rose were released without charge and returned home, although their children remained in foster care.

Authorities were frustrated by Louise and Anna Marie's decision to remain silent. They had wanted more than anything to bring these two vile human beings to justice. But as we shall see, despite this setback, the story was only just beginning. Police instead focused on Anna Marie's insistence that they track Heather down, suggesting that her sister might be more willing to give evidence against her parents. After all, it was because of the abuse she had suffered that she had run away from home in the first place. But police could find no trace of her; no bank account, no credit card activity, no record of employment, nothing. It was as if she had simply dropped off the face of the Earth.

After months of investigation and still no evidence to suggest that Heather was alive, police began to consider that Fred's threat to his children, which suggested that she was buried under the patio, may indeed be true. This would be enough to secure a search warrant, which would allow them to excavate the back garden of 25 Cromwell Street, and when police officers served this notice to Rosemary West on 24th February 1994, she turned pale and almost collapsed. Fred was working away in Stroud at the time but returned home that afternoon and immediately went to the police station to protest their actions, a futile endeavour to say the least. Officers were stationed at the property around the clock and that evening, Fred and Rose were seen looking out over their back garden, whispering in hushed tones.

On the morning of the 25th, Fred West—recognising the inevitability of his situation—once again visited the police station, this time to formally admit to the murder of his daughter, saying that she was buried under his patio after all. He pleaded that her death had been an accident and that he had killed her in a fit of rage during an argument. On the 27th February, police discovered a human thigh bone in a section of his back garden, which somewhat corroborated this confession. However, what at first appeared to be little more than a domestic argument that had gone terribly wrong, soon turned into one of the most sickening cases in British criminal history, which would stun and utterly outrage an entire nation.

Later that same day, the forensic pathologist attending the scene was called over to an excavation point near the bathroom of the property. He jumped down into a hole to retrieve more remains of a human female, which had been found buried three feet beneath the mud. But when he noticed that these remains included two thigh bones, he looked up at the superintendent and said, "We have already found one thigh bone, these two make three altogether, so either Heather had three legs, or we're dealing with more than one set of remains."

When police questioned Fred over this later that afternoon, he casually told them that there were in fact two other bodies buried in his garden besides his daughter. Indeed, two more sets of remains were located on 28th February, and two days later, Fred was charged with all three murders. Throughout all of this, Rose West claimed that she had no knowledge of the killings, and her husband confirmed during interviews that he had acted alone. In the meantime, she was moved to a safe house whilst authorities made the decision to thoroughly search the entire property. Over the next two weeks, police would discover a further six sets of remains buried beneath the house at 25 Cromwell Street. All were young females ranging from the ages of 15 to 21 and all had been dismembered before they were buried, including West's own daughter.

Although all the bodies were heavily decomposed—they were little more than skeletal remains at this point—authorities were able to ascertain that most of the murders had been committed for sexual gratification. The majority of them—again including West's own daughter—had been bound and gagged before death and other signs indicated that they had been sexually abused and even tortured; all of them were missing finger bones and some were even buried without their kneecaps. Fred had admitted to all of these killings before the bodies were even located by police. This was due in no small part to the pressure of facing constant and intense questioning, sixteen hours a day, seven days a week, and Fred's eventual resignation to the fact that the bodies would eventually be discovered anyway, whether he confessed or not.

He told police that most of his victims were hitchhikers and local girls he had picked up at bus stops. He also indicated that there were a further three bodies buried at other locations in and around Gloucester, two of which were his first wife, Catherine "Rena" Costello, and his stepdaughter Charmaine West. This made a total of 12 murders altogether and authorities began to wonder how Rose could possibly have been oblivious to so many killings whilst married to Fred. She was arrested on 20th April 1994, initially on charges of sexual abuse, but was later charged with participation in at least ten of the murders. Fred West would ultimately retract his statement that he had acted alone and would, in fact, go on to say that Rose had been far more culpable for the killings.

Just who were Fred and Rosemary West? And what situations had arisen during the course of their lives that had steered them down such a dark, depraved, and deadly path? As the story goes, Fred was born in Much Marcle, Gloucester, in September of 1941. The eldest of six children, he was raised on a farm in the post-war years, at a time when the country was struggling economically and, as a result, his family toiled well below the poverty line. His parents were strict disciplinarians and each of their children was assigned chores to help with the farm's upkeep.

Fred would state in his police interviews that at the age of 12 he began an incestuous relationship with his mother, and that his father would regularly rape his younger sisters, but his siblings would emphatically deny this in later years. Classmates described him as a scruffy kid, dim-witted and always in trouble, but that he had an aptitude for woodwork and construction. At the age of 17 he purchased a motorcycle, which he crashed less than two months later, fracturing his skull in the process. He lay unconscious for seven days, but otherwise made a full physical recovery. However, something in Fred's personality changed; he developed an ingrained fear of hospitals and became prone to flying into fits of absolute rage.

He suffered yet another head injury two years later when a girl he had groped punched him the face, resulting in him falling two stories from the ladder he was stood on. Later that same year, at the age of 19, Fred was arrested following an accusation by his 13-year-old sister that he had raped her multiple times. When questioned by police, he freely admitted this, saying that he'd been molesting young girls since his early teens. Appearing nonplussed by his arrest, he casually responded to the charges by asking, "Doesn't everybody do it?" Unfortunately, the case against him was dropped when his sister refused to testify, but from that point onwards, his immediate family had nothing more to do with him.

A year later, Fred would marry his first wife, Rena Costello, who was pregnant with another man's child. The couple were married in November 1962 and relocated to Rena's native Scotland. His stepdaughter, Charmaine West, was born the following March and another child, Anna Marie, would follow shortly afterwards in July 1964. By all accounts, Fred was an abusive husband and father, regularly beating Rena and locking his two young children away in a cage during the evenings. During this time, he worked as an ice cream man and in this way, whilst on one of his rounds, he met a 16-year-old runaway by the name of Anne McFall, whom he invited to come and live with him and his wife, and work as a nanny to their children. Having nowhere else to go, she accepted his offer on the spot.

In November 1965, Fred ran over and killed a four-year-old boy whilst on one of his rounds and, although cleared of any blame, he feared reprisals from the local community and so relocated the family—including Anne—to Gloucester. Unable to cope with the constant abuse from her husband, Rena returned to Scotland in mid-1966. As she was unemployed, she had no choice but to leave her children in Fred's care, something that deeply unsettled her for obvious reasons. In the meantime, Anne McFall fell increasingly under Fred's spell and the two of them began an affair, resulting in her falling pregnant with his child.

In the summer of 1967, Anne suddenly vanished, and as she had only maintained sporadic contact with her family, she was never reported missing by Fred or anyone else. When asked by friends of her whereabouts, Fred simply replied that she had returned to Scotland. She was in fact buried at the edge of a cornfield between Much Marcle and Kempley after Fred had bound, tortured, raped, and then killed her, extracting her unborn foetus in the process. And there her dismembered body would remain undisturbed for 27 years.

In February 1969, whilst at Cheltenham bus station, Fred met Rosemary Letts for the first time. She had recently turned 15, meaning that Fred was more than 12 years her senior. She was initially repulsed by his advances, but eventually agreed to go on a date with him a few weeks later. Although intelligent, Rosemary had performed poorly at school. She was a moody child who was prone to daydreaming. Her mother had suffered severe bouts of depression whilst carrying her and as a result, she had been subjected to electroconvulsive therapy, which some believe may have inflicted prenatal damage on Rose.

Growing up, she was constantly abused and raped by her schizophrenic father. Eventually, she became so desensitised towards his attacks that she became a willing participant in these interactions. Rose began dating Fred shortly after meeting him, something her parents vehemently disapproved of as she was still a minor. Her father threatened to report their relationship to social services, but this did not deter them. As soon as Rose reached the legal age of consent—16 in the UK—she moved in with her much older lover. In doing so, she became stepmother to Charmaine and Anna Marie West, and at first, seeing that they were in a state of neglect, showed them compassion.

She soon fell pregnant with Fred's child and the family moved into a ground floor flat in Midland Road, Gloucester. Her relationship with her stepdaughters deteriorated rapidly during this time and she became just as eager to beat and punish them as Fred was. On 17th October 1970, she gave birth to her first child, Heather West. Rose would commit her first murder just eight months later, whilst Fred was serving a six-month prison sentence for theft. She apparently killed eight-year-old Charmaine West in a fit of rage after she had misbehaved, an incident many have put down to the pressures of raising three children alone at the immature age of just 17.

Charmaine's body was stored in the coal cellar until Fred's release, after which he buried her in the back yard at the Midland Road address. The couple would go on to tell family, friends, and neighbours, as well as Anna Marie, that Charmaine's mother, Rena, had taken her back to Scotland to live with her. When Fred's ex-wife came knocking two months later, on one of her frequent visits to see her children, she demanded to know where Charmaine was, a course of action which would ultimately cost Rena her life; Fred and Rose would subsequently beat her to death with a metal bar and bury her body in a nearby field. Although it is speculated that Fred had already developed an appetite for killing by this time, there is no doubt that this was the point where Rose developed a pleasure for it herself, as almost all of the subsequent murders had a sexual motivation behind them.

The couple eventually married in January of 1972 and moved into the house at 25 Cromwell Street shortly afterwards. Rose turned to prostitution in order to supplement her husband's meagre income and it was rumoured that one of her most regular clients was her own father. Over the next ten years, she would give birth to a further seven children, the last being born in 1983, with at least three of them being fathered by her regular clients. Nevertheless, Fred accepted them as his own. Over time, he extended the family home and turned rooms on the top two floors of the property into bedsits in order to bring in extra income. Between 1973 and 1987, Fred and Rose West would rape, beat, torture, and kill nine young girls, and leave their bodies to rot beneath the house where their family lived. The victims' names were as follows:

- Lynda Gough, aged 19. Lynda was found buried beneath the ground floor bathroom. She was a lodger at the Wests home. It is believed the Wests murdered her in April of 1973.
- Carol Ann Cooper, aged 15. Carol was found buried beneath the cellar. Her skull had been bound with surgical tape and her limbs had been tied together with cord and braiding cloth. She

was last seen alive boarding a bus in the suburb of Warndon in November 1973.
- Lucy Partington, aged 21. Lucy was a cousin of the famous novelist Martin Amis and was abducted from a bus stop on the A435 in December 1973. Her body was buried beneath the cellar.
- Thérèse Siegenthaler, aged 21. Thérèse was a Swiss national who had travelled to the UK to study sociology. She was abducted whilst hitch-hiking from South London to Holyhead on 16th April 1974. Her body was found buried underneath a chimney breast in the cellar.
- Shirley Hubbard, aged 15. Shirley was last seen on 15th November 1974. She was abducted from a bus stop in Droitwich as she was travelling home from a date. When Shirley's body was exhumed from the cellar, her skull was found completely wrapped in gaffer tape with a three-inch tube inserted into her nasal cavity, which would have allowed her to breathe.
- Juanita Mott, aged 18. Juanita had briefly lodged at the Wests household but had subsequently moved in with a friend. She was abducted in April 1975 whilst hitch-hiking along the B4215. She was the last victim to be buried in the cellar.
- Shirley Robinson, aged 21. Shirley had lodged with the Wests and had begun an affair with Fred. She was eight months pregnant with his child when she lost her life. Her murder was not sexually motivated, and police believe she was killed by Rose as she threatened the stability of the family. Fred would later state that his wife had cut the unborn foetus from her womb after death. Her body was then dismembered and buried in the back garden. She was last seen alive in May 1978.
- Alison Chambers, aged 16. Alison's was the last known sexually motivated murder. She was a child living in foster care and had become acquainted with the Wests in the summer of 1979. She went missing in August of that year. When her remains were exhumed from the garden 15 years later, a leather belt was found looped around her neck.

- And finally, Heather West, aged 16. Heather had begun to tell her school friends about the abuse she was suffering at home and had applied for a job at a holiday park in Devon as a way of escaping her parents. Fred and Rose had seen this as a threat and had murdered her in order to keep her silence. Although Fred would claim her death was an accident, her remains were found buried with a length of rope, suggesting she had been bound before death.

In 2004, one of the West's youngest children, Barry, would claim that he had witnessed Heather's murder, saying that she had been tied up, physically and sexually abused, and that Rose had finally stamped on his sister's head until she ceased to move. With Fred having taken his own life in January of 1995, Rosemary was left to face the prosecution alone. She maintained her innocence during the trial and does so even to this day, but the evidence ranged against her was overwhelming. The jury heard recorded confessions from Fred, describing how he and Rose had tortured their victims; tying them up and suspending them from ropes in the cellar, a room where no one could hear them scream as they had had their fingernails extracted, the ends of their fingers cut off with pruners, their genitals beaten with blunt objects amongst other unspeakable acts.

They heard testimonies from other women who had survived their ordeals with Fred and Rose, and most heart-breaking of all, from their own children. Anna Marie finally came forward to testify against her own mother, and as she sat there looking across at Rose with a yearning, apologetic expression full of love and pain, it capsized the whole courtroom. Tears streamed down her face as she reluctantly told of the abuses she had suffered, saying that whilst Fred was the most sexually perverse of the two, her mother was easily the most violent and calculating, and was likely responsible for the majority of the killings. Rosemary West was found guilty on ten counts of murder and subjected to a whole life tariff, meaning that she will never be released. Anna Marie would later try to take her own life out of the guilt of still loving her parents despite everything they had done, to her and to others because, she explained between sobs, they were all she had.

There is no telling how many more people the Wests killed, but police estimate there could be as many as 30 plus, that the address of 25 Cromwell Street was just the tip of the iceberg. West's son, Stephen, claimed that his father had admitted this once whilst visiting him in prison. Apparently West told him that "when everyone else went to sleep, he used to go to work" and that his crimes were "far worse than anyone could imagine." When Fred was living in Scotland during the 60's, he had rented an allotment, one quarter of which he never cultivated. When his neighbour asked why he never grew any vegetables there, he simply replied with a slight smile that it was "reserved for something special".

Police were never able to search this location as a section of the M8 motorway was built over the top of it during the 1970's. The building, which had served as the Wests home for more than 20 years—their "house of horrors" as it was dubbed by the British press—was demolished in 1996, and every single brick destroyed. A public footpath now rests over the site today.

One of the most prominent questions we try to answer in writing this book is whether monsters exist. We believe this case decisively proves that they do and that we can never truly know what goes on in some people's minds, even those closest to us. It is not so difficult to ponder, as you drive through the rows of streets and houses of any town, what awful secrets might lie beneath the surface of those otherwise idyllic scenes. We must spare a final thought for the victims of Fred and Rosemary West, both known and unknown. It is difficult to imagine the pain and suffering they must have endured. May we take solace in the fact that their killers were eventually brought to justice and hope that their souls can now rest in peace.

Printed in Great Britain
by Amazon